JUST TROUBLE

THE CARPE DIEM CAFÉ
BOOK 1

DEBORAH COOKE

THE CARPE DIEM CAFÉ

The Carpe Diem Café is a series of steamy small town contemporary romances. When Merry opens her own bistro in the sleepy small town of Empire, there's more cooking than her daily farm-to-table specials. Merry's café is named for her philosophy ('*Carpe Diem*' or '*Seize the Day*') and once her doors are open, Empire will never be the same.

1. Just Trouble

2. Just Like Starting Over

———

JUST TROUBLE

1

———

DAPHNE

I hear the motorcycle on Tuesday morning, its throaty roar echoing along Queen Street like an announcement—or a wake-up call. It's April, one of the prettiest months in our little corner of the world. Spring is bursting out all over, welcome flashes of bright green on every corner, flowers emerging from the soil and birds chirping merrily. The tulips and daffodils are in bloom, not just in gardens but in window boxes and pots outside our offices. On this perfect spring morning, the cloudless sky is that shade of blue that looks like forever. The wind is crisp off the lake and winter seems long ago.

(It's not.)

I'm annoyed, having had The Discussion with my father for the hundredth time, and lost right again on schedule. We don't argue or fight, my dad and I—he just overwhelms all objections with his affability. He's so calm, so reasonable, so sure, that I end up backing down every time.

And it bugs me.

So does the seemingly endless pile of paperwork on my desk.

It's part and parcel of dad being on retainer for Cavendish Enterprises. Seasonal foreign workers come. Seasonal foreign workers go. In every possible instance, there are forms to file, and as the most junior lawyer at Weatherby & Bradshaw, I win the grunt work.

I've poured myself a fresh coffee and opened the top folder when I hear the engine. The town is so quiet that the sound of the bike is jarring. I assume it's a scout for a motorcycle club, an older grizzled guy looking for a place to congregate on Friday the thirteenth, and am not thrilled that Empire might be a candidate.

The roar gets louder. It reminds me of a certain hot guy, the one who rode his bike out of town sixteen years ago and never came back. (Of course, it does.) It makes me reconsider the wisdom of my own return to bucolic Empire. Should I have stayed in Toronto? The work was more interesting and it could be argued that my social life was, too.

I didn't feel stalled or on the shelf either. I wasn't bored.

I sigh without meaning to and get to work. Forms don't fill themselves, despite my wishes to the contrary.

Against every expectation, the motorcycle stops in front of my dad's legal office, idling for a minute before the engine stops. I make it to the window in time to catch a glimpse of a long-legged man in black striding to the door and my heart skips a beat.

No. It can't be.

Even Mrs. Prescott sounds flustered when the door opens to the street, which is a big clue to the new arrival's identity.

A bigger one is the low rumble of his voice, still thrilling after all these years, still evocative of melted chocolate and dissolved inhibitions. Of course, it's familiar. I've listened to all of his band's recordings, memorized more than a few, and had that smoky ballad as the ringtone on my phone for ages. I retreat behind my desk, hoping, not hoping, feeling all of fourteen years old again.

Luke Jones must have come to see my father, to get himself out of some epic trouble or other. I won't need to even see him...

Yes, I mean *the* Luke Jones. You've heard of him, of course, and his über-famous band, those rockers who have made millions—their music is good, but they're also sinfully photogenic, all four of them.

Well, three now. And not much of a band anymore, but that's another story and one that isn't my business. (My browser history isn't yours to peruse.) I won't be feeling sorry for Luke because he doesn't have to wade through piles of lingerie on the stage five nights a week and clearly adore every minute of it.

It's too easy to envision his sultry smile and bedroom eyes, smouldering looks—and that little smile, the one that steals over his lips when his dark lashes are falling, hiding his thoughts, making you think he's remembering a private secret. A panty-melter, even virtually.

If he does that here, live and in person, my lingerie might spontaneously combust.

But I'm not the teenager who was in awe of Luke, not anymore. I've learned that guys like him might be easy on the eyes, they might know all the right moves, make all the right promises and have charm to spare—but in the end, the only thing they care about is themselves. They're not potential partners. Great-looking guys say and do whatever is necessary to get whatever they want, then move on. I have the unworn wedding dress as a souvenir.

I straighten at the sound of a deep male voice in reception, proof positive that I've guessed right. Luke has this baritone that sounds as if it's coming from the ocean floor and in real life, it's rougher than in the band's recordings. The sound works for me in a big way.

My heart skips as if I'm going to be caught in some crime. I read the top form twice without comprehending a word before Mrs. Prescott taps once then flings open the door.

"Mr. Luke Jones to see you, Miss Bradshaw."

And there he is. He *is* back.

Right here.

Let me tell you that Luke's a thousand times hotter in real life, and better looking than I remember. Man not boy now and it makes all the difference in the world. He's taller and broader, filling the doorway and not caring a bit. He exudes presence and confidence. He owns the room before he steps fully into it—and it's *my* office. He's wearing jeans and a black leather jacket, his helmet under one arm and a leather satchel in the other hand. I feel as if Sin has stepped into my office to issue a personal invitation.

I'm tempted to accept.

He has what looks like a day's growth of beard, dark and even, which makes him look like a rebel. They always said he was just trouble. He takes off his mirrored sunglasses and I see that his eyes are just as vividly blue—one Cavendish legacy he wasn't denied—but his gaze is a lot more assessing than it used to be. His gaze sweeps over me, leaving tingles in its wake, but I step forward and offer my hand as if unaffected.

Crisp. Professional. Dispassionate.

It's what I do. The moat is filled and the gates are closed. Always and forever. Lesson learned.

It's when his hand closes over mine—warm, firm, a solid grip—that I notice it. It's Luke but *not* Luke. Sure, he's broader and older, and looks a bit more disgruntled than I ever remember him being. Determined, maybe. But there's another change, something I can't quite name. His lips are firm and drawn in a tight line right now, as if maybe he wanted to see my dad and is displeased to be forced to face the junior partner instead.

I could explain the merit of making an appointment to him, but I have no words.

He seems...wounded.

Oh.

There's no oxygen left in my office after Mrs. Prescott shuts the door behind him, and not nearly enough space for two when one is Luke. "How about that," Luke rumbles, sparing me a glance as he puts his helmet on my desk. "Abbie said you'd come back, but I didn't believe it." He's talking about his sister and my best friend. The corner of his mouth almost lifts in a smile, one that makes me hot and cold. It's the gleam in his eyes, the way he's treating us like allies before I even know what he wants. I'm reminded of sleek predators—panthers maybe—who pounce on their victims before anyone even knows the hunt is on. "Don't tell me you missed our hometown."

"I did," I say crisply. "Looks like you did, too."

"Not a chance, Daph," he says, making my name his own. I'm tempted to correct him, to tell him that everyone here calls me Ms. Bradshaw and that my friends call me Daphne, but I let it go.

For now.

What hurt him so badly? I want, against every speck of good sense I possess, to fix it.

His very presence shorts my circuits, proof positive I need to send him on his way ASAP.

"You could say I'm here for a good time, but not a long time."

Excellent. We already agree on something.

He glances at the chair for clients and I invite him to take a seat with a gesture, then sit down behind my own desk. He pulls out a document from his portfolio. He's watching me, but pretending not to.

I'm intrigued that he's uncertain what I will do. I'm not the unpredictable one here.

"I may not be available for your schedule," I say, hating how prim I sound.

Luke's smile flashes, dazzling me for a moment. "Or you might be." He nods at the document he's holding. "Never take a pass on something before you're certain what you'll miss, Daph."

It's not bad advice and I have no quick answer.

I take the document.

It's a list of addresses.

"It's not a huge obligation, Daph. I want to buy these five properties from Cavendish Enterprises, and I need some help with both the offer and its execution..."

He's referring to the corporation run by his father and brothers, which makes my reply automatic. "That would be a conflict of interest, as Cavendish Enterprises has Weatherby & Bradshaw on retainer."

Luke pauses, impaling me with a very blue glance. It gives me shivers of the most excellent variety. "That's your dad, though, right?"

"He is senior partner here since Mr. Weatherby retired."

"What about you?" He braces an elbow on the chair and studies me. I wonder what he sees—or how much—and I don't dare blink.

"What about me?" I repeat politely. "Cavendish Enterprises fill all of my billing hours." I shrug, gesturing to the pile of paperwork. "Sorry to disappoint."

"Are you?" he asks under his breath and I flush, even though he isn't expecting an answer. Luke shakes his head, still studying me, as if he can't make sense of my presence at all. "You know, I didn't believe Abbie. I was sure you'd have a big shiny condo in Toronto and a great job. Or maybe have a successful lawyer destined for great things by your side, and two adorable toddlers, a massive house in Lawrence Park. Maybe an even bigger one in Moore Park or Rosedale if the mister was doing well." I'm surprised that he knows that much about Toronto real estate. "But you're *here*."

"I like it here." I'm a little too vehement, but it's done.

"Nobody likes it here," Luke counters, impatient with the idea. "Anyone here just hasn't figured out how to escape yet." It's a stunning condemnation of our hometown, but there's truth in it too, enough truth to silence my objections. Empire isn't what it was. It's faded and become tired, a place of resignation, not of opportunity. I hate that. Luke fixes a look on me. "Did your lovesick lawyer follow you home?"

"No." Too late I realize I should have denied the existence of said lawyer.

"You're here, working for your dad, and indirectly for Patrick, and single, too?" He feigns surprise and I want to throw something at him. "Oh, Daph, what are we going to do to shake you free of all of this?"

"I don't want to shake free," I inform him coldly, disliking that he put his finger right on it. "I worked hard in high school to get accepted at the university I wanted to attend, busted my butt there, worked hard articling, then passed the exam and was invited to the bar, just to come back to Empire and do exactly this." I tap the desk for emphasis, which is maybe a little much.

We both know it.

Luke surveys my tidy office so slowly that I become keenly aware of how small it is. It's also due for a repaint. I hear my endless dispute with my father one more time, but it feels like a betrayal even to think about it. "Is that paperwork for foreign workers at Cavendish Enterprises?"

I nod. There's no point in denying.

"So, with all your accolades and top marks, you're filling in forms like a clerk."

"Perhaps we could get to the point of your visit." I sound frosty, but what does he expect?

He leans back and takes another slow look. "I always thought you were a bit of a puzzle, Daph, but this takes it. You're not back here for love or money, and I don't see any other attractions. I thought at least you'd be out on your own, building your own practice as you fought the good fight, bringing justice to all. I seem to remember you being an idealist."

It sounds more like admiration than mockery but the truth in his words burns all the same. "It makes more sense for me to work at Weatherby & Bradshaw, and subsequently inherit a viable business," I say, hating the sound of my father's own argument falling from my lips. "But that's not your concern."

"No," Luke agrees easily, his gaze unswerving. "It's not. I'm just trying to figure you out."

"There's no need."

"Maybe I like the challenge."

When he looks at me so intently, it's like he can read every thought and secret I've ever had. I drop my gaze to my desk, telling myself to hurry this consultation to its end. "Your father isn't going to sell any property," I inform him. "He likes owning as much as he does."

There's an understatement. Patrick Cavendish owns most of Empire and he does nothing with most of his holdings. Buildings sit empty, lacking even tenants, as they disintegrate into the ground. It makes me angry, but he just wants to own it all.

Luke starts to smile. "I think that annoys you, Daph."

Of course, he noticed the subtext. "It doesn't matter if it annoys me. It *is*."

"But it doesn't have to be this way."

"Because you will just take over the titles of five properties? How? Private citizens don't have the right to expropriate property from other citizens or corporations."

"I'll buy them." I blink as he continues, remembering a bit late that he's rich. "I've been reading the bylaws of Cavendish Enterprises and if all the board is in agreement, they can divest of properties deemed to be unnecessary."

"You're not on the board."

"A detail that Patrick made sure I understood," Luke says without the bitterness I expect. I'm trying to name what's different. He seems resigned, maybe disappointed, or less sure that the world is his oyster.

What did happen to that bandmate of his?

Taylor. The huge blond guy with the man-bun, who played the guitar like a god. He was as radiant as the sun, and just as golden, a stark comparison to Luke's dark good looks. They looked fabulous together on stage and were said to be great friends. It was never reported how Taylor died, just that he did, and as I look at Luke, I wonder.

He flicks a look at me, catching me, and our gazes hold for a potent moment. My throat tightens.

"You should just ask Patrick to sell them to you then," I say.

Luke laughs and it's not a merry sound. "I did. He refused. He wouldn't even listen to me."

"He's on the board, too, and has the power to veto anything."

He sits back, eying me, his disapproval clear. "So, you're saying I should just give up and go away, give Patrick what he wants."

"It's easier."

"Someone once told me that if you want a specific outcome, you have to be prepared to influence results," he says grimly.

I wonder then what he has planned.

But Luke is done. He rises to his feet, shaking his head, exuding disappointment. "I've got to say, Daph, that I was hoping you'd at least listen, but I guess you know which side your bread is buttered on."

"What does that mean?" I ask, bristling, even though I know.

"That I knew he owned most of the town. I didn't think he owned everyone in it. Someone has to think Patrick isn't all that, and I expected Abbie's friend to be on my side. You used to be interested in what was *right*." He shrugs and reaches for his helmet, not even seeing how that barb hits home. "But I was wrong. My mistake. Have a great day." He turns away and I can't stand it.

"Tell me," I invite and Luke glances back.

"Why?" His eyes narrow. "Going to bill me for it?"

"Not unless it takes you an hour to explain."

He hesitates only a moment then returns to his seat. To my surprise, Luke doesn't launch into an explanation but sits there, tapping his fingertips on one knee. I expected him to have a smooth story prepared, that there would be patter and persuasion, but he seems to be having a hard time choosing where to start. I wait, mustering my own defenses, knowing that if he tries to charm me, my moat will be breached and my drawbridge will fall.

The gates will burn.

If he doesn't try to charm me, I'll once again feel like the only female on the planet who doesn't interest him.

I remind myself that I don't care, then he looks up suddenly again, and our gazes lock.

Caught.

"Once upon a time," he begins in his low rough drawl. I'm surprised by his choice of beginning—but not as surprised as what he says next. "I was a dick."

"You might still be," I say without thinking about it, then bite my lip.

Luke grins, though, untroubled. "You sound like Abbie, or does she sound like you?"

I shrug. "I suppose you have an example to illustrate your point."

"Brr, Daph. It's cold in here." He pretends to shiver and I just wait until he gives it up with a shrug.

I will not be teased.

"A good example," Luke acknowledges then, averting his gaze. He looks uncomfortable with the confession he's started to make, which is interesting. I never thought Luke had regrets. I thought that was his anthem, in fact. *Never look back. Never apologize.*

Maybe he *has* changed.

"The articles governing Cavendish Enterprises were drawn up when we were in high school," he says, changing direction so abruptly that I frown.

"I remember. My dad put in a lot of hours on them."

"And Patrick gathered everyone together, even yours truly, to walk us through the way he'd endowed his three older legitimate sons with all the power for the future. He made sure Abbie understood that she was cut out of the deal because of her gender. There was zero doubt that I was omitted because I'm not a real son."

"You look real enough to me."

"'Born out of wedlock' was Patrick's dismissal, as if my existence had nothing to do with him."

I nod. It doesn't make sense to me that Patrick has had affairs whenever and wherever he chooses, but he never thinks that any children who result from those relationships are his responsibility. He doesn't even treat them as his kids. He certainly doesn't pay support to their mothers. Everything Luke inherited from the wealthy Cavendishes was genetic.

I realize again that he doesn't sound resentful. "You used to be really angry about that."

"I did. I hated him. Still do, actually, but the difference is that someone pointed out that I was acting a lot like him." His brows rise as his gaze swivels to mine. "Ouch."

I don't believe it. "You?"

"Me. I was accused of taking what I wanted and not caring how much that cost anyone else." He grimaces. "It's not untrue, although if people voluntarily offer something and you take it, I'm not sure how much obligation you have beyond any good time you have together."

He's talking about fan-girls. He has to be. Ever since he

confessed in an interview that he loves women and lingerie, the stage has been knee-deep in bras and panties by the end of every performance. The finale of the show is always Luke wading through the offerings to invite one female fan onto the stage. She always squeals. He always drops to one knee and sings that ballad to her, the one that made them a fortune, the one that strikes at the heart and fills your thoughts with promises of forever. It's a great way to end a concert. Brings down the house every time.

And when that woman follows Luke off-stage, it's no mystery what happens next.

I am not the only person who has ever fantasized about what it would be like to be that fan.

I can't be.

I realize a bit late that he's watching me. When I straighten, startled, he resumes. "I didn't believe that I had anything in common with Patrick, but my friend said I needed to have more balance. I needed to take responsibility for what I've done, intentionally or not, and I needed to do my part to make the world a better place. He told me that I had to identify the prime mover, the incident that tipped the first domino, then fix it."

"And that's why you've come back to Empire?"

"No, I laughed at him. I thought he was crazy." Luke's expression hardens and he looks bleak. "And then he died," he adds quietly, a break in his voice.

I stare at him in shock.

He clears his throat, then resumes, speaking more quickly. "And it was my fault. Then the band fell into chaos and broke up, and that was my fault. Then we lost a bunch of sponsorships." He jabs a thumb into his chest, anger now making his eyes vividly blue. "*My* fault. The dominos kept falling. I knew that everything would keep going to hell unless I took his advice and *fixed* it." He winces and runs a hand through his hair. "The problem was that I couldn't figure out how to make a change, much less where to start." He fixes me with a look. "Don't laugh but I think my friend got impatient with Fate and took on the job himself."

I nod, knowing he's talking about Taylor but keeping my questions to myself for the moment. I'll ask when he's finished his confession.

"I ended up at this restaurant in Toronto. A friend recommended it, said the food was awesome but the neighbourhood stunk. Right on both counts. I would never have found that place on my own, but it was amazing. The incredible part, though, was that Sylvia Kincaid was working there."

"Sylvia Kincaid? The same Sylvia who was supposed to marry your brother Mike?"

"The very same. And he's my half-brother."

Right. I nod at the distinction.

Sweet, pretty, spunky Sylvia. I wonder how she's doing. At the end of high school, Sylvia just got on the bus and left town. Even though her grandmother still lives here, I haven't caught a glimpse of her since.

Why not? Why did she leave? I always assumed she just wanted to get away, but Luke's attitude makes me wonder if there's more—and if he knows the story.

"I haven't seen her since high school," I say.

"Me neither. But that didn't stop her. She marched up and dumped a pitcher of ice water into my lap."

I have to fight my smile as I see the point of his story. "Because of your dickness at some previous point in time."

He points at me in triumph. "Exactly."

"We return to the topic at hand. Always liked Sylvia."

He nods ruefully, unoffended. "And I treated her badly. It really didn't have much to do with her, which is the worst part of it."

I fold my arms across my chest. "What exactly did you do to Sylvia?"

"I seduced her, of course. It's what I used to do with every female in my proximity. I'm surprised you don't remember that, Daph."

I do. He never tried to get it on with me, though. I don't say it. *Used to.*

"I didn't think you'd stopped," I say instead.

"I have, actually, but that's recent and irrelevant to our discussion."

I think it's very relevant, but take a warning from his hard glare. That subject is closed, at least for the moment. "But Sylvia was engaged to Mike then."

"Yes. And stopped being so because of me. I'm not proud of what I did, and I won't blame Mike for being a contributing variable to my choice. I should have known better. I should have *been* better, but I wasn't. And that means I need to fix this."

"Fix what? It's been sixteen years."

"She's waiting tables, Daph." He's outraged by this, which makes me wonder how much exactly was between him and Sylvia. "The owner of the place calls her front-of-house, but she's waiting tables and that's what she's been doing since she left."

"Her choice," I venture.

"She could have been married to Mike all this time!"

"Maybe she didn't want to marry Mike." I do a good Devil's Advocate. Perhaps it comes with the territory.

"Or maybe I screwed up everything for them. Does Mike look happy to you? Has he had a relationship since Sylvia left? I'm pretty sure Sylvia's departure broke Mike's heart, and maybe it broke hers, too. I was a dick, Daph, and I'm going to own it. Don't try to make excuses for me."

"I'm not."

"Good." His eyes are blazing.

"Did you plan to mess them up, or was it just collateral damage?"

"No. No! Of course not. They were happy. I was just…"

"Being a dick."

"That's it. There was way too much Jägermeister involved in whatever decision I made then. I was angry and feeling provocative and Sylvia had the bad luck to be in my vicinity." Luke gets up to pace, perhaps sensing that I'm not entirely with him on this. He's as restless as a tiger.

"How does it make you different from Patrick to meddle in other people's lives?" I have to ask.

Luke grimaces as he pivots to face me, so intent that he could be an avenging angel.

If he was, I'd give him my soul voluntarily.

"Haven't you ever made a mistake, Daph?" he demands, an appeal in his tone that I can't ignore. "Haven't you ever done anything you wish you could erase completely, or that you could have a do-over and make a different choice?"

"Yes," I say without hesitation.

He steps closer. "Well, what if you *could* fix it?"

I avert my gaze because I have this weird feeling, like I can have anything I want just for agreeing with him. It clouds my thinking in a big way. I have the urge to make a wish and I know what it would be. Does he? "How is buying five properties from your father going to fix anything?" I ask, knowing my tone is hard.

Luke holds up a finger. "That is the brilliance of the plan, the one I need your help making a reality."

"I'm *not* buying a bridge in Brooklyn."

"No, but I'm going to buy a diner," he says, then points out the window. "*That* one. And you're going to thank me for doing it."

I follow his gesture, not understanding. Leon and Dotty's diner has been closed for ten years. They sold the property to Patrick to fund their retirement to Florida. It's been sitting there ever since. I'll guess that even the cockroaches have moved on.

"You're going to buy a diner?" I repeat.

"Yes. And Una's house, too. And you're going to help me." He smiles and my panties smoulder, right on cue. "Please."

Luke's so determined that I wonder if he's lost more than his friend.

I wonder if he's lost his mind.

Please.

I've lost this battle before he even begins to make his case, and I have to wonder just how smart that is.

2

———

LUKE

Daphne Bradshaw is looking at me like I'm a lunatic, and I can't entirely blame her. I could have presented this idea more coherently if I hadn't been so surprised—and distracted. I knew, of course, that she'd grown up, at least in theory, but I wasn't expecting the reality.

She's as brilliant as ever. Intimidatingly so. I'll bet that she's just as idealistic and principled.

But she's also gorgeous.

And inscrutable. She's watching me like I'm an alien specimen, one that defies all logic. Maybe I do.

I was ready for her to be smarter than me, but this new combination is throwing my game.

And that's a novelty, too.

I love women. I love how they smell and how they feel, how they think and how they taste, and how so many of them make little sounds when they're surprised. I love how different they are from me and from each other, and I could argue that I've had a plan to appreciate each and every one of them individually. I'm not intimidated by women and even the most beautiful of them never throws my game.

But then there's Daph. I have no idea what she's thinking, and that worries me.

It undermines any strategy I might have. It's prompting me to tell her more than I should, because my thoughts have gone straight to the gutter. She's one person I should never ever mess with, she's always been off-limits, and yet...and yet, I think being with her would be awesome.

Even more incredible is that this side of me died along with Taylor. I haven't been with a woman since that night. I don't think I've looked at a woman since—well, not in that way, anyway. (Granted, I looked at Sylvia when she gave me a very cold bath, but there was nothing sexy about that exchange.)

Daph has jolted that back to life again. I could very easily become fascinated by her—which would be exactly the wrong tactic. She's not the kind of person who responds to charm, who can be seduced or beguiled or persuaded by anything other than cold hard logic. I'm trying to get Spock to help me here and she has the advantage.

I remember that seriousness about her. I remember a girl with braces, a cloud of red hair and legs that went on for days. I remember a good girl with a little secretive smile, one that hinted she wasn't always such an angel. I was intrigued by her, my sister's best friend, but knew better than to get close. She was beyond my reach, and even if that was the very best way to get my attention back in the day—it still works pretty well now, evidently—I knew better than to mess with Richard Bradshaw's daughter.

And here she is, sleek and professional like she's corporate counsel for a Fortune 100 company. Her hair has darkened to auburn and is twisted up in a sleek updo. Her silver-gray suit is conservative, polished and expensive. Her legs still go on forever, and when she folds her arms across her chest to give me a look, the pose hints at some sweet curves hidden away.

Does she know that suit perfectly matches the gray of her eyes?

Does she ever wear purple or teal, or any other rich tone that would make her a knock-out?

Is her hair still long and wavy? What is it about that pale pink lipstick that makes me want to eat it off her? (Hint—it's the lips beneath it.) I want to know all the details and more—what kind of lingerie does she wear, and will I ever get to see it?—but alienating the only possible ally I might have in this venture is every kind of stupid.

I've been a lot of things in my time, but I've never been stupid.

I push impulse aside and focus on the plan. I can smell her skepticism, but even if it's at record levels for Daph, she's got nothing on Patrick and my half-brothers.

"Let me backtrack a bit," I say.

She looks at her watch pointedly and I start talking faster.

"So, Sylvia is still mad at me. Fair enough, if surprising. I called Una to find out more, maybe to learn how I could make amends."

"Sylvia's grandmother."

I nod.

"Inspired by your friend's 'do better' talk."

Exactly. We're on the same proverbial page, at least. "And Una, I've got to tell you, needs more people to talk to. I listened to her for an hour and she wasn't nearly done."

Daph bites back a smile. "When you live alone in the forest and never leave home, conversation can be hard to come by."

"True enough. She told me two salient things." I count them off on my fingers. "First, she has cancer."

Daph straightens and I get a peek behind the mask. She's

concerned. I'm glad for any sign that she's alive in there. "I didn't know..."

"No, she's not telling anyone, least of all Sylvia, because she doesn't want Sylvia to feel compelled to come back to Empire for any reason."

"Oh, but that must be so hard for her. I'll stop by and talk to her tonight, see if there's anything I can do to help."

"No, you can't. I promised not to tell anyone and she'll know then that I did."

I get a look for that. "Then you shouldn't have told me."

I shrug. It's for the greater good. And I trust Daph to keep the secret, even if she's looking daggers at me now. "Two. Because of the cost of her treatment, which is something not covered, she had to sell her cottage."

"But that's her home."

"And she sold it to Patrick."

Daph's eyes flash with fury and I'm glad I'm sitting down for that sight. She's electrified and smoking hot. "He should have loaned her the money instead!"

"That's not how he rolls and you know it."

She frowns. "Why would she even go to him?"

"Lack of options, I'll guess. The bank wasn't in a hurry to give her a loan and she was friends with Dianne."

Dianne was Patrick's first wife, the one he cheated on with my mom, and mother of his three golden sons and one daughter. I wasn't easy on her back in the day, but she was a nice woman. She must have picked up some truly awful karma in a past life to have ended up married to Patrick.

Daph looks at the list I've given her. "This is Una's house?" she asks, pointing to the first address on the list, and I nod. "I never knew it had a street address. I still don't understand the diner."

"That restaurant in Toronto is going under, despite the amazing food. I went back and talked to the chef when Sylvia wasn't there. She wants to open her own place but doesn't have the capital. I could have loaned it to her, or even given it to her, but Meredith MacRae isn't having any of my charity."

"Her words?"

"Pretty much. And though there was a time I could have created a line outside her door just for posting the place on my socials, those days are gone. I'm essentially no one now."

Daph gives me a look that is way too perceptive. "Doesn't seem to bother you."

"It was never about the money."

"It was about the women," she guesses.

I wince. "It was about the music and the concerts and the band. We had such a good time, every time, and there's a kind of magic in making your living at something that feels more like play than work."

Daph looks away and I know she doesn't feel that way about her own job.

What's her one regret? I'm dying to know, but continue with my presentation, such as it is. "So, I thought, what about offering opportunity instead?"

Daph, no slouch, glances toward the empty diner across the street.

I lean forward in the hope that my enthusiasm might be contagious. It's a long shot, with her eyeing me like a new species of beetle—one that might be such a threat to humanity that the world would be better off without me—but there's no backing out now.

"I'd sell it to her at a bargain price, easy terms. A hundred bucks a month over ten years, but she has to pay the utilities. I'll even pay the property taxes to sweeten the deal and toss in some cash for renovations."

"You'll lose a bunch."

"It's penance. It's supposed to cost you."

Her eyes narrow just a little and she looks like an exotic cat.

"But the real price here is that you have to ask Patrick for something."

She's too smart by half.

"And he will say no. He did already, without even hearing me out. Just because it was me asking for something." I open my hands to her. "And that's where you come in, Daph. You'll be presenting a purchase offer from an interested party who prefers to remain anonymous. It's not a conflict of interest, because the divesting of the properties would improve the financial position of Cavendish Enterprises."

"How could you know that?"

"I asked Jake."

It is satisfying to see her astonishment that I spoke to my oldest half-brother at all. I dig into my portfolio again. "The structure of Cavendish Enterprises requires the entire board to agree upon the selling or disbursement of any property held by the corporation, so I went and asked the board." I place a document on her desk and she leans forward to read it. "Here's Jake's signature on the proposal."

Daph picks it up, reading it through. "Is it real?"

Of course, she remembers. "Once, Daph. Only once."

"Seems like you have a lot of only onces."

"Some deeds don't bear repeating."

"One and done," she says under her breath, naming my mantra with an accuracy that shakes me a bit. She gives me an expectant look.

I produce the next document. "Austin. On board."

She reads this one, too, her gaze lingering on the signature of Cavendish son number three. "He never cared about any of it."

That's so true that there's no good reply. I move on. "Abbie."

"Not a board member," Daph notes, her voice as hard as Patrick's heart.

"She should be."

"But she isn't."

"But she still likes the plan." I wait while Daph shrugs, then hand her another document. "Mike. On board."

She's really surprised this time. "But Mike runs the greenhouses. He has the most time and energy invested in Cavendish Enterprises."

"And he wants change."

"Did you tell him about Sylvia?"

"No! That's for them to work out. Otherwise, I'd be meddling."

She has to fight a smile and I'm glad to see it. She can't keep her eyes from twinkling. "Even though you're scheming to get Sylvia back to Empire with this whole complicated *meddle*. You *have* inherited some tendencies from Patrick, whether you want to hear it or not."

I really don't like the sound of that comparison, but it just spurs me to try harder and do better. "What do you think?"

"There are three other properties." She taps the list. "This is Margaret's house. It's close to my dad's place. Pretty house."

That's not half of it. The house Patrick grew up in, and his mom before him, is a Regency cottage made of cut stone. It might be the oldest house in Empire, and even I remember it surrounded by perennial flowers instead of weeds. It's a disgrace to keep it empty and let it rot, instead of having someone live there and love it.

I know who would be perfect.

"Patrick's mother's house, where he grew up. Sitting empty and neglected." I can't hide my disgust.

Daph is philosophical. "The lawn gets mowed, at least."

"That's not loving a house. Abbie adores that place. You know she would come back if she had a place of her own."

Daph stares at me for a long moment. "That house would suit her," she says finally and I have no clue what she's concluded. Her fingertip is moving down the list and I notice that the pale pink polish matches her lipstick. Does she paint her toenails? I'm such a sucker for painted toenails. (On women.) "This is a legal description for a piece of property. Where is it?"

"It's a small parcel between the Cavendish greenhouses and Rhodes Vineyards. Adding it to my list was Mike's price for signing off. I started with just four properties, but am rolling with it."

"Not the land that Augustine Rhodes and Patrick are arguing about?"

"The very same. What do you know about it?"

"More than I want to," she says with heat. I watch her eyes as she gets up from her desk. If Daph had any idea how clear her thoughts are when she's agitated, how the truth is in her eyes, she'd shut that down in a hurry. For the moment, I feel like I have an unofficial window into her soul, and I love it.

She paces back and forth, and I get to watch.

"Both men claim they own it, and the titles are a mess. Nobody wanted it until a year ago, because it's sloped and has bad drainage. It's an irregular shape, too. Cavendish Enterprises can't build a greenhouse on it or even use it for a pond. But it's south-facing and last year, Mackenzie Rhodes discovered that the soil is exactly the right acidity for her to plant more grapes for ice wine."

She raises a hand. "We won't talk about the argument over her taking a soil sample for that test. Then the *battle royale* began. It's been Hatfields and McCoys up there, both Patrick and Augustine calling the cops all the time, not to mention lawyers. I suggested a survey, but the stakes keep moving in the night, though no one knows anything about it. And we still can't prove which ancient title includes that chunk of land that no one cared about until now." She sits down hard, her lips tight. "It's a hot mess."

"And Mike wants it solved. The plan is that I buy the parcel from Patrick and give it to Augustine."

"Good luck with that. Augustine thinks he already owns it and your father will never sell it."

"I was hoping you'd be more persuasive than that, as my representative."

She gives me a simmering look that makes my mouth go dry and taps a finger on the last property listed. "This is the little place at the other end of Queen Street, the one that used to have Albert Foreman's accounting business downstairs and an apartment upstairs."

"Maybe I want a place in town of my own."

She purses her lips. "You should know that no one rents apartments in downtown Empire, at least not anyone who pays their rent."

"I kind of assumed that."

"Are you staying then?"

"No. Not unless hell freezes over while this is getting done."

Our gazes lock for a hot moment and I know she's not going to give it up easily.

"I added it in so he'd have something to edit out," I say, which is plausible if not all of the truth. I do have a plan for the place, but Daph isn't ready to hear it yet.

I need her to take the job before I can talk about her compensation.

She has to want to hang out her own shingle. There's a pile of folders on her desk, stuffed with paperwork. Having her do all the forms and filing for agricultural workers at Cavendish Enterprises is a serious waste of her abilities, and I don't think she believed the party line any more than I did. Truth be told, it annoys me that someone as clever as Daph is pushing forms around her desk. She must want more. She must have had more in Toronto.

I can't figure out why she's even back in Empire.

It's got to have something to do with that regret.

In the meantime, she's going through the signed proposals

while she decides. I know better than to make another appeal, because I don't want to seem pushy or desperate—even though I'm pretty much both.

That leaves me with nothing to do but wait and study here, which does zero for any resolutions I might have at this time.

Who would have believed Daph would have become this woman in sixteen years? She could be a robot for all the emotion she shows, though—which just makes me want to unpin her hair, peel her out of that suit and give her an orgasm that makes her scream loud enough to wake the neighbours.

Get someone to call the police. Ha.

I love a challenge, and she might be the toughest one ever.

The fact is that I'm wired to want the one thing I can't have, whatever it is. Right now, that's Daphne Bradshaw, wrapped around me, digging her nails into my back and begging for more. I want her teeth marks on my shoulder, I want the slick heat of her on my fingers and my tongue. I want to lose myself in everything she is. I want her incoherent with pleasure, quivering around me.

Oh *yes*.

It's a distracting vision, as well as a very good one.

I'm both shaken and stirred.

And Daph couldn't care less.

That has to be the sound of Taylor laughing. (Too bad I'm the only one who can hear him.) He always said that one day, I'd meet a woman who would turn me inside out and enjoy doing it, one who would walk away and leave me with dreams that couldn't be fulfilled. I never believed it would happen. I never expected it to happen in Empire.

I never thought that woman might be Daph Bradshaw.

The worst thing is that I suspect she's going to turn me down. She's going to toss me out on my ass before I can regroup and make a better argument.

And still, I have nothing.

"You have to know that this plan might not come to fruition," Daph says finally. "Sylvia might not want to come back to Empire, even if you are trying to create a job for her to make it financially feasible. This chef—"

"Meredith MacRae."

"—might not want a place badly enough to take on Leon and Dotty's diner, such as it is." She fixes me with a glare that would have made Medusa proud. "If you have a solution that you're determined to inflict upon the participants, it's not that different from the way your dad plays."

Ouch. It's an observation worthy of Taylor.

And it's true.

"Can't I facilitate a possibility and let people choose?"

She smiles and it's like the sun rising over the tundra. "Of course," she says and there's a warmth in her tone that hasn't been there so far. "I just think you should be prepared for the possibility of being turned down."

"I am." I'm in Empire, after all.

"I'll have to do some due diligence," Daph says then, meeting my gaze steadily. Alas, the ice queen is back. "I want to be sure these signatures are genuine before I take on a job like this. If and when I do, we'll talk more specifically about compensation." She names her hourly billing rate, which doesn't surprise me at all—if anything, it's low—and gives me a round estimate to cover her efforts, if there are no surprises along the way.

The wave of relief nearly flattens me. The signatures are real, so I'm almost sure it's a go. "I suppose we should shake on it," I say and she glances up.

There's that little smile again, the one that is half-wicked, the one that always intrigued me. What *is* she thinking? Her gaze lingers on my mouth for the barest moment as she smiles and she's the hottest thing I've seen in half of forever. Before I can think of what to say, the smile is gone and Daph's composed again—as if I imagined that look.

Maybe I did.

She offers her hand. "Thank you for stopping in, Mr. Jones," she says, a big fat hint that it's time for me to make myself scarce.

I do. I don't want to mess this up now, even though it's only a partial victory. I shake her hand, liking the cool strength of her fingers, pick up my helmet and my portfolio and leave. I'm well aware of how the receptionist watches me go, and I wonder how many people she's already told about my arrival in town.

I put my sunglasses on, then stand beside my bike looking around.

It's a bright sunny morning in Empire and I have absolutely nothing to do, nowhere to go and no place to stay. My mission, such as it was, has been accomplished as much as it can be. I could visit my mom in Havelock, but I'm not ready for that just yet.

The bike starts right away, a sign of its recent visit to the shop, and I hope that Daph is watching me through the glass. I can't see into her office, as much as I'd like to have one last look. I walk the bike back to the road, noting that I don't have to yield to a single vehicle, then open the throttle as I ride out of town one more time.

I guess all the satisfaction comes with the first time you do something. Today, leaving Empire feels a bit flat.

As soon as I see the sign for The Maple Leaf Motel, though, I know where I'm going. Once again, the universe is steering me right, because that can't be anyone other than Bruno DeLuca crouched down beside a Harley in the parking lot of the motel his folks owned when we were kids.

It can't be the same bike, can it?

Speculation has me slowing for the turn. Contrary to local lore, I did not ride out of Empire on my motorcycle and never look back. I sold my Harley to Bruno so I could buy a plane ticket to the

States. He gave me my last ride on it when he took me to Havelock to get the bus to Toronto.

"Don't tell me you haven't got it running yet?" I ask as I pull to a stop alongside him. There are engine parts lined up on a sheet of newspaper spread on the pavement, just the way he's always worked, and his hands are black with grease.

"Luke!" he shouts loud enough for the whole town to hear. I get off the bike, enduring a hug while he keeps his hands away from my clothes. And then, it's all about the bike as we turn to survey it together. It *is* the same bike. I recognize a couple of scratches and the dent in one fender that was entirely my fault. "I've never been able to keep it running the way you did. Maybe you have the touch."

"Maybe I didn't teach you all its secrets." It's been a while since I've gotten my hands dirty and I'm looking forward to it.

"What brings you back?" he demands, then continues before I can reply. "Can you stay for a beer?"

"I'll stay longer than that if you've got an available room."

"Of course! Special offer for a friend."

"No, Bruno, you've got to charge me. I'll pay the full price." He starts to argue and I raise a hand. "Seriously. Let me."

"Okay, then you take the best room, the one we renovated last year, and you have to come for dinner tonight."

I'm surprised to feel all warm inside. "Deal. Now, what about this bike?"

"Let me get you a beer first."

"I'm up for that."

"Nothing fancy, now. I've got a two-four of Blue, just like always. You're probably used to some European boutique beer."

I grin. "Blue sounds great." I check out his progress on the bike as he gets the beer. He brings back two bottles, glistening with sweat.

"Are you in town for long?" he asks, after we've toasted each other and taken a swig

It tastes like tradition.

"Maybe a week," I say and he nods. "I'm not sure. I have some things to get sorted."

"Fair enough. We don't have many bookings before July, so take your time. Now, what's the deal with this engine?"

"It's always been the timing." I chuck off my jacket and crouch down beside him to get to work. I know this bike like the back of my hand. I feel like I worked on it just yesterday, that I was here, in this parking lot, taking apart bikes with Bruno just last week. The dates on the newspapers were different but not much else. He's losing a bit of hair on top and has put on some weight around the middle, but he's the same amiable, kind, generous guy I remember from high school. "Your folks still here?" I ask as we get to work.

"Nah, they retired to BC and gave us the motel. It's not making us rich, but we like it. Marissa will be excited to see you. She works in Havelock now."

"Marissa Talbot."

"Nuh uh. Marissa DeLuca," he corrects me with a grin.

"Prettiest girl in high school."

"You just say that because she's the one who turned you down."

"You beat me to it."

He laughs. "Good thing, too."

"You look like a happy man, Bruno."

"How could I not be?"

"I'll guess there are kids," I say because he's bursting to tell me.

"Three," he says with pride, handing me a wrench. He tells me about the kids and their activities in excruciating detail—which is actually quite sweet—and the kids themselves start to appear when we're on our second beer. By the time Marissa arrives, I've been pulled into the warm hug of their family like I never left at all.

There's lasagna and five conversations happening at once, a crowded table with mismatched cutlery, a red wine that's not half bad, and the coziness of their kitchen in the end unit, which I remember so well. The pictures of his folks are on the wall, smiling as it they're at the table with us, too. Marissa makes her lasagna half with meat and half without, so I have the middle daughter to thank for being able to stick to my dietary choices without any bother at all.

The conversation ebbs and flows, and I just sit, eat and enjoy, appreciating them both so much my heart hurts.

Maybe there is something I've missed about Empire, after all.

3

———

DAPHNE

Luke's gone with a roar, no doubt leaving a cloud of dust in his wake. He might have been a mirage or a figment of my imagination, but I can still smell that cologne of his, the one I like too much.

I have hot shivers and goosepimples for no logical reason at all. He's just a man.

But no matter how I rationalize it, there's no 'just' about Luke. His name should be written in capitals. He should be twenty feet tall. He's too bold, too imposing—too vital—to even occupy the same universe as we mere mortals, never mind sitting in my office, which has been entirely too small and too warm this morning.

Worse, he still has that superpower, that ability to make me not only aware of him but to feel so intensely that I lose track of everything but him. It's like he jolts me to life, just by showing up.

And he's *here*. Back in Empire, trying to hire me. His very presence is at odds with everything I know to be true. I stare at the chair for clients where he was just sitting. I can still see him clearly there in his jeans and his black leather jacket, his biker boots and his tight T-shirt. (The black suits him. It makes his eyes look more blue.) I saw the end of a tattoo on the back of his wrist and want to know what it is. He didn't have it before. He was wearing a silver ring on his right thumb with a Celtic knot on it and a silver bracelet on his left wrist.

It's not crazy that he's haunted my dreams since I returned to Empire. A harmless fantasy spurred by location, one that I never expected to be tested by an actual meeting. Maybe that was part of its appeal.

But today, he's not only here, but challenging my expectation that gorgeous guys only care about what they want for themselves.

Could there be an ulterior motive behind his plan? If so, I can't see it.

Luke is a Cavendish, whether Patrick likes it or not. One look at Luke and his connection to the patriarch is undeniable. Both coloring and confidence. Luke is his father's son—in appearances, anyway.

In every other way, he's defied that man since day one.

And given nothing, or close to it, he left town and made millions all on his own.

Which is admirable. Patrick Cavendish likes to manage everything and have it all his way. He has a will of iron and insists all his kids do as they're told. They're not kids anymore, and some of them have to hate that affluence comes with such a price.

But Luke, Luke was the only one to do anything about it.

And now, evidently, he wants to challenge Patrick again.

I can't help thinking about that one forged signature, the one that made all hell break loose in town. It was audacious, the kind of challenge that only a teenage boy would make, although really, other than Patrick's pride, not much had been hurt.

It certainly gave everyone something to talk about.

I take a deep breath, scan the single page proposal to buy five properties from Cavendish Enterprises again. It's an interesting idea, in a way. Out of the box. So unexpected that it just might work. I have to like that the other board members are agreeable—if, indeed, they are.

A bit late, I realize I have no way of contacting Luke. No phone number. No idea where he's staying. No real conviction that he *is* staying. (He said he was leaving, just not when.) I take a deep breath, telling myself that he'll be back when he chooses and to just accept that reality.

I really *really* hope that none of these signatures are forged, but I know better than to believe they're genuine before I verify them.

I call Jake first.

The oldest of Patrick's legitimate sons is a finance guy in Toronto, making buckets of money. I always assumed that Jake was interested in having all the goodies himself, that maybe he hadn't been that pleased to surrender his status of only child at the ripe age of two, so I'm curious about his agreement to Luke's scheme. I don't remember them getting along very well.

Jake answers on the first ring, crisp and efficient. Maybe impatient at the interruption. He listens, though, without interrupting me.

"I appreciate your due diligence, Ms. Bradshaw," he says. "And I certainly understand your reservations, but this is perfectly legitimate. Luke came to see me last week to present his proposal and I agreed."

"Why?"

He sighs. "I've been bugging Dad for years to divest of some of these bits and ends of property. He and Cavendish Enterprises would be better served having that asset in cash, instead of tied up in properties that leech money."

"Insurance," I guess.

"Property taxes. Maintenance, such as he does. Legal fees if there are ever any tenants. It's a lot of trouble and completely unnecessary."

"I see."

"And with Cavendish Enterprises rapidly expanding, it would be prudent to have more cash in reserve. Things happen unexpectedly." I nod and he clears his throat. "I trust that detail will go no further."

"Of course not. We have experienced some uncertain times of late."

"Exactly."

I think he's going to end the call, but Jake hesitates for a moment. "Anything else?" I prompt.

"I just want to note that I appreciated the idea of Luke wanting to provoke change. I saw no harm in encouraging that."

"Why not?"

Jake laughs a little. It's a rueful sound. "Well, it's an exercise in futility, isn't it? Dad is never going to agree. Luke's heart might be in the right place, but it's not going to matter in the end. Dad will nix it all."

"Then why did you agree?"

He considers this so long that I think he isn't going to answer. "Because Luke drew the short straw," he concedes finally. "It's not his fault, but he's paid the price of being an outsider over and over again. I know I've been a part of that and I was glad he came to me. I saw an opportunity for change between us, which I welcomed. We had a good talk, which is new, and I'm optimistic that things might be easier between us going forward, no matter what Dad does."

"And if Patrick does agree?"

There's a full beat before Jake answers, as if he can't even wrap his mind around that possibility. "Then Luke will finally get something he wants. Whether that's a good or bad thing remains to be seen." I hear another phone ring. "Is that everything? I've got to go."

I add Jake's admission that Luke was always an outsider to

Luke's comment about Mike being a contributing variable to his choices with regards to Sylvia, and decide that as rich as they were (and are), the lives of the Cavendish clan haven't been all sunshine and roses.

But then how could they have been, with Patrick as their father? The patriarch sets the tone and when he's as domineering, demanding and inflexible as Patrick, there's not going to be a lot of kindness going around.

I think about Luke's mom then, without expecting to. Such a pretty woman. Louise worked at the hair salon in town and never seemed to catch a break. She never said anything against Patrick either, which maybe means she's a saint. I wonder where she is now.

Back to business.

Mike is next. Unlike Jake, he's slow to come to the phone. They page him and I wait, then they page him again. He must be in that enormous greenhouse. It literally has acres under glass, and there are more greenhouses beyond that one, too. The workers ride bicycles to get from one end of the complex to the other.

I have time to wonder whether I should say anything about Sylvia, then decide against it.

Mike sounds even more impatient than Jake and though I can hear someone yelling in the background, I can't understand the words. It could be Spanish. I hear him drumming his fingers while I explain the reason for my call.

"I signed it." He gives a wry laugh. "I suggested that he add that piece of land that Rhodes Vineyards wants to his list and when he agreed, I was sold. I'd give anything to get Augustine Rhodes off my back. That man is making me almost as nuts as Dad is over this. It's a small parcel of land that's useless to us. Those two just like a fight more than I do. I don't have time for this crap." He clears his throat, evidently realizing who he's talking to.

"Everything has been within the law, of course, just a steady drip of annoyances, like water on stone."

"But the rest of Luke's proposal?"

"I didn't even read it. If Luke has a plan that will make Augustine Rhodes go away, I'm all for it."

So, Mike might not have even noticed Una's house on the list of properties.

"Of course, Dad's never going to agree to any of it. I wouldn't want to be the one who gets to present it to him." He pauses. "Who's going to do that? Luke? He won't even manage three words before Dad turfs him out."

"Apparently Patrick already declined to hear his proposal, so I'm going to present it on behalf of an anonymous party." I decide that, right then and there, and not just because Mike is probably right.

"Well, good luck to you, Daphne. Set your phaser on stun, at least."

I smile despite myself at the warning. "What do you think might convince Patrick to agree?"

"Nothing! I've been trying for a year to get him to agree to cut loose that one property. I swear, he thinks he's going to take it all with him. I'm out of ideas." His voice sharpens as I hear more Spanish. "Is that all you need from me? Things are a bit crazy today."

I thank him and end the call, then sit looking at my phone for a long moment. They both signed, partly because they thought Patrick would never agree.

I have no way to reach Austin, given how famous he is, so I text Abbie. Her reply is immediate.

> Daphne! Of course, I agreed, but not for the house.
>
> Tho it was sweet of L to think of me.

Why, then?

Who am I to trash his emotional recovery?

???

My phone rings. It's Abbie.

"Didn't Luke tell you?"

"Tell me what?"

Abbie backpedals. "Something happened."

"Like what?" I'm pretty sure I can guess but it would be better to know.

"It doesn't matter. Luke wants to make a difference. He wants to change. That's the important bit and if I only need to sign one document to help, I'll do it."

I think whatever had that big of an effect on Luke Jones' worldview does matter. "Was it Taylor's death?" I guess.

She sighs but doesn't answer. "It's his story to tell, if he wants to, but he convinced me. I know this plan is crazy and I don't think it will work out, but I'm hoping I'm wrong."

"Your dad won't agree."

"That's what we all think. Luke won't be able to change his mind, but Daphne, could you?"

"I have no idea."

"I suggested that he come to you. If anyone can do it, it's you, Daphne. Promise me that you'll try."

Of course, I promise, even if Abbie's view of my skills is unjustified.

I call Austin, using the number Abbie gave me. Apparently, he's in California, filming yet another episode of *So You Think You Can Cook*. You've probably seen it. All these ambitious chefs pitted against each other, three judges to pick apart their creations —and them, if they're unlucky. Austin is the miserable one. He's sarcastic and tough, kind of funny if you like that sort of thing. He does it so well that he must come by it naturally.

Again, the legacy of Patrick casts its shadow. No one learned the power of praise and encouragement in that house.

"What?" Austin demands when he finally comes to the phone.

They were all out of charm when he got to that line, I think but I don't say it out loud. It sounds like something my mom would say.

I start to explain, but Austin interrupts me.

"You're calling from *Empire?* From the end of the world? You're interrupting my day with a question about my half-brother's half-assed scheme to improve our wreck of a hometown and the lives of people I don't even know? Do you think I have nothing better to do than listen to this kumbaya garbage? Who *cares* about those properties, other than Luke?"

"Did you sign the agreement?"

"Of course, I did. It doesn't matter what happens in Empire. Give it all away, my father will have a heart attack from shock, and life will instantly become simpler." He sighs. "It's never going to happen, though, Ms. Bradshaw. Luke is ridiculously optimistic. The old bastard doesn't even get rid of his fingernail clippings."

There's an image I don't need. I thank him and look at my list.

They all knew.

They all willingly agreed.

Luke didn't lie to me.

I spin in my chair and review the whole thing one last time. On the pro side, I like the idea of the world being a better place. I like the idea of Empire getting another chance. I like all the ideas of Abbie getting her grandmother's house, of this awesome chef in Toronto owning her own restaurant, of Sylvia spending time with her grandmother while she (hopefully) heals, of Una not having to worry about losing her house, of Mackenzie planting those grapes to make more ice wine and build on success.

I really like that Luke sees the power of change in women. Did he do that on purpose?

I also like the idea of having a great place to go for lunch in town, right across the street.

I like fresh starts.

I like making a difference.

I like a challenge.

And I think I'm going to like being in league with a self-appointed agent of change just fine.

All I have to do is get Patrick's agreement.

That's not going to be easy.

In fact, that, and the need to actually present this plan to him, is the only con—but it's a big enough one that someone fainter of heart than me might take a pass.

Not me.

———

I ONLY KNOW Patrick Cavendish by sight. (He'd probably say the same about me.) That's an amazing thing when you consider it. Abbie and I were best friends from kindergarten on. We were in and out of each other's houses all the time, having sleepovers, going to dance class together, all of it. You'd think I'd know her dad pretty well, but Patrick was never there. At the time, we were told that he was working, but my mom's lips always got tight when my dad made Patrick's excuses. Maybe he was working some of the time, but a lot of the time, he was spending energy and money else-where. Dianne, wife #1, was concurrent for a while with Luke's mom but blissfully ignorant of her competitor's existence. When Dianne died, Patrick married again, but to Candace Knowles, not Luke's mom.

I've resented Patrick on Abbie's behalf for years. The summer I spent picking tomatoes in the Cavendish greenhouses gave me an appreciation for his...frugality. The company was much smaller then and so were the greenhouses, but they were driven to get the fruit harvested according to schedule. It was hard work and long hours, and the pay wasn't particularly great. (My father used to like telling me that I was lucky I never had to pick tobacco, as his father compelled him to do one summer. No doubt he also walked barefoot in the snow to school, uphill both ways.) Patrick occasionally appears at my dad's offices, but usually my dad goes to his client. Minions travel to the king, of course, not the other way around.

And they play golf, every Tuesday, weather permitting.

Today's weather permits, so I know where to find them both. I check the time and guess that they'll be finishing up the front nine by the time I get there.

The Empire Golf Course is fancier than you might expect. Patrick is on the board, naturally, and one of the endowing partners. The membership is tightly controlled and consists primarily of professional men, mostly from Havelock and beyond. The course was designed by a PGA champion and is scrupulously maintained. The restaurant is predictably mediocre. I have to like that even Patrick hasn't been able to change that.

I check in at the front desk, my dad is located, and I head out the back of the clubhouse to the tenth tee, glad that I changed to my flats.

They're waiting together and laughing, my handsome father and his client. Or the king of Empire and his crown vizier, who knows it's smarter to laugh at the regent's jokes. Neither of them look their age: both are trim and tall, perhaps not as slender as they once must have been. You'd probably guess my dad was the older of them.

In fact, Patrick has a few years on my dad, but his hair is still mostly dark and he has a restless energy that I realize reminds me of Luke. He watches me all the way across the lawn, eyes narrowed against the sun, his scrutiny as sure as the weight of a hand on my shoulder. Pushing me down, of course. Some would call him handsome, but he reminds me too much of a hawk for me to think he's attractive. All the right features are there, the chiseled profile and the firm lips, but he looks like as ruthless he is.

I wonder for the first time whether my amiable gentleman of a father loses deliberately to Patrick when they play each week, just to keep the business. I wouldn't put it past him. As I've been told multiple times, there's precious little opportunity in Empire for legal work and my dad does love his Benz.

"This is a surprise, Daphne," my father says, his tone cheerful. I hear a wariness in it all the same, and know that he's suspicious of my appearance.

"I didn't want to interrupt your game, but there's something I think you should see, Mr. Cavendish."

My dad lifts a brow, a question in his gaze. I ignore it. Heart in throat, I give the document to his companion.

Patrick hands off his club to my dad, as if my dad is his caddy, and takes the proposal from me. He reads it, all of it, his dour expression speaking volumes. He shakes his head when he's done and hands it to my dad, whose eyes widen as he reads. Then he shakes his head and gives the document back to Patrick.

"What do you think, Richard?" Patrick asks, his gaze fixed upon me. "What's your little girl trying to stir up here?"

I bristle at the diminutive. My dad shoots me a warning glance. "It looks to me as if Daphne has been retained to act on behalf of an anonymous client to present an offer to purchase," he says mildly. "She is fulfilling her obligation to her client by presenting this proposal to you, as requested."

Relief floods through me that my dad is defending me and I'm ashamed that I wasn't sure he would.

Patrick snorts. "Anonymous, my ass."

My father glances at me.

"Is your client Luke Jones or not?"

"Client privilege…" I begin but Patrick scoffs.

"Bull. This is Luke's doing, and I know it." He shoves the proposal toward my father, not waiting for my reply. "What do you really think of it?"

My dad flicks through the agreement. "I don't think these properties are key to your business, or that their ownership is particularly material. You could be agreeable, at very little cost to yourself, and, in fact, add to your capital assets."

"Agreeable?" Patrick laughs. "I thought you knew me better than that, Richard."

They laugh together and my dad hands the proposal back to me, as if the matter is closed.

I don't take it.

"This is an offer to pay market price for five properties in your possession," I say calmly. "The other members of the board have agreed to the sale."

"Because they're fools."

"The opposite could be argued, if you insist upon holding onto properties for which you have no use, or no future plans."

My father's eyes narrow, but I ignore that, too.

Patrick is glaring at me. "How I choose to run my business, Miss Bradshaw, is my business alone."

"But I'm curious. Why wouldn't you take the chance to make a difference to the town where you live?"

"I don't technically live in Empire. My house is in the township, not the town."

"Yet you've reduced the town to a shell of its former self by leaving properties empty and untended. It could be said, Mr. Cavendish, that you've taken but you haven't given back."

His eyes flash and my dad starts to say something. Patrick gestures him to silence. "Who are you to know what I've taken and what I've given? This town survives because I've given people the support they need." He gestures to the list. "Una Kincaid needed money and she knew where to come for it."

"Maybe what Una needed was compassion," I reply. "Maybe what Una needed was a break."

"Oh, is that how we do business now?" he sneers. "We give everything away to those who ask for it, until there's nothing left to give? That's not how anyone succeeds, Miss Bradshaw. That's not how legacies are built."

"And what will your legacy be, Mr. Cavendish? A business that draws heavily on the infrastructure that people in Empire pay for and you utilize?"

"You have a nerve..."

"The very few residents of Empire would have no need to upgrade their water system or install windmills to generate power, not without the draw on both utilities by Cavendish Greenhouses." His lips tighten but I'm not done. "It's not unlike this golf course, built for rich people from somewhere else. Do people from Empire even get service jobs locally? We know they don't get work in your greenhouses."

His nostrils flare. "People in Empire get what they choose to for themselves. I don't owe people jobs who don't get an education. I don't owe anything to anyone."

"Yet we all owe whatever you want to you."

My father inhales sharply but is ignored.

Patrick shakes his head. "Luke's done it again, hasn't he? Charmed some woman who could be useful to him. Don't go thinking there's any future for you with Luke Jones. He's been trouble ever since he was born, making waves for their own sake, and if he's back, that can't be good news. You should be smart enough, Daphne Bradshaw, to recognize that there's only one thing he ever wants from a woman, and you're not going to be any different."

I'm tempted to say that Luke came honestly by that inclination, but I remember his own claim that he's been celibate. I bite my tongue hard.

Patrick laughs. "Not what you wanted to hear, is it? He's got you stirred up and on his side, because he wants to play. Okay. Let's play." He grabs the document and turns to the list of properties. "It's time Luke had a lesson in how the real world works. I'll make you a bet, Richard, that I'll have it all back in a year." He puts out a hand and my dad gives him a pen. "But a couple of changes first."

I watch, wondering what he'll do.

"I don't want to sell Albert Foreman's building," he says and puts a line through that item. Funny, that's what Luke predicted he would do. "Why does he want my mother's house?"

"He thinks Abbie should have it."

"Women don't need real estate," Patrick says. "They need husbands. And Abbie doesn't need a house in Empire since she's chosen to live in Vancouver," he says, breaking my heart with a stroke of a pen. He taps another item on the list. "Augustine Rhodes will only have that parcel of land over my dead body," he adds and draws another red line.

I'm tempted to suggest that it could be arranged.

He writes a number on the bottom of the document, where there's a space for the price.

"That's too much," I say. I know the price of real estate in Empire. I just bought a house here.

"When you come with an offer like this, you can expect to pay a premium," Patrick says. "Luke can afford it, unless he's forgotten to look out for number one and has wasted all his money away like the loser he was born to be."

He looks at me and I shake my head, hoping like hell that Luke is good for it. I also hope that Mike won't withdraw his support with that parcel of land removed from the proposal.

Would it really matter? It's clear that Patrick makes all the decisions.

He and my father exchange a glance, my father shrugs, Patrick initials his changes and signs the document. "Take it or leave it," he says. His gaze is as cold as ice and I hate that I have to fulfil his expectation.

I take it, just the way he knows I will. There's the diner, which gives that chef her chance, and Una's house, which is for Sylvia. It will make some of Luke's agenda come right. I remind myself that this really is the heart of his suggestion, to make amends to Sylvia, and that's been preserved. The prime mover is being addressed. I hate losing any of the plan, though I know that there's no blood to be had from this stone.

"Thank you, Mr. Cavendish. I apologize for interrupting your game."

"You're making a mistake," he warns. "That boy will lead you astray. You can count on it. He's never been any good."

I don't answer. It seems to me that I've been talking to the trouble behind all of this. I walk away, reminding myself to be content with a partial victory.

I'm not.

Not even close.

I thought I was in before, but Patrick has redoubled my commitment. Now I'm determined to make Luke's plan work.

Whatever it takes.

4

LUKE

I'm so full of lasagna that I go for a walk after dinner.

Actually, I go for a walk because I'm curious as to what Daph has discovered and/or done.

Can I find her?

I head back down Queen Street and immediately notice that the pewter Honda that was parked outside the law office earlier is gone. I decide immediately to do some detective work to figure out where Daph lives. Empire isn't that big. I can walk it all inside of an hour, so I get started.

What can I tell you about my hometown?

The road from Havelock comes from the east. It twists around a bit then becomes Queen Street, straightening out at The Maple Leaf Motel. I leave the motel parking lot and walk past the Petro Canada gas station just west of the motel, a brand new place with very bright lighting and no service. I don't even have to look to know that the chip truck beside it is open. I can smell the fat a hundred meters away. Across the street on the north side is the United Church, solid brick and a century old, the sign reminding us all that services are at 10 each Sunday morning.

On the left, the south side, is Weatherby & Bradshaw, the first building in Empire's downtown. The lights are out and nobody is home there.

Queen Street runs roughly east-west. There's one major intersection ahead at Erie Street, which heads north, past several streets of houses, ultimately finding its way to the Cavendish Greenhouses and Rhodes Vineyards a couple of clicks out of town. (That's kilometers, in case you aren't sure.) Erie Street also runs south to (surprise) Lake Erie and Empire's sister town, Port Cavendish. Once Port Cavendish was the big town and Empire the offshoot. It was the other way around for a while, and now both are quiet.

The intersection of Erie and Queen is a roundabout, with a huge sugar maple planted in the island. Big Red is over a hundred years old and an absolute knock-out each fall. It's bigger than I remember, its leaves now the bright green of springtime and new growth.

After I pass the law offices, I check out the current state of downtown retail. It's bleak. Across the street is an antique store, which might be better called a junk store from the offerings in the window. There are more empty stores before the closed diner that I want to give a future.

There's also a bunch of papered windows between the law offices and the old Odeon theatre, which shut down sometime after I left town. They used to play *The Rocky Horror Picture Show* at midnight on the last Friday of the month, even though that trend had been well over—just not in Empire. I smile in recollection of all of us doing *The Time Warp* (again and again) and would bet there are still pieces of toast in the darker corners.

Next to it, on the southeast corner of the circle around Big Red is The Emporium, a department store of sorts from Empire's early years, also closed and empty. The post office is across the street on the northeast corner.

It's amazing how quiet it is. I can't hear any cars or other traffic. There's a bit of music floating through the air, like someone is listening to oldies in their kitchen with the window open, but otherwise, I could be out in the country. Or maybe in a ghost town. I hear an owl, which is enough to make me stop and try to spot it. (No joy.)

There aren't many cars parked on Queen Street or any litter blowing down the street. Maybe Empire *is* a ghost town. Most of the buildings are two storeys, retail on the street level and residential units upstairs. The majority of that retail space is empty, too. I don't see many lights, although there's a television or computer on in the apartment over the antique store, casting blue light at a ceiling. No signs of movement, though.

I suppose some towns would have a war memorial in the middle of the roundabout, but Empire has that maple tree in pride of place. The town has always been small. Maybe there weren't enough local sons who went to war. Maybe they had lucky charms in their pockets and all came home. I don't know, but Big Red isn't going anywhere soon.

I look up Erie Street to the library on the west side just a bit north of Queen Street. Like so many towns in the area, Empire has a Carnegie library. The Anglican Church is beside it, on the northwest corner, claiming the prime real estate, followed by a run of closed stores on Queen Street west, including one that I remember as a small grocery. The street looks sadder than I remember. There's a thrift store at the very end, then the road narrows and turns to gravel. I know it carries on to the town cemetery, out of view, a site for a lot of late night shenanigans then and maybe now.

Are there even kids here? Teenagers? The silence is almost eerie.

I cross the road and head back on the south side of Queen, passing the convenience store, which is open, neon light flashing, and a taco truck, which is not open. The taco truck is new and I check the hours on the sign, planning to drop by Friday if I'm still in town. Empire seems an unlikely place for a good taco, but then again, a lot of the seasonal workers in Patrick's greenhouses are Mexican.

Next to the convenience store is the Canadian Legion. There are a few cars there now, cheap beer having an eternal appeal. I hear a bit of laughter and some old rock and roll, but am not tempted to go in. The Grand Hotel beside it might once have been spectacular, but now it's dreary. Technically, it remains open, but I can't believe anyone would choose to stay there.

There's another empty storefront of no particular distinction, then The Golden Lotus Chinese & Canadian Cuisine, which occupies the former Bank of Montreal building on the southwest corner of that main intersection. I smile at the sight of it, remembering a lot of late-night eating at Mr. Chang's. It was the place to go when we had the munchies, and if it was close to closing, Mr. Chang let us eat as much as we wanted of whatever had already been prepared.

To my right, Erie Street heads south, curving past an auto repair place and a bicycle shop before heading to Port Cavendish. I make the circle around Big Red all the way to head north on Erie Street, and turn right on Caledonia Street.

Caledonia runs parallel to Queen, followed by Britannia immediately to the north—somewhat higher in terms of altitude and more expensive in terms of real estate. They're both filled with houses and I'm guessing Daph lives on one or the other. I can't imagine her in the trailer park at Port Cavendish, but she might have a surprise for me.

Most of the houses are neat and modestly sized on Caledonia. They are a mix of styles and vintages, and there are a few in dire need of repair. Forest Drive is a short street at the end, running south from Britannia past Caledonia and ending in a circle. You could cut through the trees there to get to the United Church when walking.

I spot the pewter Honda parked in front of a two-storey house with a porch. It's on the east side of Forest Drive between Caledonia and Britannia. Behind it is a forest that merges into the provincial park just outside of town. Somewhere in that cluster of trees is the cottage owned by Una. I pass the house where Daph must live, deciding what to say and do, and turn down Britannia while I plan. I walk it to the very end, past Erie Street, past the house where Daph's dad must still live. There's a big Mercedes sedan parked out front and lights on inside. A couple of doors down is Margaret's house, the Regency cottage that looks as abandoned as it is.

That's the house I want Abbie to have, and I study it for a long moment, knowing it would suit her perfectly. On the other side of Britannia are newer houses, including some from the 70s that look like they host extensive macramé collections. There's a footpath that leads down to Caledonia and on to Queen, but the ground is uneven here. To the west is a creek and though there are a couple of walking trails, it's dark as Hades out there. This time of year, the mosquitos will be thirsty, so I take a pass and head back toward Daph's place.

And there you have it. You've seen Empire, such as it is.

Small, but not particularly mighty.

And I've stalled as long as possible. Time to get the verdict.

The upside is that it's another chance to see Daph.

―――

I STEP up to Daph's porch, wondering suddenly if there are more pewter Hondas in Empire than I realize. The house is neat to the point of austerity. I expected fluffy chick stuff for a woman living alone, but then, Daph does have that Vulcan thing going on.

Does she own the place? Maybe.

The porch runs across the front of the house and is simple. The lack of curlicues and gingerbread, the plain cream paint, makes me suspect I'm in the right place. The door has a new coat of paint, too, a deep blue that looks great with the creamy trim. There's no cutesy welcome sign or wreath of arranged flowers on the door, just a wooden bench for two under the front window. It's a light green, closer to lime than mint. The front garden is almost non-existent—I'm thinking that some ancient and overgrown shrubs have been torn free of the earth, and guess that there are plans for this year—but there are tulips growing on either side of the steps. Pink ones. The aesthetic is kind of Scandinavian and would photograph well.

I knock on the door and shove my hands in my pockets when I hear footsteps.

When the door opens, I catch my breath.

Daph has not only gone casual, but she's mad as hell.

She's wearing dark leggings that show her fabulous legs to advantage, and an oversized cream cabled sweater that falls off one shoulder. I can see the hollow of her throat and enough skin that I know there's not a bra strap. I drag my gaze back to her eyes.

They're all silver fire, an even better view than the one offered by the sweater.

Damn. I have to look away to compose myself.

"He's an asshole," she says and I'm not going to dispute that, knowing exactly who she means.

"Patrick said no?" I guess.

"He took out the Foreman place, just like you expected." She frowns. "Wait. How did you know where I live?"

"I looked for your car."

Surprise lights her eyes for a moment, then she pivots. She leaves the door open and marches back to her kitchen, which I take as an invitation.

I follow her, closing the door behind myself, sweeping a glance over the interior. It's beyond neat. I shed my jacket and boots, leaving them at the door.

The house has to be close to a hundred years old, but it's surprisingly modern inside. Almost austere in its minimalism. There's a fireplace in the front room, polished hardwood floors throughout, a packed bookcase in that front room that I want to explore. (Yes, I want to know Daph's secrets as revealed by her choice of reading material.) The furniture is teak, vintage gems with new upholstery in shades of silver and blue. The area rug is creamy white and thick, more than a Berber. The overall look is elegant, just like Daph.

There must have been a dining room once between the kitchen and front living room, but it's become part of the kitchen. The structural beam reveals that a wall is gone. There's a table for four, then a counter with bar stools, and a new kitchen where Daph is slicing a lemon with enough enthusiasm to lose a finger. I like the talavera tiles on the kitchen backsplash, all blue and white with hints of yellow, and the open shelving. There's a door at the back, one with a half-window, but I can't see anything beyond it. Her place backs onto the forest, so there'd only be shadows out there at this hour.

There was a staircase opposite the front door, leaving up to probably two or maybe three bedrooms and bath. It's a small house, but it is both inviting and cozy.

She takes the knife to some asparagus spears with a savagery they can't possibly deserve. "And he red-lined Margaret's house."

Ah, that's what's fired her up. Truth be told, it annoys me, too, but I expected it.

I tell her so.

She shakes the knife at me, obviously having no clue how amazing she looks. Her eyes are blazing, practically shooting sparks in every direction. Her cheeks are a bit flushed, too. She's taken down her hair and shoved it into a messy bun instead, which proves that it's both long and wavy. I can see the back of her neck, all smooth silky skin, and want to taste it. Her feet are bare and her toenails—be still my heart—are painted that same pale pink that her lips were earlier.

I could eat her up with a spoon.

Or without one.

I lean on the counter and remind myself that I'm not that interested in women anymore. I didn't even have to swear off them when Taylor died. I didn't care. Not about women. Not about sex. Not about pushing my hands through thick tresses of silky hair and taking a deep breath of any woman's scent.

Until now.

Until Daph.

Come to think of it, her place smells humid and sweet. I realize that her hair looks damp and that the scent is shower gel. Jasmine and vanilla. I'm a dead man. (Well, not all of me.) My mind immediately conjures an image of Daph in the shower, of hot water and suds, a vision that does nothing for my ability to coherently continue a conversation with her.

Of course, I catch her looking at me. "What's wrong?"

"Just disappointed," I lie. "I was really hoping to give that place to Abbie." That part's true.

"I know. He went for the diner and Una's place, though. I'm telling myself to be content with small victories."

I wince that Rhodes Vineyards won't be getting that piece of land. "But you're not."

"Are you?" She puts the lemon slices on a piece of fish without waiting for an answer. It's already on foil on a sheet pan. I realize there's a pot of rice on the stove and the asparagus is ready to be added to the sheet pan. She winces when she follows my glance. "I hope you're not hungry. I only have this one piece of fish."

"No worries. I've had more lasagna than is reasonable, but when it's homemade, I can't resist."

I get a look for that. "Where did you get homemade lasagna in Empire?"

"I took a room at The Maple Leaf Motel. It's worth it to be invited for dinner at DeLuca's."

She smiles and I bask in the sight, glad I could improve her mood. "I'll have to ask Marissa if she takes orders." She puts the fish in the oven, sets a timer and puts a second glass beside the one already on the counter.

"This your place or do you rent?"

"Mine," she says with an increment of pride. "That's one good thing about Empire. Cheap real estate. I could never have bought my own house in Toronto."

It's not nearly a good enough reason to live beyond the end of the world, but I don't say it.

She raises a finger. "Speaking of which, the properties you listed have comparatively high prices." She gets the paperwork from her briefcase and offers it to me, retreating to check on the fish.

I read it, like I'm supposed to, shake my head at the number Patrick has scribbled on it, and smile.

"You're not surprised."

"I was guessing he'd go ten per cent more. Maybe fifteen." I take the pen she offers and sign.

"He made a bet with my dad that he'd have it all back in a year."

"Then your dad should brace himself for the win."

She's watching me. "You really hate him."

"I'm thinking he's not one of your favourite people either."

"No, but that's not a great thing to have in common." She gets a bottle of white wine from the fridge, one that's already been opened, and pours.

I toast her. "To incremental progress," I say. "Thanks, Daph, for riding to war on this."

"Sorry I didn't do better."

"You got more than I would have done. He refused before he even knew what I wanted when I tried to ask."

"He knew this offer was from you."

"Probably one of the golden boys spilled the truth."

She leans a hip against the counter, watching me. "Have they always closed rank against you?"

I shrug. The truth is self-evident.

She sips the wine, eyes simmering again. "It's so unfair," she says under her breath. I have to love the idea that Daph is feeling protective of yours truly, but she probably just hates to lose.

It's almost worth ticking her off just to see her like this. You know I'm wondering what she looks like when she comes. You know I'm wondering if I'll ever have a chance to find out. She's making me feel like my old self, but not quite.

What's new is that I'm only interested in this one woman. Is it because she's unavailable to me? I do have a history of hankering after anything I know I can't have. The very fact that I'm standing in her kitchen with a glass of wine is proof that she doesn't find me either interesting or threatening. I'm just another job, or maybe a favor because I'm her BFF's brother.

I take another sip of wine, telling myself to get over it, which means I have a mouthful to choke on when Daph surprises me again.

"So, what exactly happened to Taylor?" she asks, glancing over her shoulder after adding the asparagus to the tray. She pivots and braces a hand on her hip, her gaze boring into me. "Why are you so sure it was your fault?"

My recovery isn't graceful and she hands me a tea towel, not giving it up for an instant. The options run through my mind at lightning speed.

"Does it have anything to do with your new tattoo?"

I must look like a fish gasping for air. My thoughts spin through the possibilities.

I could deflect the question.

I could lie.

I could avoid confronting the loss that has flattened me, just the way I've been ducking it for more than a year.

Or I could seize the opportunity and tell someone about it. Once this deal is done, chances are very good that I'll never see Daph again. She's determined to stay in Empire, for whatever reason, and I'm set on leaving, forever this time. (I have to think the chances of hell freezing over are comparatively low, especially in the spring.)

She's a good candidate for a confidence even without that consideration. She won't tell anyone, maybe not even Abbie. She's a clear thinker and will ask good questions.

She's perceptive and isn't afraid to call me on anything.

I could do worse, a lot worse.

I drain the glass and put it down, indicating that I don't want more. Then I sit on one of the bar stools and start to talk. It's surprisingly easy to find a starting point. Maybe Daph's a really good listener.

Maybe it's just time.

5

DAPHNE

I don't expect Luke to confide in me, but he does.

He doesn't even protest.

Good thing dinner's ready and I can sit down, pretending that my meal has my undivided attention. There's something about having him in my house, about him filling this space—*my* space—that is disconcerting. It's more unsettling that he seems to belong here, but that's just me making excuses for enjoying his presence.

(Fact: I have been single too long.)

Luke even matches. Black hair, blue eyes, T-shirt the same colour as the bookcase in my living room. I could have chosen him to coordinate with my décor, which makes me smother a smile. If I picked Luke, it wouldn't be because he looked good in my kitchen.

But I'm *not* choosing Luke.

"I'll trade you," he says and I look up to find him watching me. "My story for yours."

"I don't have a story to tell."

"Sure, you do, Daph. You said you knew what it was like to

regret something. If I tell you what I regret, it's only fair that you do the same."

It's too reasonable an idea for me to argue, or I'm too agitated to think straight. Having Luke lean close like there's no one else in the world but me makes me *feel*, and that eliminates any clear thinking I might otherwise do.

Feeling is such a big mistake.

Feeling leads me down unreliable roads.

The only thing worse than feeling is letting emotion rule your choices.

"Deal," I say, just to make him look away. "But you first. I'm eating."

"And it looks good." He turns on the stool, just as I'd hoped, seeming to check out my place. I already know the new Luke well enough to realize that he's composing his confession. He flicks me a quick look as if he's heard that thought. "I want to do it right this time," he says. "After botching the story earlier."

"You didn't botch it."

"I could have made a more coherent and compelling argument."

He's annoyed with himself, as I might have been, and that makes me wonder what threw his game. Is it possible that he was unable to concentrate because of me?

No. That's crazy. This man has seduced so many women that I can't believe my gender matters. Maybe he felt too strongly about the plan.

Maybe he really hated being back in Empire, challenging his dad all over again.

That I can believe.

"It all comes back to Taylor," he muses, his voice low. "The way he was, as opposed to the way I am." He spins to face me, his eyes a vivid blue. "Taylor trusted everybody, because he saw the good in everybody. He used to say that the world gives you what you expect of it, and that if you expect good things, you'll get good things."

Luke smiles and shakes his head. "Oh, we used to argue about that. I told him it was crap, that the world gives you whatever it's dishing out, regardless of your perspective. He believed there was a rhyme and reason to everything, that each choice we make brings us closer to our destiny. And he was sure it was all good." He falls silent then, staring across my living room, maybe out the front window to the quiet street beyond.

"That's kind of tough to reconcile with his sudden death," I say because it seems as if he won't say more.

"No. No, it's not. Taylor never indulged too much. He was a pretty strict vegetarian, and he only drank the occasional beer. If we went to a party, he insisted it was about the company and the energy. He always wanted his experience to be honest. That was a big word for him. Honest."

"Sounds like he grew up in a commune."

"His grandparents are very...groovy." Luke grins. "Taylor was raised by them while his folks worked, and they had a great relationship. Very kind and mutually supportive of both Taylor and his younger brother." He nods and I see a shadow of regret, maybe that he didn't have a similar upbringing. "My point is there's a lot of indulgence when you're in a band. You play in bars at first, so there's alcohol, and people are always offering you stuff. But that wasn't for Taylor. He would smoke a joint once in a while, but even that was a rare thing. I maybe saw him do it twice in the years we knew each other. And we were in each other's pockets when we toured. Taylor and I shared one bus, and Brent and Zach shared the other."

I know he's referring to the bass player and the drummer in the band. I nod. "Bus?" I ask, giving him a way to talk about something easier.

Luke braces his elbows on the counter. "That goes back to our first tour. We had a manager then, and he booked us into hotels at each venue. We toured and we partied, we had room service and five-star accommodations, and we had a great time—"

"Even Taylor who got high on the company, if nothing else."

He nods and I see that these are happy memories. "Even Taylor. And when it was all tallied up at the end and the manager took his cut, we owed money. Eight months on the road, playing to sold-out crowds, and we were in the hole." Luke shakes his head, still incredulous. "There was a lot of fast talk, but I knew it was garbage. The manager bought himself a red Ferrari."

"Big clue there."

"Exactly. We kicked him to the curb and I dug into the math while we recorded a new album. When we went on tour next time, we had two custom buses for the band and the crew stayed in lower key accommodations. A couple of them bought RVs instead. We all wanted to be healthier, so we had a PA who shopped for us and we cooked every night, instead of ordering in. We even wrote some songs on that tour, almost a whole album because we were hanging out together, and ka-ching, we made good money. We had a new formula and even though the tours got bigger, the system kept working."

"Not so many parties then."

"But always one after the last show of the tour to wrap it up. Kind of a celebration. At the end of our last tour, though, Taylor and I had a fight. We never fought, but that day, we really got into it. Maybe we were just tired. It was a long tour. Maybe we were fed up with living so close to each other. Doesn't really matter." Luke frowns and shakes his head. "I know I said things I shouldn't have, but I was furious when he said I was like my dad."

"Maybe he thought he shouldn't have said that."

"Maybe. But we parted badly, and the rehearsal and sound check was awkward, and I don't think we played our best that night. The balance between Taylor and I was compromised. I like to end the tour on a high note, and I was angry enough to blame him. I just left with the chick from the last song." He shakes his head. "Don't give me that look, Daph. I got her a cab and said goodnight outside the stadium. I was that mad. I went back to the bus, but Taylor had gone to the party."

"Maybe he expected to find you there."

"Maybe. Maybe he needed to let off some steam. At any rate, I stayed on the bus alone. And meanwhile, someone offered him a joint and he took it, trusting in the goodness of the world." Luke levels a look at me.

"I don't understand." How bad could one joint be?

"The pot was cut with meth and some other garbage too. He went into cardiac arrest and died before anyone realized what was happening." Luke snapped his fingers. "Just like that, he was gone. They came and knocked on the door of the bus, and I couldn't believe it."

I put down my fork, horrified.

"When I heard the story, I knew it was my fault."

"You can't blame..."

"I *can* blame myself, Daph, because I was the one who distrusted everybody. Whenever Taylor wanted a joint, I got it for him. I made sure the dealer was reputable and that everything was on the up-and-up. I would never have even taken a gift from someone I didn't know and trust, because the dealers who give the stuff away are the ones who slide a little bonus in to get you hooked. It's a plan to build their client list. But I wasn't there, because I was angry that he told me the truth, and because I wasn't there and because he trusted everyone, he died." Luke looks away, his throat working. "I wasn't even there to see that it was going sideways and intervene. I let him down. He was my best friend, and because I was too much of a loser to tolerate the truth, he died." He shakes his head and stands, restless with his agitation. "I will *never* forgive myself for that."

I don't know what to say.

He pushes a hand through his hair and takes a quick breath. I gesture to the wine bottle, but he shakes his head.

"That won't help. I've tried."

He walks the length of my house and back, bristling with pent-up energy, anger that he doesn't know how to dissipate, and stops in front of my bookshelf. "I like this," he says, nodding at it with approval. "It looks really good here."

"Thanks. I knew when I saw it that I had to have it."

"Instinct," Luke agrees. "You just recognize truths, even when it's just the right bookcase, and you need to follow on them." He spins to face me. "I knew Taylor was right, even when I was furious with him."

"Maybe that's why you were furious with him."

"Probably," he cedes. "And I'm here because I had to act on that. I had to find the prime mover that made everything go sideways, but for the longest time, I didn't know what it was. Not until I saw Sylvia. I knew that the universe was giving me a chance to fix what I'd screwed up—which sounds like the kind of stuff Taylor used to say, but I believe it now."

"Maybe Taylor was giving you a mission."

"Maybe." I can see that he likes that idea. "But I know I have to do it. I've no idea whether it's going to work. Maybe Meredith can't make the diner profitable. Maybe Sylvia doesn't want to come back here, no matter what's in the offing." He raises his hands. "But I have to try. I feel like he's counting on me."

His urgency is impossible to miss. "I can probably drive to Toronto Thursday, if you want me to present the idea to this Meredith MacRae."

"Yes," he says immediately and emphatically.

"You can think about it," I say, my tone teasing.

"I don't have to."

Right. He's in a hurry to solve this and leave town.

"You'll need to tell me where to find her, and I'll need you to sign off on the offer for her. I can draw it up tonight and print it at the office in the morning." I think for a minute. "Maybe Dad will let me borrow his car."

"What's wrong with yours?"

I pretend to balance things in my hands. "Renovate the house I just bought or buy a new car. Since I don't drive far and I eat daily, the kitchen won."

He casts a look over it. "It's a great kitchen. I like the tiles."

"Me, too." I smile at him. "I brought them back from Mexico a few years ago. They were intended for a different kitchen, but they look better here."

"You were going to buy a different place?" He slides back onto the stool.

"I was going to move into a different place, then put my mark on it."

His eyes narrow to blue slits. "What does that mean?"

"It means I said yes to the dress, then he said no to me." It's surprisingly easy to confess, but maybe that's the wine.

Luke is staring at me—and really, I'm kind of shocked, too.

I never talk about Justin.

I'm so over Justin.

But I realize in this moment that *not* talking about him is as bad as talking incessantly about him.

So, I toss out some more truth. "That's what I'm doing back in Empire. I wasn't ready to keep working with the jackhole I'd thought I was going to marry, and see him every day at the office, not after I knew he had been screwing around on me; and subsequently was going to marry her instead. She can buy her own tiles to update the kitchen in his house."

Luke looks across the room and back again, visibly composing his reply. "You can't regret not marrying such a jerk."

"No, but I can regret that I ignored all the little signs I saw along the way. I can regret being gullible, and believing all the ridiculous explanations that made no sense at all." I take my plate to the sink and scrub it clean with vicious gestures, my voice dropping low. "I can regret being stupid and putting my trust where it didn't belong." The plate is cleaner than it's ever been when I put it in the rack, and my utensils follow it quickly. I halfway wish I had the pots and pans from a turkey dinner to scrub, because I don't like having nothing more to do.

On the other hand, it felt good to say it out loud. I *am* over Justin. My anger is with myself. He lied, absolutely, but I chose to believe him despite my own observations.

"Maybe you're more like Taylor than I'd thought," Luke says and I realize he's right behind me. He's not touching me but I can feel the heat of his body, close, so close, and I'm tempted to just lean back. I know he'll catch me. I doubt I'll regret whatever happens next.

But that's because no one's going to make any pretty promises.

Maybe that's because I know what and who he is, what he does, what he will do—and I still find him incredibly attractive.

And maybe, maybe a little something for right now is what I need today. More than a future or a promise, much more than a lie, just something honest exchanged in the moment.

Mutual solace.

The idea has resonance, like it's the perfect notion at the perfect time. Looking for forever with your one true love is all good. But maybe along the way, you just need to be appreciated a little. Maybe a little physical satisfaction without expectations has its place.

I spin and meet his gaze, quick enough that I catch the admiration in his eyes. He's been looking and he seems startled that I saw.

He almost smiles. "Caught." He looks guilty and wicked, not apologetic at all. "Sorry, not sorry."

"You're not the only one," I admit, watching surprise light his eyes.

They darken then, his lashes sweeping down to hide his thoughts as the corner of his mouth lifts, just a little. My heart skips a beat then takes off at a run. "Aren't I?" he murmurs, a low purr that is the sexiest sound I've heard in a while.

"Not even close."

His smile widens a little and his eyes gleam. "Aren't you full of surprises, Daph?" he says in that deep rumble and doesn't move.

He's waiting for me to make the first move.

Is there anything better?

And that's when I remember Justin, telling me that something I've done without thinking is the sexiest thing he's ever seen.

On impulse, I do it, but it's not about catching Justin's attention.

Not this time.

I watch Luke as I part my lips slightly and slide the tip of my tongue across my bottom lip, very, very slowly. He seems to be frozen in place, his gaze locked on my mouth. I'm not even sure he's breathing before I see him inhale sharply, then his gaze flicks to mine, checking that I'm not putting him on.

His eyes are brilliant blue, his voice deeper than the ocean.

"Careful what you wish for, Daph," he warns, but I don't need to be warned off the one thing I want. In this moment, I want a kiss, and I want it with all my heart and soul.

I want it from Luke.

So, I slide my tongue back the other way, counting on not having a chance to do it a third time.

I'm oh-so-very right on that.

6

———

LUKE

Bloody hell.

I never thought of Daph as a temptress, but clearly I have it all wrong. She looks sultry and seductive, a siren whose call I can't resist. When something seems too good to be true, it often is, so I take my time easing closer, savoring the view.

She doesn't move away.

Her expression doesn't change.

The ice queen has evidently been given her marching orders.

If anything, Daph's smoky eyes fill with anticipation.

I put one hand on her waist, letting my fingers curl around her, and she sets a hand on my shoulder. She gives me a little squeeze, checking out the shape of me, and I'm glad I haven't given up on my daily work-outs. We take it slow, slower than slow, staring into each other's eyes like we're both mesmerized.

There can only be one first kiss. I'm going to make it one to remember.

She looks like she has the same plan and I like it.

Two minds as one.

My other hand is on her shoulder, my fingertips sliding to the exposed skin at the neck of her sweater. She's soft, of course, soft and warm and smooth, and my fingertips ease higher of their own volition. I feel the tiny hairs on her nape and push my hand into her hair.

Daph reaches up and pulls out the clip, shaking her hair free so it falls in waves around her face. She looks disheveled then, even more inviting, and I can't resist her. My hand is wrapped around her nape, her hair tangled around my fingers, and I lean in to capture her lips in a kiss. She's trapped between my hips and the lip of the farmhouse sink, which means she has zero doubt how much I'm loving this.

She wriggles her hips, message received, which sends a jolt through me. That's nothing compared to the moment she opens her mouth to me, flicking that mischievous tongue across my bottom lip. Seductress in spades. I pull her up to her toes and slant my mouth over hers, claiming her with a kiss that demands a response.

Daph gives me one, arching against me, kissing me back with an enthusiasm I didn't expect. I slide my other hand beneath her sweater and find bare skin under my hand. I can smell her shower gel and her arousal, and it's the most potent aphrodisiac known to mankind. I deepen the kiss and she's right with me, her hands locked in my hair pulling me closer, her foot rising up my leg, then her leg twining around mine. The heat of her is right against me and she rolls her hips again in silent demand, making my blood run white-hot. I find her nipple beneath the sweater and it's both bare and hard as a pebble. I tease it with my thumb and she gasps and moans into our kiss, grazing my mouth with her teeth as she leans on the sink and wraps her legs around my waist.

I'm thinking about the sturdiness of the counter, before I catch myself.

This is *Daph*. This is my lawyer, my sister's friend, the one person who is trusting and helping me. I break the kiss and remember that her windows are bare, that the whole town could see us if they were looking.

I want more than sex, more than this minute.

I want special.

Her cheeks are flushed and her lips are swollen, her eyes shining and her expression welcoming. We could do this thing, maybe without regrets—probably not slowly enough, given my recent abstinence.

But then it will be over, and it won't have been enough.

I straighten, tucking a strand of hair behind her ear, pressing a kiss to the corner of her mouth. "You need some drapes," I whisper to her and she almost laughs. I lift her up and set her feet on the floor then she studies me.

"That's not really the problem, is it?" she asks, her own voice husky.

There is something impossibly hot about smart perceptive women, something I've never appreciated until this moment.

"I want more," I say, not knowing how else to explain it, and immediately see that she's taken it the wrong way. I've said it the wrong way, but it's too late. She's straightening her sweater and slipping away, combing her hair with her fingers and twisting it up again. If she knew how much I want to kiss the back of her neck, she wouldn't be presenting it to me like this, but I look and yearn and keep my mouth shut.

Funny how I've always known the right thing to say to women, until Daph.

Until it mattered.

"I'll draw up the paperwork tonight," she says, all business again. "If you can stop by to sign everything, I'll visit Meredith Thursday in the city."

I pull out my phone and give her the address, ridiculously pleased that the transaction results in my having Daph's cell phone number. "I don't think she'll be around in the morning."

"Good. I'll have time to meet a friend for lunch first." She's avoiding my gaze and I know I've hurt her feelings but I don't know how to make it right. My own reaction is too chaotic and new for me to manage that.

"Nine?" I suggest and she flicks me a look. Her gaze is cool again, and even though I should have expected it, it's like a knife to my heart.

"Nine," she agrees.

It's clear that I'm supposed to leave now. I head for the door, tug on my boots and shrug into my jacket. "It's not you, Daph."

She rolls her eyes. "Don't give me that it's-not-you-it's-me garbage."

"Even if it's true?" I hold my ground, needing her to know this. "There was a time that I would have taken whatever you would give, right there on that counter, then walked into the night and never seen you again." Her lips are tight and her arms are folded across her chest, but she's listening. "But I'm not that guy anymore. I don't want that anymore." Her gaze drops pointedly to my jeans and I shake my head. "I don't want *just* that anymore. I didn't know it until tonight, until you, until this." I wave at her house including her and our conversations in the gesture. "And I don't know what it means, not yet. But I do know that I don't want to mess it up."

"Maybe there's nothing to mess up."

"Maybe not. But I'm not going to have you think later that it was pity sex because you were sad about this Justin jerk…"

"I am not sad about this Justin jerk." She bites off the words and I know she's mad.

"I'd like to be sure of that." I look out the window and back at her. "There's something going on here, Daph, something more, and I don't want to rush it."

She looks across the room, her lips tightening, and I know she doesn't believe me. That's fair. It just means that I'll have to convince her that I mean what I say.

"Tomorrow at nine," I say and she nods without looking at me. I turn and leave, knowing I'm doing the right thing, but feeling like I've made a mistake all the same.

How could anyone toss her back?

How could anyone mess around on Daph and lie to her about it?

On the other hand, if Justin the Jerk hadn't done that, she'd be married to him, living in Toronto, making babies and living the good life.

That means I owe the moron.

I'm just not sure how much yet.

––––––––

I DON'T SLEEP. I spend the night staring at the ceiling of my room at the motel. There's a big tv, apparently with satellite service, but I don't turn it on. I don't even turn on the lights. I just crash on the king-sized bed in my T-shirt and skivvies, thinking about Daph.

No. Haunted by that kiss.

By her.

I'm not surprised very often, not by people anyway. Events, sure, they catch me off-guard. Death is particularly good at that, but I don't want to think about the grim reaper right now.

I want to think about Daphne Bradshaw.

I want to *fantasize* about Daphne Bradshaw.

I'm hot inside, that perfectly delicious combo of impatience and a conviction that the experience should be prolonged. I can't be sure where this is going. I have ideas, but Daph is the kind of person who will have some of her own. I like that, too. I love that she's not afraid to set me straight or share her view, but that means doubt.

The very essence of romance is uncertainty. Yes, Oscar, I see now that you were on to something there.

I want to make the uncertainty last, draw it out, seduce Daph as slowly as possible—if that even can be done—and that desire contrasts with the need to know right now what it feels like to be with her. That's an imperative.

I need to kiss her again. No, I need to do more than kiss her. I need to know what she likes and what sounds she makes and how she moves—and I need her to want me back. I want her wrapped around me, telling me what she wants, demanding more.

Again and again and again.

I want it all. I want to fall into her and drown, losing myself in what we're like together.

I shiver and run my tongue over my lips, tasting her again, thinking of the dangerous little move with her tongue. Who would have guessed?

Not me.

It's gratifying to have a good surprise. It's good to feel the rush of adrenaline again, to feel alive, to be interested and intrigued in something—or better yet, someone.

When was the last time a woman destroyed me with just one kiss? I'm not sure it's ever happened. Maybe my first kiss ever, the novelty and all that, but I can't even remember who it was with. So, it was the sensation of a kiss, not the kisser herself, who made an impression.

This time, it's the other way around.

Funny thing. I couldn't get enough of the women when we had the band. They were everywhere. They were pretty and enthused. They flung themselves at us, and I thought it only decent to catch as many of them as I could. I was insatiable and apparently their numbers were infinite. If I'd realized my joke during an interview about my fondness for lingerie would have the stage knee-deep in lingerie at the end of every performance, I would have made it sooner. The only thing better than a lacy treat of a bra is one filled with breasts of whatever size and shape—and the only thing better than that is setting them free, and worshipping them. Thoroughly.

But I haven't been that way for thirteen months. When Taylor died, my best friend left me, the band fell apart, fame slipped through our fingers—and a part of me died. I couldn't sleep for months, I have no music in my heart and mind, and I haven't had sex since.

When everything is shit, temporal pleasures are irrelevant.

Maybe I was sleepwalking. Maybe I was drifting. I sure didn't care about much of anything.

Until today.

Until Daph.

Is it possible that I only arrived in town this morning? I look at the alarm clock, the numbers glowing red in the darkness. Not even twenty-four hours ago.

Impossible.

And yet true.

What has she awakened—and why did it come out of hibernation for her? I don't even want to think about it. It makes one kiss seem way too important. Sure, Daph is great, but I remind myself that all of those women were great. That truth rings hollow. I didn't want more of any of them. The once was enough.

So, why did I step back from Daph tonight?

I try another argument. Daph's just the right woman in the right place. Maybe I was due to shake off my grief. Maybe it was time, and any woman's kiss would have provoked this change.

Nope. All of those sound like rationalizations, too.

The sad fact is that you can't expect different results by making the same choices over and over again. I've seen where surrendering to temptation repeatedly gets me. It certainly yields a measure of short-term satisfaction, but nothing that endures. And when the bit that was enduring—the fame, the money—went away, so did everything else. I learned from Taylor what it was like to have a friend who was indifferent to my circumstances and I want another one.

His death has left me lonely.

There. I said it. Or at least I allowed myself to think it. And I haven't felt a connection with anyone in thirteen months, not until Daph shook me awake. She did it even before we kissed. She doesn't accept the easy answer. Maybe that's the secret. She sees through me and demands more. That reminds me of Taylor.

She's tough and smart and beautiful...

And I like her. I really like her.

I want to know *everything* about her.

Of course, I want a hook-up—I'm still human—but I'm thinking about more than that. I'm pretty sure that once with Daph might not be enough. She's got layers of secrets, and though I generally don't worry about unraveling anyone's mysteries, she's different.

Her kiss was different. It gave and it took. It hinted. It definitely enticed. She met me halfway and led me on. We were in it together.

I like that.

A lot.

So I'm awake, wondering a perilous and unfamiliar thought.

What if the songs are true?

It's a crazy notion, one I've never considered before, but it's persistent in the way that unexpected insights tend to be.

Could this be what we write songs about? (*All* the songs.) I've written a bucket of them myself, maybe out of yearning, maybe out of optimism. I don't think I ever really believed in love and forever, but what if it *is* a real possibility?

That's a gamechanger.

It's certainly enough to give your world a hard shake.

What if you can fall in love with someone who turns out to be your partner and your lover both? What if eighty-four million love songs are true?

It should be too terrifying a prospect to be given serious consideration.

But I can't stop thinking about it.

That kiss.

Maybe Daph's The One.

I can't believe this thought has even come into my head, but I can't shake it. Taylor was the only who believed in kismet, that there was one true love out there for everyone, that paths would cross when the moment was right for both. I always thought that was nonsense. Maybe wishful thinking.

What if he was right?

I can't help thinking about a love song, the ballad Taylor wrote that was our finale at every show, the one that ached with yearning, the one that was so transcendent that women stormed the stage, wanting all we had to give. The song was what brought them to their feet. Its sentiment brought out the cigarette lighters in the sea of darkness—that was Taylor's interview confession, that he loved to see the lights. After that, we sold branded battery-powered lights by the thousands before every show. It was magical to look out and see them all swaying in time to the music. I sang that song thousands of times and it always felt new.

I hum it to myself in the darkness, unable to stop wondering if its words might be true.

It seems infinitely more probable that I've lost my mind.

But what if I haven't?

What if I'm in the right place at the right time to have my dream—the one I didn't even realize I had—come true?

It's no wonder I can't sleep.

———

IN THE MORNING, I'm right on time. I'm wearing my last clean shirt, the one with our band logo across the chest. I always liked this one, since it has silhouettes of each of us cut out of the block letters. I'm in the upright of the M serenading the microphone, Taylor is in the B with his guitar, Brent is in the D bent over his bass and Zach is triumphantly waving his drumstick in the K. The shirt is black, the letters white.

When I arrive at the law office, the receptionist has the paper-work for me to sign. She sits me down in a small conference room and I start reading. Never sign anything without reading it and understanding every single word. I can hear Daph talking to someone in the office with the closed door. Her dad, undoubtedly. The Honda is parked out front beside the Mercedes sedan that I saw outside his house. There are more papers to sign, contracts to read, funds to transfer.

When they emerge, her dad is polite but distant. A gracious gentleman and I can see where Daph got some of her good looks. He's not out to make friends with me, but then if some dickweed had cheated on my beloved only daughter and effectively jilted her, I'd be giving the side-eye to a whole generation of guys, too, particularly any who were in her proximity.

Daph is glacial. I guess I deserve that, but it's not like I can explain as her dad and his receptionist circle around. Just before noon, her dad leaves to have lunch with Patrick while Daph heads to Havelock to finish up the title transfer. I thought they did all that online, but apparently not when you're in a hurry. The recep-tionist, Mrs. Prescott, firmly ushers me out the door and locks it behind us, marching down the street after a curt nod to me.

She must go home for lunch.

My day yawns before me, devoid of commitments or errands. I'm supposed to come back to get keys etc. but not until the morning. I wander down Queen Street, impatient and hungry. I'm tempted into the thrift shop, and pleased to discover a lot of vintage T-shirts for sale. There are more than a few in my size and it's tough to choose. I pick the purple one with Queen's logo in silver across the chest, the Rolling Stones one in red, the INXS one in a blue so dark it's almost black. I also found a great pair of running shoes that look new for a crazy cheap price. That they're in my size means they should be mine.

The tattooed and pierced girl behind the counter is singing along to Tracy Chapman and doesn't appear to recognize me.

Give me one reason to stay here.

Exactly, Tracy. Exactly. My thoughts to your lips.

Tell me that you have a soundtrack for your life, a mix that follows you wherever you go and provides the background to all your significant moments. I do. I've always had one. Even before there was the band, there was the music. And it's funny, but being back in Empire has conjured up that old playlist of eighties and nineties hits.

It's not as good as the playlist I've had since, the one of our band's songs and the songs I was writing, a glorious mix that was ours alone. The best, though, is when a new song appears in my thoughts, tempting me to listen, taunting me with possibilities, a melody that has to be coaxed and urged toward a full song. I haven't heard one of those since that fight with Taylor.

The music is gone.

I'm suddenly aware of the void within me. I refuse to think about it, not here in this store. I think of that old playlist instead.

Tracy Chapman was on it. The Rolling Stones (*Can't Get No*) *Satisfaction*. INXS *Devil Inside*. Billy Idol's *Rebel Yell*. I smile, realizing they're all songs of teenage mutiny. My anthems, at least while I lived here. I have time to think that my T-shirt choices are right in sync with that before I see the anomaly.

I'm in Empire by choice this time. In those days, I wanted to get out of Empire more than anything, but I decided to come back. I could drive right out of town right this minute and no one would care.

It's jarring to realize that Tracy is singing for a different version of me.

Even weirder, I have no firm plan to leave, even though I can.

Disconcerted, I head for the cash counter.

"Mad, Bad & Dangerous 2 Know," she says, correctly interpreting the initials in the band logo on my T-shirt. "Aren't they over?"

Ouch. I hide my flinch, but just barely. "Think so?"

"Oh yeah. Ages without a new song." She chews her gum, blows a bubble and pops it, then nods at the shirt I'm wearing. "I'll give you ten bucks for it, or fifteen credit. Vintage and all."

Vintage. *Vintage!* This shirt was brand new a year ago and this is the first time I've worn it. I had to work up to flaunting the logo again, and right now, it's working for me. Being back in Empire makes me feel MB&D2K, for sure. I'm ready to kick down some doors, wake people up, provoke change.

Not sell the shirt off my back.

Okay, maybe I haven't changed that much.

"Thanks. I still like it, though."

"Suit yourself. I'm all for a little nostalgia." She rings everything up and I pay. "Someone told me the front man was from here," she says as Tracy finishes the song.

"I heard that, too." I manage this deadpan.

"Yeah? Maybe it's true then. I thought she was putting me on." She flashes a smile. "It's not like he'll ever come back."

"You might be surprised," I say, but she shrugs and starts singing along to the next tune.

Roxy Music, in case you're wondering. *More Than This.* Not on my playlist but a good song. Evocative. I ask her what radio station she's listening to, and it's the one from Havelock we used to listen to in high school. They must be playing the same music, which is okay.

I linger until the end of the song, then she's giving me the side-eye so I leave. It has been a while since anyone thought I was a shop-lifter, but that happened in Empire, too.

I treat myself to a sad-looking tomato-and-cheese sandwich from the convenience store across the street. There's a boombox on the back counter, banging out salsa music so loud that I can't hear anything the guy says to me. There are no other options for lunch in town, at least as far as I can see, and this sandwich hasn't reached its best-before date. Call it a win. White bread, though. I eat it on the way back to the motel, thinking.

The thing is that if love is real, then it's still untrustworthy. Love, or the illusion of love, is the justification for zillions of mistakes.

Like me. There's a truth that's tough to avoid in this town. I exist because of the folly of love—and its effect on my mom.

Is it a mistake for me to fall for Daph? The result might not be good for either of us, as much as I hate to admit it. I should be amused that I'm feeling so protective of her—Daph can fight her own battles, I suspect—but I am and it feels right.

Maybe that's part of the package.

No, if I need a reminder of the price of love, then I should visit my mom. It's a sound plan and a better way to spend the day than hanging around, waiting for Daph to come back.

Mom'll probably let me do some laundry, and I have to believe there's something better to eat in her fridge than the sandwich I just inhaled.

It's time I visited her, too.

7

———

DAPHNE

If Luke found it was cold in my office yesterday, he must be fighting frostbite today.

Not that anyone would have been able to tell. He sits there, reading contracts and asking questions, as if we're perfect strangers.

Not as if I invited a kiss and he declined to continue it.

Yes. I'm mad. What's the point of asking for what you want if you don't get it? Why wouldn't he take what I was offering? What particular kind of plague do I have? Luke isn't shy and casual hook-ups seem to be his forte.

Just not with me.

Message received.

More. That word makes me livid. I was awake all night, fuming, and rolled into work like a tropical storm about to wreak havoc on anyone or anything dumb enough to get in my way. I can't remember ever being insufficient for anyone, and I don't like the change.

That Luke doesn't even seem to notice my mood is icing on the cake.

And then—too late—he gives me all the right words, presenting it as sincerity when I know better. He didn't have to prove to me that good-looking guys are all the same. Was he trying to get a second chance after turning me down? What kind of game is that?

It's one I'm not going to play.

It helps absolutely nothing that my heart keeps going skippity-bop when I hear his voice, all low and rumbly, making all my sensitive girl bits tingle in harmony. It doesn't help that I admire the thoughtful questions he has and the way he sees through the words to the legal implications. He's no fool, that's for sure. Even my father raises his brows and flicks me a look after one discussion, impressed.

Luke'll be gone soon.

That the thought leaves me with the taste of disappointment makes everything that much worse.

I grind the gears of my beloved Honda backing out and have to talk myself down. It's good that I won't see Luke until the next morning. It's good that this transaction is likely to be short and sweet. If I go to Toronto to present his proposal to Meredith MacRae tomorrow, he might disappear right after that. He'll never come back to Empire now and I tell myself to be glad.

Maybe I will be, later.

As I wait on the clerk, I compose a list. Wednesday means that tonight is my turn to play hostess. I might as well take advantage of my unexpected trip to Havelock to buy some groceries, the likes of which are unavailable in Empire.

Tonight, I will create a charcuterie board to spawn legends. That should be enough to improve my mood.

Funny, but it's not.

———

WEDNESDAY NIGHT IS the very best night of the week.

Every time.

Because that's when I meet up with my friends. It is the ultimate girls' night, held weekly, filled with wine and snacks, gossip and love. It's the highlight of my new life.

These three weren't always my friends, but that's how it works, right? Abbie came up with the idea of our club in high school. It was Abs and me, Mackenzie Rhodes and Willow Forsythe. In high school, we hung out all the time. You never saw a more unlikely group of BFFs but it worked.

Maybe it was because we were so different. Mackenzie is the math whiz, the overachieving heiress to the throne of Rhodes Vineyards. If anyone was ever all work and no play, it's Mackenzie—though she says that when you love what you do, work seems like play. (Where have I heard that recently? Maybe she should jump Luke's bones. Two of a feather, etc. Grr.)

Willow is the creative genius who can turn any problem on its head to find an unexpected solution. She sees everything from a different perspective, which makes her unpredictable and interesting.

Abbie was always pretty and popular, the rich girl who everybody liked and who knew everyone.

And then there was me, quiet and serious, a socially awkward nerd who could lose herself in the details—or a good book.

Abbie and I went away to university, but when we came home for holiday breaks, there were Mackenzie and Willow. We always picked up where we'd left off, as if no one had ever been gone. Mackenzie went to a winemaker's program in France for a year in the middle of our absences from Empire. Willow never left, just dabbled in online courses and hobbies and part-time jobs. Abbie took a job in Vancouver when she graduated and never came back. We keep a chair for her, just in case.

Damn, but I wanted her to have that house. Oh well.

A year ago, Cameron Sinclair just walked up and knocked on my door one Wednesday night. She'd bought the house next door, having discovered that real estate was significantly cheaper in Empire than in Havelock where she works. She's not the kind of person to let a detail like not knowing anyone in town stand in her way. She'd noticed us getting together and self-invited. She's a nurse and I like her. She seems aloof, even reserved, when you first meet her, but she slides in these wicked little comments that crack me up every time. She also has a gift for finding the only single guy in a crowded room/bar/event and charming him so completely that she ends up taking him home.

Every time.

After Cameron joined us, we tried to have a theme. We were a book club first, but then we couldn't agree on what books to read. I like mysteries. Cameron is into thrillers, preferably of the medical variety so she can red-line all the technical errors. Willow loves romance. Actually, Willow loves pretty much every genre of fiction. She's our official free spirit, filled with love for everything and everyone in the universe. (Thanks to Luke, that's now reminding me of his description of Taylor.) Mackenzie never gets around to reading. (We have a joke that our book of the month should have always been *The Seven Habits of Highly Effective People*, because then Mackenzie would not only read it but quiz us on the content.)

We were a knitting club for a while, but I had too many scarves in a hurry. Cameron prefers to crochet and Mackenzie is still knitting a pair of fair isle mittens she cast on in 2014. They'll be perfect if they're ever finished, worthy of a blue ribbon somewhere, but they may never be done. Willow makes fuzzy amigurumi by the dozens and sometimes leaves them in unexpected places. There was a perfect plump crocheted penguin in my freezer the last time I hosted, waiting on the ice cube tray for me to discover him. The expression on his face is priceless.

I'll put him back in the freezer today so she can discover him there. That always makes her giggle.

I wouldn't miss our weekly gathering for the world. I still miss Abbie, but this helps.

Willow is first to arrive tonight. She's brought a spinach and artichoke dip that has to be heated up and gets busy in the kitchen. We've done this often enough that there's no ceremony. We know each other's kitchens and just dig in. I'm already setting out cold cuts and olives, cutting cheese into bite-sized pieces and generally admiring the layout of my masterful platter of goodness. Willow hums as she works and that always makes me smile. She's the niece of Jim who runs the antique store, which is where she works sometimes. Mostly she repaints vintage furniture while he's out picking, attending auctions and estate sales. I always wonder if it bugs him that some of her repaints go for more than the antiques.

My big bookcase is one of hers, the turquoise blue one in the corner of my living room that provides the perfect pop of colour. It makes me think of the Caribbean or maybe the trip to Greece I've always wanted to take.

Now it's always going to make me think of Luke admiring it last night. How can he have infected my life in just over twenty-four hours? He'll be the ghost at the banquet forever, but I'm not moving again, not just to exorcise him. (And I'd keep that bookcase anyway.)

The bell rings and I see Cameron waving through the window in the front door. She's tall with dark hair that's always cut short—she says it's practical—but you know when she's off-duty because she wears red lipstick and dangly earrings. I open the door, she charges in, hugs me, and manages to shove a wine bottle at me at the same time as she takes off her coat. She chucks the coat in the general direction of my coat rack, and it snags a hook, seemingly of its own volition, then confronts me.

"Did I buy the wrong thing?" she demands and I look at the

label on the wine. "The guy at the liquor store in Havelock recommended it, but it is entirely possible he was just trying to get lucky."

Willow laughs. Cameron waves to her. "I hope it wasn't expensive," Willow says.

"He's always recommending stuff to me," Cameron complains. "He comes out of nowhere every time I set foot in the store."

"Maybe he's on commission," I suggest. "Is he cute?"

"Not bad," Cameron says. "But it feels like mixing work and pleasure."

"You don't work at the liquor store," Willow notes.

"But it's a cornerstone of my existence. I don't need any complications when running errands." Cameron eyes me. "Well?"

"This is from Rhodes Vineyard. It's a vintage. How could it be wrong?"

Cameron makes a face. "But why is it still there? Does this vintage suck that badly?"

"Oh no, this one won awards. I remember. It's in demand." I show her the list of accolades on the label.

Cameron dismisses them with a gesture. "We know all that marketing crap is bullshit."

"Don't say that to Mackenzie!"

"Wouldn't dream of it, but I brought another bottle of Italian plonk just in case."

Can an Italian primavera even be plonk? I'm outside my sphere of expertise and just take both bottles.

"We might need both, since *he's* back," Willow says with a smile. I know exactly who she means and I hate that I blush. Cameron doesn't miss a thing. She looks between us, expectant. Willow brings her dip to the coffee table. It smells great. She winks at Cameron as she slips into a chair. "And the *only* person he went to see was Daphne."

"Who he?" Cameron demands.

I return to the kitchen to get the charcuterie tray. I get down the wine glasses while I'm there, upgrading to my better ones just because.

Okay, they're in the cupboard on the other side of the kitchen, which means I can turn my back to my guests for a minute and compose myself. Sort of.

Willow meanwhile is filling in Cameron, the two of them leaning over her phone as she shows Cameron who she means.

"Luke Jones? *The* Luke Jones?" Cameron stares at me. "He's here and he came to see you?"

"Yes." I nod as if it's no big deal. "You want to open the wine?"

Cameron will not be distracted, even though she's twisting the cap off the Italian red. "The Luke Jones who has vanished from the world stage without a trace—" she blows at her fingertips "—is here, in backwater Empire, and he came to visit you?" I nod again, because it's true. If I try to evade the truth, Willow will provide it. Cameron's eyes narrow. "Why?"

"He has this plan. He wants to make things right." I frown. "I agreed to help because I thought it might bring Abbie back to town. By the time I figured out that wasn't going to happen, I was angry enough to help make his plan happen, despite his father's garbage."

There is a beat of silence while they stare at me, Cameron with an olive between finger and thumb, almost in her mouth, and Willow's eyes wide. They've both heard that my version is heavily edited and I wonder which of them will call me on it. Cameron definitely will, but Willow might be faster this time.

"Is that supposed to make sense?" Cameron asks.

I sigh and perch on the edge of the couch. "We should wait for Mackenzie, so I don't have to repeat it all." They nod reluctant agreement. "He needed a lawyer and I won the lottery."

"Not a lot of candidates in town," Willow says.

"And my dad is on retainer for Cavendish Enterprises."

Willow's eyes round. "This is about family matters?"

"Forget that. Let's talk about the important stuff," Cameron says. "Tell me you're not doing him," she entreats me, clearly hoping I'll say otherwise.

"I'm not doing him," I say.

"I mean, tell me the truth about whether you're doing him."

"I did."

They exchange a pitying glance. "Maybe you should rethink that plan," Cameron says under her breath and Willow nods agreement. "He came to see *you*, here in Empire."

"He needed a lawyer."

"And there are none of those between wherever he was and here." Cameron tosses back a measure of wine, her gaze unswerving. "You must know him. He came looking for you."

"Details have been withheld," Willow says in an undertone.

"Critical details," Cameron agrees. "We need the entire backstory and we need it now."

Mackenzie knocks at the door, saving me from the Inquisition. She looks harried and a little less composed than usual. I take her coat. "Screw Patrick Cavendish," she says by way of greeting and there's a universal cheer of agreement.

"You first," I say and she laughs.

"Daphne is going to be too busy doing his son," Willow provides, her manner innocent when I glare at her.

"No?" Mackenzie says in a whisper that is part horror and part delight.

Willow nods and offers dip.

"Wait!" Cameron demands, the one who is not from town. "Luke Jones is the son of Patrick Cavendish?"

We nod in unison.

"But why is his name Jones?"

"Wrong side of the sheets," Willow says. How she manages to

say something like that looking both wise and innocent at the same time is beyond me.

Cameron chews another olive. "Patrick Cavendish is the one who owns everything, right?"

"Including one piece of dirt that I need more than anything in the world," Mackenzie says with heat. "And I'm pretty sure he stole it."

Cameron looks confused.

"Patrick not Luke," Willow and I tell her in chorus.

I distract Mackenzie with the bottle Cameron has brought and she falls on it like she's greeting an old friend. "This! This has been sold out of our cellars for ages. Where did you find it?"

Cameron tells her and Mackenzie shakes her head, incredulous. "They must have been saving it. Or maybe they lost a case in the backroom. I'll go over there tomorrow and see if I can buy the rest."

"Maybe he'll only sell it to Cameron," Willow says, her expression sly.

"I am not doing the liquor store guy, even to get more of your wine," Cameron says. "He's not that cute. Open it already so we can taste it."

But Mackenzie is doing her sommelier thing. I watch her, amused that she doesn't even realize it. Her entire life is about wine and work, and in this moment, there's nothing in her world but the wine in that bottle. She draws out the cork and examines it, sniffs it, touches it, puts it aside. I hand her a freshly polished glass and she pours a bit into it, holding the glass up to the light to check the color, swirling the wine around the glass and sniffing it.

"I'm dying of thirst here," Cameron says but Mackenzie ignores her.

I will say that the process builds anticipation.

Mackenzie takes a sip, rolls it around her mouth with her eyes closed. I can practically hear the patter.

"Apples and pears, a touch of nutmeg with a strawberry undertone," Willow says softly, as if she's doing the voice over at a golf game when the leader takes his putt, and we all crack up.

"No nutmeg," Mackenzie says. "Not even cinnamon." She takes a breath, mouth open. "Touch of vanilla maybe. It's aged well." She admires the bottle as she savors another sip. "Really well." I hand her more glasses and she pours, then we all toast.

"To fine wine," I say.

"To good friends," Willow says.

"To liquor store guys who want some action badly enough to surrender the good stuff," Mackenzie says.

"To the full story of Luke Jones being back in town," Cameron says and they salute me in unison before we all drink. I'm thinking we'll fall on the charcuterie and demolish it—after suitable admiration—but no.

We might have conjured Luke up, by force of will.

Maybe he knows we're talking about him.

(Maybe he expects all women to.)

Either way, no sooner do our glasses clink than there's another shadow framed in the window of my front door. The shadow is male, tall, broad and I have no doubt who is casting it.

It's not a fixation. There aren't that many possibilities. (Says she, defensively.)

There's a collective 'ooooo' as I get up, proof of the paucity of candidates.

I open the door and Luke grins, looking so much like a hungry wolf that I can't think of a thing to say. "Want to get some dinner?" he murmurs and the contingent of women behind me inhale. It must be Cameron who makes a little growl of approval. His gaze flicks over my shoulder to my guests. "That's got to be good wine, to render everyone speechless simultaneously. Either that, or it's really bad."

"Bite your tongue. It's excellent," Mackenzie says. She pours another glass and offers it to him, making the decision for me of whether he should join us. "Welcome back to Empire."

And Luke, being Luke, saunters right into my house, takes the glass and salutes us all.

"Mackenzie," he says, his gaze flicking over her. "Is this one of yours?"

"One of our best," she admits.

He mimics her tasting routine almost perfectly, sniffing, swirling, sipping, studying my guests all the while. When he sips, he gives the mouthful of wine his undivided attention, much to Mackenzie's obvious approval.

Maybe she'll be the one to take him home.

"Willow Forsythe?" he asks and she beams at him for remembering. "Abbie said you were giving new life to some of Jim's acquisitions."

She gestures to the bookcase.

"This is your work? Really? I love it. The colour is great."

"That's what Daphne said."

He turns to Cameron. "I don't think we've met."

"There's always time to make up for that," she says. "Cameron Sinclair, right next door. That way." She points. "That house."

Luke nods politely, then toasts us all and sips the wine again. "Damn," he says after he swallows and Mackenzie beams. "That's amazing."

"Thanks," she says and sits down. Luke takes a seat, everyone else finds a place and I end up on one of the barstools at the kitchen counter.

There is a noticeable and awkward silence.

Cameron, being Cameron, puts down her glass, reaches under her shirt and does that miracle move of unfastening her bra and hauling it out her sleeve in record time. She tosses it at Luke and I laugh that he looks so surprised.

That doesn't stop him from catching it one-handed. It's bright pink and he glances at the label. "La Perla," he notes. "Very nice." Then he tosses it back at her.

I have a lump in my throat, for no reason at all. At least that's what I tell myself as I make wine go away. I have no claim on Luke and he doesn't want one on me, and Cameron is how she is.

Their one-and-done is pretty much inevitable.

The wine isn't agreeing with me, oddly enough.

"Now, you've got to sing to me," Cameron says, triumphant and expectant as she drains her glass.

The hush behind me is complete.

I look.

Luke is suddenly very, very serious and very still. "Haven't you heard?" he asks softly, maybe even dangerously. "I don't do that anymore." Then he puts down his glass. "Keys in the morning?" he asks me and I nod before he murmurs something polite about seeing them all again, gets up and walks out the door.

"What did I say?" Cameron asks in the quiet that follows.

I don't know, but I'm going to find out.

8

———

LUKE

That move of Cameron's, that moment, it takes me right back to a place I don't want to go. Ever. I'm shaking a bit when I get to my bike and I know I shouldn't ride just yet, no matter how badly I want to escape.

Of course, Daph doesn't miss a thing.

To be honest, I was kind of hoping she'd follow. I can trust her. I can talk to her.

I can admit that things are not okay, just to her.

And I've been missing her all day, missing her something fierce. It's another reason I'm off-kilter. Things are out of balance between us and I came here tonight to make it right. I didn't expect her to have company. I didn't expect to have to wait even longer to talk to her.

I know that's unreasonable. Of course, she has a life. It would be nice if I didn't keep making the wrong choice around Daph. It might give me a snowball's chance.

She stops behind me without saying anything, but I feel her presence. I know she's watching me and I like my conviction that she'll wait.

It's good to have someone to count on again, even if it's just for this moment.

"Sorry I didn't appreciate the joke," I say without turning.

"Not very long ago, you might have found it funny."

I nod, my throat tight. "Times change."

"Is that yours? I didn't know." Her tone is light, teasing even, but I don't turn. "What else is wrong, Luke?"

I spin then, surprised but not surprised that she's asking. The light from the house is behind her, so she's in silhouette, her face in shadows. I hate that I can't see her eyes. Her tone is gentle though, understanding even. "The last time that happened was at that last show, and you'd be right in thinking that I loved it. Then."

"But now?"

"Everything's gone. It's all gone," I admit, and the beat of silence tells me she doesn't understand.

"Taylor? The band?"

"Everything, Daph. Not just Taylor. Not just the band. Not just the fame and the revenue. The music is gone, too. I haven't sung since that last show. I haven't written a song in a year and a half. The music used to be with me all the time. I had my own soundtrack, playing all the time in my thoughts, and now—" I put out my hands. "Crickets."

She waits. I see her fold her arms across her chest, but she's listening.

I stare at the ground and say it. "I'm broken, Daph."

I sense her nod and risk a glance her way. She hasn't moved and I still can't read her expression. Her tone is even softer, though, when she speaks. "Are you okay to drive?"

"More or less. The motel's not far."

"Leave the bike," she suggests. "Come back for it in the morning."

"I don't want it to be in your way."

"It won't be. Tomorrow I'm going to borrow Dad's car to drive to Toronto."

I take a breath. "But someone will see."

I hear the smile in her voice. "And they'll all think I'm getting some action. Of course, they probably already think that but we both know how wrong they are."

There's something in her tone, something a little raw, and I realize that I've hurt her feelings. How? By wanting more than a night? "I hate small towns," I say, though that's not what I'm thinking. I'm wondering if I've screwed up completely.

"It's kind of sweet when you think about it. People looking out for each other."

I peer at her shadowed features. "You're way nicer than I am."

She laughs and that's got to be a good sign. "Maybe I'm having a moment."

I take a chance and ask what I've been wondering all day. "Tell me you aren't insulted that I stepped away last night."

She bristles, proof that she is.

"More," she echoes, mustering her inner ice queen so quickly that I know I've made a big mistake.

"Yes, more. Not more than you. More *with* you." She's startled. I reach out and snag her hand. "I don't want something quick, Daph. I want you, you have to know it, but for the first time ever, I want more."

"More?" This time, the word is less charged, a sign of progress.

"More than once. More than sex. More than one-and-done." I gesture vaguely. "I don't know how it works. I don't have a map, but I don't want to ruin everything." I squeeze her fingers, just a little. "But don't imagine for one minute that I don't want you with all my heart and soul, because I do."

She's quiet for a long time and I feel her studying me closely. I wonder what the verdict will be, and know that if she sends me away, I'll go, just because it's what she wants. Have I ever given anyone that much power over my choices? No, but it feels exactly right.

I trust her.

Completely.

And there's something magical about having said the words out loud. I feel like I've put down a burden. It could be a first step. I feel like I can be better.

I want to be better.

"What about what I want?" she asks finally.

"Well, that's going to determine how we go from here."

"You'll do whatever I ask?"

I nod and she tilts her head to study me. "I don't believe you, you know. Guys say whatever they need to in order to get what they want." I might protest, but she raises a hand. "But it doesn't matter. I don't believe in forever anymore either."

That's the saddest thing I've heard in a long time.

"Bad timing, since I'm just starting to wonder if all the songs are true."

"Oh Luke," she says with a sigh and I love the sound of my name on her lips, even when it's not a shout of joy. "You don't have to mess with me, or tell me stories."

"Not a chance."

"If there's going to be anything, it has to be honest, no matter how it goes."

"Of course." It's only an increment of what I want to give her, but she's right. Honesty is a cornerstone.

"No stories, no promises, no nonsense about forever."

My throat is tight because I can feel now how much that loser hurt her. "If that's how you want it."

"There you go," she says, shaking her head.

"What do you mean?"

"That's an implication. It sounds like a promise, like you don't want something that simple."

"I don't. I told you."

"More," she says under her breath. She's still wavering, deciding whether to give me another chance.

I wonder if I'm asking for one thing she can't give.

"Don't you see, Luke? It's just words, words that sound good in the moment. Don't bother with them. I'm done with words, and promises, and lies."

She was burned. I get it. This Justin Jerk said all the right things but didn't follow through by doing all the right things.

Actions speak louder than words.

I can own that.

"Just think about it," I say, and when she doesn't reply, I kiss her palm. I fold her fingers over the place where my lips touched the softness of her skin, and recognize the power she already has over me.

Daph does something to me, makes me gallant, makes me want to be a better man than I've been in the past. I want to make her proud of me, even proud to know me. I want us to be together, but only if she wants to be with me.

I'm ready to earn that, whatever it takes.

And yes, I want to restore her faith in forever.

One step at a time.

Maybe The One is the person you admire so much that you'll do whatever it takes to make things work between you. Maybe romance isn't about uncertainty, Oscar, but about putting in the effort to earn the result.

"Good night, Daph," I say, knowing that once I would have come to her door in the middle of the night after her friends were gone, that once I would have charmed my way inside her house and into her bed, that once I would have made her shout in pleasure—then disappeared by morning.

I'm not that guy anymore.

I don't want quick satisfaction this time.

I don't want to vanish.

Our fingers and gazes cling for a long moment, then Cameron's laugh echoes from the house and I pull away. My equilibrium is restored sufficiently that I don't want there to be rumours in town about Daph, about us. (I don't think gossip is sweet.)

So, I start my bike as she steps onto her own porch, wave, and head back to the motel. I'm well aware that she's standing there watching until I turn the corner and pass out of sight. Like a guardian angel.

Will I sleep?

I don't think there's a chance, but I'm wrong. It's lights out as soon as my head hits the pillow.

———

THE MAGIC HAPPENS in the morning, when the sun is rising.

I can hear a stirring in my mind, something that hasn't been there since Taylor died. I roll to my back and keep my eyes closed, not wanting to spook it.

It's the faint warble of a melody. It's not complete. It's only a bar or two, really, but it's *there*. I know it's too soon to try to capture it. Even as I listen, trying to catch the notes, it flickers and vanishes.

But it was back. A song is elusive and has to ripen in its own time. Not all of them do. But just the fact that I heard it again is a glorious gift.

Maybe Daph'll be my muse.

9

DAPHNE

I'm jangled in the morning, and not just because of the congestion on the drive into the city. I end up arriving downtown a little later than planned, but even that's not what is throwing me off balance.

It's Luke.

The way he looked at me the night before, the things he said—well, the one thing he said—kept me awake. It made me wonder about possibilities and probabilities. It made me hopeful, then I felt foolish for being optimistic. Was he just telling me what I want to hear? Was he spinning a story?

I can't believe it, but at the same time, I want to believe in him.

I would have slept with him, no expectations, no strings attached. But after last night, I understand that he thinks he doesn't want it that way. It'll be full-on, shooting for forever, and I'm not sure I've got another leap like that in me.

No, it's not the leap that would finish me. It's the crash at the end, when it inevitably ends, when he walks away and forgets me. I'm not sure I can handle being jilted again.

Maybe Luke believes in forever, but I don't.

Maybe Luke is wrong about his own intentions—this forever thing is all new to him, after all. Maybe it's an idea he finds appealing, in this moment, but the attraction will fade.

I'm afraid that's right.

Yet I want him anyway. Even being sure it wouldn't end well, even knowing it can't have a chance of being more than a one-off, I still want to know.

Am I crazy?

Let's face it—taking a chance is all new to me. Luke's not the only one who doesn't have a map to this territory.

My friends stayed late, though we avoided the topic of Luke. It felt to me like he was the elephant in the room. My impression was proved right when I discovered that Cameron had left a brown paper bag full of assorted condoms in my mailbox this morning.

What made me smile was the little crocheted hedgehog that someone—undoubtedly Willow—left on my kitchen windowsill. It reminded me of the power of friends.

That's why I sent Rafe a text first thing, asking him to meet me for lunch. We were best friends in law school and articled together at the same firm. We definitely should have been rivals. Instead, we became really good friends. Rafe always tells me the truth, even if he knows it will hurt. He's the one who told me about Justin cheating. (I didn't believe him, but he didn't let it go until I did.) He's a friend who goes above and beyond, and I need a bit of that today.

I always called him 'the pirate king.' It was one of those jokes that stuck. (I also told him he could make a fortune posing for romance novel covers, but he didn't find that as funny.) I watch him approach as I wait outside the restaurant he's chosen and am reassured that I had it right.

Rafe Rossetti is a beautiful man, with his dark hair and dark eyes. He could have posed for a Renaissance sculptor, and taught any one of them a bit about life's fleeting pleasures. It's obvious that success agrees with him—even in a bespoke Italian suit, a white shirt with French cuffs, shoes that undoubtedly have leather soles and a massive diamond solitaire in place of the gold earring that prompted my moniker, Rafe looks expensive, reckless and completely irresistible. He could be running guns for a dictator or defending hitmen. Who cares? He's such serious male eye candy that women turn to stare after him in awe.

I can tell by the way his eyes are dancing that he loves every minute of it. He's the adored baby boy of his family, the only son with four older sisters who doted upon him and a mom who thinks he hung the stars and the moon. Rafe has no lack of confidence, and yet, he's a very sweet man.

It's good to have some fixed variables in your world, and Rafe is one of mine.

"The glorious Daphne," he purrs, seizing my hands then kissing my cheeks in turn. He smells really good and he winks at me, up close and personal, still bent over my hand, when I take a deep appreciative breath.

"Who is she?" I ask.

"On what evidence have you based this conclusion?"

"You changed colognes. I thought that would never happen."

"Doesn't matter. She's gone but it's not." He spins me around outside the restaurant, making me laugh and women gawk. "Look at you! I love this suit on you. So chic. Why are you in town? Job interview?"

"Work."

He lifts a brow.

"An errand."

Rafe makes a skeptical sound. "With that bra? I don't think so."

I glance down. "You can't see it."

"Underwires." He cups his hands and makes an appreciative growl. "The shape...Mmm." He shakes his head. He's having too much fun and I'm blushing to my toes. Apparently, Luke isn't the only male with a fondness for lingerie. "I have it on good authority that you only tolerate underwires for special occasions."

"Where did you hear such a scandalous rumor?"

"From you." He guides me to the restaurant. The maître d' is watching with a gleam of indulgence in his eyes that tells me Rafe is a regular.

"Maybe I changed my mind."

"Mmm hmm." He leans down to whisper in my ear. "Maybe you're getting some."

I laugh at him to deflect the question. "Jealous?"

"How could I not be?"

"That must be because you aren't getting any."

He raises a hand to his heart as if I've dealt a fatal blow, and the maître d' guides us to a table. It's a corner table near the front, as if we're being displayed to prospective diners, and I smile because we probably are.

"Damn, we look good together," Rafe says playfully. "Think of the beautiful babies we'd have."

"We?" I demand, just as I always do. "You stop by for the fun part then I get all the work? Thanks, but no."

He winks. "I'd be diligent about the fun part."

"It can't possibly make up for the next twenty-some years."

He pretends to pout. "I keep hoping you'll change your mind."

"No, you don't. I'd make you change the diapers in the middle of the night. You want someone you can wrap around your finger."

Rafe laughs, unrepentant.

We're left to peruse the menu after being informed of the specials and I look him in the eye. "When exactly are you coming to visit?"

He cringes at the suggestion just the way I knew he would. Rafe is an urban creature. I'm not sure he'd survive even the drive to Empire. All those open fields. He's twitching because I'm thinking of them. "I will. One day."

"You said you would come last summer. You promised."

"Is that why you're here? To harass me?"

"No, I just miss your sparkling company."

He smiles again. "I'm guessing there's not a decent hotel in town."

"A motel." I wait for him to grimace. "But I have a house and a sofa-bed."

"Be still, my heart." His eyes glint. "Is there a copier, at least?"

Once again, I'm blushing. Rafe and I almost got it on once, when we were articling together at the firm where he is now partner, in the copy room, on the copier. We were tired and desperate and stressed, and while it was fun for a few moments, we both agreed to cease and desist.

I do not recommend copier machines for intimate liaisons, by the way. They have hard corners and buttons. It does, though, add a certain *je ne sais quoi* if one of the participants inadvertently hits Copy. I thought I was going to get sunburn in a very personal location and that's what brought us back to reality.

"We have inkjet printers," I say and shake my head sadly.

He laughs heartily, making more than one person turn to look.

"I should despise you for that," I say and he grins.

"But it's just not possible between friends with so much common ground." He picks up his menu. "Even though I did make partner six months ago. Any news of your pending partnership from the hinterland?"

"You know there isn't." I hear my dad telling me again about ten years of service before being offered a junior partnership. I sigh. "I'll be forty before it happens, if it even does then."

"I'll be running this place by then," he says with relish.

He probably will be.

I glare at him.

He smiles. "But my infinite charm keeps you from resenting me. That is friendship."

"Nah. Your burn rate makes me pity you."

"I like nice things. It's not a crime."

"You can't possibly be earning enough to afford that suit."

He holds up his fingers.

"Five? You have *five* suits like that?"

"One for each day of the work week. I think I need another, just to mix it up."

"How much *do* you make?"

He drops his voice to a whisper to confess and I feel my eyes fly open.

"That's outrageous."

He brushes an invisible speck of lint from his lapel. "I'm worth every dime and don't you ever doubt it."

The truth is that Rafe probably *is* worth it. I never met anyone with such a quick mind. He's more than clever. He's devious, too. He works harder than he plays, and just because he makes it look easy doesn't mean I don't appreciate his mad skills.

He was born to be a lawyer. I was just expected to become one. It's different.

I look at the menu. "Well, if I can't pity you and you're that rich, I might as well eat. You're buying."

"Of course. Have the lobster ravioli. It's great."

"And dessert?"

He raises his hands. "Have it all."

I will. We quibble the way we always do over ordering in restaurants, making sure we each choose something we both will like, because sharing is part of our jam. Once that's negotiated, we order and are left alone again.

Rafe locks his hands together in a gesture so familiar that I smile, braces his elbows on the table and leans his chin on his fingertips. He fixes me with a look intended prompt my every confession. "The truth now," he orders. "Why are you in town today?"

"To bask in the glory of your radiance."

"Besides that. Come on. This has got to be good to merit that bra."

I tell him the whole story of Luke's restaurant scheme, which sounds so bizarre in the telling that it makes him laugh. (My impressions of Patrick don't hurt in that regard.)

In the meantime, lunch is served. It looks and smells divine. We dig in appreciatively, then share bites, just as we have since law school.

"So, you're on a quest. What's the name of that chef?"

"Meredith MacRae, apparently."

He lowers his fork. For the first time in a long time, I think I've surprised Rafe. (There should be bonus points for that.)

"Oh. That changes everything."

"Changes everything how?"

He taps a finger on the table. "Let me know whether you convince her or not."

"Why do you care?"

"Because she's brilliant and if she sets up shop in Empire, I *am* coming to visit."

"No, you'll be coming to eat."

"Details, schmetails," he says, stealing one of my ravioli. "Oh, by the way." His casual tone is the only warning I get. "Heather moved out."

My heart does a somersault. I know which Heather he means.

Rafe winces. "So, Justin is single again. I'd bet good money he deserved it but that doesn't change the fact that he asked about you."

Now I put down my fork. "No." I don't think I'll be able to eat another thing.

"That's what I said. No, no, and no. Anyone who pees in the pool is banished forever."

I fight a smile. "You didn't say that."

He looks grim, just for a moment, a pirate king who has no regrets. "I chose a more colourful verb." I get a fierce look. "And that, by the way, is why I asked you to meet me here instead of at the office. I didn't want there to be any chance of him seeing you and even trying to make a move."

I appreciate when Rafe gets all grumpy. It makes me feel like I've qualified to be another of his sisters.

"Thank you." I reach across the table and touch his hand.

"What else is a friend to do?" he demands, then gestures to my meal. "Didn't I tell you this was great? Oh, you haven't tried my risotto yet. It's worth every extra minute in the gym."

———

MEREDITH MACRAE IS ALONE in the restaurant, or what used to be a restaurant. The sign is blacked over and the place is empty. It's about three by the time I get there, but I can see someone moving around inside and I guess it's her. I have to bang on the door and convince her—with hand signals—to unlock the door.

Only then can I see her clearly. She's tiny but I have a sense of a forceful character. She has a cloud of curly red hair that falls to her waist and probably eludes most efforts to tame it. Her eyes are green and her gaze shrewd. She looks both worldly and innocent, probably because of the freckles across her nose and cheeks.

I have the definite sense that only fools underestimate her and am not getting in that line.

"There's no more money," she says bluntly, unlocking the door just a crack. "Take it up with the owner. I'm just packing up."

"Where are you going?"

"Why should you care?"

"Because I have a suggestion for you."

She braces a hand on her hip. "A suggestion," she repeats, as if I've just said I could levitate a city block.

"Maybe even an offer you can't refuse." I smile, which only seems to increase her suspicions.

"I'm really good at refusals."

"It's a deal on an empty restaurant. Kind of a rent-to-buy offer."

She looks me up and down. "Kind of."

"It's not really rent. Every payment goes toward the principle."

"Debt."

"Ten thousand dollars and the restaurant is yours."

"I don't even have that kind of money." She starts to close the door and I wedge my foot in the door.

"A hundred dollars a month for a hundred months. You have to pay the utilities and property taxes, though."

She stares at me. I fumble for the folder with the contract.

"A couple of hundred dollars a month should cover them, but the patron could cover them for the first year for you if that's a dealbreaker."

"What kind of crazy person would make me an offer like that?"

"My client prefers to remain anonymous at this time."

She's wary but curious.

And she doesn't close the door. I conjure a card and introduce myself, shoving it through the space and watching her read it.

"A hundred dollars a month," she muses. "That's the net on four dinners. In a month."

"If you say so."

"Even being closed Sundays and Mondays leaves between twenty and twenty-two days to sell those four dinners."

I nod my agreement of this impeccable math and she holds my gaze, then frowns.

"There are other expenses than the food, of course."

"Of course, but a lot fewer of them in this situation."

She looks at my card. "Empire. Should I know where that is?"

"North of Lake Erie, most of the way to Windsor."

Her eyes narrow and her eyes flick, as if she's reviewing some private map of her own. "There are greenhouses down there."

"Mostly tomatoes and sweet peppers. Cavendish Enterprises."

"And a vineyard."

"Rhodes Vineyards is the biggest one."

"There's another?"

"One of the Cavendish clan has a start-up with fruit wines."

She dismisses this with a gesture. "Other farms?"

Belatedly, I see what she's getting at and feel dumb. She's a *chef*. She cares about local sources of food. "Oh, yes. The farmers' market in Havelock, the next biggest town, features organic produce, locally-made cheeses, meats raised without hormones locally, and a lot of heritage varieties..."

She opens the door so abruptly that I almost fall over, then waves me inside with impatience. It's cool and dark, and the emptiness echoes a little. Tables and chairs are stacked to one side and the floor is big enough to dance. "They're picking up the chattels tomorrow," she says, inviting me to take a seat. "I'm just packing up my own things today." She fixes me with a look. "I had a feeling I should be here."

"Are you psychic?"

"No. I just smell when opportunity might come knocking." She smiles. "Sometimes I wait too long for it to show up. Tell me about this place you're trying so hard to unload."

I do. I have the pictures I took of Queen Street, the front of the diner, even Big Red. I show her the parking space behind the diner, the loading dock, the empty apartment on the second floor, everything else before the diner itself. I'm worried that the sight of its neglect will nix the deal, but she pounces on the pictures of the interior. She rattles off questions faster than I can answer them, demanding to know how many seats, how much fridge and freezer capacity, is that a pizza oven, how long has it been closed, when was the wiring last updated, how big is the town, and just when I think there's no way she'll go for it, she pauses and sits back.

"What other restaurants are in town?"

I wince. "None."

"None?" She's visibly incredulous.

"We don't have a donut shop or any fast-food places."

"You have to have a Tim Hortons."

I shake my head.

"No Golden Arches?" She's incredulous, like most teenagers in Empire.

Again, I shake my head. "People have to go to Havelock for that, even for a grocery store. There's a convenience store in town that has some essentials and there's a taco truck there on Fridays." I point it out on my map but she's not interested. The glance at the map, though, reminds me of something. "Oh, and The Golden Lotus is open Fridays."

"The Golden Lotus?"

I point it out. "Chinese-Canadian smorgasbord."

She smiles at that, although I don't know why.

"It's a buffet," I explain. "Or it used to be. All you can eat."

"I know what a smorgasbord is, but that's a Scandinavian word. It should have pickled herring and rye bread, not beef chow mein or General Tso's chicken."

I see her point. "Well, that's what they've always called it. But Mr. Chang died and Mrs. Chang wasn't doing so well on her own, so one of their sons came back from Toronto. I think Phil has a lot to manage with his mom's care, so he's only open for take-out on

Friday nights, but not always even then. That's why I forgot about it. He's an engineer, but his dad taught him to cook."

This is way too much information and I know it, but I'm not sure what she wants to know.

She tilts her head to look at me, reminding me of a bird. "Where does he shop?"

I blink. I've never seen Phil in the grocery store in Havelock. "I don't know."

"I'll have to ask him then." She looks around the empty restaurant but I know she's not really looking at it. She's thinking. I wait in silence, following her gaze and deciding it must have been an attractive place with lights, tablecloths and such. Crummy neighbourhood, though. I was glad it was daylight when I parked the Benz, and more glad that I got a spot right out front.

I look. The car's still there.

"I have an unofficial partner," she says finally. I nod, wondering if I should tip my hand that I know it's Sylvia. "It's only fair to check with her."

"Of course." I hide my anticipation. She's actually thinking about it! I've got butterflies in my stomach and they're cavorting happily in anticipation of good news.

I avert my gaze and stare out the window as she makes her call. When she starts talking, I get up and move to the window, gazing out at the quiet street without seeing it. I guess the rent here was comparatively cheap. Evidently, it wasn't cheap enough.

I'm thinking all of this, my thoughts running like a gerbil on a wheel, in an attempt to *not* eavesdrop.

The strategy fails.

"The lawyer's name? Daphne Bradshaw. Why?" Meredith's voice sharpens. "What do you mean, you *know* her? How could you know her?"

There is a pause as she listens, one that seems tense.

"That is seriously against the odds. What do you know about this Empire place that I should know?"

Oh, I wish I could hear Sylvia's response.

Meredith laughs a little. "Okay, keep your secrets. What do you think? It's looking to me like the proverbial offer I can't refuse." Another pause. "Depends who's asking. What does that mean? Are you going to explain? No, you won't and I know it. Hang on." Meredith raises her voice. "She wants to know who your client is."

"I can't tell you that."

"Even if it's a dealbreaker?"

I shrug. Luke said not to reveal his name, so I won't. I never considered that she might decline, just because the benefactor's name is a secret.

"No dice. She won't tell," she informs Sylvia. She rolls her eyes. "She wants initials."

I shake my head. "Still a breach of client confidentiality."

Meredith's eyes start to sparkle. "She wants to know if she can give you initials, and you can either agree or disagree."

"This feels like high school."

"There is that," Meredith cedes. She listens, then looks up at me. "Is it someone with the initials M.C.?"

M.C.? Mike Cavendish? It makes sense Sylvia wouldn't want him luring her back to town after she broke off their engagement. But then, why would he? And why now? How would he even know where to find her? The offer was for Meredith and, unlike Luke, Mike didn't hop into Toronto for dinner. I wasn't sure he ever left the property of Cavendish Enterprises.

Who else?

M.C. Martin Carmichael. He's the old guy who runs the auto repair shop. I can't imagine he'd even know Sylvia.

M.C. What's the name of Phil Chang's younger brother? I'm drawing a blank.

"Well?" Meredith says, reminding me that she's waiting.

"No."

She searches my gaze then turns away. "She says no. I trust her. You do, too?" She glances over her shoulder, smiling a little. "Daphne Bradshaw couldn't tell a lie if her life depended on it." She's obviously repeating something Sylvia said and it makes her smile. "Is that so? Why do you make that sound like a bad thing?" My ears are burning, but Meredith laughs, says something quietly then ends the call. She tosses her phone on a table and goes to a cash register I hadn't noticed. She presses a button and the drawer opens. She takes five twenties, then returns to put them on the table in front of me, her hand flat on top of them. "First payment."

"I thought there was no money left."

"There isn't much. I figure this much of it is mine. Where do I sign?"

I pull out the agreement, those butterflies doing a mad tango that I do my best to hide. She reads it through, earning my respect, then puts out her hand for a pen to sign it. I exhale when she does, then witness the signature with my own and date it. Luke already signed all three copies, though his signature is tough to decipher. That's maybe a good thing. I take one copy, fold it and put it in an envelope, then present it to Meredith.

"The other two?"

"Your patron and my files."

"All official."

"Pretty much."

She makes a note of the address on her phone, and I guess that she's checking the GPS. Then she nods approval.

"I'll be there tomorrow," she says.

So fast! So comparatively easy!

What will Luke say?

What will he do?

I can't wait to find out, but I keep it business-like. "Give me a call when you're on the way and I'll meet you there. My office is right across the street." I hand her the keys to the diner, not missing how her grip closes around them. I remember that satisfaction when I got the keys to my house.

"You'd better call me Merrie," she invites with a smile that makes her look like a demon leprechaun. "Everyone else does."

We introduce each other again and shake hands. She looks down at the keys and I watch her smile as she fingers them. It's as if she can't believe it. I know that feeling, too.

"What are you going to call the restaurant?"

Her smile broadens. "The Carpe Diem Café," she says, as if she's been dreaming of this place for a lifetime. Maybe she has. "A Farm-To-Table Bistro."

"Seize the day?" I translate.

"That's it. Call it my philosophy." She laughs a little. "And I'm following it today."

"I like it." I pack up my briefcase and stand. "I might be one of your first customers."

She suddenly snaps her fingers. "Wait. How did you get here?"

"I drove my dad's car." I gesture to the sedan parked at the curb and her eyes light. I've no idea why my car is so welcome until she speaks, and then it's obvious.

"Take some stuff back for me?"

An hour later, I'm back in the Benz, the trunk and back seat loaded with saucepans and dishes—even I know she would never trust me with her knives—before I remember I need to text Rafe. It's almost four-thirty. The 401, that fat snake of a highway that runs across southern Ontario, is bumper-to-bumper heading west, stop-and-go, all eight lanes of it. It'll be like this through Milton, if not Guelph or Kitchener, but because I only have to do it this once, I don't mind. It gives me another reminder of why it was good to leave the city.

As I come full-stop in the gridlock, I text Rafe. His reply is a thumbs-up emoji, repeated over and over again. Looks like I'll have a houseguest soon.

I send another text to my dad to let him know I'll be late and why. Then I load up my tunes and settle in.

I can't help thinking about Merrie's philosophy. Seize the day. Leap and believe the net will appear. Take a chance. Not my speciality, but maybe it's time for a change.

If I take a chance on Luke and his pursuit of more, what's the worst thing that can happen? He already turned me down and I survived. He might seduce me. I might seduce him. I can't believe I'll regret either option.

Maybe it's worth taking a chance on what you want, just to see what happens next.

Maybe it's time to find out.

I could stop at the Maple Leaf Motel on my way home, but I decide on a shower and change of clothes first. Maybe I'll wear my hair down. Maybe I should stick with the underwire bra, though. You only get to seduce a man for the first time once, after all.

And the prospect of that makes me smile.

10
———

LUKE

Here's one thing I've learned in my time so far on this spinning rock: you have to protect whatever is important to you and your survival. You can't count on anyone else to do it. You need to look out for threats to its continuation, even at risk to yourself. And if it's important to you that a person be in the world, you need to protect that person from harm.

I fell down on that once and I'm not going to do it again.

So, even though it's getting dark in Empire and Daph isn't back from Toronto, even though the uncertainty of whether she succeeded in persuading Meredith MacRae to take the deal may just eat me alive, I'm not going to text or phone her.

Chances are good that the one person in the universe who doesn't text and drive is Daph, but I'm not going to take any chances. I don't need it to be my fault that her car ends up wrapped around the underside of a tractor trailer.

I need her in the world. It's a purely selfish perspective when I think of it like that, but I'm still working on a broader view. She's my ally and the key to making this whole scheme work.

More than that, beyond the Empire-rehabilitation plan, I need her.

She might end up being my muse, my friend or my lover. She might be my salvation. I want the chance to find out, and I'll do whatever has to be done to make it so.

So, I sit on her porch and wait, like a dog faithfully awaiting its owner. (Or its dinner.) Once I've thought of the comparison, I can't shake it, even though it's not the most flattering perspective of yours truly.

What do I want from Daph? Easy. Pretty much everything.

What am I prepared to give up for the privilege?

I can't see that it's costing me very much, at least not yet. I'm surrendering secrets, which isn't that easy for me, but she hasn't demanded my soul or every cent I possess, my last breath or even my pride.

It would be very easy to fall head-over-heels with Daph.

It would probably be smart for me. Would it be smart for her?

I'm pondering this when a familiar silhouette comes into view, strolling up Forest Road. I'm surprised to see her dad walking home from the office, but then I remember that Daph took his car. His footsteps turn up her drive and if he's surprised to find me on the porch, he hides it well.

He puts his briefcase down on the top step and stands there, looking at me.

I give him a jaunty fingertip wave and he nods acknowledgement.

He's choosing his words and I let him take his time. I'm not going anywhere soon and I've known since this morning that he has something to say to me.

"I suppose it's old-fashioned to ask after your intentions," he says finally.

"Maybe, but the impulse is a fair one."

He nods just a little, staring across the lawn. His posture is relaxed, his manner indifferent, but I'm not fooled. If I'm protective of his daughter, Richard Bradshaw is a thousand times more so. I have to wonder if he ever had a little heart-to-heart with Jerk Justin.

"And so?" he invites.

"You know my plan for the diner."

"I'm talking about my daughter and I think you know it." Mr. Bradshaw waits but I don't leap in. I can appreciate that he wants to know, but I'm not ready to tell. Whatever is between me and Daph feels fragile and private. I don't think she'd be happy with me talking to her dad about it either.

"Perhaps your plans aren't my business," he offers, clearly checking the temperature.

"I seldom make plans anymore."

This amuses him. "So, when you steer your ship out of the harbor..."

"I put up the sails and let the wind take us where we need to be." I deliberately speak in the plural and the slight narrowing of his eyes proves that he didn't miss it.

"There are those who would suggest that you should have grown out of such impulses."

"They're probably those who don't know me very well."

He turns to face me then, his gaze sharp. "Why did you include the Foreman house in your list?"

Interesting question, and unexpected.

I hide my reaction. "To give Patrick something to eliminate, of course."

Mr. Bradshaw shakes his head slowly, his gaze fixed upon me, and waits.

Daph comes honestly by her intellect, it seems.

I lean forward, bracing my elbows on my knees. "There are people who are very principled."

"There are."

"And those people, sometimes, are underwhelmed by mere money, even if it's fair compensation offered for a task they will do well." He lifts a brow and I nod. "If you have wealth, they may think that you throw money around, that cash isn't important to you. If they're principled or idealistic, or if you ask them for something that takes a little more, they might appreciate some other form of compensation." I pause for a beat. "Something they think costs you more than just cash. Something...more interesting."

He's watching me and listening.

"And in my experience, what makes such people particularly happy is the chance to have whatever it is that they really want. Even better, they love if you figure it out without them telling you, and you offer their heart's desire."

"Instead of just cash."

"It might cost less than their usual fee, or it might cost more, but the fact that you thought of it gains their support. It makes the exchange more than a contract or an agreement."

"It creates a bond of understanding," he says and I nod.

"Exactly. I didn't expect Daph to be impressed if I paid her fee, whatever it is. I knew for her to really think well of whatever we achieved, she'd want more than a timely payment in full."

"And what exactly is my daughter's dream that you intend to facilitate?"

"Her own practice, here in Empire." He's not surprised by the suggestion, but I think he's surprised that I named it. "I was going to give her the title to that building as her compensation, to do with it whatever she wished. I thought she might set up shop on the main floor and rent out the apartment."

"She has no reason to set up her own practice..."

"So, I've heard. She explained it all to me the first day I arrived, how it made sense to be your junior lawyer and wait to inherit the business, but you know, it sounded like she was repeating someone else's argument instead of making her own."

He straightens just a little and stares down the road again.

"I was surprised to find her here," I admit. "Abbie was always telling me that Daph was top of the class all through high school. She said she graduated *summa cum laude* from U of T."

"Top percentile on the bar exam," he adds with a touch of pride.

"Articling and then working at one of the big firms in the city." Again, I watch him nod. "On the fast track to a successful future, until some loser broke her heart and she came home to heal."

Now he looks at me, surprised that I know this.

"But why would she stay here?" I ask when his gaze meets mine.

"She came home..."

"Yes, she came home to heal, and not to see the jerk again, and that's fair. But after she finds her footing again, what's going to make her stay?"

He frowns.

"What's here for Daph? What's going to challenge her and interest her? She's not the kind of person who will be happy filling in paperwork forever."

"She has friends here. She has a house."

"A nice house, that didn't cost much comparatively and might sell quickly, even in Empire. The new kitchen is great. And she has other friends, like my sister in Vancouver. Would she really stay here if someone offered her a great job, one far away from the offices of her former fiancé?"

He winces though he tries to hide it.

"She needs more and you have to know it, even better than I do."

"She might marry."

"She might not."

His brows rise. "I'm beginning to realize why Patrick thinks you're so much trouble." He eyes me. "You don't care how much truth you tell or who you challenge."

I shrug.

"Are you staying?" His gaze is searching.

"I'm here for the moment, until I finish what I've started."

"And then you'll hoist your sail and let the wind take you where you belong," he concludes. "I see. Thank you for your honesty, Mr. Jones. I hope your venture is successful."

"But it's not my venture," I correct before he leaves and he stops to glance back. "If Daph convinces Meredith to take on the diner and Meredith makes a success of it, that won't be to my credit. I'm just creating an opportunity and whatever comes of it will be due to Meredith and to Daph."

He shakes his head a little, and I continue.

"I think the most meaningful thing I can do is open the door to possibilities and I'll keep doing it as long as I can. I love watching people flourish. I love watching them grab opportunity with both hands and take it places I could never have imagined." I take a breath. "I like having a teeny tiny part in making people happier, maybe even in making the world a better place. Imagine if we all tried that once in a while, if we all gave someone a hand when we could." I pause for a second. "Imagine what the world could be."

Mr. Bradshaw stares at me, and I think for a minute that he looks like a man awakened from a dream. I can see that he's never considered this before and I wonder if I've made a convert.

Then I remind myself that he's in Patrick's pocket, today and every possible tomorrow.

He hefts his briefcase and starts to turn away, then glances back. "Daphne texted me that she was stuck in traffic. She didn't expect to be back before eight."

"Thank you," I say and mean it, because relief is flooding through me.

She's okay.

He must hear some of that in my tone because he gives me another look, a long considering one, then he nods and heads off. I sit and watch until he's out of sight. He walks with purpose, not rushing, and I see him wave a greeting to someone on the way.

Then the evening closes around me again, the astonishing quiet of Empire on a spring evening. I can almost hear the frogs in the river in the woods behind me. Someone has lit a wood fire because I can smell it and I hear the distant crack of sparks. Is it Una? Daph's house hides the woods behind from my view. I sit and I think, and I smile at the little bit of melody chasing its tail in the back of my thoughts, hoping against hope that it won't vanish unexpectedly.

And so, when the big silver car finally pulls into her driveway, I'm immediately on my feet. Daph swings those divine legs out of the car. She doesn't realize I'm sitting on the darkened porch: she rolls her shoulders and stretches like a cat. Then she reaches back into the car, slings her briefcase over her shoulder and heads for the door, sorting through her keys. She's wearing a black suit with a straight skirt, which gives her a retro look with her hair twisted up. A few strands of hair are loose, silhouetted against her neck by the streetlight. I feel a wave of desire that is primal and almost potent enough to take me to my knees.

She's okay.

"Well?" I say, stepping into the puddle of light from the streetlight.

She jumps, then smiles. "Done," she says softly and I give a hoot of triumph that makes her laugh.

Her laughter is all the encouragement I need to let loose. I jump off the porch and catch her up to swing her around, ignoring her protests. I shout and holler and she laughs like I'm insane and maybe I am.

"You did it!"

"It was your plan."

"But you made it work."

I put her down and she smiles up at me. "She was easy to convince. I think you offered the one thing she really wanted."

"That is the key to success," I say with enthusiasm.

"Maybe it is." Her gaze dances over me, something in her eyes that encourages me to take a chance.

I lean so close that our noses almost touch. I smell her skin and hear her gasp, and suddenly there is only Daphne Bradshaw in my world. "She really signed?"

"She really signed." She reaches into her pocket and offers me five wrinkled twenties. "Down payment. She said she'll be here tomorrow."

"You are amazing!" I kiss her before she can even think about arguing, because it's the only possible way to celebrate such a victory. I kiss her, intending that it will be short and sweet, not that her lips will be soft and seductive, realizing too late that I'll end up wanting to scoop her up and carry her off, spending all night seducing her.

But she puts her hand on my chest, flat, and gives me a nudge. "You don't have to do this, Luke" she says, her eyes dark. "You don't have to pretend."

"What exactly am I pretending?"

"That you want this. That you want me. Remember about honesty? It's okay..." she starts, but I lean in and steal another quick kiss. I feel her melt toward me and I know that she needs this as much as I do. She's delicious, welcoming...

I break the kiss reluctantly, then kiss her ear, grazing her skin with my teeth. "I want this," I whisper. "We're consenting adults, so if you want this half as much as I do, it's your move."

"But yesterday..."

"I was trying—and failing, it should be noted—to be a gentleman."

"You didn't fail. You walked away."

"Only possible way to manage it."

She smiles a witchy little smile, one that lights her eyes and is all glorious mischief. "Maybe gentlemanly restraint just isn't your style," she says. Her hand slides down my chest at the same time and I catch my breath when she reaches the front of my jeans. She hesitates then, and it's fair to want a little reassurance.

"No one but you Daph," I murmur. "Not now."

Maybe not ever, but given her skepticism about the long game, I don't say that part.

Her eyes glow with pleasure and she lifts her chin a little, inviting me to kiss her again. I'm not going to decline. I bend down and capture her lips, the taste of her almost making me dizzy. I'm not expecting that she'll open her mouth a little, much less that I'll feel the tip of her tongue.

It destroys me completely.

And then there's no chance of anything short and sweet. I spear my fingers into her hair and hold her captive as I deepen my kiss, loving how Daph makes a little sound of capitulation, how she drops her bag and wraps her arms around my neck in surrender.

She doesn't drop the money. She jams it into the pocket of my jacket, then locks her hands in my hair, kissing me back as if her life depends upon it. I swing her up into my arms and head for the door, bending to scoop up her briefcase on the way. I turn around so she can get the door unlocked, even hung over my shoulder, and that makes her laugh. I carry her inside and she shuts the door, turning the deadbolt before I let her slide down into my arms.

She looks disheveled and wonderful, her eyes sparkling and her cheeks flushed. "I need a shower," she says but I crush her into the wall, almost devouring her. It's a great hungry kiss, one that goes on for half of forever and isn't nearly enough, one that lights my blood on fire.

"You need an orgasm, not a shower," I growl against her throat and kiss her again.

"Can't I have both?" she demands, breathless, when she has a chance. I don't have time to agree because she slides her hands under my jacket, then beneath my shirt, the feel of her fingers on my skin enough to make me spontaneously combust.

I pull her toward the stairs and we start stripping each other, kissing all the while. Daph kicks off her shoes and I shed my boots and jacket. Her jacket is flung over the couch and I tug the pins from her hair as she wriggles out of her blouse. Her hands are on my belt buckle and I'm unfastening her skirt, then I stop cold to admire her lingerie.

Black lace. Her skin is as pale as alabaster and almost glows in the partial light. Her hair is a loose tumble of auburn over her shoulders and her lips are swollen a little from our kisses.

"Irresistible," I murmur then trap her against the wall with my hips. She feels so good. She smiles as she slides her hands under my T-shirt again and pushes it up, hands spread flat against my chest. She tosses it away, bending to kiss my nipple, eyes dancing with mischief. She's wearing that pink lipstick again and her eye make-up is all smoky—just like the sultry expression in her eyes. She's a temptress, a siren, a pin-up girl, a fantasy come to life and I want everything she has to share.

"Me first," I growl, holding her gaze as I lower my head and flick my tongue across her nipple through the lace. It tightens immediately, as if in welcome, and I smile as I cup that breast in my hand, loving how perfectly her curve fills my hand. I kiss it and worry it, teasing it until she moans in my ear. I love how she's gripping my hair, how she's squirming between me and the wall, how I can smell her arousal. My hands slide around her and I find the clasp of her bra, flicking it open and watching as her breasts spill into my palms.

I catch my breath at their perfection. She's watching me, her eyes dark, her satisfaction clear. "I'm going to eat you until you scream," I threaten and Daph grins. "And then I'm going to do it again, until you come and come and come."

"Promises, promises," she says playfully. She flicks my nipple with a fingertip. "I can be very hard to please."

She's teasing and I know it, but I'll take that challenge. I pick her up so quickly that she gasps in surprise and toss her over my shoulder, heading up the stairs in my jeans. She's wearing her panties and stockings and one shoe, but it'll take me seconds to strip her bare.

She laughs at me when I toss her on the bed, then picks up a brown paper bag tossed on the floor. She reaches into it and tosses a colourful collection of small packages at me. Condoms in every size and colour, ribbed and not, lubricated and not. All the options are present and accounted for.

"Courtesy of Cameron," Daph says.

"She thinks we need two dozen, does she?" I strip off my jeans, aware of Daph's assessing gaze. "Well, I wouldn't want to disappoint your friends," I growl, then ease down on top of her, my hands on her thighs. She tastes like heaven and sighs exquisitely when my mouth closes over her. It's like we're exactly where we need to be and I believe it with all my heart.

And that's the last coherent thought I have for quite a while.

11

DAPHNE

The sex, in case you have any doubts, is phenomenal. Best ever. No contest.

I do scream.

Twice.

Luke makes some comment about ensuring the neighbours call the police then I straddle him and he's not even capable of being a smart-ass for a while. There's nothing better than that groan he makes when he finally lets go, the one that goes on and on and on, as if his release is being torn free of his soul.

The third time starts in the shower and ends up on the bathroom counter, then I'm so exhausted I can hardly stand up. Luke carries me to the bed as if I weigh nothing at all and tucks me in. I sigh with contentment and murmur 'good night.' I expect him to let himself out and disappear forever.

Instead, he slides into the bed behind me and wraps his arm around me. He kisses the back of my shoulder then nestles in, his breathing getting slower as he falls asleep. He's warm and rock-solid and I have no complaints that he's challenging my expectations.

It's lovely.

I sleep like the dead and awaken only at the sound of my front door lock.

Luke, I think, *heading out, never to be seen again.*

But then I realize that Luke is still dozing against my back, the weight of his arm around my waist. In fact, his hand is on my stomach, fingers splayed, and his thumb is doing this delicious swirly thing that is melting my knees and turning my brain to a tangle of spaghetti. I'm not even awake and I'm so turned on. He has to know it and I wriggle against him, just to be sure.

He's huge and hard, exactly what I want to make up to, so I reach back and close my hand around him.

He makes a little growl that proves he likes the situation as much as I do. He rolls me to my back and leans in for a kiss. How can he taste minty fresh like toothpaste already? I have no time to ask because his kiss is gloriously distracting and I love how he's pressing me down into the mattress...and the keys jingle again.

My eyes fly open. Friday!

It's *Friday*.

The trouble with really great sex—especially if you haven't had any sex in a while—is that it blurs your thoughts to other possibilities. Sensation has a way of making me forget reality, and the better the sensation, the more details I drop.

After the night with Luke, it's amazing that I remember my own name.

What I've forgotten is this: my dad and I have a weekly meeting every Friday at this breakfast place in Havelock. (It's called Eggs-traordinary. Really. The entire menu is filled with puns and dad-jokes. My dad loves it. He sits there chuckling away, each and every week, as he reads the menu.) You would think that I also would have remembered that his car was in my driveway, that it was full of Merrie's pots etc., and that he has keys to my house.

I yelp as I sit up. Breaking contact with Luke's hand means I instantly remember everything.

Shit.

Luke lounges against the headboard, eyes gleaming. "Expecting someone?" he asks in a silky murmur and I know he's enjoying my reaction.

I swat him and he grins, unrepentant.

"Competition?" he asks, clearly knowing he has none. He reaches over and caresses my nipple, rolling it between finger and thumb.

Traitor that it is, it tightens to attention and I close my eyes in rapture...

"Daphne! Sleeping in after your drive?" my father calls from the foyer.

Then there's a silence, one that makes me remember the detritus shed in every direction as we undressed each other. Luke's boots and jacket. My skirt and jacket.

My bra.

My father clears his throat delicately, apparently having noticed said detritus.

Of course, my father must know that I'm not a virgin anymore, but being aware that something is probably true and stumbling unexpectedly onto the evidence are two different things.

I look at Luke, who looks more like mischief than should be humanly possible, and he smiles wickedly. He cups my breast, leans in and kisses it, sending shivers right to my toes.

I have no script for this moment and don't know what to do.

In fact, Luke's caress is removing all vocabulary from my mind, replacing it with wonderful sensations and even better urges. Luke catches me around the waist and rolls me beneath him in one smooth move. His lips are against my ear again, his breath warm and his hands more than a little distracting.

"I'll hide," he whispers and I don't believe it. I pull back to look at him. He nods and crosses his heart with a fingertip.

Those eyes, though. They're twinkling with devilry.

"What price?" I mouth and he pretends to laugh silently.

I do not trust him. Not one bit.

My soul is gone forever. I'll owe Luke sex on demand whenever he wants it—and I can't regret the possibility much.

"Hi Dad!" I call, knowing I sound ridiculously cheerful. "Sorry I overslept." I try to get out of bed, but Luke pulls me into his lap. He turns me around, bending to kiss first one nipple and then the other, even as I stare down at the dark tangle of his hair. He moves seductively, slowly, and once again I'm drowning in sensation, everything else forgotten. I feel his lips close around one and his teeth graze the taut peak gently, so gently that I nearly moan out loud.

He glances up and tips his head toward the stairs, his expression expectant.

My dad. I forgot.

Again.

"Why don't we cancel this week?" my father calls. "I see that my car is a bit full."

"Oh, yes, I'm sorry. I'll get it sorted out today. Sorry!"

Luke spreads his fingers and slides his hand down my belly. I'm on fire and he knows it—and quite possibly my dad does, too.

"No problem," my dad replies cheerfully. The moment feels surreal. "I know it's a long drive. See you at noon?"

"Yes! I'll be in the office by then. Thanks, Dad!" The door clicks as he leaves and I fall back against Luke with relief. I twist around to face him, jabbing a finger into his chest. "You. Are. Wicked."

It's not exactly news and he doesn't look chastened.

In fact, he looks proud of himself.

"Guilty as charged," he cedes easily. "Now come here and do something about it."

"Why should I?"

His eyes glint. "You don't think I'll make it worth your while?"

"I think you want what you want and everything else is immaterial."

He sobers. "Guilty as charged, counsellor." He gives me a smouldering look, entwining his fingers with mine and I roll to my back again. He braces his weight over me as he gazes into my eyes. My heart skips a beat and he can probably feel it. I have no idea what he's going to say or do, and even that is exciting.

"I have a confession to make," he rumbles.

"Talk, talk, talk," I complain and his grin flashes before he sobers again. His gaze locks with mine and he's so serious that I'm a little bit worried.

"I thought you were gorgeous the other day when I came into the office, Daph," he confesses and my chest squeezes tightly. "All sleek and polished, polite and cool. It made me want to shake your composure. I thought you were pretty much irresistible."

He steals a kiss, a slow sweet one that takes my breath away.

The man defines 'irresistible.'

"I wanted to wake you up and shake you free," he whispers in my ear, giving me shivers. "I wanted to feel you wrapped around me, to make you come and hear you lose it."

"You did," I whisper.

"But I was right. Once could never be enough."

Another slow kiss that pushes every sensible thought from my head. I have no coherent reply, so I just kiss him back.

"Twice wasn't enough," he confesses and I know he's right. "And that makes me want to do it all over again."

"No complaints," I manage before I'm drowning in another of his bone-melting kisses.

He smiles down at me when he finally lifts his head. It must be a million degrees in my bedroom and time has stopped. There's only Luke and his oh-so-blue eyes, his little knowing smile and his tangled dark hair, his lashes sweeping down as he surveys me with satisfaction.

"I thought you were gorgeous then, but right now..." He lowers himself down, interlacing our hands and stretching mine over my head. I swallow when he whispers in my ear, his whiskers grazing my skin and his breath making me shiver. "With your hair all tangled and your skin flushed, your eyes shining..." He kisses me, all slow seductive heat. "You're blowing my mind, Daph," he concludes, his voice so husky that my heart squeezes tight.

We stare at each other for a long hot moment, then I deliberately smile to break the spell. I roll my hips beneath his and feel him get harder. "Is that your mind all the way down there?"

He grins slowly, hungrily, the wolf at my door, his eyes glowing with a heat that warms me all the way to my toes. I twine my arms around his neck and pull him closer for a kiss that takes no prisoners and demands everything he's got.

It's hot and hungry and a little rough, demanding and impatient. Luke moans then feasts upon my mouth, surrendering to sensation all over again. It's exactly what I wanted, what I needed, what I yearned to have, so I wrap my legs around his waist, loving how sharply he catches his breath.

Fortunately, noon is hours away.

———

THE NEXT TIME I wake up, it's almost eleven and I'm alone in bed. I stretch and yawn, acknowledging that I have precisely zero regrets.

We didn't use up all of Cameron's condom supply, but there's a respectable dent in the inventory. I sweep the rest into the top drawer of the nightstand and head for the shower. I hardly recognize myself in the mirror. I look happy—no, I look sated. Relaxed.

Everyone will know with a glance what I've been doing and I don't care.

In the shower, I remind myself that I can't expect more from Luke than I did from Justin. If Mr. straight-and-narrow, who had incidentally put a ring on my finger and written our wedding date in his calendar, couldn't be expected to be exclusively mine, then I can't anticipate that my bad-boy rock-star lover will be. In fact, I don't expect Luke to stick around. He said he wasn't going to. He might not even say goodbye.

He came to Empire, after all, to arrange for this diner to open and Sylvia to return. The wheels are in motion. Will he even stay to see the result? If so, will he linger after that?

No, it's even money that he's already gone.

I tell myself that it's okay and I almost believe it.

I choose jeans and a blouse. Not quite business-casual but it is Friday and I have to unpack the car when Merrie arrives. The diner can't be a clean place, either. Maybe I'll stay and help her get started on the cleaning.

When I go down the stairs, I notice two things.

My favorite black bra is tossed over the back of the couch.

And Luke, barefoot in his jeans, is making coffee in my kitchen.

I like the sight of him there. I like it a lot.

And the coffee smells great.

"I never expected you to have domestic inclinations," I say and he chuckles. I put my arms around his waist in the kitchen and he turns, giving me a very thorough good-morning kiss. Still minty-fresh, or maybe again.

"I have skills beyond expectation," he says. "Hidden depths." He lifts a brow. "I like coffee. And I can be trained, with the proper encouragement."

"What encouragement is that?"

"I don't think you need any tips from me in that department. I found bagels in the freezer." I get a questioning glance and I nod, seeing that he already has one in the toaster. There are bananas in the bowl on the counter and I get the cream cheese in the fridge. By the time the coffee is ready, we have breakfast laid out on the counter, and we eat contentedly for a few moments.

"You look like a cat in the sun," I say. "Or the one who got the cream."

"I wonder why." He wiggles his brows and I laugh at him, just the way he's expecting me to. It's warm and easy and comfortable, but I tell myself not to get used to it. "Did Meredith say when she was coming?"

I shake my head. "I told her to call me when she's close."

"Today, though?"

"That's what she said."

He nods, considering his bagel as if it holds the mysteries to the universe. He looks up suddenly, pinning me to the spot with a perceptive look. "So, when are you going to tell me the whole story about Justin?"

I do not drop my mug, and I'll count that as a win. "I told you already."

Luke shakes his head slowly. "No. You told me that he messed around on you after you were engaged."

"Isn't that the important bit?"

"I don't think so. How did you end up with him? What drew you to him?" He sips his coffee watching me. "What convinced you that he was the guy for you, Daph? I have a hard time believing that you misjudged anyone that badly."

I feel my eyes narrow. "You think I *chose* him knowing he'd be a douche?"

"Maybe you didn't really want to get married and do all that traditional stuff. Maybe he was the best option available, or the one you thought was good enough."

I put down my mug hard. "Do you think I would get engaged to just any guy? I *loved* him."

His gaze flicks over me. "Why?"

I'm outraged by the question, but I can see that Luke is genuinely curious. He's not being a prick, not on purpose anyway. He's just asking a tough question, one a whole lot like the one Rafe asked me once upon a time.

Why Justin?

And I'm floundering, because all the answers that come to mind are pat. They could be somebody else's answers, not mine.

Why Justin?

I get up and pour the rest of my coffee down the sink.

"Getting chilly in here," Luke says, like he's trying to lighten the mood. "I should head out."

"No, wait," I say, putting my hand on his arm. That new tattoo is under my fingers and I trace it with a fingertip. I couldn't see it clearly the night before, and to be honest, I wasn't looking. Now I see that it's a tangle of lines that covers his left forearm from elbow to wrist, a tendril trailing over the back of his hand. It looks like part of a whole, an image partially veiled from view. It makes me think of the moon behind clouds, of Celtic ruins, of druids and carvings in stone. There's something fluid about it, and mesmerizing, and I look closer.

Yes, it's part of a labyrinth.

"Daedalus created the labyrinth to trap the minotaur, the monster of Thebes that devoured the children of Athens." Luke is speaking softly. "Theseus killed the monster and escaped the labyrinth, with the help of Ariadne and her thread."

"Which he followed to find his way back out," I remember, seeing a spider in his tattoo as well as a spindle of thread and a distaff. There's a small bull near his wrist, and its tail is what appears on the back of his hand. There's a sword worthy of a hero, too.

"And since the Middle Ages, the labyrinth has been a path for introspection and study, a meditative path for introspection."

"They're in churches."

Luke nods. "Taylor and I visited the one at Chartres. He was fascinated by labyrinths and the notion of looking deeper inside yourself to improve."

And I understand the new tattoo. "This is for Taylor."

"He had a tattoo of the labyrinth at Chartres, right over his heart." He smiles crookedly, watching my finger. "He used to say that he'd know the woman who was for him, because she'd not only recognize it but know how to navigate her way through it. It would be their common ground."

I nod, thinking of Justin, wondering about common ground. It feels heavy and hard to face this truth, harder even than acknowledging that I wasn't really surprised to learn about Heather. "He was really good-looking," I admit. "Smart enough and successful enough. He came from money and had a certain flair. Everyone admired him and I just got in line. It seemed like the obvious thing to do." I shrug. "He pursued me. He said all the right things." I sigh. "I believed him."

Luke is watching me but remains silent.

"My dad liked him." I wince. "My mom didn't. So maybe there was a bit of rebellion there, too, or at least a desire to prove that I could make my own choices. You're supposed to go away to university, fall in love, get married, get a job and make a new life. It's on the schedule and part of the plan. Maybe he was just in the right place at the right time. Maybe I was for him, too, because he was persistent. Nice."

"Nice," Luke echoes, making his view of that clear.

"And then there was all the wedding stuff. It's so easy to get caught up in that, to want that ritual and fuss. Princess for a day. It becomes a goal in itself."

"The dress."

"The dress, the flowers, the venue, the bridal party, the invitations, the honeymoon. It's an epic extravaganza, at least our wedding would have been, and I wouldn't be the first person who was more interested in the idea of the wedding than the marriage."

"Ouch," Luke says, raising a brow.

"Of course, you wouldn't take a back seat to anything."

"The whole point is that you're binding your lives together. Shouldn't the other person or your love be the focus of everything?"

I have to cede this. "Of course, but there's so much to do, and he left it all to me. I didn't have time for everything."

I get a look for that. "Do not tell me that you're blaming yourself for him messing around."

"No," I say, but I wonder if on some level I did. Hmm. Something to consider later. "It was easy to be with Justin." I take a breath. "He always looked good and had the answer. He wasn't very demanding."

"You're not making a persuasive case for this life-changing romance, Daph."

"But that was it. He wasn't so exciting that I felt out of control. It felt steady. Predictable. The stuff of long stable marriages." I take another deep breath and meet Luke's gaze, admitting what I never wanted to say out loud. "Safe."

He looks floored. "And that's what you wanted? To be *safe*?"

"It felt like the responsible choice."

"Sounds boring, in all honesty."

"It was boring," I admit, feeling like a traitor even now. It takes me a minute to confess the next bit but once I do, I feel better. "In a way, it was a relief not to have to go through with it."

"And you still have the dress," he notes. "Or don't you?"

I gesture to the spare bedroom upstairs. "A complete waste of money and effort. Three fittings. Silk." I sigh, my heart squeezing as I remember the Great Hunt. That's what we called it. The quest for the perfect dress. It was the last thing my mom and I did together, although neither of us knew it at the time.

We had such fun.

Even though she didn't like Justin. I avoid the memory of the one time she spoke her mind, not wanting to dwell on the fact that I was warned. I'm too busy remembering how she looked in different shops, how she tried on hats everywhere, how we both knew that this dress was the right dress.

She cried when she saw me in it and my tears are welling now.

"So, why keep it?" Luke asks. His voice is gentler, so he's noticed my tears. "Going to use it next time? Or keeping it in case you change your mind?"

"No!" I never thought of this and it probably shows. "It was expensive. It's my dream dress."

It's a little piece of my mom.

"But what exactly is the dream, Daph?"

I blink. "To be happy?" It's more than that, so much more. To be cherished, to be trusted, to have a haven in your marriage and a surety against all the uncertainties of the world. To know that you're not alone, that someone will have your back and stand at your side, lift you up when you're down—and that you'll do the same for him.

Exactly what Justin was never going to do.

My mom warned me and I didn't listen. I turn away from Luke because a tear is going to break free.

"By marrying some guy you find boring to be with? That doesn't sound worthy of you."

Part of the seduction was the fantasy, I know. The vision of myself floating down the aisle in that dress, en route to happily-ever-after forevermore. The wedding was going to solve everything, set my place in the world, establish the boundaries of *my* world. Getting married meant one less thing to think about, one less thing to manage, one less worry to have. It probably meant a whole suite of new worries, but I hadn't gotten that far. It was a decreed step forward and I had been taking it.

Justin appeared to be a good choice of spouse. He was handsome, fit, courteous, successful—and I thought he was reliable. Did I love him? Sort of. Certainly not madly or deeply. I've proven that I can easily live without him. He's proven that he was never going to defend anyone's interests but his own. He never gave me butterflies the way Luke does, nor did he give me the kind of orgasms Luke has prompted.

But he was safe.

And safe, I realize, was what I always wanted to be. I wanted security more than adventure, contentment more than passionate love, certainty over uncertainty. Despite my mom's misgivings about Justin, I was prepared to compromise to be sure of my place in the world.

What a terrible reason to get married.

That I could ever think that, that I still yearn for that kind of haven, should be proof enough that Luke is exactly the wrong person for me. One night was fine—actually, it was great—but I can't let myself be seduced into hoping for more. I will be, if he sticks around. And the result is inevitable. If—when?—Luke breaks my heart, I might never recover.

It's inevitable that he will.

I meet his gaze, knowing he's been watching me, wondering how much he's seen.

"You're right. You do need to go, and I need to get to work."

"And I'm getting frostbite again," he rumbles, his eyes narrowing. He looks stubborn and I have to admire that he's ready to fight for what he wants—even if I know he's wrong. "Talk to me, Daph."

I'm already heading for the door, jingling my keys. "This can't work. It'll never work."

"I think it worked pretty brilliantly last night." He stops beside me where I'm standing at the door and grabs his jacket. His lashes do that thing, sweeping down to hide his thoughts, and I wish I knew what was going on in his heart and mind.

"One and done," I say briskly. "Now we know and can move on."

"It's not that simple, Daph," he growls, stepping past me onto the porch.

"It is," I insist. "It has to be."

He nods, looking across the lawn. "Did Justin do everything you told him to do? Except, you know, for the messing around part?"

"What difference does it make?"

"Just makes me wonder if that was part of his appeal. Some women like men who do what they're told, like trained puppies." He gives me a look so hot that it sears my soul. "While others prefer to feel alive, to be surprised, to celebrate every damn day." His gaze sweeps over me and leaves me simmering. "Did you ever find out why your mom didn't like him?"

I shrug. I don't have to offer up that confession and I won't. Even thinking of saying it out loud feels like a betrayal of her memory, a breach of trust. She confided in me, said she had to say it but she wouldn't mention it again.

My mom was a great judge of character. I ache at the memory of her gentle words. *I want only the best for you and maybe no man is good enough. I want you to be cherished, the way your father has always cherished me, not chosen because the two of you look good together. A man concerned with appearances might not continue to believe you're the best choice, not when you're older and it shows, not when he doesn't love you for who you really are. I'm afraid, sweetheart, that he's going to hurt you...*

Now I am going to cry. It's raining a bit this morning, the air filled with mist and fog rising from the ground. I feel like the weather is echoing my feelings.

Luke, though, has turned away from my silence. He flips up his collar and strides away, his steps so long that I'll never catch up to him. His back is straight, his posture stiff. I watch him go, noticing how the rain beads in his hair, how it glistens on the shoulders of his leather jacket, an emptiness inside me that might never be filled.

Why are the right things always so hard to do?

I tell myself not to even try to catch up to him or call after him, then remember the car is full of Merrie's stuff. By the time I back out of my driveway, Luke has vanished into the woods behind the United Church.

I remind myself to be glad. I tell myself to be proud that I've done the sensible thing.

But I can't help feeling like I've let something precious slip away. I have the definite sense that my mom would be disappointed in me.

She'd know that I've sent Luke away because I'm afraid.

No wonder it doesn't feel good.

12

LUKE

afe.

Safe.

I'm outraged by a single word. Safe! Who wants to be safe?

Sheep are safe. Savings accounts are safe. Staying inside the house and hiding from the world is safe. Who would have expected Daph to want that?

Not me.

I thought she'd be fearless, diving into this new experience like a skydiver, ready for all the sensation and all the thrills.

But she prefers *safe*. I can't make sense of it. She should be audacious, ready to take on the world, demanding that her every wish comes true. She could be a superhero, a warrior queen, a vigilante for justice, or just plain courageous.

I could have been the asshole and pointed out that Justin the Marvelous hadn't been that safe a choice after all, seeing as he'd mucked around on her, but I hadn't been able to do it.

Daph's expression softened when she talked about him and

her voice dropped low. She wasn't able to look me in the eye, so lost in sweet memories.

Still in love.

I saw that tear.

That sight was a knife to my heart. Does she really still yearn for that loser? Or is it the contrast with me that's making him look good?

Safe. I want to snarl at someone, howl at the moon maybe, rev the engine on my bike and go roaring out of town.

No, I want to convince Daph to come with me.

By the time I reach the motel, I'm getting soaked. I leap up the stairs, needing a really hot shower. Time for some clean clothes and maybe a fresh perspective. Last night was awesome in every way, but surely that can't be it? I'm not nearly done with Daph.

Is she done with me? My reaction to that is instinctive and immediate, but that doesn't mean I'm right.

I have to wonder what I've done to spook her. Shaken her awake? Frightened her with the prospect of really living? Maybe she can't deal with a lack of control. But I'll never be anyone's pet poodle. I can't really understand why anyone would want to control their partner or companion.

I meet my own gaze in the mirror and allow the scary thought.

Maybe Daph's not really The One.

I can't believe it. I don't believe it. I know she's the only woman for me.

But maybe I'm the only one who's falling fast and hard. That's not difficult to believe, since I'm an all or nothing, all-in kind of guy. I leap before I look, every time, and follow my impulse, wherever it leads. No one would ever imagine that I'm a safe choice, the cautious one, the sure bet. On the other hand, I've done a lot and seen a lot in my time so far. Mostly, I've had a great time. No one could accuse me of sitting back and waiting for anything.

Would I wait for Daph? Absolutely.

Could she fall for me the way I am? I have no clue.

The trick is that I'm going to have to convince her to take a chance on me, and I see that it's not going to be an easy sale. (Thank you, Justin.) I'm going to have to dig in and make a conscious effort to win her over. I can't assume that things will fall into place, not this time, it's too important. I have to believe I can make a favorable impression in comparison to Jerk Justin.

I mean, the bar is low.

But Daph's expectations are high. What have I done to challenge them? Hired her and seduced her in less than forty-eight hours. Jumped right in like this is one-and-done.

No wonder she thinks there's no future in this. I even told her that I was going to leave. Why would she expect me to hang around?

That wouldn't be *logical*.

I need to court her. It's an old word but a good one. We need to date and talk, cultivate some romance instead of just satisfaction. I need to show her that I'm not a one-hit-wonder with one foot out the door. I need to prove to her that it's not just about the sex—even though the sex was amazing.

Can I do it? Can I win the war without my most reliable asset? I'm pretty sure I could convince Daph to invite me home again, but that's not nearly enough. I need her to trust me. I need to prove that I have the stuff to go the distance.

Maybe, we need to abstain until she's sure.

If ever there was a thought to shake me up, that's it—but it also echoes with truth.

What she distrusts are words. Promises. Lies. What I need to provide is tangible evidence of my reliability. (Yes, that has to be Taylor laughing again.)

Fortunately, I'm not a guy who backs away from a challenge. If Daph sends me away, I'll go, but until she does, I'll argue my case as well as I can.

While I strategize that campaign, I have stuff to do. Merrie is coming today, but first I want to tell Una the good news.

———

THE LAST TIME I went to Una's place, a few weeks back, I didn't use her driveway. I rode into the provincial park to the east of Empire and approached from behind, coming through the forest to avoid the town. This time, I walk up to Daph's place, take a right at the two-track leading into the woods, and go for a more conventional arrival. I've scored a big black umbrella from Bruno and am enjoying the soft patter of the rain. It's tranquil in a way that I'm not.

Una's driveway is an unpaved two-track that hasn't seen a vehicle in a long time. The grass is already long on either side of the worn pathways, both beaten down so hard that nothing grows in them. One is wider than the other so it must be her footpath of choice. In between, there are small pink flowers emerging like little stars. Right now, they're glistening with raindrops. The path bends a bit, making its way around larger trees that obviously weren't worth felling, even when the house was built. As a result, the trees quickly close behind me. I could be a million miles from anywhere, if not for that worn path leading me deeper into the woods.

There were trilliums in bloom the last time I was here, gleaming white in the shadows of the forest on either side. They're finished now and something yellow has come into bloom instead. The trees are in full leaf now and the shadows on the forest floor are speckled with sunlight. I hear a lot of birds calling, then see that there are feeders hanging from the trees at intervals, all close to the path. A blue jay screams at me for interrupting his meal, then flies away, leaving the feeder swinging in his wake. I don't take more than half a dozen steps past the feeder before I hear claws on metal, and look back to see that he's perched there again, gobbling seeds as the feeder swings like a metronome from the force of his landing.

Una's house could be something out of a fairy tale, in that it's a log cabin, hewn out of the surrounding forest. The foundation is fieldstone, a collection of rocks in various sizes, undoubtedly collected from the local fields. The roof is ribbed metal and steeply pitched, one guarantee that snow will always slide off. There's a tendril of smoke rising from her fieldstone chimney, a reminder that she's off the grid and proud of it. It could be a cottage and maybe it was once.

When we were kids, we always speculated that Una was a witch, that she ate children and mixed potions, that she cast spells turning people into frogs and toads. The dares were plentiful to go knock on her door alone at Halloween, despite the fact that she never had a bad word to say about anyone. Bruno and I took the dare one year and discovered that she had full-sized chocolate bars for trick-or-treaters. After that, we were Team Una (although we did debate the merit of continuing the rumour to score more chocolate for ourselves.) I don't remember Sylvia being around then, but maybe there was a phase in my life when I didn't care about girls. (Impossible. She must not have been here.)

Today, Una is sitting on her porch, sheltered from the patter of rain. Her porch is closed in and extends across the entire front of the house. I can see her there through the screens, the sunlight making the fat braid cast over her shoulder even more silver than it is. She's frowning at something, and as I get closer, I see that she's knitting—or she's counting stitches and not liking the answer very much.

"Back twice in as many weeks," she says by way of greeting. "There must be something in Empire that's caught your attention."

Is it so obvious that she's right? I don't know what to say and she smiles, indicating that I should come in. I leave my umbrella at the door, then sit in the other chair and wait. She counts the row again, then puts the work aside with a grimace.

"What can I do for you today?" Una's eyes are pale blue and her skin is fair. She looks both delicate and powerful, a woman confident in what she knows and who she is, a woman who has looked in the mirror and come to terms with the battle she must wage.

"I thought you had chickens," I say, indicating the empty coop.

"I did. A coyote took the last one, just after you were here."

"You could get a couple more."

She shrugs, looking tired for a moment. "Not now. I have to save my strength for the next while." Then her eyes brighten and she fixes me with a look. "But you didn't come to talk about chickens, did you?"

I didn't come here to talk about cancer either.

I shake my head and give her the copy of the property transfer and title from Daph. She straightens her glasses and peers at it with as much concentration as her knitting, then eyes me.

"What's this?"

"Just what it looks like. You own your house again."

To my surprise, she slaps the document into her lap and glares at me. "You can't do that."

"I just did."

"Why?"

"Because I wanted to make something right, and that became part of it. Aren't you pleased?"

Her expression changes, softening as she casts a glance over the interior of the porch and the chairs there. They're wicker chairs that have been painted bright blue, and they have patchwork cushions on them. The inside of the roof is unfinished and the floor is just sanded wood, worn from footsteps and rain. The rain falls steadily on the roof, making me feel that I've stepped out of time.

"Of course, I'm pleased," she says gruffly. "This is my home." Her eyes narrow. "This is about Patrick, isn't it?"

"No," I say and it's true. "It's about me, figuring out where I stand."

She watches and waits, but I don't admit any more. I want her to be surprised when Sylvia arrives. I also don't want her to have a chance to call Sylvia and convince her to stay in Toronto.

Maybe I am a meddler like Patrick.

"I could refuse," Una says finally. "I could decline to be in your debt instead of Patrick's."

"But you aren't in my debt. It's a gift, free and clear. All yours."

"You didn't think that might hurt my pride?"

I didn't and it probably shows.

Una laughs at me and pushes to her feet. She pats my arm. "I'm not going to turn you down, but you have to tell me what I can do for you in exchange."

"Nothing."

She snorts as she passes me, on her way to the door. "Don't refuse so quickly, Luke. You never know when you might need a friend."

It's good advice and I'll take it. "You didn't say you were offering friendship," I say lightly. "That changes everything."

She grins and I see a younger woman in that expression, a mischievous girl more than happy to issue a challenge. "All right then," she says. "I always make a cup of tea for my friends when they visit, so you'd better come in."

I do, and even though it's linden flower tea, I drink the entire cup.

The things we do for friends.

———

WHEN I GET BACK DOWNTOWN, it's after noon. Daph has parked her dad's car in front of the diner. There's no sign of her, so I'll guess she's at work. I have a second set of keys, so I open up the place to do something useful—well, more useful than talking to a woman in love with a loser who isn't me. The diner smells like dust and solitude with a base note of old grease.

But I'm charmed all the same.

I love that I remember this place when it was bustling, full of kids ordering a plate of fries after school or an ice cream. I remember the whispered confessions in the booths and the squeak of the vinyl seats that sounded almost—but not quite—like farts, and how we boys cackled at that. I remember spinning on one of the stools at the counter and am saddened that they've been removed and likely sold.

And I particularly love that it's one of two properties in Empire that Patrick doesn't own anymore. His price was higher than anticipated, given that it was just for two places of the five listed, but I would have emptied my accounts to make this happen. I'm still in good shape financially, thanks to years of royalties that accumulated and weren't spent, but the inflow of cash is a lot less than it was. As landlord, I'll need to invest in this place even for it to pass the health code. Maybe that will clean me out. I don't much care.

I've never owned real estate before. Never felt the need. But this, this kind of feels good. It feels like a solid choice, permanence, roots and a plan. An investment in the future, maybe, or at least a step toward figuring out what that future is.

At least so long as Meredith doesn't take one look and run screaming back to the city.

To avoid that, I hang my jacket on a hook by the door and leave the umbrella to drip there. I fill an ancient pail with hot water in the industrial sink and try to make this place a little cleaner before she arrives.

Thank goodness Daph thought to get the utilities turned on again.

No one has entirely emptied the place, even after all this time. It looks like Leon and Dotty assumed the diner would be taken over and run by someone else. They left some cleaning supplies and unmarketable chattels like this huge old metal pail on wheels. The tables and chairs are gone, probably sold, and everything that remains is ancient. Turning on the lights does the place no favours, but it can only look better when it's cleaner.

I get to it. Floors first. I think the linoleum tiles are set in a black and white checkerboard but it's past time to find out for sure. The detergent is wickedly effective and I consider that it's probably been banned during the time the diner was closed. It's good, though, and I have to appreciate how quickly I make visible progress.

That's motivating.

It rains all day, and the weather perfectly echoes my mood.

I see Luke arrive and head into the diner. I know he has keys so that doesn't surprise me. What's unexpected is that he doesn't come back out. There's movement inside and I wonder what he's up to, even as I try to concentrate on the forms in front of me.

I think about going over there. I think about emptying Dad's car, but I know I won't be able to spend time with Luke and just leave things be.

What can he possibly be doing in there?

I watch, incredulous, as he begins to wash the windows from the inside. He comes outside eventually and goes after the grime with impressive determination. Maybe the rain has softened the dirt. Maybe he's really good at cleaning windows. Either way, the difference is impressive. The windows are sparkling when he vanishes inside again. I can't see him anymore, though I really want to know what he's doing.

I pounce on my phone when Merrie calls me at four and my heart jumps that she's close by. I head across the street to meet her, hearing the approach of a vehicle. The rain has stopped, although it's still humid and gray. I stop on the sidewalk to wait, wondering if Luke has noticed, then notice the line of green between the curb and the sidewalk.

It's a line of little plants, no bigger than half an inch tall. They're all the same, as if someone deliberately seeded this little gap filled with dirt. I can see green all the way past Jim's antique shop and west toward Big Red.

I'm spared further consideration by Merrie's arrival. She has an older Jeep Cherokee and parks right in front of Dad's car. It's full to the roof inside, just enough space left for her in the driver's seat. She gets out and looks up and down the street, then marches over to shake my hand, unable to completely hide her excitement. "It's really here," she says.

"It's really here," I agree and she almost rubs her hands together with glee.

Luke opens the door and leans against the frame. He's dirty after his efforts of the day, a streak of dirt on his cheek and his hair tousled. How can he look better than ever? "Welcome to Empire," he drawls, pulls off a yellow rubber glove and offers his hand.

"That guy," she says, apparently referring to the water dumping incident. "You're *that* guy. The one who got a bath."

"I'm that guy," he agrees as they shake hands. "Otherwise known as Luke Jones."

"Not M.C.," she says and gives me a smile.

"Not even close," I agree, though Luke frowns in confusion.

"Mr. Patron, it's nice to meet you." Merrie eyes him warily. "Why me?"

"Because I can give you a chance. And because Sylvia works with you."

"I *knew* it," she says, untroubled, and turns her attention to the diner. "Let's see the worst of it." Luke stands back, gesturing to the open door with a bow, and she heads in, looking left and right.

Where I see dirt and old fixtures, she seems to see opportunity. We go through the whole place, front to back, the apartment upstairs and the basement below, the parking spaces out back in the alley and even the empty flat roof. I can see the excitement in her eyes. I'm also keenly aware of Luke's presence and how often I find his gaze on me when I glance up.

"How much leasehold improvement are you in for? Mr. Patron?" she asks, running a hand over the old counter.

"Just talk to me," Luke says. "I'll tell you what's too much. When I got in here today, I looked at the electrical panel." He makes a face. "So, there's an electrician coming tomorrow to see what needs upgrading. He couldn't make it during the week, but is working us in. We'll need to update the walk-in fridge and freezer, as well as the stove..."

"Two stoves," she says. "One with burners and one with a grill. Gas, of course, and a broiler, too. A deep fryer with two reservoirs." She's walking through the cooking space, indicating fixtures with her hands. "Double sinks here as well as the ones over there. A bar fridge here and a wine fridge on the other side. Pizza oven here. Stainless counters, shelves here for plates. This counter needs to be higher and I'll need better ventilation. That wood floor needs refinishing and I want tiles in the kitchen...

"I should go," I say, but they both turn on me.

"I'd like you to stay," Merrie says.

"Me, too," Luke agrees. "You'll have ideas about who can help out."

As much as I want to be part of the solution, I'm wishing there was a more personal reason he wanted me to stay.

And this is illogical, given what I said to him this very morning, so that annoys me too.

"Tables, chairs, bar stools. Not new or cheap," Merrie says. She gets a portfolio and opens it on the counter Luke has wiped down. She spreads out drawings and Luke and I gather closer.

"I've been dreaming about this opportunity forever," she admits, then looks around and catches her breath. "This place will work beautifully."

When I get past the fact that I'm standing so close to Luke that our arms practically brush, I see that there are clippings and pictures mixed with the drawings. It's a beautiful vision-board and I understand what she wants immediately.

"It has to be earthy and welcoming, a little upmarket but not intimidating," she says. "I want people to feel like it's their place, like they can hang out here all the time."

"Copper, wood, candles," I say and she nods. There are sample menus mixed into the clippings, a picture of wood-fired pizza oven, lit candles and wineglasses without stems. Linen napkins and dark wood tables. The images are so elegant that I want to invite myself in.

"Farm-to-table, local ingredients presented at their best. Pizza of the day. Soup of the day. Good fresh food done right doesn't have to be expensive. I want to have regular clientele, people who come weekly if not more often, people who always stop for lunch. I want to be a neighbourhood fixture."

"I love it," Luke says. "When do you open?"

She laughs. "That depends on you. Help me."

"Okay." Luke frowns and starts making a list. "We have the electrician. We'll need a plumber and a carpenter, someone to paint…"

I pull out my phone and start sharing phone numbers. There's the guy who painted my house inside and out, the woman who tiled my bathroom and kitchen, the contractor who moved a wall for me. Luke grabs a pencil and paper, sketching the dimensions of the interior as the two of them talk, then locating elements and details. I find a kitchen supply in Havelock with the search engine. Luke wants to have the windows replaced—one is cracked and the others are single pane—as well as the door. We confer over who might be able to do that.

Merrie, meanwhile, has been scrubbing down the rest of the counter with fearsome energy. It wouldn't dare refuse to gleam by the time she's done.

The aesthetic of Merrie's vision-board reminds me of Willow, so I call her and she comes over to consult. She and Merrie confer, then she goes back to Jim's shop. She comes back in thirty minutes, her phone loaded with pictures of furniture. In the meantime, we've emptied Dad's car, and Merrie has squirreled everything away upstairs until the renovations are done.

Willow's grabbed pictures of some hammered copper panels that Jim scored at a sale but hasn't known what to do with since, and Merrie is thrilled by the possibilities. "Are there enough to top the whole bar with copper?" she asks and Willow starts measuring.

"Who could do that?" Luke asks me, leaning closer as I do a search on metalworkers and artists. I want to touch him more than I've wanted anything in a while, but he doesn't touch me. He talks to me and listens to me, soliciting my thoughts and considering my views. Even without touching me, he's making me burn for more of what we did the night before.

It's dark outside the windows by the time we stop for breath.

Luke's stomach growls audibly and he apologizes for it. "Tacos?" he says. "The truck should be open tonight."

"What about the Chinese smorgasbord?" Merrie asks and Luke looks surprised that she even knows The Golden Lotus exists.

"I'll call Phil." I do and he's open. I tell him what we're doing and he's immediately interested. "Any chance you could join us for dinner?" I ask and Merrie nods so hard that her curls seem to have a life of her own. "Merrie wants to ask you about suppliers."

"It's a dead night, but could you come here?" Phil says. "My mom's a bit restless and I don't want to leave her."

I ask, they nod agreement, and I tell him so.

"Any special requests?"

"Tell him to make what he'd eat, given a choice," Merrie says. I tell Phil and he laughs.

"You mind spicy?"

"Of course not. Bring on the heat."

"Oh, I will. Give me forty minutes. I do have a couple of orders to get out the door."

"See you then."

And so it is that in a little more than half an hour, we're all walking down the street together, talking as if we've been friends forever. The enthusiasm is palpable, and the smell that wafts out the door of The Golden Lotus is divine.

Mrs. Chang rushes forward to urge us toward the best table, just the way she did when we were in high school. She might be lost in those days again, but she's as charming and sweet as ever. Phil manages to convince her that this is a friendly dinner and she joins us at the table, dictating to everyone to take more as if we're family.

We don't need a lot of encouragement. The food is awesome. I'm sure that none of these dishes are on the menu. The dumplings are the best I've ever had. Merrie and Phil are apparently kindred spirits, and she's making notes on her phone as he tells her about the mushroom guys just outside of town and the best place for heritage green vegetables. She wants to know what's in every dish, her passion for food impressive.

And the whole time, I'm aware of Luke beside me, passing one dish or another, his gaze catching mine once in a while. He smiles at me then, like we're co-conspirators in some great plan and I feel almost like we are.

Or we could have been, if I hadn't been afraid.

Is it too late to change my mind?

14

SYLVIA

Empire is so much more dismal than I remember.

I almost turn around when Queen Street comes into view, empty and abandoned, wet with spring rain. We might have driven off the edge of the world. Sierra was bouncing the whole way from the city, complaining when her cell phone service gave up, vibrating with impatient energy until finally she fell asleep.

I'm glad she'll miss my disappointment in this first glimpse. There were also changes to the countryside on the drive down from the 401, but I expected that. There are still fields on either side of the road, still old farm houses and barns, some falling into disrepair. One change was entire subdivisions of new houses, looking modern and out-of-place amidst the fields. I can almost hear Una complaining about the failure to protect valuable farmland.

There are windmills, too, lots and lots of them. They're also sleek and modern, huge silver structures spaced across the fields at regular intervals. They turn lazily in the early evening, some turbines stopped completely, looking alien on the land I used to know so well. It's flat here, flatter than I remember, strikingly flat after Toronto's ravines and hills.

I roll down the window and welcome the familiar smell of manure being spread on the fields. Perfume of my childhood. I hear Una calling it *Chanel Number Five* and smile.

There are greenhouses, too, but not like the ones I remember. There were always greenhouses and market gardens, thanks to the rich soil and the sunshine. These new ones are taller and larger, enormous areas of land secured under glass. The walls are wavy, so I can only glimpse the green of the plants inside. If those are tomato plants, they're big ones, easily fifteen feet tall, probably grown vertically and hydroponically.

I will not think about anyone who works in that business.

For the hundredth time, I wonder why I agreed to this move.

There are good reasons and I remind myself of them while Sierra dozes. I miss living in a small town. I miss knowing my neighbours and even the guys who sleep rough in the bush. I miss seeing Una all the time because talking on the phone doesn't nearly compare. I miss the smell of the lake and the feel of the wind. I miss the sense of freedom I had when I lived here.

It's true that I chose to leave. No one forced that on me. But I wonder sometimes if I should have toughed it out and stayed, let the cards fall as they would, given Sierra a childhood more like my own. I loved growing up in Empire.

Even now, it'll be cheaper to live here, that's for sure, and I'd love to be able to worry a bit less about what Sierra's doing when I'm working late. Of course, there are creeps everywhere, but I have a hard time believing they're quite as numerous here as in the city.

The inescapable fact is that I suspect I'm missing something. There's been an edge to Una's voice, the one she gets when she doesn't want to tell me something. It's been there a while, sometimes a little stronger and sometimes so faint that I can convince myself I hear it at all. But in my heart, I fear that something is wrong.

I was thinking of coming down for a visit before Luke showed up.

And when I looked across the restaurant that day, my thoughts were in Empire. That's maybe why I saw a Cavendish with his back to me. His posture and silhouette were unmistakable.

I was sure it was Mike, come to mess up my life all over again, and I just saw red.

I should have realized Mike would never come looking for me. He's had plenty of chances. He has my address. But then, Luke Jones isn't exactly an innocent bystander.

I have no regrets, but I wonder who is behind this offer to Merrie. I can't believe Daphne would lie, but then, who else but Mike would care about me coming back to Empire.

Except I know that Mike *doesn't* care.

Of course, Merrie would seize the chance. She's wanted her own place as long as I've known her, and of all the chefs I've worked with, she's the most brilliant. Mercurial, of course, but that's the chef temperament. She's passionate about her work, and she's so good at what she does that you'll forgive her anything. I do. Plus she's loyal beyond all expectation. She's had my back when no one else did.

I want Merrie to have her dream come true, and if that means moving back to Empire, well, maybe it's time that I put the past where it belongs. Maybe it's time I stop running and face my truth.

That all sounded great until I turned onto Queen Street.

I know exactly where Leon and Dotty's diner is, of course. I spent most of my teenage years there, scooping ice cream during the summer at first, then had my first job waiting tables. Eggs over easy, ham or bacon, white or brown toast, I can recite the menu by memory even now. It was worlds apart from the magic Merrie makes—she doesn't do breakfast or eggs—but a great training.

There's a new gas station and the Maple Leaf Motel looks as if it's been spruced up a bit. Big Red is bigger than I remember even from a distance, but it has been fifteen years. The only cars parked on Queen Street are in front of the diner, the first one being Merrie's green Cherokee. I'd know it anywhere with that replacement back gate in metallic gold. Behind it is a big silver Mercedes sedan. I park behind it and touch Sierra's arm.

"We're here," I tell her and she sits up with a jolt, taking in the view with wide eyes.

I watch her face fall. "It's nowhere."

"Pretty much."

Her eyes narrow in an increasingly familiar expression of teenage dissatisfaction. "If Una lives here, how come we've never come here?"

"Because she wanted to come and see us instead." I get out and stretch as Merrie comes out of the diner, grinning ear to ear.

"I hope you brought mouse traps," she calls. "We've got a colony."

"Gross," Sierra mutters.

"A whole carton, just like you asked. Good thing you called before we got past Havelock."

"Excellent. Come and see!"

Merrie's followed by Daphne Bradshaw, who is at least partly responsible for our relocation, and Luke Jones, who smiles at the sight of me and waves a greeting. No hard feelings, evidently.

"You know them?" Sierra demands, then Daphne and Luke turn, maybe just realizing that she's there. They realize more than that and in a hurry.

I see Luke's eyes widen.

I watch the colour drain out of Daphne's face.

And a little bit too late, I realize what they're thinking.

Funny that in all my imaginings of what might happen when we got to Empire, this assumption didn't even cross my mind.

I can work with it, though.

In fact, it just might be the solution we need.

15

———

DAPHNE

It's almost nine when Sylvia arrives. We're back at the restaurant after dinner when she parks out front. She has an older Subaru, its red paint faded, and it's loaded to the roof. She gives a cheerful wave when she gets out and Merrie bursts out of the restaurant to greet her.

The thing is that Sylvia's not alone. There's another woman in the front passenger seat, one with her head bowed over her phone so that her hair hides her features. She looks up when the two women embrace and I catch my breath.

Not a woman. A girl.

And a Cavendish.

It's obvious with one glance. Her thickly lashed eyes are blue and heavily lined with black. Her skin is fair and her long hair is almost black where it isn't tinted vivid purple. She gets out of the car and tosses her hair over her shoulder, revealing that she has the tall lanky build of all the Cavendish clan. She's dressed completely in black with attitude to spare. She surveys me, then Luke, who has apparently been struck dumb. And the fire of rebellion lights in her eyes in a way that is painfully familiar.

Sylvia notices the confrontation, or maybe the frigid chill, and smiles tightly as she steps forward. "This is my daughter, Sierra," she says, sounding as if she's deliberately keeping her tone level.

"I didn't realize you had a daughter," I say in the yawning silence that follows. "Nice to meet you, Sierra."

"Whatever," she replies, holding up her phone with a grimace. "Is there a decent signal anywhere near here or have we really driven off the edge of the earth?"

"Sierra has never been to Empire before," Sylvia says, giving Luke a look.

His mouth is open. His brow furrows like thunder gathering and he pushes a hand through his hair. I've never seen him at a loss for words and I know he's come to the same conclusion as me.

"What the actual—" he begins, then he glowers at Sierra and falls silent.

Her eyes narrow and she smirks at him, exuding disdain the way that only teenagers can. "I know the word," she informs him, bracing one hand on her hip. "And I won't need my smelling salts if you say it out loud. In fact, I can explain it to you if you need help, old man."

I look between them, unable to deny the resemblance, and brace myself for Luke's reply.

It may leave a crater in Queen Street, judging by his expression.

I understand suddenly why people stand and watch accidents happen. I should leave. I should look away. I should do something to avert whatever is going to happen next.

But instead I stand there and watch, unable to even blink.

16

LUKE

I can't believe it.

I *cannot* believe it.

Sylvia has a daughter, a teenage daughter, a daughter who is clearly a Cavendish. That one night had greater repercussions than I'd realized. The jug of ice water in my lap makes a lot more sense now, but not sixteen years of silence.

Merrie is making introductions like we're at a bloody cocktail party, Daph is watching me warily, but I don't care.

"How old are you?" I ask the girl, who is startled for only a beat.

"Fifteen," she says with defiance. I patented that tone when I was a teenager. "What's it to you, old man?"

I turn to Sylvia. "Fifteen? *Fifteen?*"

"Sixteen in February," Sierra provides.

Which means she was conceived in the spring. In May.

I fathered a child and *I don't even remember*.

I did the one thing I always swore I would never ever do, and I didn't even know it for sixteen years. There's a failure of epic proportions.

The revelation makes me livid.

"What was in your head?" I demand of Sylvia. "How could you do this? How could you not *tell* me?"

She bristles, folding her arms across her chest. If looks could kill, I'd be a dead man. (Maybe Daph took pointers from Sylvia.) "It was none of your business," she says, exuding enough frost to freeze half of North America.

"How can you say that?" I'm roaring now, not just because Daph has turned away. "How can you imagine that I didn't have a right to know..."

Sylvia jabs a finger into my chest. "You. Did. Not. Turn around, Luke, and walk away. My life doesn't concern you. It never did and it sure doesn't now."

I am incredulous. That she could cut me out of the life of my kid, that she would deliberately not tell me, is beyond every measure of decency. "You, you..." I'm sputtering. "I deserved to know."

"Do you? Do you even remember that night?" she asks, her gaze hard.

It's like she read my mind. I don't. I remember running into her. I remember that she was upset with Mike for something. I remember encouraging her to come with me so we could pay Mike back for whatever he'd said or done.

I remember waking up on the porch at Una's place, tucked under a quilt. (I remember puking in the woods.) I've never been able to stand the taste of Jägermeister since.

The next time I saw Sylvia was in Merrie's restaurant in Toronto.

She shakes her head in disgust. "How can you imagine that I would change my life for a night you don't even remember? It wasn't an incident worth shaping my future choices." I wince at her tone and she notices. "Be serious, Luke. We're adults. I made choices for the good of my daughter and they weren't your concern." She turns then, puts her arm around Sierra's shoulders and leads the girl away.

Sierra looks back. "He's my dad?"

"No," Sylvia says, her voice hard. "You don't have a dad. A dad is there when you need to be rocked to sleep. A dad is there when you have a fever, when you scrape your knee, when you get a good report card, when you ace your dance recital. A dad loves and cares for you, protects you and makes sure you're safe. A dad cares. A dad *remembers*." She tosses me a look. "You don't have a dad, sweetheart, although I wish sometimes it was otherwise."

"You didn't tell me!" I bellow. "And I wasn't hard to find!"

"Deal with it," Sylvia says and the pair of them vanish into the diner.

I turn away, shaken, and find Daph watching me. She looks like she's going to carve me up and toss me to the tigers.

"You knew," she says.

"I had no idea. I didn't guess. I *didn't* know. I didn't even wonder."

She nods, looking after Sierra and Sylvia. "Well, then, you've got a lot of time to make up."

And she goes around her dad's car, gets in, starts it up and drives away. I watch until she makes the turn at Big Red and the tail lights disappear.

I'm left with Merrie—and all of my shattered assumptions.

"Are we still good?" she asks and I can't believe she's wondering about the diner.

"What difference does it make?"

"It makes all the difference in the world," she informs me. "I need to know if we're still on here."

It's the last thing I care about in this moment. "Of course, we are. We signed a deal."

Her satisfaction is complete. "Good." She nods. "I think I'm going to like it here."

"But Sylvia..."

"Has to do whatever she has to do. Doesn't her grandmother live here?"

"Una," I provide. "She, um, has cancer."

Merrie is walking toward the diner door, but she spins to face me. "Does Sylvia know?"

"I don't know. I don't think so. Una didn't want to be a burden."

Merrie props a hand on her hip. "How many people's lives were you intending to mess up here?"

I fling out my hands. "I was trying to fix things!"

"You need more practice, then," she says, then actually whistles as she ducks into the diner.

I don't know whether to follow her or not but she makes the decision for me. Merrie turns the deadbolt in the door, just as the rain begins a cold steady onslaught.

And Bruno's umbrella is inside the diner. I can see it but when I knock on the door, no one hears me. The women vanish into the back together, and I look up and down the abandoned street.

In this moment, it's easy to remember why I wanted to leave this place so badly.

———

WHAT'S incredible is that I don't remember.

I have a great memory. I remember the smell of the little salon where my mom worked as a hairdresser. I remember the dandelions in the yard of the house my mom rented when we first moved to Empire, the squeak of the rusted swing set abandoned there, the smell of the bathroom that had something wrong with its plumbing. I remember the taste of blood when Jake decked me for saying we were brothers in school. I remember how cold the winter wind is when you have only a thin coat, or one that's not quite big enough this year for you to zip shut.

I remember the sensation of freedom when I rode my bicycle out of Empire and down to Port Cavendish—without permission, of course—and how I learned to cobble together that bike of spare parts. I remember the sound of mocking laughter from other kids, whose bikes had been purchased new, with all the parts matching. I remember my mom trying to hide her tears in the kitchen when Patrick called her a whore, his wife standing by his side. I remember things about Empire that I'd rather forget.

But I don't remember being with Sylvia that night.

At all.

My memory offers glimpses of many women, but not Sylvia. She's completely absent, and I can't figure out why.

I should go to sleep but I can't. The enormity of my mistake is going to keep me awake forever. Is Taylor laughing at me now? Did he guess that there was something this epic for me to fix in my past?

It's past three in the morning when I give it up. I wander down Queen Street. I don't have the stones to go to Daph, not now, and it aches to have lost whatever that might have become before it really got started. The street is empty, the rain making it seem black and white, like I've stepped into a Fellini movie. I see in the distance that there are a few guys hanging around the taco truck and they sound as if they've been drinking. I'm not in the mood for a fight so I duck around the back of the Golden Lotus and walk down the alley. Someone is putting out the trash there, it must be Phil, but I wait in the shadows, avoiding any contact, until he goes back inside.

I met Sylvia in front of the Grand Hotel that night. I remember that. It was senior prom and there was a party there, in the bar, a celebration before the dance for those old enough to drink. She'd come out of there in some floaty long dress, tears on her cheeks, and I caught her when she stumbled.

She asked me to take her away. "Anywhere," she said. "Just not here."

I lean against the wall of the Grand Hotel, trying to remember. I could hear the party breaking up. They'd be moving on, going back to the school for the dance itself. It was maybe eight-thirty. I had no intention of going to prom and was just restless.

Like tonight.

Maybe looking for trouble.

Maybe I found it.

I stand in the alley in the rain and look back toward Queen Street, staring down the passageway between the Grand Hotel and the Legion. It's narrow and empty, puddles gleaming. There's a Dumpster behind the Legion, which is just as fragrant as I remember it being then. The one behind the Grand Hotel is empty, the lid thrown open. Is it really an empty shell now? I look up and there's only one light in the entire hotel, in the window of the apartment at the back.

Cole Henderson inherited the Grand Hotel, while he was in the military. I remember my mom telling me that. She still kept up with some of the news from Empire, and she'd imagined him renovating the place. That hadn't happened.

I can see barbed wire along the top of the two-storey addition that contains that apartment and the silent kitchen, and it's new. Maybe you can leave Afghanistan, but Afghanistan might not ever leave you. Living alone in that huge space can't be good for him, but I don't remember Cole ever being interested in advice.

I remember Sylvia instead, following toward me down this alley. Her hand was cold in mine when she reached me and made her appeal. Her dress was peach and gauzy. All sorts of floaty layers, then beading on the front. Flowers. She looked like a fairy princess, hardly even real.

She asked me to take her away from there, so I did.

I keep going, passing behind the Legion, hoping this exercise will help me recall what is undoubtedly my worst mistake. Someone is stacking cases of empty beer bottles behind the Legion in a container that locks and again, I keep out of sight. I catch a glimpse of a raccoon doing pretty much the same thing, but it vanishes to the south in the shadows. The convenience store is quieter than it was earlier, its lights bright against the night. The salsa music is going strong.

I pause behind the Foreman place. Here. I brought her here. I'd forgotten that, but now I remember. It was empty even then and the closest place I could think of where no one would see her. I pick the lock, just the way I did that night—my misspent youth has to be good for something—and the back door creaks as I open it.

I remember that, too, as well as the sense of doing something illicit. Sylvia caught her breath, I recall now, and her grip tightened on my arm. I ease inside, thinking. The bottle of Jäger was there, on the floor, proof that I wasn't the only one who had ever taken refuge in this place. I would have never bought something like that—I was all about beer in those days—and it felt like winning the lottery. Sylvia laughed and said Una drank that junk at Christmas.

So, we took it upstairs, exploring as we went. The old floors creaked then, just as they do now. The building is empty, filled with shadows, lit by the streetlights on Queen Street. There was an old wooden desk on that night, a creaky chair with torn upholstery. A pair of plain plastic chairs in the front room. They're all gone, now, maybe scored by some picker because they were vintage, and my footsteps echo in the emptiness.

I climb the stairs, feeling as if I'm lost in time, neither in the now nor in the then. Sylvia was wearing perfume. I remember smelling it once we were inside. Something floral and sweet. Maybe lavender.

At the top of the stairs, the door is open. I step through and I look around. It's an empty apartment, just the way it was then. Living room at the front, facing over the street. Bedroom at the back on one side. Kitchen at the back on the other side, with the bathroom in between front and back, opposite the top of the stairs. It's tiled in black and white, little octagonal white tiles that seem to glow in the darkness. There's a door in the kitchen that must have once led to a porch, but now it's boarded over.

We went in the front room that night. Dust stirs as I walk in there, hinting that maybe no one has been here since. I sit down, back against the wall just the way we did then. I remember the herbal taste of the liqueur and how much I disliked it. It had a heat, though, and a serious kick.

No bar service tonight. There's just me and the darkness, and the realization that I recall nothing after that first sip. I woke up on Una's porch, so I must have left under my own steam.

How can I not remember something so important?

What am I going to do about it?

I have a daughter. Even though Sylvia never told me about her, the responsibility is real. She might have expected that I'd be like Patrick and deny the results of my own actions, but that's one thing I'll never do.

Sierra is my daughter. Just because I haven't had anything to do with her life so far doesn't mean it has to stay that way. As much as I'd like to get to know her, that might not be possible. I'd never mess with Sylvia's custody, but some time together might be a good thing. I feel even more responsible for her financial situation than I did before, but I can make it right.

Making a mistake doesn't mean I can't make amends.

There is a resonance in a right answer and I hear it in this one. I'll pay support. I'll ask Daph or her dad how such things are arranged, what amount would be appropriate, how to orchestrate that.

There's one cornerstone to my life, and that's my resolve to make different choices than Patrick has made. I've fallen down on that here, but it isn't my fault. I didn't remember and Sylvia didn't tell me.

But I'm on a quest to straighten out the past, and I'm not going to stop.

I'm thinking about this when I see the flashing red lights of the cop cars coming down Queen. I figure something is going down at the taco truck and look out the front windows with curiosity. No sirens, but the cars stop right in front of me, parking at the curb. I can hear their radios, but can't see the taco truck from this angle.

I'm not expecting to have a light shine suddenly up at the window, much less to have someone speak from behind me.

"Hands in the air," says the cop who has come in the back way quietly. "Let me see them."

I do as I'm told and turn around, realizing I've been busted.

Just like old times.

17

DAPHNE

I hear zip from Luke all weekend. I don't catch a glimpse of him either.

I know I shouldn't have expected otherwise, and I didn't—but I did.

No doubt he's ridden out of town when I wasn't paying attention, content that he has set all to rights as he planned. He told me right up front that he'd leave and he's evidently followed through on that. He's probably forgotten all about me and Empire and Sierra by now. Maybe he's even forgotten about the new café.

Maybe he's calling Merrie and not me.

Maybe he's calling Sylvia.

Maybe he's *with* Sylvia, sorting out how they'll be a happy family together. That's the knife I twist in the wound in the middle of the night.

The truly crappy thing is that now I'm the one who wants more, and it's too late.

And that's what I get for believing people—well, one man—and *feeling* instead of thinking. Following impulse always leads me wrong.

We're supposed to learn from our mistakes.

If I'm going to seize the day, I need to be faster.

I grumble about this to myself all weekend long, going through my usual routine. I clean the house on Saturday morning and do my laundry. I drive to Havelock and pick up some groceries in the afternoon, then have my weekly talk with Abbie. She's annoyed about someone at work so I mostly listen. When she asks about Luke, I manage to deflect the question and admit nothing. I go to my dad's for dinner on Saturday and he barbeques steaks. It's almost warm enough to eat on the patio but not quite. He's in a great mood even if I'm not.

I stay in bed to read on Sunday—wishing there was someone around to make coffee, someone whose butt I could admire while he was doing that—then Cameron texts me to go for a run on the beach at Port Cavendish. It's such a beautiful sunny day that I go along, even if it means ignoring her questions and pointed glances.

I do check my phone a little bit obsessively, not that there's any reward in that.

On Monday morning, I confront my sorry self in the mirror, tell myself to let it go, and head to work. My motivation is non-existent. I remind myself that I expected Luke to vanish. I expected once to be enough for him—even though I was wrong about it being enough for me. I expected him to be trouble—but I never expected him to be a delinquent father.

Well, that's it and it's huge.

It's also stupid, because condoms fail, but still, I feel betrayed.

And that feels even more stupid. I barely knew him sixteen years ago.

My father is at work already, of course, and offers a cheery wave from his office. He seems to be highly amused, although I'm not in on the joke.

No one has mentioned the previous Friday morning, which is

just fine by me—especially after Friday night's revelations. I'm not sure anyone else knows about it, other than my dad. There is a bustle of activity across the street and I see Willow heading toward the bistro with purpose.

It seems my part in this particular drama is over.

Mrs. Prescott clears her throat, then indicates the office answering machine. (Yes, we still have an actual answering machine, a little box that sits on her desk with a red light that blinks when it's done its job.) "I believe this is for you," she says primly, pushes the button then goes into my father's office. Normally, I'd be amused that she goes through the motions of giving me privacy to listen to a message that she's already played, but not today.

Because it's Luke.

"Hey Daph," he says, his voice surprisingly rough. My heart does its caged bird thing, right on cue. "Looks as if I need an angel of mercy and I only know one good candidate. I'm a guest of the Havelock police, at least until someone helps me out, and I'm hoping it will be you. Thanks."

I play it again, just to be sure, then straighten to find Mrs. Prescott watching me with undisguised disapproval.

Suddenly, I understand what my dad was smiling about.

I duck my head around the door to his office. "I have to go to Havelock this morning."

"Oh?" He is not surprised. He's enjoying himself—too much.

"Luke's been arrested and told them I was his lawyer."

My father chuckles. "Your young man," he teases. "He's more interesting than the last one, I'll give him that."

"He's not my young man. He's my client," I correct and Dad laughs out loud. "Why is this funny?"

"It's not funny." He sobers with an effort but his eyes keep twinkling.

"You look like you're planning to have a good chuckle with Patrick about this."

"Not me," he says with such resolve that I believe him. "But I was recently reminded that clever people need challenges to feel as if their efforts matter. I never expected this young man to step up so effectively."

I'm going to ask who offered that advice—if that's what it was —but the phone rings and Mrs. Prescott intervenes.

"Mr. Cavendish for you, sir."

"Of course. Right on time for our call." My dad reaches for his phone before indicating that I should shut his office door behind me.

Why is Luke in jail? What did he do?

When did he do it? Is this the reason he's been AWOL all weekend? Or am I making excuses for him? Why would he call the office instead of my cell phone?

I'm in my car before I realize that Luke could have called his mom for help. She's right in Havelock. Should I be flattered that he called me instead?

No. His mom isn't a lawyer. I'm more *useful*.

And of course, he'd want to protect her from this truth.

———

BREAKING AND ENTERING. At the Foreman place, against every expectation. Why there? It's been empty for years. Also, Patrick is the owner of the building. Did that contribute to Luke's decision?

To the cop on the other side of the desk, it's not complicated. A neighbour saw suspicious activity around an empty building and called the cops. They arrived, found Luke where he shouldn't have been, and arrested him.

But there are no damages and nothing missing. To my amazement, the property owner doesn't want to press charges. That seems out of character for Patrick, but I'm not going to complain. Even the neighbour doesn't care anymore.

I do tell the officer which Luke Jones he is, and it turns out that Luke has fans in Havelock.

We agree that it's mischief, that it won't happen again, and that if it does, the repercussions will be more serious.

A big cop walks me down to the cell, I think maybe because he wants an autograph. The Havelock police station isn't huge and it's not stuffed to the rafters with dangerous criminals. There are a couple of holding cells, one of which is empty on this Monday morning.

I don't expect Luke to be contrite. I'm not even surprised that he's unrepentant.

I did not expect the jubilation.

But there's no denying that Luke Jones is over the moon. He's pacing back and forth, humming to himself and singing snatches of a song I don't know.

Ivan Ross, Empire's amiable town drunk, is propped up in the corner of the bottom bunk, watching Luke. Ivan looks rougher than the last time I saw him—a little puffier, a little paler, considerably less clean. You'd think the amount of time he spends in jail would loosen the clutch of his habit, but no luck so far.

"What do think, Ivan? This finale or the other one?" Luke hums something, his back to me as he waits for Ivan's verdict.

"I like the other one," Ivan says. "It sounds happier."

"But it's a ballad, Ivan. It's supposed to sound romantic, not happy."

"Ah." Ivan straightens at the sight of me, and runs a trembling hand over his stained shirt as if that will make a difference. "Mz. Bradshaw! Come to spring me?"

Luke spins to face me and his eyes light. "Daph!" My heart goes skippity-bump with such predictability that I frown. Luke's probably patented that expression of delight because it works so well on susceptible females. For all I know, it works on guys, too.

Ivan *is* watching him with a measure of adoration.

"Not today, Ivan," I say, very aware of the cop who has escorted me. I look back and he murmurs something. "I understand that a counsellor from social services is on the way." Ivan looks unhappy about this, but I'm relieved. I set that up for him the last time he was busted for singing in the middle of the night on Queen Street. He's mostly harmless, but that doesn't mean his addiction should continue untreated.

The cop remains behind me, his arms folded across his chest. I speak crisply, willing Luke to behave. It's a long shot. "Good morning, Mr. Jones."

He smiles just a little—yes, *that* smile—his gaze sliding to the watchful cop. "Good morning, Ms. Bradshaw. I apologize for interrupting your morning."

"All in a day's work, Mr. Jones."

"I wasn't sure you sprang felons free."

"Small town." I tick items off on my fingers. "I do divorces, real estate closures, power of attorney agreements, wills, bail hearings, court appearances, custody agreements, and whatever else the job demands. No criminal cases, though, so one day, you might be out of luck."

He's undaunted. "But today?"

"Breaking and entering downgraded to a public nuisance charge, which can be resolved by payment of a fee."

"How much?"

I tell him. It's nothing.

His dark brows rise. "Daph, what a shark you are," he murmurs under his breath with a certain measure of admiration.

"I'm hoping you're good for it," I say.

"I don't have any credit with you?"

I shake my head and he sobers, our gazes locking. He's dead

serious when he nods. "Understood," he murmurs. The cop unlocks the cell and he steps out, then turns to wave to his former companion. "Be good, Ivan," he says.

"And if I can't be good, I'll be careful," Ivan agrees heartily.

We head out to settle everything up, the sergeant sticking close all the while. He's young, younger than me, maybe even a rookie, but his size makes him intimidating. When everything is sorted and Luke is putting his personal possessions back in his pockets, I indicate our companion. "Sergeant O'Reilly was hoping for an autograph."

The cop flushes, crimson rising from his neck to his hairline as we watch. "For my daughter," he says.

"Of course," Luke says smoothly. He visibly searches for a piece of paper and the sergeant pats his pockets, finally offering his notebook. "What's her name?"

"Aurora," the cop says and Luke signs a blank page in the notebook before handing it back. We leave the station together, and he starts to whistle the same tune he was humming to Ivan.

To be honest, it irks me that he's not apologetic at all, much less offering an explanation. "Proud of yourself?"

"They used to know me well here."

"It's not something to be proud of."

"Old times, Daph."

"You look positively cheerful." I stop beside the Honda, unable to explain why I'm so annoyed with him.

No. That's a lie. I could make a list.

"I am." Luke winks at me. "All's right in the world, Daph, and not just because you rode to my rescue." He stops on the passenger side of my car, watching me over the roof, so obviously waiting for me to ask that I do.

"Why is that?"

"Because the golden goose is back." He flings out his hands. "I stink, Daph. I'm starving and I haven't slept, but I can hear the music again, and let me tell you, that's *divine*."

"Glad to hear there's an upside to being a delinquent father."

"I am in an awesome mood." He points at me. "While you are giving me your Medusa stare."

"Medusa stare. Why do you say things like that?"

"Because I read mythology and fairy tales, and when I see a comparative, I call it. It was a scheme to add some depth to my lyrics, but actually, I really like those stories." He nods at me. "And that expression could definitely turn a man to stone."

I glare a little harder then unlock the car when it makes no difference.

"Are you offering me a ride or am I on my own now?"

"What do you want to happen?"

"I would like to explain myself to you."

I raise my hands, inviting said explanation. Luke comes around the car to confront me. "You're mad at me. That's inescapable and so is my disappointment that I've let you down. But what you might not realize is that I am more angry with myself than you could ever be." His eyes are dark and his voice is low. "I did the one thing that I was always determined to avoid doing, and I don't even remember. What kind of garbage individual does that make me?"

He looks away, his throat working, and my anger dissolves.

"And there it goes," he murmurs. "One great mood shot to hell by reality."

"What did you do to end up here?" I ask quietly.

"I tried to remember. I retraced my steps from that night, the night I ran into Sylvia. And I remembered that she came out of the Grand Hotel, that she wanted to avoid Mike and his friends, that we went to the Foreman place, which was empty even then. Someone had left the bottle there and we went upstairs with it. After that, I have a gap. I remember being sick in the forest. I remember waking up on Una's porch. In between, nada. And as I stood there, trying to remember *anything* about that night, the cops came."

"A neighbour saw you enter the building."

"I don't doubt it. The cops emptied my pockets and took me to Havelock, and by the time I had the chance to make a call, my phone had died. I didn't remember your number. You don't have a landline, apparently, because there's no listing for you, so I called the office and left a message." He shrugs. "Not a lot of options."

"You could have called your mom."

"No." He gives me an intent look. "Where did you think I was this weekend?"

"Gone." I reach for the door handle but he stops me with a touch, his fingertips on my wrist. I look up. "You said you wouldn't stay."

"That was *before*, Daph."

Before what? Before we had sex? Before he knew he and Sylvia had a daughter? I don't know and I won't ask. Once again, I'm awash in competing feelings and that makes me want to retreat to the safe territories of logic and professional indifference.

Fill that moat.

Lift that drawbridge.

Maybe get the boiling oil ready on the ramparts.

I open the car door. "Are you coming or not?"

"Not quite so Medusa," he murmurs with appreciation. "Maybe one of the furies instead of one of the gorgons." I look up and he grins. "I'm good with you haunting me forever, by the way."

"You're incorrigible."

"I'm starving and I desperately need a shower. Both are significantly less chronic conditions."

I fight a smile and get into the car. He gets in the other side and fastens his seatbelt. The car feels much smaller than I know it is, and his proximity can't be ignored. I swear I can feel the heat of him—and he doesn't stink, despite his insistence otherwise. I'm thinking inappropriate thoughts as I pull out of the parking lot. I'm intending to drive back to Empire and drop him off at the motel when he clears his throat.

"Actually, Daph, could we make a detour?"

"Anywhere specific?"

"Somewhere a little less glacial than inside this car," he mutters, then continues before I can reply. "To my mom's. I want to get my guitar. It's maybe ten minutes out of your way, if you don't mind." He waits a minute, then continues. "I'd like also to consult you on a legal matter, so we can do that on the way, and you can bill me for it." He casts me a sidelong glance. "Win-win, right?"

I'm skeptical, but I nod. He gives me directions and I head toward his mom's house.

Whatever I'm expecting him to say, it's not what he does say.

"So, Daph, if I want to pay child support to Sylvia, how do we make that happen?"

I miss a gear, and Luke doesn't miss that.

"What? You didn't expect me to do the right thing?"

"Sierra is fifteen. She won't be a child much longer."

"I didn't know about her."

"Because Sylvia didn't want you to know."

"Well, now I do and I want to make it right. Better late than never." He sounds determined and I can't help respecting his choice.

And he *is* my client. Okay.

"Well, there would be a negotiated agreement, a payment, probably paid monthly, in exchange for either custody or visitation. Basically, your financial support of Sierra buys your access to her. Visits are usually forfeit if payments are missed."

"Sounds cold," he says with disapproval.

"By the time parents get lawyers to sort things out, all friendly avenues have usually been exhausted," I note and he nods. "Sylvia might just welcome a lump payment, given Sierra's age, or she might not want anything from you."

"She can't deny me outright, though, can she?"

"You'll probably want to request a paternity test to avoid that eventuality. It's a wise choice before you make that kind of commitment anyway," I say, sounding like the lawyer I am.

Luke is visibly indignant. "Because Sylvia wouldn't know who fathered her child? I'm not going to imply that she's a liar. She says it's me, so I'll respond accordingly."

I frown. She hadn't actually said it was Luke, though the implication was there. Before I can make that nit-pickity distinction, Luke continues.

"It sounds very carrot-and-stick the way you explain it, but does it have to be that way? Of course, I'd like to get to know Sierra and have a part in her life, but I don't want the exchange to be defined so specifically. I'd prefer to support her, and get to know her if and when she wants to know me. Is that crazy?"

"No," I admit. "It sounds nice. Respectful of her space." I slant a glance his way. "You don't have to do this, you know."

"It's *right*, Daph." He's glowering out the windshield. "Why wouldn't I do what's right? Why does everyone assume I'm an asshole?"

"Because you have been in the past?" I suggest.

"I've been angry in the past, but I'm over that."

Fair enough.

When he looks at me this time, there's a glint of humor in his eyes. "And even if I've been a dick in the past, Daph, remember, I'm on a quest to set that right."

"So, support for Sierra."

"Yes. Why wouldn't I do that?"

Ah, the Devil's Advocate. One of my fave speaking roles.

"Well, it would have been right for Sylvia to tell you, but she didn't. And it's not like you've been difficult to locate." I'm not really making excuses for him, just reviewing both sides of the issue. And, even though I didn't consider it earlier, this result isn't all Luke's fault.

His tone turns fierce. "I'm doing it, Daph."

I have to know. "Why? Sylvia's not asking for it, and she might turn you down."

"Then what happens?"

"You could sue her. There would definitely be a paternity test then and a lawsuit..."

"And all the lawyers make money," he says with exasperation. I don't argue because it's true. "Let me put it this way, Daph," he says and I feel the weight of his conviction. "I am the one person who knows how lousy it is to grow up in Empire, knowing you're a Cavendish, having everyone else recognize that you're a Cavendish, while Patrick tries to erase your existence. It's more than ignoring you. He goes out of his way to make his views known and to turn others against you. And so, okay, I survived it and maybe it made me a stronger person, but that doesn't mean that I want to stand by and watch him do the same thing to Sierra. And he will, Daph." He's grim. "He *will*."

I have to say it. "After you leave town, you won't see it."

"Wherever I am, I'll *know*. And if Sierra's well-being is the reason we finally have it out, Patrick and me, then I'm ready for it. I'll fight for her the way I didn't fight for myself."

"You don't think you fought?"

"I made trouble. I stirred things up and provoked Patrick when I could. Then I left. I succeeded despite him. That's not the same as holding your ground and fighting back." He takes a breath. "And the worst part of is that she's *here*, in Empire, within his range because I *meddled*. You were right, Daph. I should have minded my own business, but now I have another mess to fix. No one is going to stop me from doing it."

I'm impressed. And I'm touched by his ferocious need to protect this girl without knowing more about her than he does. I think that Sylvia is going to have to go some to turn him down, and I have no doubt that she'll try, but I'd put my money on Luke.

He's frowning at the streets we pass, and indicates that we need to make a turn. It's a residential area, neither new nor old. Maybe 80's. The houses are similar but not the same and when he points out the one, I'm surprised. It's a bungalow, probably the smallest house on the block, neatly kept with a tidy garden out front.

Nothing about it says 'my son is a rock star.'

"This is the house you bought your mom?"

"It's the one she wanted." I feel the weight of his gaze. "You look surprised, Daph."

"I expected a mansion, some huge fancy place."

Luke smiles and there's affection in his expression and his tone. "Then you don't know my mom very well."

I don't. She used to cut my mom's hair. I would say they were acquaintances, not friends. Friendly. I haven't seen Louise since my mom's funeral, an unexpected realization that catches me a little.

"She wanted a place she could manage herself, that she could stay in for the duration. She wanted a garden and a spare bedroom and her dream kitchen." Luke raises a hand. "This is it. She said she knew it when she saw it."

"Impulse runs in the family then?"

"Or maybe I came honestly by my inclination to trust my gut. Are you coming in?" he asks. "I won't be long, but she'll give me hell if I leave you to wait in the car."

I smile at the prospect of anyone chewing Luke out and turn off the engine. "Yes. I'd like that."

I'm curious, naturally, but that's about more than the house. I want to see Luke and his mom together.

And I'm not disappointed. Louise is clearly delighted to have a surprise visit and almost smothers Luke in hugs and kisses. He appears to tolerate her fussing, with some objections, even though he's a good foot taller than her. I can see that he's loving it. He protests that he was there a couple of days ago, but she ignores that. She tousles his hair and tells him he's too thin, then welcomes me with a radiant smile.

She's a very pretty woman and looks younger than she has to be. Perfectly turned out. Her hair is dark, too, though not as black as Luke's. More of a deep brown, and there are a few silver hairs mixed in. Her eyes are thickly lashed like Luke's and clear green. She's also tall and slim, so the genetic legacy was consistent. She's comes across as warm and kind, the kind of person whose presence makes you smile. I remember that my mom really liked her.

In no time, we're seated in her kitchen—which is cozy and yellow, with wooden cabinets and counters of veined stone with metallic flicks in it. The sunlight streams through the window and there's a line of herbs on the sill, all thriving and green.

"I suppose you've come for a reason," she says to Luke, her tone teasing.

"Actually, I came to get my guitar," he says and something in his tone catches my ear. "And to see you, of course. Daph was good enough to drive me."

He doesn't mention where he spent the last two nights so I won't either.

Louise turns to look at him, bracing her hips against the counter and folding her arms across her chest. "Your guitar?"

"Yes." Luke is obviously discomfited.

She doesn't relent. "You're taking it away."

"Yes." He's practically fidgeting.

I'm officially and unofficially intrigued.

"After all this time, you suddenly want your guitar?"

"What difference does it make?" he asks her. "I thought you'd be glad to have it out of your way."

Louise exhales, the kettle boils and she turns around to make the tea. "Where are you going to keep it?" she asks, then glances at me as if she knows the answer already.

Why does this matter?

My mom was a huge fan of Neil Simon's work. We used to have movie marathons on Friday nights when my dad was working late. *The Odd Couple. The Sunshine Boys. Sweet Charity. Barefoot in the Park. The Plaza Suite. The Heartbreak Kid.* She loved them all, the dialogue and the characterizations, and I loved them because she loved them.

That's when I have it.

The Goodbye Girl. In that movie, the heroine is finally convinced that the hero is coming back because he leaves his guitar at her Manhattan apartment when he accepts an acting job elsewhere. The last actor she loved never came back from a distant job, so she had issues.

"I'm not sure," Luke says, avoiding her gaze. "I just want to have it."

"Doesn't fit on your bike well," she notes. "Are you getting a car?"

"No." Luke sounds stubborn now. "I can take it back to Empire in Daph's car."

"And when you leave Empire?"

He gives her a warning look. "I'll sort it out."

Louise's gaze slides to me and she smiles. The back of Luke's neck is red and he pushes to his feet. "Didn't you want me to check on that downspout that keeps disconnecting itself?"

"It's probably the neighbour's cat, knocking it loose on his midnight rounds."

"I'll put a couple of screws in it," he says gruffly then makes what is obviously an escape.

"Take a shower while you're here," she shouts after him and I hear his grunt of agreement. Louise smiles at me. "And I'll make lunch."

I smile back. "Thank you," I say and mean it. "That would be great."

But what I'm really wondering is where Luke intends to keep his guitar.

18

———

LUKE

Could that have been any more excruciating?

I'm thinking not. I love my mom but her match-making can make me crazy. Usually, it has no basis, but in this case, I'm afraid her meddling will mess up everything. I know I'm on thin ice with Daph, but if anyone's going to screw it all up, I'll manage that on my own, thanks.

Maybe I've come honestly by my desire to meddle, and not just from the Cavendish side.

We finally escape after lunch and too much talking.

At least she doesn't get out my baby pictures.

We leave my mom humming happily to herself—probably picking out wedding gifts, but at least she didn't say anything outright. She just knows me too well, and she knows how closely I guard that guitar. I don't have many possessions any more. I never did, always having a tendency to travel light, but I've gotten rid of almost everything in the past year. This guitar is different, though. It's my favourite one, and my mom has had custody for a while.

But if I'm going to compose songs again, I need it.

Daph—incredibly, mercifully—didn't seem to notice the

importance of my request, even after Mom made a fuss over it. To my relief, she's thawed a bit. Maybe it was the homemade bread and soup, but I'll take it. Life seems a lot easier when Daph is on my side of anything. She's a great ally, and I like the magic that happens when we put our heads together to solve anything. That analytical thing she does of considering an issue from all sides is impressive and so helpful.

We talk about the details of my pending offer to Sylvia on the drive back to Empire. There's a moment when she pulls into the parking lot of the motel, a moment when I know she has questions and I could give answers.

But Daph isn't about compromise and half-measures. I still want to be with her, but I need to get this thing with Sylvia sorted first. I need to prove my intentions. This situation demands actions not words.

The moment passes before I figure out how to explain any of that, then I watch her drive on to her office. The plan is that she'll draw everything up for me to review by the morning, so I know I'll see her then, at least.

And she's talking to me. The temperature in the car was positively balmy. Not warm. Not torrid. But my chilblains are receding.

I'll take progress where I find it.

I carry my guitar case up the steps to my room, intending to put the afternoon to good use by getting some of this elusive tune down. I don't have the bridge yet. I'm humming the chorus again, skipping over the gaps in the lyrics, and come full stop when I find a kid leaning against the door to my room.

I don't know him. He's maybe fourteen, with hair so red that his buzz cut doesn't hide the colour at all. He has more freckles than I would have thought possible and is wearing jeans and an Old Navy sweatshirt. He gives me a look that is both stubborn and a little hostile and I figure I understand this kid already.

But I have it wrong.

"I'm Noah McLaughlin and I want to interview you," he says. "I want the whole story behind your acquisition of the diner and your plans for its future *and* I want an exclusive."

"Who are you with? The CBC?"

"The Empire Chronicle."

"Never heard of it." The newspaper in town was called The Standard when I was a kid, but it must have stopped publishing. There are no newspaper boxes on the corners anymore.

"Your mistake," Noah informs me. "You'll see all the news in this town and even this county first at The Chronicle. I have a website and all the socials so you can follow the news in real time."

"There's that much news here?"

He straightens importantly. "News is where you look for it. There's always something happening, always a story that can be told."

I have to cede that.

"Shouldn't you be in school?" I check my watch. It's only two.

"Professional development day," he informs me. "It's for teachers but there's nothing saying I can't work on my own future today."

The fact is that I could use someone telling this story. I could blow off this kid and look for someone with more influence and more followers. But I like his initiative and I like that he's local. I'm thinking that if we help out each other, we could both be stronger forces for change—and that can't be a bad deal.

"The new bistro will be called The Carpe Diem Café," I say and he shoves his phone at me.

"Speak loud and clear," I'm instructed by the youngest reporter ever. "I'll upload the audio to the site."

"You need my permission to do that."

"You give it automatically by granting the interview," he says, waving off my objections.

Is one of his parents a lawyer? If so, they can't be working in Empire.

"How big is your audience?"

"Those are proprietary numbers."

"But your reach is going to influence how long I talk to you and how much I tell you."

He eyes me, considering how much to confess. I win the stare-down because he blinks first. "I just started. Traffic on the site is slow. I need a good story to launch properly. Something that can go viral, even. I don't suppose you have any secrets to share or celebrity gossip?"

"No, but I'll talk to you about the diner." I'm all for entrepreneurship and initiative, after all.

I invite him in, pull out my phone and check out his website. It's crisp and clean, well designed, loads quickly, but is lacking content.

"I want to start a podcast too," Noah confides, shifting his weight from one foot to the other. "But I need a newer phone."

"Who's paying for your domain?"

"Me. Allowance money." He gives me a pitying look, probably because I'm too old to know anything useful. "You have to own your domain to look professional," he confides. "And pay for the level of hosting that turns off the spammy ads."

I nod agreement.

I offer him the chair at the desk and I sit on the edge of the bed. "Okay. The restaurant is a new venture that I'm supporting. I think you and I can make a deal that benefits both of us. I'll give you the inside scoop, and you'll help us build awareness for opening night."

"An exclusive," he says again and I have to give him credit for persistence.

"First look," I counter. "And I'll get the other players to talk to you."

"Exclusively?"

"First."

"When's opening night?"

"I'm not sure. We could go down and ask Merrie. Maybe you can book an interview with her."

"Excellent!" Noah forgets to be cool and indifferent for a moment and I smile. "But first, you."

"First, me."

I wasn't ready for this, and in a way, Noah is a great reality check. Success, in my experience, doesn't just happen on its own. It doesn't alight on your shoulder like a blessing from above. Maybe that happens to other people. Me, I've always had to work for it. I had to do the research, put in the time, go out and coax good things into happening.

And I haven't started that with this venture yet. As I'm thinking, I reinvigorate my socials, which have been languishing for over a year. The band's stuff is off-limits for this, a personal project, but I have my own accounts. Some people will unfollow me, inevitably, but some might be interested. It can't hurt.

I get Noah's info and link to him, and he links to me. I make a mental note to ask Chelsea, who managed social media for the band, for some advice, then do a search on The Carpe Diem Café. Ha. Merrie is ahead of me. She has a website, still bare bones, but it's there and it's searchable. I hook Noah up with it and feel like we're rolling.

"The story," he says firmly. "I want the story."

"All right. Let's do it." He holds out his phone as I try to choose where to begin. "I'm Luke Jones. I grew up in Empire and after I left, I started a band called Mad Bad & Dangerous 2 Know with my friend Taylor Tate. You might have heard of it."

Noah nods, his expression hinting that I'm in his mental file of historic personages, like Abraham Lincoln and Queen Victoria. Columbus. Well, I am setting sail for new worlds.

"When Taylor died, just over a year ago, the band stopped touring and recording. I've been trying to think of a way to honour his memory, to pay tribute to what a terrific person he was, and that brought me back to Empire."

I wasn't entirely sure what I'd say to Noah, but once I find this thread, it makes perfect sense and I follow it. I'm not going to talk about Sierra and Sylvia. I'll leave them out of the official narrative to protect their privacy, and focus on The Carpe Diem Café. I send Merrie a text to let her know that we'll probably be over, and she replies with a thumbs-up emoji.

"You see, Taylor was all about making the world a better place and leaving it in better shape than how you found it. It seemed to me that Empire, and some of the people in it, could use a little help with that. You wouldn't recognize the town I knew when I was your age, and I hardly recognize this version of it. There's a lot less going on, as well as less opportunity to support neighbours and friends, to act locally and make a difference."

Once I choose my spin and start talking, the words flow easily. It's always been that way for me and I'm glad I haven't lost that bit.

"That diner, for example, was run by Leon and Dotty, and it was busy all the time. It was where we all went, not just to eat but to hang out and talk. We walked there or rode over on our bikes. We didn't have to drive to Havelock to get an ice cream cone. I have good memories of that place."

Noah nods. "It's been closed for a long time."

"Since Leon and Dotty retired. I knew that if I'd brought Taylor here, he'd be as saddened by the changes as I am. I was trying to figure out a way to make a difference when I met a chef whose restaurant was closing in Toronto. She wanted her own place, so I had this idea. What if she opened her dream bistro here, in Empire? What if that diner got a new lease on life? What if everyone in Empire had a great place they could go for lunch, or dinner, or just to meet up with friends after work?

What if Merrie achieved her dream? What else would that change?"

"Maybe nothing," Noah says. "Maybe a lot."

"Exactly. I'm hoping for option number two. Come on. Let's go over and meet Merrie. You'll be the first in town to talk to her."

And just like that, an amazing afternoon of promotion comes together. Merrie has prepared for us. The first thing I see is the sign, carved from wood and hanging from the eaves over the door. The Carpe Diem Café. I explain what that means to Noah who rolls his eyes that I could be so dense as to think he doesn't know. "Google is my friend," he informs me loftily and I'm glad to hear big tech has some pals.

We step inside and I can't believe the transformation. The place looks a billion times better than it did on Friday. Willow is there, in overalls with her hair tied back, busily painting. There's a guy installing sheets of hammered copper on the surface of the bar, which is about two feet higher than it was. The base is being painted matte black and what's done looks fantastic. The linoleum floor has been pulled up, revealing wide-plank pine floors beneath, which seem to be in great shape. The walls that Willow has painted are a vanilla shade, and she's making the long wall deep burgundy. The kitchen area is having its stainless upgraded and there are two guys working on a fireplace that I didn't know was there. (Maybe it wasn't. Just because it looks original doesn't mean it is.) I do wonder what it's all costing me, but I'll ask later.

"First peek," I remind Noah and he starts taking pictures, beginning with Merrie's signage. Meanwhile, I spot Sylvia at the back. She takes a call on her phone, gives me a dismissive glance, then walks out the back door.

She knows I can't follow her. Not now.

Later, though. In the morning when I have the docs from Daph.

Merrie, meanwhile, walks Noah through the space, talking

about her plans, and I love how she takes him seriously. They pause for a while in front of her vision board, though she asks him not to photograph it. She uses it to describe her plan, though, and he records her doing that. She also has an agenda, something I see when she guides him right to a big ass map on one wall of the back room.

"That's Empire and surrounding area," Noah says.

"My grocery store," Merrie says with pride, urging him closer. "The whole point of farm-to-table is to cook seasonally, with what's available locally. So, my first quest is to find suppliers." There are push pins in the map in different colours and she points to one. "Red is for meat and fish. This is a farm raising boar and heritage pigs; this is a farm with Angus beef; this is a rainbow trout farm. Look how close they all are to Empire. This place is ideally located for cooking fresh."

"Green is produce," Noah guesses. "That's the main Cavendish Enterprises greenhouse."

"It is. Here's a market farmer with heritage potatoes, and other root vegetables like parsnips and beets. Here's one with rhubarb and blackberries, blueberries and strawberries. Here's an orchard with apples, pears and more by season, and here's an organic mushroom farm."

"Lots of green pins," Noah says.

"Lots of research for me to do. I'm loving it. Yellow is dairy. Here's a goat farm that makes their own chèvre and also sells the milk. Here's an indie dairy that makes butter and cheese from local milk. Lots of people with free range eggs—" her fingers fly over the map, touching a sequence of pins "—and chickens raised organically. I love how many farms are selling at their gates. Blue is for other ingredients."

"Rhodes Vineyard," Noah says, identifying a pin by its location.

"Mackenzie Rhodes came in to see me yesterday, with a

sampling of their wines. They'll be featured on our menu and in our pairings. Here are three micro-breweries I intend to check out. This place here dries fruit and vegetables, and mixes their own herbal teas from dried local ingredients. This guy works with native plants and ingredients traditionally used by indigenous peoples. I cannot wait for that appointment. Here's a mill, grinding local grains." The enthusiasm is coming off her in waves and I wonder how she's going to check out all of these places.

"Why heritage varieties?" Noah asks when she pauses for breath and Merrie launches into a soliloquy that would make Taylor proud, listing the advantages of old varieties of plants, their flavours and distinctions even within each type.

"Apples are great, sure, but what about all the specific kinds? I'm going to do something different with a Crispin than a Spy, with an Empire or a Jonathan instead of a Macintosh. There are hundreds of varieties of apples, some ripening late, some early, some storing well, some for cooking and some best for eating fresh. The possibilities are fantastic." She surveys her map with obvious anticipation. "Stir that up with classic French bistro cooking, simple foods, great ingredients, comforting flavours and sometimes surprising combinations."

"Isn't that going to be expensive?"

"No! The menu will have a range of options, something to suit everyone. A daily pizza. A daily soup and sandwich. A dinner special. I'm thinking of a fixed price special with soup or salad, the daily special dinner and dessert. Crème brulée with local butter. A fruit crisp with a mix of berries, served warm with locally made ice cream."

"So, you'd be featuring local farms and their products."

"Absolutely. Farm-to-table is about fresh. And in time, I'd love to add a retail area, where you can pick up a carton of that ice cream on your way home to enjoy later. I want people to have a great meal, to feel like they can come here and discover something new, but also that we're all learning more about our neighbours and what they do. I'm going to put a bulletin board just inside the window, where anyone can post a flyer about a local event. I'm not from Empire but I want to be part of it."

"You have big plans."

"I have plans. I *love* plans. What about a farmer's market in town? What about a grocery store stocking all the ingredients I use and more, or a cooking class once a week, or a food box delivery featuring all this good stuff? What about kids learning how to cook after school? What about *everyone* learning how to cook? We are in the middle of an area offering a bounty of great food. Let's dig in. Let's appreciate it. Let's eat well together."

Damn. An impassioned Merrie is impossible to ignore.

"When are you opening?"

"The Thursday before the holiday weekend."

"May 15?"

"That's the one. Reservations are available on the website. We open for dinner at six."

Noah wraps up the interview, visibly excited, and Merrie agrees to share the link on her new website. We part ways with plans for more interviews and I pause before I head back to the motel.

My guitar is calling, that song demanding that I work out the details and write it down. I stare at the law office across the street, though, wishing I could celebrate this moment with Daph.

I'd even risk frostbite, because she's not wrong to be disappointed in me.

How could I do the one thing I always insisted I'd never do, and not even remember? There is no comeback. There's only penance and the need to make it right.

Until I manage that—if it even can be done—I'll leave Daph alone. I want to go back to her with everything together, and I want to start over, show her what it means to want more.

Tomorrow I'll pick up the paperwork from her and take it to Sylvia. I'll bet Daph leaves it with the receptionist for me, and maybe that will make it easier to keep my resolve.

For tonight, my company will be my guitar. That's not all bad. The music is back because of Daph, and this first song is for her.

It feels right and I'm going with that.

19

———

DAPHNE

Tuesday starts off hectic and only gets worse. I barely see Luke when he comes to get the proposal because I'm on the phone with the feds about paperwork from Cavendish Enterprises. It's my dad who walks through the details with him and sends him on his way.

I'm still on the phone when Luke leaves.

The day drags out, filled with cross-checks on documents for the feds. I talk to the human resources coordinator at Cavendish Enterprises several times, checking dates and details that are somehow different between various forms. We're getting it all sorted when she asks me to hold.

A moment later, she's back. "If we're done, Daphne, there's someone who'd like to talk to you."

"I think we are," I say, curious.

"Mike Cavendish here, Daphne." He sounds embarrassed, which is odd.

"Hi Mike. Is there a problem?"

"No, no, not that. I was, um, wondering how things worked out in Havelock yesterday."

I sit back, intrigued. "You mean with Luke?"

"Yes. That is exactly the situation I mean."

How strange that he's being obscure. "Is someone listening?"

"Absolutely," he says heartily. "I'm glad you don't mind me checking on this."

"All's well that ends well," I say. "Since Patrick didn't want to press charges."

Mike coughs and puts a hand over the receiver. "Be right there!" he calls cheerfully to someone, then lowers his voice. "I didn't pass the message along," he confides. "I thought someone was due for a break."

I spin a little in my chair. Curiouser and curiouser. The Cavendish boys are breaking rank with Patrick. Not a lot, but I never expected them to do that at all. "You sound like Jake."

"Yeah, well, we had a talk over the weekend. No time like the present to make a change."

"Patrick will find out."

"Not in time to influence the result, clearly."

I smile a little. "Is this a secret?"

"Probably smarter for it to be," Mike agrees and I think I can hear a smile in his voice. "Thanks for all you've done, Daphne."

"I didn't do it for Cavendish Enterprises."

"I know. It's time someone had other interests in mind." There's a shout and he excuses himself, leaving me with something to think about.

I don't have long to consider it because my phone gets a text.

From Rafe.

OMG! May 15

This is followed by an entire line of emojis, conveying great excitement.

What on earth is he talking about?

I call him and he answers right away

"I'm coming," he says with heat. "You can't stop me."

"Bit of an intimate conversation opener, don't you think? Maybe too much information?"

"Daphne!" Rafe chortles. (He actually chortles.) "The Carpe Diem Café opens on the 15th for dinner. I have to be there. I have to have a table. You have to make us a reservation."

"Can't you do it?" I'm not Rafe's secretary or anyone else's, thank you very much.

"Of course, I can, but you have to go over there. You have to get the best table. I don't know the layout of the place. I want to see the kitchen. I want to watch her."

"Should I tell Merrie that she has a stalker?"

"I'm not a stalker. I'm a *fan*."

I have to razz him, just a little. "So, this isn't a date?" I pretend to sound disappointed. "You aren't coming to see me?"

"God, no. You were just here."

I laugh. "Thank you for that."

"Ask somebody else to join us if you feel compelled to match-make. I don't care. I'll be eating."

I spin in my chair considering who I might fix up with Rafe. He's not bad, even though he's not my type, and some women might love how much money he has. Cameron would definitely take him home. Mackenzie? Tough to say. Willow would despise him on sight. "Speak to me of your plans for the evening," I say.

"Dinner and then dessert."

"In terms of the company."

"Conversation optional. Shared plates imperative. Eye candy is always welcome, which is why you're invited."

"Sport sex?"

"You are not offering."

"I am not offering. But I'll choose which of my friends should join us based on your reply."

"How can I say yes or no with no more information than that?"

"A scale then. Ten is absolutely. Zero is no chance."

"Six," he says with resolve. "Because it depends and even though I might be distracted, I am not dead. Am I allowed to state a preference for blondes?"

"Are you going to be a gentleman?"

He laughs. "Always, Daphne. Always."

He is. I'll ask Mackenzie.

"Meet you there. Six?"

"Six," he agrees.

"And you're paying, Rafe."

He heaves a great sigh. "Oh, don't I always?"

Then we laugh together. "How did you find out anyway?"

"She's got a website and shared an interview. Honestly, Daphne, I'm salivating already. Whoa. I've got to go."

And he's gone, dispensing justice to someone somewhere. I follow the breadcrumbs from an online search to Merrie's new website, from there to The Empire Chronicle's site—which I've never heard of before now—which has posted a pair of audio interviews. One with Luke and one with Merrie.

Go ahead. Guess which one I listen to first.

———

GIRLS' night is at Cameron's this week, which means an evening of pampering. We bring everything for manicures and pedicures, facial masks and scrubs. We wear our fluffy robes and light candles and dance around her living room to the oldies. It's so much fun.

There's no question of my missing it, even though I dread the inevitable interrogation.

Maybe there won't be one. Maybe they'll read the truth on my face.

"So, are you doing him yet?" Cameron asks when she opens

the door to me and I wait just a minute to let her look. Clearly, she expects me to say no.

"I did," I say mildly and step past her into the house. She gasps and nearly drops her bottle of nail polish. Mackenzie makes the save, then they both stare at me. Since Mackenzie is wearing a facial mask, she looks particularly alarmed.

"No," she says.

"Oh, yes," I repeat.

"Told you!" Willow calls from the kitchen as Cameron demands details.

I tell them a bit but not a lot, because I'm still hugging it all close. I don't know what the future holds for Luke and me.

"I'll have what she's having," Cameron says.

"You're always having what she's having," Mackenzie notes.

"I think Daphne is having doubts," Willow says and they all look at me.

"Why?" Cameron demands. "It sounds great."

"He says all the right things..."

"But she doesn't know whether to believe him," Willow says, finishing up my sentence.

"Do you have to believe him?" Cameron asks and I blink. "Just go with it. Enjoy them the way they enjoy us."

"Absolutely," Mackenzie says with approval.

"You don't have to expect everything in exchange for some satisfaction," Cameron insists.

"You're shameless," I say to her, not really outraged at all.

"And my stress level is nonexistent. Try it. You might like it."

I change the subject by asking Mackenzie about meeting me and Rafe for dinner, which means I have to tell them about Rafe—and Cameron wants to call in sick to work so she can check him out. I look for pictures of him on my phone—there has to be at least one—then we all confer about Willow's hair. She likes Sierra's hair and wants to do something similar. She's brought a selection of hair colour products and Cameron makes a plan.

Willow's hair comes out amazing, but that's the power of teamwork.

Much later, I walk home across the lawn in my sandals, admiring the glimmer of my freshly painted nails against the darkness of the grass. It feels like it might rain and the skies are overcast, but for the moment, it's dry enough. I've just worn my big fluffy bathrobe home, and my face feels all tingly from the facial mask. I'm relaxed and there's only one thing lacking in my world. I'm ready for a little *carpe diem*.

I see a shadow move on my porch and my heart leaps, because there he is.

"Hey," I say.

"Hey," Luke replies in a soft drawl. "Love the look."

I laugh and take the seat beside him. I study him in the shadows and see uncertainty lurking in his eyes. Has he come to tell me bad news? If so, let's have it. Diving in is officially my new philosophy.

"I thought you'd be with Sylvia," I say and his surprise shows.

"Why? There's nothing between us, Daph. I just want to do right by Sierra."

"I haven't seen much of you this week. I thought that was why."

"No." He's emphatic. "I don't want to offer you damaged goods. I want to get this sorted first." His gaze bores into mine. "You're the principled idealist, remember? I'm the one who breaks all the rules. And I don't know if Sierra is a dealbreaker for you."

"It's complicated," I cede, sitting back. I can feel the tension emanating from him, and I'm relieved that he's so worried about the halo effect of his actions. "I wasn't thrilled when you seemed to be a deadbeat dad, but you aren't." I meet his gaze. "And I admire how you're stepping up. Not many people would do that."

His smile dawns slowly, lifting one corner of his mouth and then the other before it lights his eyes. "I thought you might smite me dead," he murmurs and I can't help but smile.

"There's still time."

Luke laughs. It's rare for him to laugh so long and so loud and I end up staring at him, smiling. "You should do that more," I say and he grins.

"But if I told you to smile more, you *would* smite me."

I have to cede that. Our gazes lock for one of those electric moments and I smile right into his eyes, a veritable welcome mat. He takes the hint and places his arm around my shoulders, leaning in to nuzzle me beneath my ear. He sighs contentment. "You smell good, Daph."

"So do you. I didn't expect to find you here."

"I was missing you." He presses a kiss to the top of my shoulder and I don't care which parts of me he was missing. If he's just here for sex, that's fine by me. I'm going to make the most of his presence, for as long as it lasts. Those lashes sweep up and his gaze bores into mine. "But I'll go, if you'd rather."

I love that he gives me the choice.

"I was missing you, too," I admit, watching his eyes light.

His gaze clings to mine. "Huge relief."

"I'm not that scary."

"Don't underestimate yourself," Luke replies in the low growl that makes me flutter.

I don't understand how it can be both reassuring and thrilling to sit with him like this in the shadows, but I'll go with it.

"You could have texted me, Daph."

"Sex on demand?"

"If that's what you want."

"Not what you want?"

"Not *all* that I want." We eye each other and then he kisses me, one of those smouldering slow ones that could start a conflagration. It certainly sets a fire in me.

He's the one who pulls back and clears his throat. "Have dinner with me?" he asks finally.

"Oh. Boo. Just dinner?" I feign a pout.

Luke chuckles. "Daph, I'm trying to be a gentleman and court you…"

"Court me?" I sit up to look at him, assuming he's joking. He looks completely serious. "How nineteenth century of you."

"Court you," he repeats with resolve. "I want more than a hook-up and I want you to know that it's about more than sex. I didn't make that clear by jumping right in, so we'll start over."

"I want more, too," I admit and hear him catch his breath. "How are we starting over?

"With a dinner date. Friday night, if you're free."

I'm surprised and pleased by this. I like that he's not taking me —or sex with me—for granted, and I can tell by his manner that this is important to him.

I have no objections to courtship, it turns out. "Okay."

"I know just the place. You can't wear a skirt."

"Why not?"

"Because I'm driving." I realize he means we're going on his bike, and that doubles up my anticipation. "I'll pick you up at six."

"What if it rains?"

"Then we'll get wet. Suit up appropriately. Such are the limitations of motorcycles."

I don't tell him that Cameron calls them 'donorcycles'. He's probably heard the term before. "I could drive if it rains."

"Live a little, Daph. Ever been on a bike?"

"No."

"Trust me then. It's good, even in the rain."

I smile. "Okay. See you then."

He leans closer, his arm tightening around me. "I do like the look," he murmurs, his gaze roving over me before he bends closer and gives me a kiss. I can tell it's supposed to be a quick sweet one —a courtship kiss, maybe—but I have an opinion about that, too. I lean into it and deepen the kiss, tangling my fingers in his hair to pull him closer. He makes a little groan of capitulation and pulls me closer, our tongues tangling as the temperature rises on the porch.

Luke pulls away with obvious reluctance, his eyes dark. "You're not playing fair, Daph," he says with quiet heat and I smile.

"It is my diabolical plan to get you naked again," I admit.

He gives a mock roar and swings me up in his arms, kissing me once more before he puts me on my feet in front of my own door. "Friday. Six," he says, as if I could ever forget, and then he jumps off the porch and strides into the darkness. He's moving with purpose, as if he knows he won't go if he lingers any longer, and I watch with a smile.

It's so good to know that I'm not the only one in lust.

I can't wait for Friday.

———

FUNNY HOW TIME can pass both quickly and with excruciating slowness when you're looking forward to something. I see Luke coming and going on Thursday. There's a constant stream of tradespeople at the café, and Willow must be working there full-time.

Friday morning, my dad and I have our routine breakfast meeting. They have a quiche special at Eggs-traordinary so I go for that, reasoning that I'll skip lunch.

My dad has been quiet but once we've ordered, he slides an envelope across the table to me. I must look wary, because he smiles. "Go on. Open it."

"What's this?" I ask as I flip it open. There's a copy of a property title inside and I feel my eyes narrow as I read the address—on Queen Street in Empire.

"Me being reminded of a basic truth," he says, stirring his coffee then taking a sip.

I'm counting buildings and trying to identify the address. "Is this the Foreman building?"

My dad nods. "Last Thursday night, I noticed your young man waiting for you on your porch and spoke to him."

"He's not my young man, Dad."

It seems like such an old-fashioned way to refer to Luke that I have to protest.

On the other hand, I can't say to my dad that Luke's my lover. Not out loud.

Even though he knows.

Dad raises a hand and continues. "Whether he is or not, he knows something more about you than I did. Or maybe he just understands you better."

"Luke?"

"I asked him why he'd included that property in his list for Patrick."

"So Patrick would have something easy to eliminate."

My dad shakes his head, taking another package of sugar. He's trying to cut back, but it's a battle he loses with his first coffee. "Luke planned to give that property to you."

I blink.

"He has this idea that there's merit in giving someone what they most desire, or the opportunity they want most, rather than just paying them in cash. He wanted to give you the opportunity which he believed you must want." My dad meets my gaze. "That is, to set up a practice on your own."

"We talk about this all the time," I remind him, my heart in my throat, and he nods, his expression a little rueful.

"We do, but I haven't really listened to you. I was sure that I knew best, that it would be the smartest choice for you to learn my business and eventually inherit it." My dad empties that package of sugar into his coffee and stirs it again. He nods approval when he tastes it this time, then he looks at me again. "I was reminded that you are a clever and ambitious woman, and that the weakness of my plan was your inevitable boredom. Luke reminded me that smart people need challenges and purpose, and that paperwork for Cavendish Enterprises was unlikely to offer that kind of fulfillment."

"He did?"

"He did." My father takes a long drink of his coffee. "And I was disinclined to agree with him, at least before I arrived on Friday morning and realized that Luke Jones perhaps knew more about my daughter than I'd guessed." His eyes are sparkling and I'm mortified. "I went to see Patrick that morning, instead of coming here for breakfast, and he agreed to sell me that property."

"Because he thought you were right?" I realize that it wouldn't have mattered if Mike told Patrick about Luke breaking into the house, since by then, Patrick didn't own it.

I look down. I did, though only my dad knew as much at the time. Patrick thought my dad owned it.

My dad shrugs. "I think he was looking forward to Luke returning to him to ask for it again, and being able to say that he no longer owned it." He becomes serious. "Patrick is not an easy client, but he's a good one. He generates a lot of revenue and he pays his bills on time. It's not always easy to remember which side my bread is buttered on, but overall, ours has been a profitable relationship."

I caress the envelope. "I thought women only needed husbands."

My dad chuckles. "Maybe in Patrick's world."

"What about Margaret's house? Luke wanted that for Abbie."

My dad frowns. "That will be a more difficult achievement. This property was disposable to Patrick. He doesn't care about it either way. But Margaret's house is very important to him, as he grew up there himself."

"Why wouldn't he want someone living there, then, someone like Abbie?"

Our meals come and we fall silent for a moment, waiting for the waitress to leave again. "The thing you must understand about Patrick is that he loves control. He wants everyone to defer to him about everything. For me, that's comparatively easy. I just call him about every decision, no matter how small, and this makes him happy. For his kids, that's tougher. Of course, they want some autonomy. Of course, they might wish for a few crumbs to fall from his table. I think he wants them to ask, or even to beg."

"I think Abbie knows that."

"Which might be why she never came back. But the very fact that she didn't come back means that he sees her as beyond his control. He doesn't suffer that circumstance well, so he won't be generous to her. She would have to come back and defer to him."

"And even then, it might not matter," I conclude. I can't see Abbie doing that, either way.

"Exactly. I'll try to nudge him on that, but I can't make any promises, Daphne."

"Bread and butter," I say with a smile and he smiles back.

He taps the envelope with a fingertip. "I didn't realize how much of Patrick's view I'd taken onboard, not until Luke challenged me. I'm sorry, Daphne. Of all people, I should have recognized that you needed more than I was offering."

I grip his hand and thank him and he beams at me. My throat is tight with relief and excitement, and the awareness that Luke has provoked a change in my life that I won't soon forget.

————

I WANT to tell Luke but there's no chance. I get back to another lot of questions from the feds and I work though lunch to get it sorted. I see him drive off in Merrie's Jeep in the afternoon but don't see him come back.

I know he'll be on time, though. I leave the office early so that I can have a shower and change before six. I'm jumpy with excitement and anticipation.

I arrive home to find Sylvia on my porch. She has a stubborn look about her, as if she'll wait through the end of time to have her say.

"What's up?" I ask, fingering my keys as I stand on the steps. I have very mixed feelings about her seeking me out. I don't want to think about her and Luke together, even sixteen years ago. I don't really want to think about the complications that are likely to ensue. I want my date night, plain and simple.

"What do you know about it?" Sylvia asks.

"Luke said he seduced you and you left town." I shrug.

Sylvia smiles and looks across the lawn. "Did he tell you he was drunk?"

"He implied that he might have been. Something about Jägermeister."

"Lots of it," Sylvia said. She pats the bench beside herself, her manner so inviting that I have a better feeling about the whole thing. I sit beside her, putting my bag on the porch. I'm expecting her to tell me something I don't know but she still astonishes me. "I was pregnant before that night with Luke."

"What?"

Sylvia nods. "I knew it. Mike and I had been fighting a lot. I wanted –" she sighs "–I wanted him to propose even before I told him. I wanted him to want to marry me without knowing about the baby." She gives me a look. "Our baby."

M.C. = Mike Cavendish. I feel stupid for missing it.

Sierra isn't Luke's daughter.

I'm glad to be sitting down, given the power of my relief.

"We had just fought again when I saw Luke that night. Mike made some comment about Luke being unworthy of being a Cavendish or similar crap. I was already mad at him so I left. And I approached Luke because I was angry, and I went with him, just to be anywhere else. We went to the Foreman place. It was empty and I guess someone was using it to keep a stash of booze. He found the Jäger there, a new bottle. I knew better than to mess with that stuff. It's fierce."

I watch her, thinking how weird it is that I own this building now.

Sylvia sighs. "You have to know that I went with Luke because I felt safe with him, and that never changed. He never came on to me, not at all. That's why when he passed out, I couldn't leave him there. I managed to get him walking and took him home to Una, because I knew she'd know what to do. He barely made it to the house, but Una made him drink a lot of water then tucked him in on the porch. I went to bed. Alone. Not exactly the prom night of my dreams." She frowns and I touch her hand.

"I'm sorry."

"Me, too. But the worst part was that Mike came around in the morning. He was disappointed that I never showed up at the prom, even though I was supposed to be his date. I was mad that he didn't miss me enough to even look for me. He came looking for a fight and he found one. We both said a lot of things." She swallows and looks away, clearly remembering every word.

"There was a lot of resentment between the brothers," I say, wanting to mitigate this for her.

Sylvia shakes her head. "I know, but that argument helped me decide to leave. I had no idea how hard it would be, but once it was done, it was done. I went to my aunt's, in Toronto, and she helped me. After she passed away, I just stayed in the city. I never said anything to anyone about that night, not until now and you."

"But why did you dump the pitcher of water on Luke?"

She smiles. "I thought he was Mike. From behind, they resemble each other. He was sitting with his back to me and I hadn't seen either of them in years. I just saw red. By the time I realized it was Luke, the pitcher was empty." She grimaces. "And then when he wanted to give Merrie the chance she's been dreaming about as long as I've known her, I thought, well, what's the harm in it? Everyone will guess that Sierra is a Cavendish and Mike doesn't want any part of her. Luke will just leave, so no one will be hurt by letting people believe he's her father."

Sylvia shakes her head. "It wasn't right, Daphne, and I'm ashamed that I ever thought it could be. I just wanted to come home again. I was tired of losing everything because I was ashamed, while Mike stayed here and had everything. I missed Empire and I missed Una and so we came back." She looks at me. "I never thought he'd offer to pay child support and want to actually become involved. I mean, we're talking about Luke Jones! He's supposed to be the irresponsible one!"

"He's also the one person in Empire who knows what it's like to have your father deny you," I remind her gently.

Her eyes widen and her voice drops. "Of course. I never thought of that."

We look across the lawn together, a poignant silence between us.

"I'm sorry, Daphne. I owe an apology to you and to Luke. I was just thinking of Sierra." She pauses. "And I was being unkind, without thinking it through." She holds up an envelope that looks familiar. "I can't sign this. I can't accept this. He deserves to know the truth."

"I'm glad you aren't going to leave Luke twisting in the wind."

"Well, that's the other thing. He's arranged for me to be here and I could resent that, but I'm so glad we came. Una is stubborn.

She never told me about her test results, she never wants to impose, but she really needs us here."

I smile because Luke is making things right everywhere he goes.

"So, should I tell him?" Sylvia asks. "Or would you like to do the honours?"

"I think you should tell him. You're the most reliable source of information, after all."

Sylvia nods but doesn't move.

I have to ask. "Are you going to tell Mike?"

She grimaces. "He knows. I wrote him, every year at Christmas and on Sierra's birthdays." Her throat works. "I sent him pictures and told him about her. I thought that even if he didn't really love me, he had to love her. She's so awesome." Her voice is husky. "But he never even answered me, Daphne. Not one reply in almost sixteen years."

"Maybe he didn't get the letters."

"He got them. I called once and asked the housekeeper. Mrs. Wilson." Her lips set. "She even told me to stop bothering him, that he had more important things to do."

"Did you?"

Sylvia's expression is fierce. "No! I kept writing him. And he kept his silence. So, now, here we are, and we have to figure out how to all live in the same town again." Her lips tighten. "It's not going to be easy, but I'm glad to be back. I've missed it. And a childhood here was Sierra's legacy. I gave it up once, but I'm not giving it up again. I'm sick of running and hiding, of being ashamed that I loved so hard and so much that I conceived a child by the man I expected to marry. And if Mike Cavendish has ideas about that, I've got some ideas of what he can do with them."

"If you need any help legally, just let me know."

"Aren't you and your dad in Patrick Cavendish's pocket?"

"Not any more. I'll be setting up on my own, at the old Foreman place." It feels audacious to even say it out loud.

She nods and straightens. "That's good to know. I may need you. Thanks, Daphne." We share a hug, one I sure wasn't expecting when I got home. "Where do I find Luke? He left the café earlier this afternoon and didn't come back. I thought he might be staying here."

"No, he's at the Maple Leaf Motel." I check my watch. It's another hour before he's picking me up, so maybe he is there.

"Okay. Thanks." She gives me another smile, then heads off, walking with purpose toward the end of Forest Drive. No doubt she'll take that shortcut behind the United Church.

Luke isn't Sierra's father.

Luke didn't do the one thing he'd always vowed he wouldn't do.

And yet still, Luke tried to do the right thing. One thing's for sure—I think a lot more of Luke's character than that of his brother, Mike.

Now, I just barely have time for a shower before Luke arrives. Maybe I'll have time to change the sheets, too.

A little optimism never hurt.

———

RIGHT ON TIME, Luke pulls to a stop in my driveway, looking more like trouble than anyone I've ever known. What is it about him? I have to wonder if his effect on me will ever change.

I zip up my jacket and lock the door. He smiles as he surveys me, from my leather jacket to my black boots. I've conjured my best biker-chick-in-leather look and I see that it meets with approval.

"Yet another variation of Daphne Bradshaw," he murmurs.

I lift my hands and turn around to show off. My jeans are

black, just denim not leather, and a slim cut. I'm wearing a charcoal turtleneck under the black leather jacket, just in case it's chilly in the wind. I love these short boots, too, with their pointy toes and spikey heels. Willow calls them my witchy boots.

Luke gives a low whistle, which makes me smile. He has another helmet, a cherry red one, and he helps me to put it on. I see that he has a red helmet, too.

"Borrowed them from Bruno," he says. "He and Marissa ride together." He puts his on, then taps the side by my ear. "Can you hear me?"

"Yes! How do you feel about not being a dad after all?"

He grins. "Relieved. I hated that I could have forgotten something so important." His gaze searches mine and he doesn't have to ask out loud.

"Relieved," I admit. "But proud of you for making that offer."

His eyes gleam. "And you say that when I can't kiss you. Part of a plan, Daph?"

I laugh because I'm supposed to, but I feel lighter and happier than earlier in the day.

Luke straddles the bike then helps me into the seat behind him. It's wonderfully sexy to be crushed right against his butt, my legs wrapped around him. I slide my arms around him and flatten my hands across his chest, my move making him chuckle.

"Behave yourself," he growls. "We need to get there and back in one piece."

"Yes, sir," I say and just hang on as he turns out of my driveway. I feel I've lived a very sheltered life since I've never ridden on a motorcycle before. I've actually never had the urge. Safe Daphne, securely on the straight and narrow path.

Hmm. Even my boyfriends were safe choices, driving safe vehicles, safely to our dates.

No wonder Luke is irresistible. He's exotic.

A little bit dangerous.

And if there's going to be a first time for anything, doing it with Luke is the way to go.

He accelerates as we head out of town and I realize why he likes the bike so much.

It feels like freedom, the wind buffeting us and the bike humming beneath us, the strength of Luke beneath my hands. In a way, it's indecent to be wrapped around him like this, and in another way, it's primal and just perfect.

It's addictive, just like he is.

He turns into the parking lot of a little restaurant on the other side of Havelock far too soon for me. It looks like a casual Italian place and smells really good. Wood-fired pizzas are advertised on the sign. I reluctantly get off the bike and when I take off the helmet, the clip comes out of my hair. Luke bends to retrieve it for me, then smiles down at me.

"Now you're a siren," he murmurs, brushing his lips across mine. He looks into my eyes and smiles, his own glowing. "Leave it down?"

"Your wish is my command," I joke and he grins. "Maybe you've let the djinn out of the jar."

"Careful, Daph," he growls. "You could end up in dangerous territory." He doesn't wait for an answer, just grabs my hand, and I match my step to his.

I'm thinking that there's nowhere else I'd rather go, at least not if I can go with Luke.

Going with the flow is all new for me, but I like it.

I could even get used to it.

20

———

LUKE

A date.

An actual date.

How long has it been? Truth be told, I'm not sure I've ever gone on a date. It's just been hook-up after hook-up for all of my adult life, and while I liked that just fine at the time, I'm ready for something different.

Ha. Maybe I'm becoming an adult.

Maybe Daph is good for me.

Either way, I knew this had to be the place. My mom and I usually come here when I'm in town. It's one of her favourites and with good cause. Family-owned for a couple of generations, good food at good prices, friendly and clean. I like that Daph is a little unpredictable tonight, maybe feeling punch-drunk like I am after Sylvia's confession.

I still want to have Sierra's back. I still want to support that kid, whatever she has to face in town. But I am relieved that she's not mine. I feel that I can start fresh with Daph.

And there's something different between us tonight, something electric and powerful. It shouldn't be this way. We've been together already. One-and-done should have killed the tingle of anticipation. There shouldn't be any mysteries left.

But there are. There are thousands of them, just waiting to be unravelled.

The theory that she could be The One is gaining ground.

How is it that I had no clue she looked like a goddess in jeans and boots? How could I not anticipate how she would wrap herself around me on the bike, shifting her weight instinctively, like we'd been riding together for years? How can it take my breath away when her hair tumbles in auburn waves halfway down her back? Her eyes glow when she looks at me, and I feel astonished by her all over again. She's beautiful and smart and mischievous, both logical and passionate. I'm so honoured that she's with me, and I never want that awe to vanish.

Tonight, she's the bold twin of the sleek professional I've been seeing at the office. She's tougher and more urban than the enticingly soft—but fierce—woman who seduced me that first time at her house. How many thousands of women are part of Daphne Bradshaw? How long will it take me to meet them all?

We sit at a corner table, our knees bumping underneath, and just talk. It's easy, the conversation flowing readily. I tell her about progress at the café, then show her some pictures on my phone. I tell her about Noah's pitch and love that I can make her laugh so hard. She tells me about Mike keeping the news of my arrest from Patrick and I'm surprised.

We share a big salad and a pizza that's ridiculously good. I pass on the wine because I couldn't bear to make a mistake on the drive home and she has water, too.

I'm more surprised when she tells me about her dad buying the Foreman place and giving it to her. I never imagined I could have any influence over someone like Richard Bradshaw, but I think it's his love for his daughter that's driving everything.

I'd love to have had a dad like that.

I want to *be* a dad like that.

"You look concerned," she says, not missing a thing.

"It's Sierra," I admit.

"Aren't you relieved?"

"Yes and no. I know how it might be for her in Empire." I falter to silence, unable to put the tumult I'm feeling into words.

Daph's hand closes over mine. "And you feel protective of her."

"How can you know that?"

"It's what you do." She smiles. "I admire that."

"But she's not my daughter."

"That doesn't mean you can't be friends. That doesn't mean that she can't count on you for anything."

"Why would she?"

"Maybe because you offer."

It's such a simple solution, yet one that makes perfect sense. "She can choose."

Daph smiles a mysterious little smile.

"What? What did I say?"

"It's another thing you do that I like a lot. You let women choose." She sits back, that little smile making me want to chuck her over my shoulder and carry her away. "It's very hot, by the way."

I look away to regain control over the direction of my thoughts, something that cannot happen when my gaze is locked with Daph's and she's smiling like that. She shouldn't be allowed to say things like that to me in a public place, but on one level, I appreciate how much she enjoys provoking me.

When I look at her again, she's the one averting her gaze, pushing around the last piece of pizza, the one that neither of us want. "Are there others?" she asks quietly, her gaze lifting to mine, and I have to respect that she asked the tough question.

"Not that I know of. I suppose it's not impossible." I lean closer. "But I'll do the same as this time, if I learn otherwise."

She nods with welcome confidence. "I know. You're nice, Luke."

Nice?

"I am not nice," I reply. "I've never been nice and I don't want to be nice."

"What then?" She's teasing me, but I'll play. Anything to bring back any one of her smiles.

"How do you think the band got its name?"

"Mad, Bad & Dangerous 2 Know."

"That's what Taylor called me."

"You don't seem that dangerous to me."

"Maybe I'm getting over it. Maybe I want to be something else."

"Like?"

"Honourable," I say on a whim, the first word that rises to my lips, but it's right. I follow impulse and say the next bit. "And maybe one day, a good dad."

Her brows rise.

"You can't change the past, Daph. But you can own it, and you can take what you've learned to change the future."

"They write songs about that."

"Michael Jackson. *Man in the Mirror*. Too high for me but a solid strategy." I scroll through my playlist on my phone, noticing how much it's changed, then add that one.

Daph turns her head to read it. "Simple Minds *Alive & Kicking*," she says. "R.E.M. *Stand*. Dream Academy. *Life in a Northern Town*."

"Love the chorus," I say. "Serious earworm, though. It should have a warning label."

"What's that?" she asks, noticing what I'd rather she didn't.

"Nothing."

"Not nothing. That's my name."

Do I have a playlist for when I'm thinking of Daph. Yes, yes I do. Don't shoot. I sigh, open it and let her look.

"Fine Young Cannibals. *She Drives Me Crazy*." I get a smile for that one. "Roxy Music. *More Than This*. Berlin. *Take My Breath Away*. Chris de Burgh. *Lady in Red*." She gives me a look. "I don't wear red."

"It's the sentiment, not the technicalities."

She smiles a little, letting me have that one. "Roy Orbison. *Pretty Woman*."

"Mercy," I murmur and we smile at each other for a long hot moment.

"Tracy Chapman. *Give Me One Reason*."

I get a searching look for that one before she gives me back my phone and our fingers brush. "I, uh, don't suppose you have a playlist for me."

It can't hurt to ask, right?

"Just one song." She leans back in the booth, as inscrutable as ever. "The one you sing to someone at the end."

"Used to sing to someone." I feel the need to correct her on that.

She studies me, her eyes darkening as her voice softens. "I can't be the only one who ever wondered what it would be like."

I am struck dumb that Daph could have ever been thinking of me—but in a good way.

She's watching me, probably reading me like a book but I can't guess her thoughts. "My dad calls you my young man," she says.

I have to smile. "I would have expected him to call me something else."

Daph shakes her head, her eyes shining. "He likes you."

"No accounting for taste," I say, just to make her laugh and it does. We're high on each other and that makes me think of Taylor.

I tell her a few more stories about him and she holds my hand when my throat tightens.

"I'm proud of you," she says softly and I feel like my heart will burst.

"Your fault," I say, my voice husky. "You make me want to do better."

"You know, this might be the wrong thing to say," she begins.

"Go for it, Daph."

"But Patrick might have done you a huge favour."

"Never!" I protest but she shakes her head.

"Think about it. He could have married your mom, and you wouldn't have been able to escape him."

Bloody hell. She's right.

"Maybe I should send flowers," I say and she laughs.

We do that thing of smiling at each other for a thousand years, then the waitress brings the bill, breaking the spell. We're heading out, her hand in mine, when the owner steps forward. They've recognized me and want autographs and selfies. Daph nods and steps aside, watching as I do the honours. It doesn't take long and they're very nice, leaving Daph out of the whole thing when I ask them to. We wave goodnight and head back to the bike, where she pulls me to a halt.

"You're so good at that," she says.

"At what?"

"At talking to people. At just owning the moment. You're genuine and approachable, and so gracious. Don't you get tired of fans approaching you?"

"They weren't being intrusive. Most of the band's fans are like that. And they're the whole reason the band was a success."

"It's in your interest to indulge them?"

"More than that. It's a small gesture. I don't mind."

"I like how you do it. They were nervous, but you put them at ease so quickly." She smiles. "Like that interview you did with

Noah. You spoke so fluidly, like you knew what to say. Do you rehearse ahead of time?"

"No, of course not," I say but as soon as the words leave my mouth, I realize that she would. "It's another way that we're different, Daph. You plan."

"And you just jump," she says with a smile.

I pull her into my arms, loving this mutual admiration society, wanting her to smile again. "So, maybe I'll take some tips from you and learn to think ahead a bit more."

Daph catches her breath, her gaze falling to my mouth before she looks into my eyes again. "And I can be a little more impulsive," she suggests, her voice husky. Before I can reply, she leans against me, sliding her hands up my chest and throat, into my hair, then pulling my mouth down to hers. She kisses me with a power that makes me dizzy, her tongue wicked and seductive, the taste and feel of her enough to dismiss everything from my world but her.

I break the kiss with an effort and ease her hair back from her cheek with a fingertip. "We still have to get home," I remind her and her smile flashes.

"Your place or mine?"

"Yours," I say because a motel is a motel and that's not what I want with Daph. She nods and we climb on the bike, her arms wrapped around me and her heat against my back.

This is the good stuff.

And I still want more.

In fact, I realize as we approach Empire, I want it all. That's new, but it's still true.

That makes this more than a courtship: it's a new adventure.

———

IT'S FAST THIS TIME, because Daph is a tigress. Once again, I'm seeing another side of her and I'm completely beguiled. We do it twice, barely making it to the bedroom for the first time, then again actually in the bed.

Then she rolls over to look at me, her hair a tangle and her cheeks flushed. "What's it like?" she asks.

"What?" I'm stretched out beside her, wondering if a third time is in the cards. I slide my hand down the length of her, then leave it resting on the indent of her waist. I let my thumb trace circles against the softness of her stomach, having noticed how much she likes that.

She practically purrs.

"Having fangirls. Being the stuff of fantasies." She pauses for a moment. "Man-candy."

I snort. "I don't think about it much."

"You have to. All those women throwing their lingerie at you."

Does she imagine that she'll ever have any competition? If that's her concern, I have to put it to rest.

"Okay, maybe I used to think about it. It meant I tried to stay fit, but on tour, that's a given. Beyond that, it just was." I shrug, then gives me a look. "You must attract your share of attention from guys."

She winces. "When it's based on looks alone, I don't like it. I feel objectified, like a piece of meat."

I get that. "But you *look*," I say. "I look. Everyone looks. It's part of the mating process."

"It shouldn't be the sum of it, though."

"Of course not." I bend down so our eyes are level. "But I like you so I look more. It's not just about appearances. It's about the whole package."

"What do you mean?"

"That smile, for example." I touch the corner of her mouth with a fingertip. "There's a whole lot of innuendo in that smile. It's not just that you have the most luscious mouth ever. It's that expression, like you have a secret that's not at all what I expect. So, when you smile like that–" I take a deep breath and exhale. "I want to kiss you. I want to ravish you, actually, and when you do it in public, you destroy me completely."

She looks pleased by this so I'm on the right track. "You're not without your own arsenal, you know."

"Like what?"

"You don't mind me admiring your assets?"

"I'd love to be your man-candy, Daph. Look away. Tell me what you like—and what needs work. I can't imagine anything better than being the stuff of your fantasies." Her eyes are dark, his gaze so intent that I wonder if she's guessed that she owns my fantasies. Every single one.

I should tell her.

Maybe I already did, in a way. She did see the Daph playlist.

She runs a fingertip down my arm from elbow to wrist, watching its progress. "I like your forearms," she admits.

This is not what I was expecting. "Go *on*."

"No, really." She flattens her hand and strokes across my skin, then her fingertip gets lost in the labyrinth of my tattoo. "Just the right amount of hair. Muscled. Tanned."

"Glad to hear it," I say, aware of the tumult she's stirring within me. A third time is a definite possibility.

She threads her fingers between mine. "And these are hands that get things done."

I smile at the approval in her tone. "Is that right? Tell me more."

She tips her head back to consider me. "I like your eyelashes."

I laugh at that, then stop as she reaches up and pushes her hand through my hair. It's a proprietary gesture, a bit rough, and feels good.

"I like that your hair is a bit long, a bit unruly. And the colour of it." Her fingertip slides down my neck to my shoulder, then down the middle of my chest, vanishing in my chest hair. She nods approval as she walks her fingers down my torso. "I like the six-pack."

"Good thing I started working out again."

She flattens her hand again, her palm spanning my hip, and there's a definite sign of my enthusiasm. "But the vee," she whispers. "The vee is very good stuff." And she bends over me, touching her lips to my hip. Her hair falls over me, all silken softness, and I have to close my eyes to get control again.

When I open them, she's watching me, sultry and seductive.

"I'm glad to hear you approve of the packaging," I manage to say. "It bodes good results for the courtship."

She parts her lips and I think she's going to say something, maybe make a confession that I can echo, but she closes her eyes and sighs, and the moment passes.

Damn. What did I miss out on?

And why?

21

DAPHNE

Could there have been a worse moment to realize that I'm in love?

No and no.

It was that word, courtship, the way it makes me think of Jane Austen novels and wedding bells, of people pledging their undying love to each other. If Luke hadn't said that word, I might not have realized how much I want him to stay, how being in the moment is great but falls short of what I want.

I've been making love. Is he just having sex?

It's a question that doesn't fade away.

When I bite back on my confession, he knows I'm holding back something. There's a tension between us that wasn't there before, but I don't want it gone badly enough to confess the truth.

Somewhere there's a song about how much it bites to be alone in love.

I could ask Luke, but then he'd know my secret.

I have to smile at his comment about me approving of the packaging. He is gorgeous, but I know that it's not any of these things that make me love Luke Jones. Because I do love him. The package made me look; it might even have made me want. But it's the man inside who has stolen my heart. I love how Luke defends what he cares about, how he's determined to do the right thing, how much he wants to make the world a better place. I love that he's not afraid to take a chance, that he doesn't worry about the cost to himself when he decides that something needs to be done. The man is an open book, completely lacking in guile: if he says a thing, he believes it. The vee is good stuff, but it didn't make me love him.

"Your turn," I says, trying to keep it light.

He rolls me to my back, bracing his weight over me. His gaze sweeps down and even that sultry look makes me arch my back a little, wanting.

"I love your eyes," he confesses. "And how they reveal your thoughts."

"Windows to the soul?"

"If you only knew," he teases and one more time, I wonder how much he has guessed.

Then he bends close and touches his lips to my earlobe. "I like this here, how soft it is under your ear." He kisses it, then grazes the lobe with his teeth so gently that I tremble. I think of butterflies here causing hurricanes on the other side of the world. "And I love how you shiver when I touch you there."

His breath is warm on my skin, his fingertips sliding up my spine to my nape. I deliberately shut down my thoughts, close my eyes and enjoy. "I love the back of your neck. When you twist up your hair, it feels like seeing a secret." He kisses me there, his hands closing over my shoulders and pulling me back against his chest. He rolls to his back with me on top of him. I squeal in protest and he chuckles darkly. His hands slide around me and cup my breasts. "You know I like these, in lingerie or not." He eases his thumbs across my nipples and they stand up to salute.

"I think they like you, too," I say, a little breathless. Then I'm on my back on the bed again, Luke leaning over me with his hair tousled and a glint in his eyes that makes my heart skip. I watch his smile turn wicked, then I'm staring into the dark tangle of his hair as he bends to kiss one nipple. I catch my breath at the sensation.

"Too much?" he murmurs against my skin.

"Never," I say with heat. He flicks my nipple with his tongue and I shiver.

"I like how fierce you are when you take a cause," he murmurs against my skin. "I like how you're determined to do what's right, and I like that I find that infectious." He straightens and cups my head in his palms smiling as he looks into my eyes. "I like you, Daphne Bradshaw, and I like that I have so much more to learn about you."

"I like that about you, too," I admit, then he leans closer and I forget everything but his touch.

———

"I WAS LOOKING FORWARD to testing the counter," I say on my way to the bathroom much later.

Luke is right behind me and I feel the weight of his gaze.

"Drapes," he says with authority and I turn to look at him.

"What is this obsession you have with window treatments?"

His eyes narrow a little and I know that this is important to him. "You saw tonight how people recognize me and they want pictures. Fans are fine. Fans are great. They respect your boundaries. Professional photographers, not so much. It's been a long time since paparazzi followed us, but I won't have your privacy compromised."

His protectiveness always prompts a flood of heat in me. That it's for me this time means he earns a kiss. It's longer than planned, but that's all good. "There you go, being sweet again," I tease when we're done.

"It's not a joke, Daph. Once your privacy is gone, you can't get it back."

"But still the counter fantasies persist." I sigh. "I guess I'll go shopping for blinds tomorrow. Want to come along?"

But Luke shakes his head. "I have to help Merrie in the morning, then I want to talk to Sierra." He gives me a quick glance in the mirror, like a warning.

I straighten and look back, warned but uncertain of what.

"And while we're on the topic, Merrie's opening night." He bends over the sink and has to be deliberately avoiding my gaze. "Come to dinner with me."

"At Merrie's?"

"Of course. It's the launch of The Carpe Diem Café, the culmination of our partnership, the whole reason that we started to work together."

This does not sound romantic. It does not jive with the idea of courtship, given his tone.

"A business dinner then," I say, hoping to be corrected that it's a date.

"A celebration," Luke says. "A triumph." He nods at his reflection, then considers his beard.

And I understand. He's leaving right afterward. It won't be a date because it'll be the end of whatever is between us. The moment we've been enjoying is coming to an end.

Maybe it's better that way.

Maybe it will hurt less if it happens sooner rather than later.

Maybe there's nothing saying I can't turn it into one last stupendously fabulous date. I discover that I'm not quite so ready to accept what is offered and be content.

But then there's Rafe.

"I already have a friend coming from Toronto for it," I admit, and now I'm the one avoiding his gaze. "And I asked Mackenzie to join us. Should I change the reservation to a table for four?"

He turns and stares at me, but there's no satisfaction in surprising Luke this time.

I raise a brow. "Meet you there at six?"

"No," he says flatly, grabbing a towel. "I'll pick you up at five forty-five."

He doesn't stay the rest of the night but I really didn't expect otherwise.

I can regret it, though, and I do.

22

LUKE

I don't sleep. Even the music isn't haunting me. All I can do is review that moment when Daph slid away. There's something truly brutal about feeling that you're on the same proverbial page, that everything's coming together, then having the rug pulled out from under your feet.

What's worrying her?

What did I do or not do?

How weird is it that what I hoped would be a great date at Merrie's will have me eating dinner with Daph and two other women? That's seriously not what I had planned, but her friend is coming and making a fuss isn't going to win me any points.

I get up early because I'm not sleeping anyway and do a workout in my room but it's not enough. There is no music in my brain to tease me. I dig out the pair of running shoes I bought at the thrift store and go for a run. Merrie has equipment arriving this morning and I promised to help out, but first I need to think.

Daph strategizes. I don't. What issue would a planner have with our relationship?

That's so obvious that I could kick myself. I have no plan for the future, and Daph would be the first to realize as much. Plus I told her I was leaving Empire ASAP.

She's trying to protect herself—from me.

What does my future without Daph look like?

Not promising. I'm not interested in that prospect.

What does a future look like with us together?

That's tougher. It looks a lot like Empire for the long haul. Daph has a house. She has a commercial building now and will be building her own practice. She's staying, which means if I want to be with her, I'm staying.

No wonder she's concerned. I could kick myself again. I get so lost in the now, and in her, that I forget completely about tomorrow. Enough of that.

Time to lift my game.

I think about the music and the band, how ambition once drove me to greater heights. I remember a year of desolation after Taylor's death, a year with no plans or goals, a year of languishing with no objectives or energy. It was sheer hell. I don't want that again.

I run to Port Cavendish and stop on the pier, looking out across the silver mirror that is Lake Erie. The sun is rising and there are a few other people out, mostly walking dogs. One lab is leaping into the lake, despite being called back to the beach.

I think of how coming back to Empire was like being hit by lightning. Or maybe that was meeting Daph again. I think about how much I've enjoyed the last few weeks, the sense of purpose, the conviction that I was a part of something bigger than myself.

It's like the band but better. Much better.

It matters more than the band ever did.

I want more of that, too. And that kicks my brain into gear. What does the future look like with both Empire and Daph in it? What could I do here? What would feed my sense of purpose and fulfillment?

My first idea is so perfect that is seems inevitable, but I let it simmer while I consider the variables. Taylor, Taylor, was this your plan all along?

When I eventually jog back into Empire, I give Queen Street a hard look. Merrie's going to have a hard time building success here.

Maybe my quest has only just begun.

Maybe the challenge of invigorating Empire is what I need.

I am, if you must know, excited by how huge this idea could become.

In front of The Golden Lotus, Phil is helping his mom into a mobility van. I stop, stretching while I wait to talk to him. He waves as the van leaves and comes over. "It's her day at the seniors' centre in Havelock," he explains, waving again as the van passes the gas station. His mom is at the window, waving her heart out. "They have programming for people with dementia, and I get a chance to run some errands."

"It's great that you could come back here for her."

He's watching the van fade from view. "I'm glad I can do it. My brother's going to come down for some weekends this summer and help out." He turns and gives me a smile. "You're up early."

"Thinking."

"Running is good for that. I love when I can get out." He tells me about a couple of new trails, including one built along the old railway line in Port Cavendish, where the tracks were taken out.

"Can you tell me what isn't owned by Patrick on Queen Street?" I ask.

Phil exhales and his gaze goes to the end of the street. "Jim's Antiques, and now the Carpe Diem Café." I follow his finger as he continues down the north side toward us and Big Red. "The post office. The churches, both of them. The thrift store and the convenience store rent from him." He skips past the Foreman place, but I know it's Daph's now. "The Legion. The Grand Hotel. I own The Golden Lotus." He turns to look down the street to the right.

"The Odeon Theatre. Richard owns his law office. The Petro Canada station. Oh, and Bruno owns The Maple Leaf Motel."

"Who owns the Odeon?" I have the inescapable sense that everything is coming together. I don't want to spook the universe so I try to disguise my interest.

"Nate Thompson inherited it, wanted to sell it but couldn't, then refused to sell it to Patrick."

"I like him already," I say in an undertone and Phil laughs.

"Don't you remember him?" Phil continues without waiting for a reply. "Oh, no, you wouldn't. He has to be five years younger than you. It was his older sister I knew a bit."

"And where do I find him?"

"Mountain View or Cupertino. Somewhere in California anyway." Phil nods. "He was a genius boy wonder and big tech called his name. Why?"

"Think he'd sell me the theatre?"

That gets his full attention. "You're staying then."

"I'm thinking about it."

Phil nods once, then pulls out his phone. "I think I have his deets from organizing the reunion two years ago. Yeah, here he is." He gives me Nate's contact info. "Let me know how it shakes out."

"I will." I turn to run back to the motel. "Oh, and don't tell anyone anything yet. I want it to be a surprise."

Phil grins and waves. "You got it."

I jog backwards. "See you at Merrie's on Thursday?"

"I wouldn't miss it. Mom and I have an early dinner reservation. Merrie is going to slide us in at five, before it gets busy."

I give him a thumbs-up, and head back to the hotel, ideas sparking like quicksilver. I need to start making lists and calls and soon.

———

I CATCH up to Sylvia's Subaru just as she parks in front of the café. Sierra is in the passenger seat, her backpack slung into the back, and I remember Merrie saying that Sierra was going to be commuting back to Toronto each week to finish up the school year there.

"What's up?" Sylvia asks when she gets out of the car.

"I want to talk to Sierra."

Sylvia gives me a look. "I told her already."

"I figured that, but I want to tell her something, too."

Sylvia looks between us, undoubtedly noting that Sierra looks disinclined to listen to me, and heads into the café. Sierra gets out of the car with obvious reluctance, her earbuds still in.

"I don't have to talk to you," is her opener.

"No, you don't."

She is as prickly as a hedgehog. Her expression is mutinous and she's poised to flee. She doesn't want to talk to me and that message is received, loud and clear. "So, you're not my dad after all."

"Nope." I come around the car and lean on the front quarter panel while she glares at me.

"Are you sure?"

"No, but I believe your mom."

Her eyes narrow with suspicion. "Why aren't you sure?"

"Do you really want me to give you a TED talk on the perils of excess alcohol consumption?"

That makes her smile, grudgingly, but I'll call it a win. "No."

She's not satisfied, though, and I get it. "I'll take a paternity test if you want to be sure."

"You would?"

I nod and she studies me intently. It's so weird to see an echo of myself in her, all the defiance and fury. I really want to make her story different from mine, though I'm not sure how to do that.

"Why?" she demands.

"Sometimes it's good to know things, even if it isn't going to make any difference to anything."

"But why? If you're not my dad, why would you care what I want?"

"Well, I'm probably your uncle."

Her lips tighten and I cede that it's not a very compelling argument. You don't believe in the power of family when half of your kin would like you to vanish from the face of the earth.

I try to save it. "More importantly than that, I know what it's like to grow up in Empire, looking like a Cavendish but not being acknowledged as a Cavendish." She peers at me then, intrigued despite herself. "I'm the one person here who knows what it will be like for you, and so, I think it would be good for us to be friends."

"Friends?" Ah, the lip curl is so artful that I smile.

"I know. Impossible with an old man like me."

"Creepy," she says, stepping around me. She doesn't leave though, just folds her arms across her chest, waiting.

"Allies, maybe," I offer.

She shrugs. "Maybe."

"The thing is that I don't know anything about being a dad, seeing as I didn't ever have one. And I don't know much more about being an uncle, for the same reason." I hold her gaze. "But I know how to be a friend."

She gives me a side-eye. "You and me, friends? Don't you think some people would assume that was a little twisted?"

"I suppose, though I don't have any nefarious intentions. Do you really worry that much about what other people think?"

"Don't you?"

"I worry about the opinions of people I care about. The rest of them can go to hell."

She purses her lips, considering me and the possibilities. "You could be my non-dad."

"Like a dad, but not quite."

She nods. "Nothing twisted."

"A Norman Rockwell non-dad," I say and she nods. "All right. That works for me."

She smiles, but she's not amused. She's showing me her snaggle tooth and points to it in case I miss it. "I need braces, non-dad."

"Just jump right in and speak your mind," I say and this time she really laughs.

"Well, why not? I have exactly nothing to lose."

And now I grin because I know that feeling. "There is that."

"Mom said you used to be a bad kid."

"More like a rebel without a cause. Although come to think of it, I did have a cause."

"Do you know who your dad is?"

"Yes. I've always known, but it never made any difference to anything." I stop then correct myself. "Not any good difference, anyway."

"Because he never admitted that you were his."

"That's it."

She folds her arms across her chest. "Kind of like my dad."

"See? Common ground." I offer a fist and to my amazement, she bumps it with hers.

"Tell me something bad you did."

"What, I'm supposed to inspire you?" I feign indignation and she giggles, looking younger than she has thus far.

"I need to calibrate you, on a scale from scumbag to guardian angel."

"Right. Of course. Is this a non-dad credential?"

"If it isn't, it should be."

I like this kid. I like her enough that I wish she *was* my kid.

Because of that, I tell her.

"Okay, when I was in high school, we were supposed to play team sports. I didn't mind soccer, but I hated hockey."

"They can take your passport away for that," she deadpans.

"God, don't tell anybody then," I reply and we grin at each other.

She comes to lean beside me. "Why didn't you like it?"

"I like my teeth right where they are, thanks, and my brains unscrambled. I like hockey when it's not about enforcers, the way Gretzsky played." She nods agreement. "But I had this coach who really wanted me to play, who insisted on it, so I composed a letter." I have left out the bit about always getting thumped on the ice, either by a Cavendish or a friend of a Cavendish. I was targeted and no one intervened.

Is there a more lonely place to be?

Is there a better way to learn that you can't rely on anyone but yourself?

I doubt it, and I don't want Sierra to learn that lesson.

"A letter? How is that bad?" Sierra frowns and shakes her head, not understanding.

"Well, it wasn't just any letter. I stole some letterhead from Cavendish Enterprises and I wrote up a letter as if it was from someone else." I raise my voice as if quoting said letter. "*To whom it may concern: My son, Luke Jones, is hereby excused from the playing of any team sports, including hockey, by my express stipulation. If he is compelled to do so, I will ensure that all co-op education opportunities between the school system and Cavendish Enterprises are eliminated immediately. I will also embark upon legal proceedings as appropriate. Cordially, Patrick Cavendish.*"

"You didn't?" Sierra says in awe and I nod.

"I did. It was a really good copy of his signature, too."

"He's your dad?"

I nod again.

"What happened?"

"What didn't happen? Everything went boom. There was a lot of yelling. I was expelled for a term and when I came back, I had to play hockey, after all."

"What did you think would happen?"

"Well, I was fifteen, so I didn't know crap, but I thought maybe if I called him out, Patrick might contribute something in terms of support." I also leave out the bit that he married another woman, when my mom was pregnant with yours truly. "You see, my paternity was the great unspoken secret. Everyone knew he was my dad, but no one talked about it, and he never admitted it. I was tired of being invisible." I take a breath. "And I was tired of the way people talked to my mom. It takes two to make a baby."

"Huh." She thinks about this. "Was it worth it?"

"Yeah. I shouldn't say it, but I loved pissing off Patrick. It didn't make any difference in the end, but I am—or was—sufficiently petty that I enjoyed that bit."

She considers me for a long moment. "Do you think it's worse to know who your dad is or to not know?"

"I don't know. Both suck."

"Dad's breakfast," she mutters. "Days when we talk about our parents' careers. Days when parents come to school for whatever. Graduations. All those times that you're supposed to have two parents, not one. They all suck. At least if he was dead, you'd have that."

I get it. "So, okay, a non-dad can step up, if you like."

"Really?"

"Really. Been there and done that. If I can make sure you don't have to, that's all good."

"Even though you're not my dad."

"A non-dad kindred spirit."

She snorts but there's a glimmer in her eyes that means I'm wearing her down. "How does that work since you're not staying here?"

Trust Sierra to call me on that.

"I might stay." There. I said it out loud and the world didn't end.

"And if you don't, what? I call you in Berlin when I need a hand?"

"You could. Not everything is urgent. There are tech solutions."

I can almost hear the wheels turning as she weighs the possibilities. "And what else do non-dads do?"

"Talk. Listen. Share experiences." I shake my head. "You do know that I am making this up as we go along, since I've never had the honour of being a non-dad before."

That makes her smile. "Teach me to ride your motorcycle."

I laugh, because she's a born negotiator. "That's up to your mom and probably has to wait a few years." I think of a counteroffer. "I can teach you to play the guitar, though."

"All right," she says, to my surprise. "But I'm staying with my friend Lila in Toronto each week until the end of classes, then she's coming here."

"Aren't you coming back on weekends?"

"Yes. On the bus. It's kind of cool."

I know she means taking the bus alone, because there's not much cool about the old bus that limps from Toronto to Havelock and back a couple of times a day.

"Saturdays then," I say on impulse. "On Una's front porch so someone can watch over us and make sure there's nothing creepy going on."

Her eyes light up. "Deal."

"You have a guitar?"

"No." She's wary again, suspecting that I'll renege.

"I'll lend you one of mine, but if you bust it, you're buying it." This is nonsense. I'll buy another guitar, and if she has any interest, she can keep it.

"Okay!" For a heartbeat, I see a little girl, all optimism and excitement, then the jaded teen is back. She bolts into the restaurant, moving a little too quickly to disguise her reaction. I'm getting up to leave when I realize that Sylvia is hovering inside the door. From the look on her face, she's been listening.

"Thank you, Luke," she says softly and I nod. "Maybe what you'll be is a mentor."

I look at her, surprised but liking the sound of it. "Maybe. And if you ever want me to talk to Mike, let me know. It wouldn't be the first time we disagreed about anything."

"It's my war, Luke, but thank you." And she gives me a hug, a sweet platonic hug, and I know irrevocably that we've never been this close before. My body is indifferent to the feel of Sylvia and the scent of her, and that's a good thing.

Instead of one-and-done, I've become a one-and-only guy, and that suits me just fine.

I'm also a man with a mission.

Stand back.

23

DAPHNE

Is it the end or the beginning? Two weeks after Merrie's arrival in town, The Carpe Diem Café has its soft opening. Friends and fans, interested townspeople, anyone whose curiosity was piqued by Noah's coverage of the biggest event in Empire in years will be crowding through the door. No doubt the bistro will be full. The menu is posted outside the door and I've watched people stop to look all week long. There's a building sense of excitement that can't be ignored.

I've been watching for Luke, as you might have guessed, but he might as well have left town already. I haven't caught one glimpse of him.

I tell myself I'd better get used to it.

He has sent me several messages a day. Sometimes, they're links to new interviews with him or with Merrie. One day, there was a feature in a Toronto daily on the new café. Sometimes, they're pictures of the interior coming together, or photos of Merrie's recipe testing. I came back from an errand to Havelock to find several wonderful sandwiches on my desk Tuesday and Mrs. Prescott looking like judgement. My dad had already demolished his and cheerfully recommended the honey-baked ham on olive bread with Merrie's muffuletta olive relish and provolone cheese. I called Luke to thank him, got his voice mail and left a message. Later, he sent me an emoji of a smiling face with a heart.

That gave me something to think about. What did he mean?

I've beaten myself up trying to find ideas to launch my own practice, but have come up empty. Even the property taxes on the building look daunting, given the lack of renters and my prospects of generating revenue.

I miss Luke a thousand times more than I expected.

There's no point being grumpy about it, as he'll be leaving any day now. Will it be easier to miss him without any chance of seeing him? Probably not. (This week hasn't been a treat.) But I'm not going to be the one who tries to hold him back. I love him, and that means I want him to be happy.

Even if it means he leaves.

On the other hand, there's Thursday night, which is one last chance to drag him home and have my way with him.

We don't have a Wednesday girls' night this week. Sometimes things don't align and this week is one of those occasions. Cameron is working nights, and Willow is trying to pull together some last details at The Carpe Diem Café. Mackenzie decides to work late —no surprise—so I have time to plan for success.

I'm going to seize the day myself—or the night.

I'm going to play this to win, with no regrets.

———

VICTORIA DAY WEEKEND is the unofficial kick-off to summer in my corner of the world. It's a long weekend, the one closest to May 24, which was Queen Victoria's birthday. Cottages are opened for the season on this weekend, campers and tents get their first taste of the summer action. Boats are launched onto lakes and canoes get their first dip of the year. Barbeques are fired up and beaches are visited. There are picnics and outside sports and there is beer. Some people call it May Two-Four, a reference to the standard case of twenty-four bottles of beer (a two-four in Canadian) because so many of them are sold for this weekend's celebrations.

I leave work early. My dad has already gone for a golf game and I send Mrs. Prescott home at two. There's not much happening anyway and I want some prep time. It's a little inconvenient that Rafe has invited himself down for the dinner, but at least he isn't staying at my place. (I would never let him. I know what a mess he would make.)

I take the dress out of the spare room closet, where it's been biding its time alongside my wedding dress, and admire it all over again. I bought it in Vancouver in a shop that Abbie loves, and it's been waiting on me ever since. It's made of silk, in a gorgeous deep teal, a colour I would never have chosen but one that Abbie (and the sales clerk) insisted was perfect for me. It has a slim, kind of vintage cut, with a straight skirt and a neckline that swoops low. It's sleeveless, the straps leaving my shoulders mostly bare and my upper back exposed. It has a matching jacket, a cropped one that ends above the waist and has three-quarter sleeves.

It says glamour and it says it loud.

I love it to pieces.

I haven't had anywhere to wear it—I bought it after moving back to Empire, on my trip to visit Abbie and mourn everything—but this will be the night.

I shower and powder and moisturize, touching up my nail polish, too. I sweep up my hair and choose bolder colours for my make-up than usual. I add a necklace my mom bought for me. It's dark pearls mixed with beads, all strung on wire so fine that the necklace looks like a sparkling constellation, one that defies gravity.

I had to buy a new bra to wear with this dress because of the lower back. I ended up with a merry widow in black lace, which is just about the sexiest garment I've ever owned. It's a date virgin, though, as I've never put it on before tonight.

Maybe it was waiting for Luke.

It makes me look like a pin-up. With sheer black stockings—they have a center-back seam, too—there won't be any doubt what's on my mind. I'm not usually so blatant, but it feels good to be audacious.

I don't care why Luke comes home with me tonight. I just want him to do it.

We'll end in triumph.

It's not raining and even though it's a couple of blocks to the restaurant, I choose my newest most fabulous heels. They're black satin slingbacks with pointed toes. I consider myself in the mirror, little black clutch in hand, and know I've gone right over the top.

I don't care. I love to dress up.

The doorbell rings and I make my way down the stairs, my heart taking a skip at Luke's familiar silhouette. When I open the door, though, I can only stare. It's Luke but not Luke, Luke polished to a gleam. He's wearing a dark suit that is impeccably tailored, a crisp white shirt and a perfectly knotted tie. He's shaved and I think he's even had his hair trimmed. He looks expensive and still looks dangerous, and his eyes light when his gaze sweeps over me.

I feel a little bit faint, my girl bits all a-flutter.

"Good," he growls with approval. "I was worried I'd over-dressed."

It's got to be a lie. The man never worries about anything.

Before I can find my voice, he steps closer. "I know you were disappointed in me, Daph," he says with heat, his gaze searching mine. "And I think I know why. I've been working on that this week." The corner of his mouth lifts. "I'd like to argue my own case tonight, counsellor."

Oh, I like the sound of that.

"Okay," I whisper.

"Okay," he agrees with a smile.

I reach out and brush an imaginary speck of dust from his lapel, just needing to touch him. He smells fabulous, too. "You clean up well," I say and his grin flashes.

"You look beautiful, Daph," he says, sobering as he gives me another smoky look. "Are you okay to walk in those shoes?"

"Yes, but not as quickly as you usually walk."

"I have no issues taking our time."

I lock the door and he offers his elbow, escorting me from the porch. I smile, thinking about courtship.

"If you'd rather I swept you off your feet, Daph, just let me know."

"I'll keep that in mind," I say, because I will.

It's lovely to walk together on an early summer night. There's a breeze coming off the lake, cool but not cold, and the skies are clear. The sun is setting in an orange blaze of glory and I know the stars will be out later. I like walking alongside Luke, feeling his arm under my hand and his heat close to my side. That makes it feel like a beginning instead of an ending. I remind myself that now is what's important, though my sucker heart doesn't quite believe.

We talk about the weather, and our hopes for Merrie's new venture. He tells me about the manic rush to get everything done on time, but won't admit anything more about his week. Evidently, he went to Toronto for the suit, but beyond that, he's like a sphinx.

Nothing has prepared me for the solid line of cars parked on Queen Street, every spot filled on either side of the street on this side of Big Red. I can hear jazz and smell wonderful food as we approach the restaurant. I cast Luke a smile and am going to comment on that when a car door slams and someone blocks my path.

"The ever-exquisite Daphne!" Rafe roars with characteristic enthusiasm. I catch a glimpse of Luke's surprised expression, then I'm caught in a careful hug, having my cheeks kissed and my dress admired. Rafe even spins me around in front of him, ignoring Luke completely until I stop him and make introductions.

"He invited himself," I confess to Luke in an undertone, and I get a look for that.

"You said a friend," he says through his teeth.

"Yes."

"I thought a girlfriend," Luke says though his teeth.

Oh! Before I can explain that Rafe is a friend and only a friend, Sylvia is before us. "Table for four," she says and leads the way into the candlelit shadows of The Carpe Diem Café.

Rafe, predictably, leads the way.

24

———

LUKE

et's just get this straight. I'm not the jealous type. I'm not lacking in confidence either. I'm not possessive or domineering—but I do like to know where I stand. That's only natural.

And since I feel the way I do about Daph, it's imperative to know what's what.

To be fair, I didn't even wonder. I thought everything was right on track—until this guy stepped out of his black Lexus SUV with gold accents and right into our path.

Not a girlfriend.

Even the car gets up my nose. It's a huge gleaming beast of a vehicle and I swear it exhaled like a bull when he parked right in front of The Carpe Diem Café. The thing looks like a complicated watch—you know the ones that tell you the barometric pressure and the closing prices of the stock market in Tokyo instead of just the time and date. I'm sure it has every possible option. For a moment, I think the driver is some random jerk and that the choice of ride is compensating for something.

But when he greets Daph with an enthusiasm she obviously

shares, I hope the big hunk of steel gives it up in the middle of a desert somewhere sometime, just because.

Raphael Rossetti is handsome, apparently as rich as Croesus, and Daph's so-called friend.

I do not like Rafe.

This is almost purely because Daph seems to adore him. They exchange cheek kisses and a hug that lasts a little too long. They tease each other about what they're each wearing, admiring and critiquing like BFFs, then finally remember yours truly, waiting on the sidewalk. I think Rafe restrains an urge to toss me his keys, like I'm a carhop, and good thing, too.

He might have gotten them back in his teeth.

They are perfect teeth, so white they must be bleached, so straight he must have had braces as a kid. Maybe since. Daph introduces us and he shakes my hand heartily, his gaze locking with mine for a heartbeat. Was that an assessment or a challenge?

I don't like it either way.

This is her *friend?*

He invited himself? How is that supposed to make his presence better?

Did she dress to impress Rafe or me?

I hate having doubts. I hate feeling like our date has been crashed. I hate that she told me and I didn't pay attention, and that I feel like a raging bull myself. But I smile and take Daph's arm, not caring if I look proprietary, well aware that Rafe notices.

The other thing I don't like is that he's even here. It's a first for me to have a woman invite another guy along on a date. Once again, Daph has knocked me sideways and I have no script for this scene. She looks amazing and keeps smiling at me, which is a great way of ensuring that I'm a complete mess of contradictory impulses.

Have I become a jealous monster?

God. I hope not.

But I am scheming to move back to Empire forever, just to be with Daph, and it would ideal if we were in agreement about the future we haven't discussed yet.

Once again, I have the sense that I messed up and this is my own fault.

So, I try to make nice, perhaps for the first time ever.

For Daph.

Wonder of wonders, I learn when we step into the bistro that Rafe has been worshipping at Merrie's altar for a long time. She recognizes him and berates him for some imaginary crime, threatening to withhold dessert from him. He pretends to grovel and they both visibly enjoy what must be an established game.

I try to keep from rolling my eyes, and Daph gives me a jab in the ribs with her elbow.

"Be nice," she whispers, flicking me a dark glance.

"I told you I'm not nice."

"Aim for polite, then."

"Even though this is a first?" I ask, barely moving my lips.

She actually looks puzzled. Does she imagine that women routinely bring a plus-one to my supposed-to-be-romantic encounters? How pathetic would that be?

I take the chance to lean close, so close that my lips are touching her ear. She smells divine. At least she shivers, so I'm not out of the game yet. "I have never had anyone bring a date to a date before," I breathe, and she takes a step back.

"This is not a date."

"The hell it isn't. I invited you to join me here for dinner."

"But it's business," she protests. "The culmination of our alliance," she says with precision and I realize she's quoting me. She lifts a brow, waiting, and I see that's where I went wrong.

Delivery is everything.

"Does that mean you think we're done?"

"Aren't we? I haven't seen you all week."

"Daph, I've been trying to plan. I'm not that good at it yet, but I'm working on my next project." Her features don't soften. "In Empire," I murmur and her eyes widen. I nod and finally, she smiles.

She runs a hand down the lapel of my suit. "You mean this is for me?"

"It's sure as hell not for Rafe," I mutter and she laughs, the goddess who has my soul in her clutches.

She flicks a look up at me, one that is all mischief, one that sets me on fire. I realize then that her ability to drive me wild is never going to change or diminish.

"I did have hopes for a private celebration afterward," she confesses in a whisper that makes me want to forget dinner completely.

I slide my arm around her waist, inhaling the scent of her perfume. "You mean this is for me?"

She laughs. "Someone once told me that if you want a specific outcome, you have to be prepared to influence results."

A lot more than results are influenced by this reminder. I'm guessing that the gorgeous dress isn't the sum of it, nor even the intoxicating perfume, the way that her nape is bare, the perfect pale lipstick. No, she's chosen some lingerie to rock my world, and I can't wait to peel her out of it. In that very moment, she moves and my hand lands on the back of her waist. My thumb discovers a lot of bare skin and it's like a jolt of white lightning to realize that her dress is backless. Before I can think of a polite (comparatively public) way to proceed, her hands are on my chest and she's leaning close.

"I thought you were going to leave after tonight," she whispers.

"Not a chance." There's no place in the world for me other than Empire, and that's because Daph is here. I can see that I need to convince her of that. "I'm staying right here," I vow and her eyes darken.

"Did hell freeze over and I missed it?"

"No. I changed my mind." I lean closer. "Knowing you changed my mind."

"Oh, Luke," she whispers, leaning against me and giving me a kiss that almost makes me forget where we are. There's even an evil little flick of her tongue, one that would send my thoughts straight to the gutter if they weren't already there. Then she looks up at me, eyes dancing. "I'm sorry. I misunderstood. I promise to make it up to you." And then her hand is in my hair and her mouth is on mine and there is nothing in my universe but the sweetness of Daphne Bradshaw.

I am butter in her hands, in case you aren't sure.

Until Rafe clears his throat pointedly. "Are we going to sit down, or do you two need a room first?"

"That'll have to wait," I say smoothly, keeping my arm around Daph's waist. "Daph's starving." She laughs but her eyes are dark, the way they get when she's aroused, which is the most distracting sight possible. But Rafe gestures to the bench against the wall, indicating that Daph and I should sit together there, and that suits me just fine. I like having her next to me and she must like it, too, because she presses her thigh against mine.

We'll have to talk later about how she imagined this wasn't a date, because it was obvious to me all along. Maybe my communication skills aren't what they used to be.

It doesn't matter. All is right in my world, for the moment.

Mackenzie joins us then, and it appears that she's been fixed up with Rafe. Okay, I'm good with that. She looks wonderful in a little black dress, her long blond hair loose over her shoulders. Simple and elegant.

I prefer the elegant lady beside me, hands down.

I'm surprised to discover that it's easy to talk with Rafe. He's entertaining, charming, delighted about every morsel we're served, and asks just the right number of questions. He and Daph, it seems, have a tradition of sharing food, and the two of them divide and conquer the menu so that no duplicates with be served to our table. Mackenzie and I just sit back and do as we're told. We're going to try it all, and Sylvia brings extra cutlery in anticipation.

I don't miss Patrick's arrival at the door, though I don't acknowledge it. I hear Daph take a quick breath, but she pretends it doesn't matter either. Sylvia seems to get it, as she seats his party on the other side of the bistro, at the furthest possible point from us.

Of course, he's here. He thinks it's his town and he doesn't miss a thing. I notice that he's with his second wife, the one he married when my mom was pregnant, and the two kids from that happy union. Daph's hand touches my thigh in a silent sign of support that I appreciate. I give her fingers a quick squeeze, letting her know that I'm okay.

We talk about Toronto, about Empire, about the wine Sylvia has suggested. (It's from Rhodes Vineyards and is outstanding.) Mackenzie explains more about the vineyard as Rafe asks her good questions. Rafe admires the bistro and demands the story, so I let Daph tell it while I watch them both. He laughs in the right places and razzes me about being fearless after Daph shows him the before pictures of the diner on her phone.

Okay, so maybe I don't hate him.

Maybe I could even like him.

The vibe between the two of them is so mellow that they could be siblings. There's no sexual tension and I wonder how I missed that.

Testosterone, alas, is not always a friend.

The starters come and Rafe whips out his phone.

"Yes, he is that person," Daph whispers with affection and he grins, even as Mackenzie looks on with indulgence.

Rafe and I find ourselves in violent agreement about the curried lentil soup and the spring rolls, and share a lack of enthusiasm for the arugula salad with roasted figs and crumbled chèvre —which Daph loves. Mackenzie is a fan of dumplings she's ordered and I see Phil's influence in the mix of ingredients. Merrie has taken inspiration from his filling combinations and his mad skills in folding dumplings, and made them her own.

For the mains, I've chosen the tortellini with butternut squash and a cream sauce, while Daph has gone traditional with grilled lamb chops, gratin and grilled spring vegetables. The asparagus is in season, and Merrie has made the most of it, rubbing it with olive oil and salt then grilling it. I have some as a garnish on my plate and it's included in Daph's vegetables.

Rafe has chosen the mock porchetta with risotto, which looks and smells so terrific that I could consider eating meat again. Mackenzie has a stuffed supreme of chicken on a bed of all rice that is absolutely great. (Her asparagus is inside the chicken breast with some cheese.) Their sharing tradition makes a lot of sense and also breaks the ice—by the time the mains are done, we've ordered a second bottle of wine and are chatting like we've known each other forever.

Sylvia appears and whispers to Mackenzie that the foursome at the back in urban black have chosen the tasting flight from Rhodes Vineyards. She asks if Mackenzie might take a moment to give them vintner's notes. Mackenzie excuses herself and heads across the bistro to do that.

Daph goes to the ladies' room as Sylvia uncorks the second bottle.

Rafe takes an appreciative taste from the new bottle, rolls it around in his mouth, then nods approval to Sylvia. He looks like a contented lion, or an emperor savoring the perks of his position. "So, you and Daphne," he says, fixing me with a look over the top of his glass.

"Daph and me," I agree.

He purses his lips. "For how long?"

"Here through forever is my plan, but ladies' choice."

A ghost of a smile touches his lips and he nods before raising his glass again.

"You and Daph?" I ask and he almost chokes.

Then Rafe laughs, a huge belly laugh that can't have been put on. "You've got to be kidding."

I don't understand. "But you've known each other for years."

"Exactly!" He shakes his head.

"She's gorgeous."

"Stupendous." He kisses his fingertips in a chef's kiss. "Elegant, brilliant, loyal. I love her to the moon and back, but not like that. God, no."

His emphasis is a bit insulting. How could anyone take a pass on Daph? "Why not?"

Rafe frowns then, considering this. "It was never there. I'm not sure why. I thought once that maybe things just needed a little encouragement, but I was wrong. It was all wrong. I should have trusted my gut from the outset. But Daphne never held that night's stupidity against me."

So, something happened. He took a shot and was rebuffed maybe. Fair enough. "Maybe she was curious, too."

"Maybe. But there's nothing. There never has been and there never will be."

He speaks with such conviction that I wonder what I'm missing.

"You're confused," Rafe says, helping me out. "You think we're two of a kind, peas in a pod, that we each should have taken one look at the other and locked in for life."

"Something like that."

"But that's just it. We're too much the same. Maybe we understand each other a little too well. And maybe the ways that we're different don't bring us together."

"How so?"

"Daphne has opinions and views that she will defend to her last breath. She doesn't mind a fight for a good cause." I nod because it's all true. "She has dreams and goals, and isn't afraid to pursue what she wants. She's clever and articulate."

"And these are bad qualities?"

"They're great qualities. I have them, too. But the thing is that I don't want to argue with my partner. I ride to war every day. I suit up and head out to slay dragons each morning. I deal with bullies who play hard. I hold the line and try to fight the good fight, each and every day. I work long hours and I'm compensated accordingly because I'm brilliant at what I do."

He sips his wine and I think he's not cocky. He's just right.

"But here's the thing," he continues. "There's a price and it's a big one. This job, which I love, wears me out." I see in his eyes that he's serious. "So, when I come home, I don't want to debate anything. I don't even want any dissenting views. I want someone who wants what I want, just because I want it, someone who will smooth away all the irritations of everyday life so I can just *be* when I get home."

He wants a traditional wife. I didn't think anybody wanted that anymore. "You must want a woman a lot dumber than Daph."

"I want someone less challenging than Daphne. I want a beautiful, elegant woman who is demure and deferential, ideally one who is petite and blonde."

I cough that he's so specific and Rafe smiles.

"I'm allowed to want a partner who suits me, and I'm allowed to have a list of expectations. Whether they'll ever be met or not is another thing entirely." He raises his glass. "And there's nothing saying that the woman in question will be dumb, whenever I find her. She might just be smart enough to recognize a winning situation when she sees one."

I suppose everyone has their price, but I don't say it. I join his toast, raising my glass to clink it against his. "I wish you luck," I say and he chuckles.

"You and my mother. I am informed regularly that time is wasting." He grins, looking almost diabolical, and I have to think that any guy who listens to his mom has to be okay.

And that's when Patrick appears beside our table.

The angel of death is making a social call.

I missed his approach because I was listening so intently to Rafe, and that feels like a failure. Hell, everything I do feels like a failure when Patrick is in the room.

"May I?" he murmurs, then slides into Daph's seat without waiting for a reply. He eyes the wine, then Rafe—who looks both startled and affronted at the interruption—then turns his eagle eye on me.

There will be no introductions. Rafe will have to deal with that.

I'm staring straight back at Patrick, feeling my old defiance rise. He's looking at me the way he always did, like I'm something he'd like to scrape off the bottom of his shoe, something he despises, something that just keeps coming back despite his efforts to the contrary.

That look is what keeps me coming back, to be honest. I developed an affection for being a thorn in his side at a very young and impressionable age.

"Very nice," he says, sweeping his gaze over the restaurant. "And delicious, too."

I nod, waiting for the kill shot. There will be one.

"It's never going to work, though," he says with complete confidence. His gaze swivels to meet mine again, as cold and calculating as that of a wolf on the hunt. "Sure, this will be a good opening night. And the week ahead might be good, too. People like novelty. In the summer, the place might do well on weekends, at least, when visitors come into town." His gaze lingers on Rafe, who is obviously not local. "What happens in November, Luke?" he asks, his voice low and silky. Beelzebub sounded like this when he taunted Faust, I'm sure of it. "What happens in January? How exactly is this fine establishment going to survive our cruel winters in Empire?"

Another man might step up and offer to help. Another man, particularly one as wealthy as Patrick, might invest in the venture himself. But not Patrick. He exists to create lessons out of his own choices for everyone around him. I've failed in his view, and he's going to rub my face in it.

"Perhaps you don't know that Richard Bradshaw and I made a little wager the day I agreed to sell this place to you" he says, giving me a little nudge.

"I know."

He continues as if I haven't spoken. "A year. I gave you a year, but that was far too long. It won't even take six months for you to admit defeat, because the snow comes early to Empire." He smiles and I brace myself for whatever he intends to say next. "So, here's my offer. I'll buy back this place for half the price you paid me, any time before that year is out." He taps a fingertip on the table. "But you have to come to me, and you have to ask nicely."

"Half?"

"Market value. It's a sad truth that properties lose value in Empire at a steady rate."

"There's no chance in hell of that," I say softly.

"Isn't there?" Our gazes lock and hold, neither of us giving an inch. Then he clears his throat, nodding toward Daph who is returning. "We'll see."

With that, he's gone, striding back to the table where Candace, Madison and Ethan are waiting. They're both looking at me as if I'm a Martian come to visit, at least until Patrick reaches the table. He must say something because they become fascinated with their plates. Candace ignores me, which is par for the course. She makes fifty look good but I wonder whether Patrick is messing around on her yet.

"Who the hell was that?" Rafe demands.

"Patrick Cavendish," I say, then wait a beat. "My father."

I have the satisfaction of seeing Rafe's eyes widen so much that they might pop out of his head, then Daph slides into the seat beside me. Her hand is immediately on my thigh and I cover it with mine, giving her fingers a little squeeze.

"What was that about?" she asks quietly, her tone making it clear that she knows it was nothing good.

"He thinks he presented the proverbial offer I can't refuse," I say.

"And?" she asks.

I smile, having no doubt that I look a little wolfish myself, and meet Rafe's gaze. "He's wrong." There's steel in my tone because I may have finally outmanoeuvered Patrick.

The best part is that I actually don't care what he thinks or what he wants. My plan has exactly zero to do with him, or getting even, or even proving myself. It's about me and Daph, and finding purpose and charting a future. I can't wait to tell her all about it.

The music is back.

Why shouldn't the band be back?

My idea both terrifies and thrills me, still, even though I've purchased the theatre from Nate. Scheduling a performance and a comeback is like a chess game, and this one has high stakes. It's the biggest project I've ever undertaken and that's scary too. Wookie, our most reliable roadie, will arrive tomorrow to walk the theatre and give me his assessment. I trust him completely and am determined to pull this off.

Because it cannot fail. I don't want to disappoint Daph. I want to tell her everything and solicit her advice, but I want to do it when we're alone.

For the moment, there is dessert.

Sylvia brings it to the table then and I see a hardness in her eyes that echoes my own. Did Patrick even recognize her? Or did he say some asshole thing to put her in her place? I don't know and I can't ask, but I recognize that we're on the same side. I have an ally in Sylvia and I might need every one of those I can find.

There's a bread pudding studded with fruit and covered with rum sauce, a mixed berry crumble studded with nuts and topped with homemade ice cream. There is the inevitable crème brulée, not looking inevitable at all with its drizzle of blueberry coulis and garnish of fresh fruit. Rafe has some chocolate confection that looks like sin in a dish.

"Maybe a walk around town after dinner," he says, then digs in.

I have a much better idea of how to burn off these calories but Rafe doesn't need to hear about it. Daph slants me a look, proving our thoughts are as one, and I smile slowly. I watch her smile without looking at me and can't wait to get home again.

Home. When did her place become home? I don't know, but I recognize truth when I hear it and I like that just fine.

25

DAPHNE

I'm surprised that there are journalists—other than Noah, of course, who has come for dinner with his parents and sister—but I shouldn't be. I know there were press releases sent out. We finish dinner and Luke asks if I want to be part of the interviews. I shake my head and he excuses himself to take care of that business.

Word has circulated that the vintner is in the house, and Mackenzie is in demand, talking people through flights and tastings. I'm content to watch Luke and listen to Rafe grumble about cell phone service. He's cropping his pictures and uploading them to his social media accounts, showing me his progress as he goes. I'm surprised by how many followers he has as FoodFiend7 and agree for him to add a selfie of us together so long as he leaves out my name.

I'm sure that everyone I know in Empire has come for dinner tonight. Willow and Jim have a table by the window, while Bruno and Marissa arrive later. Everyone is dressed up, too, and I like that Bruno and Marissa are having a date night, too. My dad arrives just before eight with several of his neighbours and stops to chat. I introduce him to Rafe, and he smiles indulgently when he glances toward Luke.

Luke is in his element, charming reporters, posing for photographs, joking with Merrie. He makes it look easy and I'm glad when Patrick and his party leave.

"Unusual choice for you," Rafe says eventually, not looking up from his phone.

"Yes," I agree, because it's true.

He flicks me a glance. "I'm glad to see you taking a chance."

"What does that mean?"

"That the two of you are so different it's obvious it can never work out."

"How can you know that?"

"It's hot, right? The sex is great. You can't resist each other. Honestly, it's coming off the two of you in waves, and I'm happy for you, Daphne. Everyone should have at least one fling like that in their lifetime."

"Even though it ends."

"Of course, it ends. That doesn't mean you don't love the adventure of it. It doesn't mean that you don't learn something. It doesn't mean you regret it. Just hang on and see where it goes."

"I thought you were the one with the list."

"I am, but sometimes you have to chuck the list and have some fun." He gives me a stern look. "You were past due for that."

"I have fun..."

"And historically you've only dated men who were 'the marrying type'." He makes the quotes with his fingers. "There's nothing wrong with mixing it up a bit. You don't have to marry every guy you take home. If you did, there'd be a lot more work for divorce lawyers."

I smile at that.

"Kick up your heels, Daphne. Variety is the spice of life."

"The essence of romance is uncertainty."

"Oh, that's good. I like it. So go for it. Who cares if it's just one of those things?"

"Should I sing along?"

He shakes a finger at me. "And one day, when you find Mr. Right, who will probably be a lot like Justin with similar credentials but will actually have a soul, and he puts a ring on your finger and gets to the church on time, you'll have some memories to prompt that mysterious little smile, the one that will drive said man insane."

He's right. I have had a habit of assessing every guy in terms of his commitment quotient. There is something liberating about the prospect just enjoying Luke.

Is it possible that he really intends to stay?

Or are those just words, words that he knows I'll like?

Rafe nods approval of his own advice then turns his attention back to his phone. "Do you think the crumble looks better in this picture of it pristine, or the one with the bite out of it? I can argue it either way."

———

IT'S ALMOST eleven when things slow down. Willow has pitched in with clearing tables and Sylvia looks both exhausted and happy. Rafe is nodding with satisfaction at the response on his socials, and Luke saunters across the bistro to take his seat again. He takes my hand and kisses the back of it, closing his eyes for a moment.

"You owned it," I tell him and he smiles.

"I hope it's enough."

"Great launch," Rafe says, rising from his seat. "I'll stop in for lunch tomorrow before heading home."

"Thanks for coming," I say.

"Thanks for arranging the details," he replies, then nods to Luke. "Thanks for the conversation."

"Ditto." Luke stands and they shake hands.

"If you have time, stop in for lunch tomorrow," Rafe says. "I have some ideas of people you can contact for more promotion. Never hurts to reach out and with an influential foodie, a free meal might yield great results."

"Thank you," Luke says with a smile and we leave together.

Rafe drives off into the proverbial sunset with a lot of honking and waving. The Maple Leaf Motel wasn't his style, so he's gone to the Travelodge in Havelock for the night. Mackenzie is still walking Merrie's patrons through the wine flights, doing one of the many things she does well, and we leave her to it. We're holding hands as we walk and Empire is its usual quiet self.

"Good date," I say and feel Luke smile at me.

"Great date," he agrees. "Again. Maybe we should make a habit of it."

"Same time next week?"

"Something like that."

"I didn't realize you were a romantic."

"Neither did I, but a relationship can't just be a sequence of hook-ups. It's got to be more, it's got to be romantic and magical, and that means you can't just show up. You have to put *some* effort into it."

I lean against him as we walk, his words making me all warm inside. "My parents used to have a date night every month. They dressed up and went out for dinner in Havelock. Sometimes they went to Toronto for a weekend. They'd have dinner out, go to a show, visit a museum together. My mom was always so happy afterward."

"You must miss her."

"I do. So much. But I kind of feel like she's still here,

reminding me of what's important, nudging me in the direction she'd choose for me."

"Like a guardian angel?"

"Yes! Just like that." I study him. "You must miss Taylor."

"I do."

"You said you thought he guided you to Merrie's place that day."

"I do. I did." He looks down at me, his eyes vehemently blue. "And that's what's behind the new plan."

"Ah, the new plan. What *are* you going to do for an encore?"

Luke takes a breath, as if to steady himself for this confession. "I bought the Odeon Theatre this week from Nate Thompson."

I stop to stare at him. "Shut the front door."

"I did. I didn't want you to handle the sale for me, because I wanted it to be a surprise."

"It is."

"He wanted to sell, but not to Patrick. He warned me that it needs a ton of work, but he didn't want to pour cash into it himself. I bought it for a buck, Daph, and the promise to bring it back."

"Why would you want to own a theatre?"

"Because it brings everything together beautifully." He nods in the face of my confusion. I can't see the connection, but I have to wonder one thing.

"What did Patrick want?"

"To get under my skin."

"Did it work?"

"Not this time. Even though the man has a gift." He's pretending it doesn't matter, but I know better. When he bends to steal a kiss, I put a fingertip over my mouth and look into his eyes again.

"Promise me something," I say and his gaze sharpens. "Whatever you choose to do, don't choose it because of Patrick. Don't chart a course just to get even with him or to make him angry."

"What then?"

"Let it all go. Make your choices based on yourself, what you want and what you envision. Maybe he has the power to point out a failure to you, but don't give him more power than that. Act upon the information; don't respond to his provocation. It's the only way you'll ever break whatever hold he has over you."

Luke's smile dawns slowly and is blindingly brilliant. "That's what I've already done," he says and I smile, sliding my fingertip across his lips. "Thank you, Daph."

"For what? As your legal counsel, I should be giving you the best advice I can. What have you done?"

"Rewind," he says, spinning a finger. "Patrick stopped by the table tonight to point out the weakness of my plan with The Carpe Diem Café."

"And that is?"

"Location, location, location. In a way, Empire isn't any better than the site Merrie had before. It's a lot cheaper, but it has significantly less traffic. There will be people like Rafe, who make a regular pilgrimage to town just for the food, and people like you, who walk across the street once or twice a week for lunch, but she needs a stronger customer base than that. And Patrick is probably right about winter and its complete elimination of any visitors to Empire."

I don't argue that there are virtually no visitors to Empire regardless of the time of year, because he knows that.

I'm interested that he's jubilant after any discussion with Patrick. "He doesn't seem to have depressed you," I venture and Luke grins.

"Because I'm ahead of him this time. I started to think about this earlier in the week. I realized that it's not just one restaurant. We need an entire plan for the town, even to make that restaurant a success, and if I'm not just setting Merrie up for failure, I need to think ahead. I need to think bigger." He squeezes my hand. "I need to listen and learn about the merit of plans."

Oh. I like that he's sharing the credit with me, but he's the one leaping in here. Before I can point that out, he continues.

"So, we need to look at other places with seasonal traffic and learn from them. What they do is cultivate traffic during the best season, with festivals and events. They may do that in the off-season, too, but the point is that they fill the well when times are good, and that gets them through the slow months, when times are less good."

"Fair enough." It's true that we have very few festivals in Empire these days. There used to be a strawberry festival in June and a fall fair, as well as a Santa Claus parade in December, but we've rolled all of our events into the much larger versions in Havelock. If Luke plans to revive any of those, it will be an uphill battle, but I keep quiet and hear him out.

And I'm glad, because he surprises me completely.

"There's only one kind of event that I can personally organize, because I've done it a bunch of times before."

The light goes on. "A concert?"

Luke smiles and shakes his head. "Not just any concert, Daph. A reunion of the band, right here in Empire, for a tribute to Taylor."

"The band, Elwood, the band," I say under my breath and he laughs.

"Pretty much." He pushes his hand through his hair. "Brent and Zach are both up for it. In fact, they said they were waiting on me and can't believe it took me so long. I've talked to our head roadie, who is as surly as ever, and even he's excited to be on board. Once Wookie walks through the theatre tomorrow and gives me a list of improvements, I can cut our social media queen loose on the project. Chelsea is just brilliant at what she does. The gear is in storage, the buses and the trucks mothballed, but all of that can get sorted…"

"I thought you didn't want to perform anymore," I interject and he falls silent.

He takes a breath and fixes me with a brilliant blue look. "I didn't. Because I didn't think I could do it without Taylor there on stage with me. For an entire year, I couldn't hear the music and I thought that chapter of my life was over. But the music's back, Daph, thanks to you. And as soon as I had this idea, everything started to come together, as if it was meant to be. I have to do it. I have to prove to myself that I *can* do it, and I have to honour Taylor this way." His eyes narrow a little. "Does that make sense?"

I nod, because there's a lump in my throat. On the one hand, he'll be staying a little longer in Empire which is awesome. On the other, bringing the band back together probably gives him a reason to leave.

I'm going to focus on the moment and the chance to spend more time with him.

"I'm thinking about the fifth of July. That's the Saturday after Canada Day."

"So soon? How are you going to do that?"

"I don't know, Daph. That's part of the adventure." His grip tightens on my hand. "Want to meet Wookie with me in the morning? I'd love to have your input."

I squeeze his hand back, liking the suggestion that we're a team, even for a while. "Yes," I whisper, then we're at the steps of my house and I have a much better idea. I reach up and kiss him slowly, liking how his arms close around me and he abandons himself to the kiss. It feels like a celebration and a homecoming, both inevitable and unpredictable.

"I love the suit," I whisper, running a hand down his lapel. "And I loved watching you tonight."

"I was watching you," he admits, then kisses my ear. "I love the dress."

I smile. "And here I was hoping you'd help me take it off."

"Anything for you, Daph. Anything."

I love that he gives me the choice, that he never presumes what will happen between us, that he waits and lets me make the first move. I love that I'm getting bolder at doing that and when I unlock the door and tug him inside, I love the way anticipation floods through me.

It could be the first time, but it will be better than the first time. It gets better every time and that's an adventure I don't want to see end.

For the moment, though, there is Luke. I back him into the wall and kiss him as if my life depends upon it. He responds immediately, lifting me against him, kissing me back with both reverence and passion. My hands are in his hair, my tongue is against his, and his hands are under my jacket, on the bare skin of my back. He murmurs my name, the way he's made it his own, and I stop him with a touch, my hand flat on his chest. I feel his heartbeat beneath my palm a steady beat that's picking up even as I stare at him.

"No drapes," I confess, pretending to be sad about it, and the corner of his mouth lifts. "I had to order the blinds I wanted." I loop my hands around his neck. "We'll just have to go upstairs."

He glances at the stairs, then at me, and scoops me into his arms. "Challenges, challenges," he murmurs and steals a smoky hot kiss.

I kick my feet and watch him as he climbs, then tap his chin with a fingertip. "Slow tonight," I say, and he slants a glance at me. "So very, very slow."

26

LUKE

How is it possible that I love this woman so much, never mind that I fell so hard so quickly? I realize now that Taylor didn't lead me to Sylvia or even Merrie.

He was giving me a path to Daph, one that I would never have found on my own.

And here I am, a couple of weeks later, unable to imagine not having her in my life. How incredible is it that this amazing woman knows exactly who I am and lets me be in her life anyway?

Slow. Very slow. I couldn't have chosen better myself.

It could be the first time, my anticipation is that high, but it's better than the first time, because I'm learning what she likes, what drives her crazy, what makes every time better than the last. It's a quest I don't ever want to finish.

I want to have a thousand evenings like this one, a million dates. I want to come home like this all the time.

Over and over again.

It's new, this desire for permanence, this urge for roots. The Odeon is the first piece of property I've owned, well, the first one that I've kept, and I feel a raging pride in that. I can't wait to walk through it in the morning and strategize for its rebirth.

True to her request, Daph is taking her time. She turns on the lights and slides off her jacket. I'm glad she didn't do that at the restaurant, because the sight of her bare skin would have been too much. Here and now, it feels right. The colour suits her and I smile when she turns to face me, completely confident that I'm snared in her spell. She reaches up to unfasten the necklace, that sparkling confection that looks so delicate against her skin.

"I saw you wondering," Daph says when I'm hanging up

I try to play along, like we do this all the time, and take off my suit jacket, folding it over a chair. Daph turns before me, inviting my help with the zipper she can undo just fine on her own, and I slide the tab down from her waist slowly, very slowly. Meanwhile, I touch my lips to the back of her neck and inhale her scent, pure fire in my veins, then let my fingertip slide down her spine. I try to take forever to do it, but when the black lace is revealed, I move a little more quickly.

I'm only human.

She slides the dress down over her hips, revealing a fabulous merry widow, one with garters. I've noticed the sheer black stockings, and the seams up their backs, but the garters are unexpected and amazing.

She turns to face me at that delicious point of undressing, then balances on one foot while she takes off a satin pump. I could watch this woman all day and all night. And I will look.

The stockings mean she wants me to look.

That tells me that Daph was hoping this would happen, that she was plotting my seduction just the way she's casting her spell over me now.

Could there be anything sexier? Not to me.

I'm all too willing to surrender.

I whistle softly, letting my admiration show. She tosses the shoe at me and I catch it, stretching out my hand for the mate. I put them in the box, liking that they're still warm from her feet, then pull her closer to help with her garters. I nuzzle the back of her neck and her hair tumbles down. I close my eyes, savoring, and she squirms. "Admit it."

"Admit what?"

"You were wondering about me and Rafe."

"Of course, I was wondering about you and Rafe. You're friends, you say. You're both smart and attractive—although he's not my type." She laughs, peeling down a shimmering stocking and setting it aside. "Want help with that?"

"No. I don't want them snagged."

"I'm good for replacements."

She laughs and I pull her into my lap on the edge of the bed, watching as she slips off the other one. She then reaches behind herself to unfasten the garter belt. It's tossed toward the dresser, then she turns around, kneeling over me. I get a kiss that could launch a thousand ships, then she puts a finger under the knot of my tie and gives it a tug.

When she's untied it and cast it over her shoulder, she saunters toward the washroom, hips swinging.

Slow might kill me.

"Go ahead," she challenges. "Ask."

Shirt and trousers are cast aside in a hurry, because I don't care about being undressed slowly. I'm the enchanted one. I follow Daph and lean in the doorway, glad there's a big mirror in her bathroom. I'm down to my briefs and they hide none of my enthusiasm for the sight of her. "How good is your friendship?"

"We're friends, no more and no less. What did he say?"

"Same."

She smiles and turns to face me. "But you don't believe him."

"He seemed sincere. I just can't believe that any straight guy with a pulse wouldn't want you at least half as much as I do."

"What if I didn't want him, and he's gentleman enough to acknowledge that?"

"Really?"

She turns around again, loading her toothbrush. "I met Rafe when he introduced himself to me in class. He wanted to know if he could borrow my notes for the previous lecture, which he had missed because his pedicure had been rescheduled."

My surprise must show because she nods.

"Yes, his pedicure. At eighteen, he had this grooming routine that put mine to shame. He had the pedicure done separately from his manicure each week because he went to a different place, each being better at their respective tasks. He was using Botox before we finished our undergraduate degrees. He goes for manscaping weekly. His dry cleaning bills would make me weep. The man is more high-maintenance than anybody I've ever known. Worse, he's infuriatingly certain that his way is the only way and is as stubborn as a mule. Maybe more stubborn. Why do you think he isn't staying here?"

"Because you were hoping I'd come back tonight?"

"Because this entire house would be covered with his stuff ten minutes after he arrived. I was emotionally scarred by my first visit to his dorm room. It was knee-deep in discarded clothes, most of which were not dirty. They just had failed to make the cut for his daily outfit then were tossed on the floor. The mess made me crazy!" She shakes a finger at me. "But not so crazy that I'd be stupid enough to clean up after him. That is the path to Rafe's heart, becoming his willing servant, his staff, his assistant and his biggest fangirl. He has a colossal ego and can be absolutely infuriating."

"But...? I invite, feeling more reassured with every trait she gives him.

"But he's a great friend. He's loyal beyond expectation. He's the one who told me about Justin. He's also the one who makes sure I never accidentally see Justin when I'm in the city. He's a protective bear, has been a good mentor and has a heart of pure gold. If he ever falls in love, I wish the woman in question all the luck in the world dealing with him, but I hope he finds the right person one day."

"He thinks he wants a traditional wife. He has a list."

She laughs. "Well, let him have his illusions."

"What do you mean?"

"If some woman manages to steal Rafe's heart away, he'll be the one wrapped right around her finger. Wait and see."

She takes the pins out of her hair, letting it tumble down her back. I watch, fascinated. She then removes the merry widow, wriggling out of the stretchy lace in a way that is mesmerizing. My mouth has gone dry and I have no words at all.

Daph's eyes twinkle when she meets my gaze in the mirror. "Are we really going to spend the night talking about Rafe?"

"Not my plan," I admit. I step into the bathroom and pull her into my arms, inhaling the scent of her with satisfaction. She melts against me, welcoming me in that way that shorts all my circuits.

"Any better choices of topic?" she asks, her tone teasing.

"How about not talking at all?" I ask. I steal a slow sweet kiss, one that makes her melt against me and slide her fingers into my hair. She more than meets me halfway, and I know she's got me right where she wants me. The kiss gets hotter and more powerful, thrilling and new even though we've shared dozens of similar ones, and I know that I'm lucky beyond every expectation.

"I love you," I whisper into her ear, before kissing her again. She doesn't react or respond in any way and I wonder whether she's even heard me—but then the playful flick of her tongue and the caress of her hand ensures that there's nothing but Daph and this magic we make together.

Nothing at all.

27

———

DAPHNE

I've already discovered that Luke gets up earlier than me. I could get used to waking up alone, rolling over to find the spot beside me just a little bit warm, then smelling fresh coffee from the kitchen. Today, the hollow beside me is stone cold, proof that Luke was up early.

I love you.

Did I imagine that he said that?

Was it a conditional offer, one that expired because I didn't reply in kind? I don't know. This is all new territory for me. I've said the words before, of course, but I didn't mean them the way I would mean them now. I'm afraid to say them out loud and jinx whatever is going on here.

But Luke said them.

He said them so easily, and I can't help thinking that it sounds as if he's said it all before. Do I dare to believe him?

What about Rafe's advice? What about his conviction that this will never ever work, that it has to be a fling—never mind that I should just have fun.

Am I cursed to overthink everything?

Luke said it. Maybe he thought it was time to say it. Maybe he means it. Maybe he doesn't. In the spirit of the red-hot fling, I'm not going to make a big deal of it.

In the interest of being true to myself, I'm not going to respond in kind.

That's a compromise I can live with. I get up and wash up, heading downstairs in my jeans and a shirt.

I find Luke in the kitchen seated at the counter, in his briefs and open dress shirt. He's rolled up the sleeves and his hair is tousled, his feet braced on the bar stool so that his legs look taut and powerful. For a minute, I just stand and admire the view.

Then I realize that he has notes everywhere. The pad from my grocery list has been pulled into action and there are rows of sheets with notes. Some have phone numbers on them. Evidently, he is making his plan.

I go to his side, intrigued.

"How am I doing for a rookie?" he asked playfully and I smile.

"There's a lot of software that's good for this kind of thing. Maybe even apps for your phone."

"That would be great. There's so much to manage and I'm open to suggestions."

I get a coffee and lean against the counter, watching him text a reply to someone. "What's it like to grow up with no one having any expectations of you?"

"They all had expectations of me. Just not good ones."

"You know what I mean. Unless your mom had ambitions for you."

"The bar was low. Stay out of jail. Don't get yourself killed. Be home when the streetlights come on."

I shake my head, thinking it was probably a little higher than that.

"Why?" he asks, glancing up. "Was there a list of desirable achievements laid out for you?"

"Kind of. I was supposed to become a lawyer, which meant I had to get good grades." I shrug then make a little incoherent sound of satisfaction as he leans into a good spot. "I liked school, though, so that wasn't a problem."

"What did you want to do?"

"I didn't know, so following the plan seemed as good as anything else."

He puts down his phone to give me his full attention. "How could you *not* know?"

"Maybe if you're really good at one thing, it's easier in a way. That's the thing you'll do. But if you're good at a lot of things, you have to choose, and that's tougher."

"No, it isn't. You follow your passion." Luke speaks with a conviction I admire. "You do what you really want to do."

"Hmm."

He casts me a smile. "I'll guess that becoming a lawyer didn't take top spot on that list either."

I shake my head. "It's okay. I like the intellectual challenge of it. The intricacies of the law fascinate me, as well as how it got to be the way it is. Rafe is the one born to do what he does."

He puts aside the phone and turns to face me, then pulls me into an embrace. I'm standing between his thighs but I'm not going to give up that coffee. My hands are wrapped around the mug and Luke is smiling at me. I know he's listening to me, which is even more sexy than all the good stuff he can do with his thumb. "So, what's the plan for your new commercial property?"

"I'm still thinking. Because my dad's not wrong that it'll be tough to build a practice here, but I don't want to do criminal law or go back to the city." I say the thing I've never told anyone. "I actually didn't like it at the big firm. Everyone was so competitive. It felt like being a gladiator."

He chuckles. "Different clothes."

"True enough."

He's studying me, serious, trying to help. I adore how earnest he is. "There must have been something you particularly liked to do."

"I liked tutoring when I did it in high school. Helping people understand something that's eluded them to date. It's very satisfying to see the proverbial light go on."

"You're good at explaining the law."

I look at him and he nods.

"You are. You gave me the down-low on child support and custody in four sentences or less. It was impressive."

"But you must have understood it already."

"Broad stroke, never having fathered a child before or intended to." His lashes do that sweeping thing, making him look mysterious. I'm watching when he suddenly opens his eyes and our gazes lock.

"It's just what I do."

"But what about that? What about sharing your expertise? Lots of people don't understand the law. You could give a monthly class. Make it free and you'll probably end up with some clients."

"A class on what?"

He raises a hand. "Change it up every time. Understanding custody and child support. Understanding wills and estates. Stuff that everybody has to do but no one pays much attention to until they do. A real estate primer: buying and selling. Stuff like that."

I put down the mug, feeling excitement rise. "That's pretty brilliant, Luke."

"I do what I can."

"What to do when disaster strikes: understanding insurance and liability," I say and he nods approval.

"Good ones."

"Landlords and tenants," I say reaching for the pad of paper he's appropriated, and start scribbling notes. "Marriage and divorce."

"And you're off, working again," he says with affection. "That looks a lot like passion in play."

"It's a great idea."

"You're welcome."

I give him the kiss he deserves, seeing that there is more to this union than physical satisfaction. That's worth the price of admission, too, and we're well on our way to distraction when his phone chimes.

I love that he swears under his breath. He checks the message, keeping an arm around my waist. "Hey, Wookie's in Havelock already. Are you coming to the theatre?"

"I'd like to." I am wondering if the Odeon is as beautiful inside as I remember.

Luke spins off the chair and catches me up for a kiss. "Meet me there. I want to head back to the motel and change first." He spins off the stool and races up the stairs, leaving me to caffeinate. In moments, he comes charging back down, his shirt open and his tie in his hand. I get another scorching kiss, laugh at his energy, then he's gone.

I love you.

I will dream about that being true.

28

———

LUKE

Wookie is tall and sinewy, a man of indefinite age with a perpetual tan and tattoos covering every millimeter of his skin. My mom would say that he swears like a sailor, but there is no one on this earth who shares Wookie's fluid creativity with profanity.

He greets me at the Odeon with a hug and a predictable expletive, flinging out his hands to encompass greater Empire. "Have you lost it completely?"

"I don't think so."

Daph is coming down the street, right on time, and Wookie takes a good look. She smiles a greeting and I do introductions, liking how she slides an arm around my waist. Wookie takes a hint well and averts his gaze.

I unlock the door and we step inside. Daph has brought a flashlight—something I didn't consider—and plays it over the walls while we look for light switches. Wookie finds them in a maintenance area, the sound of his progress obvious from the string of curses he utters. The lights flare to life and Daph stands, looking around. She strolls through the lobby, her gaze trailing over the watermark on one wall, the crumbling plaster high overhead, the chandelier hanging at an angle, half its bulbs burned out. The carpet is stained and torn. There's a knob hanging loose on one door, its mate on the facing door is missing. The popcorn machine has been torn out, probably to be sold, without a lot of care for the resulting damage.

I see the red walls and the gilt ornamentation, the glory that was once characteristic of this place. I climb the stairs, ignoring Wookie's shouts, and stand at the top of them to view the stage.

It's stupendous, a proscenium stage with a large screen suspended near the front of it. It must have had actual footlights at one time, but the stage was updated sometime in the last century. The seats, upholstered in red velvet, are in surprisingly good shape, and the ceiling is a marvel of decorative stucco.

Wookie appears on the stage far below. "The electrical is a nightmare," he says, with a lot of extra words tucked around those ones.

I didn't expect otherwise.

"It's all got to go," he says and stamps a foot hard. "The stage is solid, but the workings back here are ancient. I'd rip it all out and start over. No matter who uses this place, they're going to need equipment they can count on, not something out of the basement of the Opera Garnier."

"Phantom of the Opera," Daph says, sliding into a seat at the end of a row.

"Eighteenth century, I'm thinking." I raise my voice. "The acoustics are great, Wookie."

"Yeah," he cedes. "These old places have that going on, at least." He nods, thinking. "Perimeter check," he says. "Basement and roof." Then he waves and heads out.

"It's beautiful," Daph says, but her tone isn't dreamy.

I'd bet my last buck that she has some kind of idea.

It may cost me my last buck to fix this place up. The scope of the repairs, even with a glance, is beyond my expectations. Have I bitten off more than I can chew this time? It wouldn't be the first time that enthusiasm steered me false, but this might take me further off course than ever.

I admit this to Daph and she smiles.

"Where does it say that you have to do it alone?" she asks. "I know you're used to doing things alone and not counting on anyone to help, but maybe it's time to mix that up."

"I don't understand."

"You'd have to incorporate, but you could sell shares in the theatre. Voting shares or not, you set up the tiers and the numbers and people invest in the project. You diminish your own risk and liability in so doing." Her eyes narrow as I stare at her, practically watching her mind work.

Bloody hell.

"Or you could take donations. I'll have to check with my dad as to how that would be set up. I've never done it before, but essentially, people would pitch in to help with the cost of the renovations. For a ten thousand dollar donation, for example, your name is permanently on the wall of the lobby. For twenty-five, your name is bigger and listed somewhere else. Maybe it's embroidered on the curtains. Maybe for fifty thousand, you get two tickets to every production mounted here." She frowns, continuing to astonish me as she thinks out loud. "Or maybe that's part of a different program. A yearly membership and maintenance subscription."

I sit down hard beside her. "Would people do that?"

"Are you kidding me?" She turns to face me and I realize how little expectation I have of those in my hometown—and it's not deserved. "Didn't you notice that pretty much everyone in town came out for dinner at the café last night?" I'm thinking of exactly that. The place was packed. Merrie said she was booked out for the week, and word of mouth hasn't even started. "People live here,"

Daph says. "People care about their homes. People love being part of a solution, especially when all they have to do is write a cheque."

I'm so blown away by this idea that I don't know what to say.

"Bad idea?" she asks, looking confused.

"It's brilliant, Daph. It's absolutely bloody brilliant." And in case she isn't sure of my enthusiasm, I kiss her senseless.

Damn. What a team we are.

Then Wookie whistles from the stage. "You gotta see this roof, Luke. It's holding together with a wing and a prayer."

"Can we fix it?"

"We can replace it. The basement's dry, though. If you're doing this, I'll need Steig and Blondie here to help, ideally Rasta and Solo, too."

"We're doing it!" I shout and Daph laughs beside me. "And oh, hey, Wookie, we have about eight weeks to get it done."

That prompts him to loose a stream of expletives that turns the air blue. Daph and I grin at each other, and I can't wait to begin.

———

IT TAKES a particular kind of insanity to try to bring a reunion concert together in just eight weeks, tossing in the renovation of an old theatre and the reunion of a band that is missing one key member.

I guess I have it.

I remind myself that the first word in the band's name has never been so apt, but I don't have time to think about it. There's just too much to do.

On the other hand, it feels as if the project has someone watching over it. I have to believe that Taylor is influencing results, giving things a nudge when they get knotty, pulling together elements with welcome ease. We avoid big crises. We have a couple of lucky breaks that are nearly miracles. Taylor's younger brother, Jason, for example, plays as well as Taylor and knows our entire catalogue. He's thrilled when we learn that and ask him to take Taylor's place for the tribute.

I have never worked so hard in my life. Touring can be grueling because each performance is demanding. Four or five shows a week means I can eat anything, and I'll still lose weight. I must sweat a metric tonne each night we have a show, but it's been over a year since we gave a performance. I start running every morning instead of once in a while, and kick up the reps on my hotel exercise program.

That's on top of the demands of the theatre building. The wiring has to go and time is of the essence, so I help out. The roof is being replaced, too, but a great company from Havelock that worked us in. The floors are sound and so are the stairs, but some of the seats need to be refurbished. And as Wookie said, everything backstage needs to be updated. A new sprinkler system has to be installed as well as smoke alarms, and it's like watching money take flight out of my bank account.

Still, it's satisfying. The first time we turn on the new house lights and see the place, we spontaneously break into applause. It's beautiful, embellished with carvings and ornaments the way no one bothers with anymore. For now, we'll get it clean and functional, but I'm having fantasies of restoring the whole damn place to its former magnificence.

For what exactly? It's a good question but I'm willing to defer it until after the concert. It seems like overkill for *The Rocky Horror Picture Show* on one Friday per month, with twenty patrons showing up to watch. (Maybe ten.)

The best part is the donations. I thought we might have a few people step up to support the project, but every day, at least one person presses a cheque into my hand on Queen Street. It's not a lot of money so far, but the spirit of it is encouraging. For the first time in my life, I feel like I might belong in Empire.

Noah, of course, is all over the concert. Again, he wants an exclusive. Again, I turn him down. Again, he'll be first. The kid has no shortage of enthusiasm. I let him into the theatre that first day, and he documents it for his *before* shots. He follows Wookie around so diligently that I have to limit his access.

We've been working sixteen hours a day and even though it's been less than a week, I'm missing Daph something fierce. I don't want to knock on her door at midnight, though. I see her in passing a lot during the day, and we make time to talk and hang out a bit, but I'm afraid she might be slipping away.

How can I do all the things at once? I'm not sure.

Tonight, I'm leaving comparatively early because I really need to see Daph. I'm locking up when I see the car.

It comes peeling out of the night, like a streak of lightning. Everyone in the county must hear the roar of its engine. It races down toward Big Red, takes the circle around the tree with a squeal of tires, then the driver gears down and heads up the hill. I hear the car turn again, but can't tell if it's turned onto Caledonia or Britannia. The driver hasn't left town. I hear tires squeal again and the engine rev and by the time I get past Jim's antique store, I see its headlights.

In Daph's driveway.

The headlights go out. The engine dies. And I hear a car door slam hard.

What fresh hell is this?

29

DAPHNE

I t's Thursday night and I'm trying to install the new blinds for the living room and kitchen on my own. It's not a one-person job, even though I am a bit handy. I don't want to ask Luke when he's so busy and I worry that my dad might have a heart attack from the exertion. We changed around Wednesday night so my friends could help.

Cameron is mostly good at giving instruction, but Willow and I got the hardware installed. Mackenzie was held up at work so she met us at The Carpe Diem Café afterward. I'd hoped we might see Luke at the restaurant, but there was no sign of him last night.

I'm not really thinking about the merit of men who come home every night right on time, or who are reliably around on the weekend. I just didn't realize that so much of our limited time together would be consumed by the Odeon's renovation and this concert.

I tell myself that I'm selfish and don't need a lot of convincing of that.

And I'm still irritable.

Missing Luke and battling drapery hardware aren't the only reasons I'm grumpy. My period has come in all its glory, and I have the usual cramps on day one, combined with an epic level of horniness—an urge that can't possibly be satisfied, whether or not I see Luke, and that just makes me more cranky.

I've just finishing hanging the second blind and am checking it out that it works smoothly when I hear a car park in my driveway. Not just any car. It's a Porsche. I know the sound of that engine all too well. In fact, there's only one person I know who owns a Porsche, someone I never want to see again.

At least I know Justin would never drive this far for anything.

But surprise, surprise. I raise the blind again and discover that it is, in fact, Justin coming up the walk to my door.

I suppose he should look good to me. He should look like predictability and all the attributes I thought he possessed before—except, you know, fidelity. I suppose he should look like a safe reliable choice and the contrast with Luke should do him a lot of favours.

It doesn't.

I recall Rafe's view of my current choice of partner and feel myself scowl. Having been with Luke means that I don't want what anyone even remotely like Justin has to offer.

I let the blind drop back into place and consider the merit of not answering the door.

Justin will just come back, though. I might as well get this solved.

He has chosen the wrong night to mess with me.

I'm in tights and a T-shirt, dusty and dirty, my hair shoved into a messy bun and my feet bare. There is no make-up left on my face and my nails are due for a buff and polish. I'm not looking my best and I'm kind of glad that Justin didn't give me any notice of his plans.

I open the door and he pauses in the act of climbing the steps. He's wearing a navy suit and I can see that he's shoved his tie in the pocket of his jacket. He was always doing that. He never folded it or treated it with care, which meant that someone had to restore it to rights. The top button of his shirt is undone, revealing that he's as tanned as ever. His hair is still dark gold and a little curly, though there might be a smidgen of silver at his temples now. Tough to tell in this light. His eyes are still green—why would that have changed?—and they still crinkle at the corners when he smiles, as he does now. He's still as confident as ever, and clearly can't even imagine that I wouldn't be thrilled to see him.

"Daphne," he says, exhaling my name. I once thought it sounded like a caress, but now it sounds like he's out of breath.

Maybe he's spending less time at the gym these days.

"You must have taken a wrong turn at Albuquerque," I say, leaning in the doorway and folding my arms across my chest. I don't feel friendly and I'm not going to fake it. "Don't tell me that what's-her-name decided to move down here."

"Heather," he supplies.

"Hmm," I say.

"That was a misunderstanding..."

"You're right. I thought we were exclusive, seeing as we were engaged and all." I wrinkle my nose. "Was I supposed to ask her to be a bridesmaid, or was she just going to coincidentally book a vacation at the same location as our honeymoon? Maybe we were going to decorate the spare bedroom for her. How exactly was that going to work?"

He steps onto the porch and shoves his hands in the pockets of his trousers, looking like a chastened little boy. "You're still angry."

"No. My anger has cooled and set into a hard slab of bitterness that will last a lifetime." Even as I say it, I realize it's not true.

I just don't care.

I have an *indifference* that could last a lifetime, and that's a very liberating realization.

Justin, I know, isn't ever going to believe it. "Daphne, you're making too much of a little fling."

"No, I think you made too little of it," I say. "But it doesn't really matter anymore. Does it?"

"What do you mean? I thought we could start over…"

"There's no way I want to do that again."

"No, Daphne, this time it would be different…"

"I don't think so." I sigh when he steps closer to make an appeal. "Give me a little credit. I'm not that gullible, Justin."

"But I love you," he says and his confession has no power at all. They're just words. Empty words. I can't help but compare it Luke's heartfelt confession.

He was telling me the truth.

"You had such an interesting way of showing your affection," I say, smiling when I see a familiar silhouette striding closer. "But then, they do say that actions speak louder than words."

The man I know whose actions are perfect in every way is closing fast and I'm glad.

Justin, of course, assumes that I'm smiling at him and that he's making progress. He takes a step closer. "Come on, Daphne." He gestures to the bench on my porch. "Let's sit down and have a talk, straighten everything out."

"How did you know where I live, Justin?" I use his name because Luke is within earshot. I see his footsteps slow and I know he's waiting for a sign from me.

Choice. He's all about giving women choices. That must be his mom's legacy because it isn't his dad's. I admire Luke so much for that trait.

"I called your dad," Justin confides with a wry chuckle. "He wasn't very encouraging, but after I saw you on Rafe's socials, I just knew we were destined to be together. I knew we had to give it another shot." He smiles, a smile that used to dissolve my knees and my reservations. Both are good this time. No surprise. "You looked fabulous, Daphne." Again, his gaze sweeps over me and I smile that he's not so fond of the transformation.

God, my mom was right about him. He'd probably kick me to the curb at forty for looking older. Certainly, I'd be shown the door at fifty. This guy is not about forever, even though he talks a good game. How did I miss that bit?

Maybe I was only looking at the surface, too.

His affair saved me from a horrible fate.

I should be grateful to him.

Funny I don't feel like saying thanks.

"Where are you staying tonight?" I ask.

Justin frowns, his gaze flicking beyond me to the interior of my house and back to my eyes. "Well, I thought, maybe, here."

"So, let me get this straight," I say. "We were engaged to be married."

"We know that, Daphne. I still have the ring, although you should have kept it."

Better and better. He's doing that endearing thing of talking down to me. Could he make it any easier to just say no?

"We were essentially living together," I remind him.

"Yes, you were going to redo the kitchen." Again, the winsome smile. "It's still waiting for your touch."

I continue as if he hasn't spoken. "I was in the middle of planning and booking our wedding, at which point you decided to become involved with another woman." He starts to protest. "Not just sex, Justin. Not just a hook-up. A full-blown ongoing affair."

"Well," he says and falls silent.

"And when I found out and broke it off, you had nothing to say in your own defense except—" I pause to give his words the weight they deserve. "—'the heart wants what it wants'." I had personally thought it was a somewhat lower part of his anatomy driving his choices, but I don't say that.

Yet.

"You don't understand, Daphne. I was dazzled by her. You were so busy and Heather was there for me. It was impulsive and wrong, and just a fling. But now it's over, so I'm back." He smiles, twinkling at me, laying on the charm.

"It's been three years," I remind him. "Did you get lost? It's maybe a four-hour drive."

"Daphne!"

"Did you think I was just sitting here waiting for you?"

"Well." He looks around, probably intending to dismiss Empire as a place lacking in dating options. Instead, he notices Luke standing on the sidewalk, hands in his pockets, listening and making no attempt to hide it. I can only see his silhouette, but he looks big and resolute, a bodyguard ready to kick some butt if I encourage it.

"And so you show up, without calling, assuming that I have nothing better to do than invite you in, feed you, sleep with you, and fill your life with joy once more."

"You make it sound like work."

"And you make the option unappealing."

He turns to Luke and speaks with some irritation. "Excuse me, but we're having a private conversation."

Luke takes a step closer. "It looks to me like Daph doesn't want you on her porch."

Justin looks between the two of us. "You know him?"

"In every possible sense," I say and smile slowly.

He looks startled then, and even a little uncertain. He looks at Luke again.

"Go home, Justin, and don't ever come back."

"You're supposed to love me!"

"If I ever did, you fixed that." I lean around Justin and wave to Luke. "You're late tonight," I say, as if he comes here every night. I refrain from calling him 'honey' but only just.

One of us would probably laugh.

"So much craziness, but it's getting sorted," Luke growls. He steps past Justin, who is clearly gobsmacked, gives him a survey.

"Nice car," he says, then smiles at me. "Sorry I'm late, Daph. Missed you every minute." I smile back at him, heart thundering, and he catches me close for a kiss that is entirely too long and too passionate for public consumption.

I don't care. I love it. He swings me off my feet and carries me into the house on one hip, while Justin gapes after us like a fish. There is something very satisfying about being carried off like plunder, especially when you really want the ravishing that comes next. Luke waves farewell to my unwelcome visitor, then flicks the door shut with his fingertips. I reach out to turn the deadbolt and we grin at each other.

"Where am I going to stay?" Justin shouts.

"There's a Travelodge in Havelock," Luke calls, his eyes dancing wickedly, then kisses me to silence again.

It's a good thing he does because otherwise Justin might have heard my laughter.

30

———

LUKE

What kind of an asshole assumes that a woman will take him back, after three years of silence, after he screws around on her while they were engaged?

I'll tell you. The particular kind of asshole who drives a silver Porsche like the one in Daph's driveway. I was seriously tempted to drag my keys along the side of that car, just because it would break Jerk Justin's heart in a way no woman ever could. Having Daph wrapped around me is a thousand times better, so much better that I barely notice the sound of the car's engine fading into the night.

I do notice it, though, and it brings me joy.

I feel the simmer in Daph, and I know she has to let it out before we can get down to business. I seat her on the counter and brace myself between her legs, touching my nose to hers. "Go ahead," I invite. "Tell me." I'm ready to be anything she wants me to be, even the consolation prize if she loves this loser forever. That's how far gone I am.

It's a bad time to remember that tear when she told me about the wedding dress.

I would have to be a lot dumber than I am not to see that she and JJ come from the same world, that theirs might be a predictable match—as ours would never be.

Her gaze simmers. "He only came because he saw Rafe's pictures."

"That's what it took for him to realize he'd abandoned the most beautiful woman on the planet? He couldn't see it when you were planning the wedding?"

She gives me a poke. "That's not all of what I'm about."

"Of course not. You're smart and sweet and sometimes funny."

"Sometimes?"

I steal a kiss. "And other times you're so perceptive that you terrify me."

"As if."

"Honest and true, Daph. I have no secrets from you. It's not even possible."

She sobers, studying me and I hope she sees whatever she wants in me. "He had a secret from me."

"And he is an asshole for that, although it might have been worse if he'd told you all about it. His keeping it secret means he knew you would have an issue with his choice."

"Of course, I did!"

"You weren't playing by the same rules, Daph, and as much as it annoys me that he treated you so badly, I'm kind of glad that you did break up, because that meant you were single when I got here."

She doesn't smile. "Are *we* playing by the same rules?" Her gaze is searching.

"I'm hoping so."

"Not the most reassuring reply possible."

I lift a brow. "You *cried* about your wedding dress, like you regretted not marrying him. Like maybe you still love him."

She looks so shocked that I'm mollified. "If I cried, it was because shopping for that dress was the last thing my mom and I did together."

Oh.

"She said he would leave me when it suited him, that he wasn't the kind of guy to stay married for the duration. She said he was all about appearances, and tonight, he proved that she was absolutely right." She shakes her head. "I feel so stupid that I didn't see it sooner."

I pull her close, more relieved than I can say.

But Daph pulls back to look me in the eye. "Is fidelity new for you?"

"Not technically. I never see multiple women simultaneously, because in the past, I've never spent more than one night with any woman."

"That's not the most compelling argument."

"I guess not." I lean my forehead against hers. "This is new for me, Daph. I think it's awesome to be with you, to keep having more and more. I don't want to screw it up, but I don't really have a map. Please tell me if I take a wrong step."

"You really mean that?"

"I do." She looks puzzled but enchanted, and I have no clue whether I'm playing this well or not. This going-for-the long-term thing is complicated.

"You should have given him one of your Medusa stares," I say without meaning to do so.

She's amused, which is progress. "But then I'd have a statue of him on my porch forever." She shudders in mock horror and then I smile. We smile at each other for one of those long potent moments and I swear, the temperature rises in the house, maybe in all of Empire. She's pleased and reassured now, her eyes glowing, her smile radiant. I could look at her all night when she's like this, but really, I want to do something else all night.

There's no mistaking the welcome in her eyes, so I bend closer, then capture her mouth with mine. We have a long sultry sweet kiss. She's flushed and her eyes are shining when I pull back a little to survey her.

"I'm thinking we should celebrate your new blinds," I say.

"What? How?"

"Right here," I whisper in her ear, grazing the lobe with my teeth. "Right on this counter. Right now."

"Oh!" she gasps. "But we can't." She retreats, putting her legs together so that I'm standing beside her, leaving me out in the cold.

But why?

"You did it again, Daph," I observe, not moving away, waiting.

"Did what?"

"Left me without a script. What's going on? Why can't we celebrate? What did I do?"

She looks alarmed. "It's not you or anything you did, Luke." She heaves a sigh. "It's me. I'm on." She wrinkles her nose. "I'm cranky and I'm sore and I'm not fit company for anyone." She sighs again. "No celebration tonight. Sorry."

Oh.

"Don't be sorry. It is what it is."

"I am sorry." She does sound grumpy and, in a way, she's adorable like this. She makes me think of a wet kitten. I remember my mom, sometimes cranky, sometimes weepy, sometimes wanting to be alone and sometimes needing contact.

"Want a massage?" I ask.

"I couldn't stand it," she growls.

My mom told me once that the most helpful thing I could do was ask what she wanted, so I go with that. "Tell me, Daph. Should I stay or go tonight?"

"I don't know!"

"Tell me how you feel."

"Irritable."

I take a chance on teasing her. "No, really? I never would have guessed."

She swats my shoulder and I chuckle at the quick glimpse of her smile. "I'm crampy, cranky, cold and sore. I smell like an abattoir –"

"Not even close, Daph."

I get a look for that. "What would you know about it?"

"Crappy job number seven, I think it was. When you think about it, someone has to clean up those places. It paid well, but not well enough."

I watch understanding dawn in her eyes. "You don't eat red meat, do you?"

"Not often. Not anymore." I smile at her and she smiles back, just a little. I lean against the counter beside her. "Go on. You were documenting your shortcomings."

"And you were refuting them."

"Got to contribute to the greater good. Be part of the solution, you know."

Her smile is fleeting. "I look like a train wreck," she says with heat. "I even have a zit." She points to her nose but any blemish is so small that I can't see it. She surveys me, a heat in her eyes that is downright erotic. "And you look so delicious that I could gobble you up with a spoon, but I *can't*." The last word is so fierce that I'm startled.

"Why not?"

"Oh, please. Don't mess with me tonight."

I turn then, pulling her into my arms. I lean my forehead against hers, my fingers finding and kneading the tightness in her shoulders. "You do not look like a train wreck." I kiss her temple, feeling her melt a little. "You're as gorgeous as ever."

"If you keep lying to me, I *will* hurt you."

I smile, untroubled, and roll my thumbs against the tightest spot in her shoulders. She sighs and closes her eyes tipping her head back and almost purring. "You've got it backwards, Daph," I murmur. Her hands have found their way around my waist. "I think you're always gorgeous because I'm crazy about you, not the other way around."

I don't give her a chance to argue. I just claim a kiss, one that quickly heats up. I'm surprised how passionately she returns it, proof positive that she is horny. Her nails are digging into my shoulder, her leg hooking around my hips to draw me closer. Her tongue is beyond wicked and I can't help thinking of the possibilities.

"Not fair," she breathes, pulling away. Her eyes are stormy. "I *want* and I can't have…"

"Why not?" I whisper and she looks at me.

"But we can't."

"Why not?"

"Um, because it's gross."

I scoffs. "Who told you that? Jerk Justin?"

"Among others."

"That just proves how unworthy they were of worshipping at your feet."

"I'm serious!"

"So am I. I can feel it, Daph, radiating off you. You're ready to go wild, and that has to be worth the price of admission. I can't wait to find out what it's like to see you lose control."

She eyes me like I'm insane. "You really think that?"

"I think it's worth finding out. And really, I'm in for anything that drives you crazy."

"But it could be awful."

"It could be great. There's only one way to be sure."

"You can't go down on me," she says.

I wiggle my hand and sing the words "I'll use my fingers."

"And your imagination." She smiles at my delight that she's caught the reference. "*Brass in Pocket.*"

"The Pretenders," I agree. I have a feeling it's the song that will haunt me for this whole encounter. I slide my hand under Daph's ginormous T-shirt and cup her breast. She shivers at my touch, even through her bra, and her eyes widen. "Aren't all the good bits more sensitive?" I slide my thumb across her nipple slowly, liking that it's already beaded to a point, and feel her shudder.

"Oh my God," she whispers, and once again, her nails dig into my shoulder.

"What about the other good bit?" I whisper in her ear, even my breath making her tremble in the very best way. She's so responsive that I'm the one who's raging now. "I've always wanted to make you shout loud enough that the neighbours call the cops," I confess. "Maybe this is the night."

"My neighbour is Cameron. That might take some doing."

I feel myself grin. "I'm up for the challenge."

"Maybe you've been training for it for years."

"If you're going to snark, I'm going to have to think of a way to keep you quiet," I threaten, then claim her mouth with a kiss that just won't stop. By the time I lift my head, Daph looks resolute.

She pushes me aside and I have time to think I've somehow blown it before she jumps off the counter. Her hands are on my belt buckle and she backs me into the counter as she unfastens it. "I've been wanting to do this for a while, but I thought I might mess up," she says and I can't believe my luck. My jeans drop and her fingers are under my briefs. I am so ready for whatever she has planned. "But you're right, there's only one way to know for sure." Her hand closes around me, the softness of her palm and the strength of her fingers against my bare skin. I almost come on the spot, especially when I see the look in her eyes.

Then she bends down to kiss me and I slide my fingers into her hair, hearing myself moan as she takes me into her mouth. It's perfect, both gentle and demanding, and when she begins to move, I know I won't last.

"I'll make you pay for this," I manage to say and she pulls away to laugh.

"I'm counting on it," she says, sounding both wicked and sweet.

She's going to own me, body and soul, and I don't even care. Maybe she does already. I can only think that it's totally worth it, just for this.

And I will make her scream the house down tonight.

Guaranteed.

31

DAPHNE

Luke is not someone often surprised, especially in intimate encounters. So, I love that he's completely floored that I want to go down on him, and that makes me want to do it even more. He's right that you can only know if you take a chance, and I dive right into that, following my impulse to seduce him.

It works brilliantly. He's in heaven and I wish I'd taken a chance on this before. It doesn't even seem possible that I could do anything wrong—every move I make, he gets harder or moans louder. His hips buck of their own volition and I get to run my hands down the strength of his bare legs. I grip his butt and he cups my head in his hands, his fingers in my hair as I tease him and devour him.

It doesn't take long for him to become taut and catch his breath quickly, just the way he does right before he comes. I love that I know the signs, that I can pull back a little, then finish him off with a flourish that has him shouting and shaking.

He swears softly and whispers my name, his eyes dark when he looks down at me with something like wonder. He's hanging onto the counter while I clean up, then he gets his second wind, tossing me over his shoulder and heading for the stairs.

"Now, you're in trouble," he mutters as he climbs them three at a time. I kick my feet in anticipation, unable to wait.

He starts the shower, then hauls my T-shirt over my shoulders, touching his lips reverently to the hollow below my collarbone. My tights are pushed down, my bra discarded. I close my eyes when his hands lock around my waist and give myself permission to just enjoy his powerful kiss.

Luke cups my breasts in his hands and kisses each nipple in turn, drawing it to attention with gentle persistence, showing me just how sensitive and tingly it is. I'm melting when he grazes his way back to my mouth, spearing his hands into my hair and holding me captive to a kiss meant to claim my soul.

The room fills with heat and steam, and I watch hungrily as he steps away to strip off his own shirt. It should be illegal for a man to have such a great butt and I reach out to give him a caress. He tugs me toward the shower, beckoning to me with a finger and a smile. I drop my panties and follow him. He closes the door behind us and pulls me into his arms. The hot water streams over us and he traps me against the tiled wall, holding me close and kissing me as his hand slides lower. I gasp when he finally touches me, arching my back and letting my head fall back. I am so sensitive. He eases his thumb across me and I moan without meaning to, a sound that is the perfect expression of my yearning.

"Oh yeah," he whispers. "Tonight, I'm going to make you wait for it."

"You wouldn't be mean when I've had such a bad day." I fake a pout and he laughs.

"I would and I will." His eyes are glittering. "You wouldn't want anything else."

I wouldn't. It's all true.

He claims a quick kiss as he laces our hands together, the

fingers of his one hand entwined with both of mine. He braces his elbow and holds my hands high over my head, so I'm stretched to my tiptoes. It feels wicked and wonderful, and when his other hand slides between my thighs, I shudder. He kisses my ear, slowly, even as his fingers begin to work.

"And when I'm done, you'll ask me to do it again," he promises in a velvety purr and I already know that he's right.

———

I END up riding him on the bathroom floor, needing to feel him inside me after I come. Luke gallantly takes the bottom against the tile and I straddle him, feeling audacious and insatiable. I see the marks of my own nails in his shoulders and even the imprint of my teeth.

And yet, and yet, he seems to be thrilled by my demands, by the new bold me, and I feel as if neither of us can get enough. I ride him hard. He watches me like I'm incredible and that only makes me more demanding. I take him almost to the edge, then relent, teasing him a little more each time so that he comes bigger in the end.

And when he does, it's explosive, his body so taut that he arches off the floor, taking me with him as he reaches for the stars.

I watch him, so glad I can do this to him and for him, then his eyes open to blue slits of amusement. "I think I just had an out-of-body experience," he rumbles.

"No, you were definitely in my body," I reply as I slide down to lie on his chest. He laughs harder than I've ever heard him laugh before. It's a wonderful sound. I wriggle my hips, still amazed that he was so huge and I was able to take him completely. "You were impossible to miss."

"Problem?" he asks and I shake my head.

"Perfection."

"Damn, Daph, it was." His tone is filled with a wonder I share.

I touch the marks I've left on his shoulders. "Too much?"

He gives a shiver of delight and rolls his eyes. "Perfection," he insists and gives me a kiss that is all that and more. Then he rolls me to my side, eyes glinting. His hand slides lower and I part my thighs, welcoming his touch. "We definitely need to add this to the playlist," he growls and I nod agreement.

I like the implication that he'll be around in a month, and I kiss him with all my enthusiasm for that concept. In a heartbeat, we're tangled together again, and I'm rocking against his hand, wanting what he gives. "Twice for you," he whispers, cradling me against his chest as his fingers drive me crazy. He's watching me with satisfaction. "Once to make you wild and once to make you sleepy."

"No. Am I that predictable?"

"Maybe not tonight." He kisses me fiercely, roughly, his fingers sliding inside me as his thumb does that really good bit. I arch my back and make a little sound of protest when he stops, one that makes him slide his knee between my legs. He's holding me down again, stretching me out, and I realize just how much I love this when he casts me into the abyss again. He swallows the sound of my release with a commanding kiss, and it takes me a minute to catch my breath.

"Damn," I whisper.

"That's not half of it," he agrees and helps me up. He starts the shower again and this time we wash each other in silence. I wonder all the things I usually wonder, then realize there's a lesson to be learned in this night's activities.

Luke's right. You only can be certain if you try.

You only know if you ask.

"You're looking very thoughtful," he says, turning me around so he can wash my back in long smooth strokes.

"Why haven't you moved in?" I ask and his hand stops for a second.

"Why haven't you invited me to?"

It appears that we have different assumptions about this and I'm glad I've asked. "This is my fault?"

"No, it's your choice. I've wanted to stay here from the very beginning, but it's your house. It's up to you if and when that happens."

"Really?"

"Really." He flings out a hand. "Just showing up somewhere, saying 'oh, I'm staying here, I'll have my eggs over easy at seven' seems presumptuous." I bite back a smile because he does a pretty good impression of Justin. "I don't even turn up uninvited at my mom's place with expectations."

"But that house is kind of your house, seeing that you bought it and all."

"I bought it for her," Luke corrects me, his eyes turning that vivid blue. "It's *her* house. It's up to her who stays there."

"That's very sweet," I say softly.

"Sweet," he echoes under his breath, his eyes no less stormy. "Not a fave adjective of mine, Daph, especially not applied to me."

"But you are sweet," I tell him. "And nice."

"Argh!"

"And sometimes a little bit spicy, too." He starts to smile. "Definitely not predictable."

"Thank God for that." He surveys me with a smile. "You are definitely not predictable."

"I thought I was."

"Not even close. I love how you surprise me." He bends down and kisses me, then washes my legs. "How did the moving in together thing work with you and JJ?"

"JJ?"

"Jerk Justin."

I laugh a little even though I don't want to talk about Justin. Luke is washing between my toes with a thoroughness I doubt is merited, but I watch him, noting how the muscles move in his shoulders, how his hands are both strong and gentle. He glances up, reminding me that I haven't answered, and I try. "I don't know. No big announcement. I don't even remember a discussion. We always went to his place, because he had a house and I had a little tiny apartment. One night, it seemed too late to go home, so I stayed." I shrug as if it doesn't matter, because I've had enough reminder of Justin today to last me a year.

Maybe a lifetime.

Luke stands up quickly beside me. "Do not tell me that you routinely left his house in the middle of the night and went home alone." When his eyes flash like that, he looks like a vengeful god.

"Why wouldn't I?"

"Because the world is full of predators, Daph. He should have taken you home if you weren't staying..."

I smile at his ferocity, then reach up and touch my lips to his cheek. He has, of course, a perfect scruffy single day of stubble, and his beard is ridiculously soft. I love the feel of it beneath my lips and think I should probably tell him how good it feels on my nipples.

"I like how protective you are," I say instead.

"It's just how I am."

"I know." I smile, knowing how he'll respond to my next words. "It's sweet."

"Let's get back to spicy," he growls but I glimpse satisfaction in his eyes before he kisses me with such heat that he steals my breath away.

Again.

This man. How is it that his effect on me only gets stronger every time we're together? Shouldn't it diminish? Shouldn't familiarity breed contempt or at least indifference? But it doesn't. I feel like he's cast a spell over me and it just becomes more powerful with prolonged exposure—and the amazing part is that I like that just fine.

I love him, always and forever.

I can admit it to myself, at least.

———

IT'S LATER and we're in bed. I'm lying on my stomach, feeling better than I ever have on day one, and Luke is kneeling behind me. His hands are on my waist, warm and heavy, and his thumbs are working some rhythmic sorcery on the small of my back. He found the herbal tea Willow gave me, the one that tastes like straw in hot water, and has made me a cup. Either it's making me feel better or the Motrin is at work. (My bet is on the orgasms.)

I'm relaxed and content, probably too relaxed and content, because my filter is off.

I start to ask him things I want to know.

I'm grabbing this take-a-chance philosophy and running with it.

"How do you know all about this?" is my first question. "About this time of the month."

"Why wouldn't I?"

"I have to think that one-and-done doesn't usually happen with the special effects."

He laughs a little, a warm and comforting sound. "My mom and I looked out for each other."

I glance over my shoulder at him, slightly horrified. "She didn't talk to you about this when you were a kid?"

"No, but I knew that sometimes she didn't feel well and I learned what helped." He leans down, his lips on the back of my neck. "Motrin, tea and hot water bottles, *not* orgasms. Nothing twisted, Daph. I wasn't that much of a rulebreaker."

I smile into my pillow.

"She told me that once, that sex helped, years later when I was…active. Maybe she thought it would ensure I didn't bolt in horror. I don't know. I never investigated until now." He bends over me again, the prickle of his chest hair against my back. "It's remained an intriguing possibility, but now, hmmm, I want it in the rotation."

"I agree." My smile broadens a bit at even a hint of permanence to our relationship, coming from him.

"What do you want for dinner?"

"You cook?"

"Some."

"Then surprise me." I wait a beat. "I'm not much good at cooking. Maybe we can take turns after you move in."

His eyes light and he freezes for a second, then smiles slowly. "Is that an invitation, Daph?" he murmurs, his voice deep and wonderful.

I nod. "It is. I think there's space for your guitar in the living room, and I can make room in the closet for your stuff." He's staring at me like I'm speaking in another language, like he doesn't dare believe it, so I take a breath and say the rest. "I'd really like you to."

I get a kiss that probably isn't intended to leave me as dizzy as it does. My heart is leaping around my chest like it's doing an Olympic gymnastics routine by the time he's done and I know he likes the idea as much as I do.

I watch as Luke saunters out of the bedroom with purpose, feeling like the luckiest person on the planet—and that's before he starts whistling.

Will it be better if he stays longer, or will that just make it hurt more when he leaves? I don't care anymore. I'm in for the experience, wherever it takes us.

And I'm going to love every minute.

32
——

LUKE

I'm heading to the theater the next morning for a meeting with the building inspector when Daph's dad passes me in the Benz, then pulls in to park in front of his office. I know Daph is down at the other end of Queen Street this morning, scheming with Willow about her new office. I've just called Bruno to tell him that I'm checking out and he's cool with me picking up my stuff at the end of the day.

I wave and say good morning, planning to just carry on, but Daph's dad has stopped on the sidewalk, waiting for me.

"When you have a minute, I'd like to talk to you."

I check my watch. Now is as good as any time, depending how much of a chat it's going to be.

"Ten minutes," he says, anticipating my question.

"Now works for me."

He gestures and we head into his offices, greeting his receptionist on the way to his office. He's a methodical man, one who can't be rushed and one who has his routines. There's a reassuring rhythm in the way he speaks to her, then hangs up his coat. She's placed the morning paper from Toronto on his desk and opened the blinds. The office itself is all dark wood and oxblood leather, with a whole wall of books that are likely legal references. It's traditional and reassuring. I feel as if everything's going to be fine, which is a great spell to cast to potential clients. Richard himself is wearing a dark gray suit, a shirt with French cuffs and a perfectly knotted burgundy tie. He's overdressed for Empire, but he fits in this room.

He offers me a seat and I take it, wondering what to expect.

"Since time is of the essence," he begins. "I'll get right to the point. It's apparent that you're spending a lot of money, particularly on the Odeon."

"It needs everything," I say, with a little bit of exasperation.

"And were you expecting that?"

"The roof was a surprise, but I probably should have anticipated it."

Richard nods. "And I have to think that the engine driving sales for a band would be either new content or public appearances."

It's easy to see how Daph comes by her intelligence. "True," I admit, waiting.

Richard chooses his words with care, a hint that this isn't easy for him. "It's not my business, but in a way, it is, since I want to do all I can to ensure Daphne's happiness. So, I wondered how you are doing financially. Such a large expenditure would drain the resources of many people."

I am uncomfortable with this question, especially as he's hit the nail right on the head. I've been fretting about my cash flow. I'm not a finance guy, adept with leveraging assets to make them work harder. I just pay my bills and make more money, but right now, my pool of assets is steadily diminishing. I've been wondering whether I'll be able to finish what I've started. There are the donations from local people and they're great, but most of them are on the smaller side. It doesn't take long for a couple of thousand dollars to be devoured in the installation of a huge metal roof, or the rewiring of a theatre.

But I'll be damned before I admit as much to my father's ally.

Richard carries on. "I thought you might, you know, ask for help. You've undertaken a noble venture here and an expensive one." He gives me an assessing look. "But last night I realized that you'll never do that. You've never been taught that you can rely on anyone else, and on those rare occasions when you've asked for anything, you've been declined. Why would you ask anyone for anything?"

He's absolutely right, but hearing it said aloud leaves me feeling naked.

"I asked Daph for help," I remind him.

"Exactly," he says with satisfaction. "And that's obviously significant to both of us, particularly as she agreed."

"And she set up the donation program."

"True. But, in the interest of being part of the solution, I'd like to offer you a contribution." He names a number that is more than enough to make everything come right. "It can be a loan, if you want to repay me in some specified period of time. It can be an investment, if you want a silent partner in the Odeon. The choice is yours and the funds can be transferred tomorrow."

When something sounds too good to be true, it often is, so I ask. "Why are you doing this? Why would you break rank with Patrick?"

Richard leans back in his chair and considers the ceiling, templing his fingers together. "You probably don't remember my wife, Christine."

"Only vaguely," I admit. "I knew her to see. My mom cut her hair."

He nods, a smile of reminiscence softening his features. "Of course," he says softly, then straightens. "We moved a lot when I was a kid, so I never felt that I was from anywhere specific. But

Christine had grown up in Empire, as had her parents before her. She had roots in this town and she loved it so much. I could never have asked her to leave it, so we came here to begin our lives together. Married in the Anglican Church right over there. Rented the apartment over Jim's Antiques until I made partner here, then lived upstairs here for five years before we could buy the house. Mr. Weatherby was very good to us, but it was tough to make ends meet in such a small place. When I tell Daphne that there's not much of a living to be earned from wills and divorces in a town the size of Empire, that's because I've been there and done that."

I nod understanding.

"And then I met Patrick. More than that, Patrick began to grow his business by leaps and bounds. He needed legal counsel on retainer, and I jumped for that opportunity. It changed everything for us, gave us financial security and ensured that I could give Christine and Daphne the lives I wanted them to have. Of course, it came with a price, and that price was and is Patrick."

He pauses for a moment and I think of Faust, making his deal with the devil. I know all about Patrick ensuring that a choice is regretted and I feel sympathy for Daph's dad.

He continues with resolve. "Christine disliked Patrick and she hated what happened to Empire as his businesses grew. It was the one thing we argued about, and the one thing we stopped discussing because it became such a sore point. I know she wanted me to step away, for the sake of principles, but I knew that we needed that money. Daphne was destined for university and a law degree, and only the best school would do. Christine never had a job outside of the home, which suited both of us, but it meant I had to be the one to provide. I had to make the choice for our future." His voice hardens when he says this, and I know it wasn't an easy decision for him to make. "I thought we'd have our retirement together to enjoy the results."

He looks away and his throat works. "And then Christine

died." His words are hoarse. "Just like that. She was there at breakfast, the same as every other day, and before lunch, the neighbour called to say that she was dead." He snaps his fingers, still looking incredulous though I know it's been a few years. "She had an aneurysm and the only blessing was that it was instant for her."

"I'm sorry."

He inclines his head in acknowledgement and continues. "I still can't believe it some days. I still listen for her when I get home. I still expect her to call in the middle of the afternoon." He shakes his head. "But that's never going to happen. I'll be honest. I was skeptical when you showed up with your big plan. I thought Patrick would win again and you would be ground under his heel. But you're tougher than that, Luke, and maybe that's what he taught you. Never expect anything from anyone, and never surrender. That's quite the legacy and I admire what you've accomplished."

He pauses for breath. "Since you arrived here, though, I realize your achievements to date are just the tip of the iceberg. I'd like to help. I'm tired of just putting one foot in front of the other. I'm tired of surviving each day so I can do it all again. I'd like to be part of the rebirth of Empire. And I'm prepared to put some of that money to work in fostering a change, for Christine's sake."

I am overwhelmed by this confession and have a hard time finding a reply. "You have to have guessed that my instinctive response is to decline your offer," I say, and we smile at each other warily. "But for the sake of Daph and personal growth and Empire, I'm going to kick that impulse to the curb."

"Good."

"Thank you, sir."

He stands up and offers his hand. "Richard," he corrects me and we shake hands. I've never had an older man take my side in anything and I realize in that moment that Richard has a wealth of experience he may choose to share.

"I'd prefer a partner," I say, "and maybe not an entirely silent one."

His smile flashes. "I'd like that a lot."

The office is filled with a warmth that takes me by surprise, yet feels so very welcome.

Daph, Daph, Daph. How is it that you have the power to heal every wound I have?

"Why don't you join us for breakfast tomorrow? We can go to the bank in Havelock afterwards and get the funds transferred."

"But that's your weekly meeting with Daph. I don't want to interfere."

"There's less business to discuss now that she's going out on her own." He gives me a look. "You and I might have more business to discuss now."

Careful what you wish for. My silent partner is already speaking up. "Really?"

"Really. I'm not alone in this impulse, Luke. A number of people in town have spoken to me about your efforts and their appreciation of it. Some will have made donations, but there might be ways you can harness that enthusiasm and even build a stronger sense of community, although whatever happens should be structured to protect everyone's interests."

"I'm listening."

"I'll work up a couple of different scenarios that we can discuss in the morning. Daphne may have some additional ideas, too."

"I'm looking forward to it." We shake again at the door. "Thank you, Richard."

"Thank you, Luke. I never thought I'd see her so happy again. That's worth the world to me."

He doesn't have to say it. I know he's warning me not to break Daph's heart, but that's not part of my plan.

And now, I have a building inspector to see, one who is probably going to give me more bad news. I'm less worried about it now, though, now that I have Richard's support.

I pass Daph on the street, loving that she's brimming with ideas and so excited. She gives me a kiss that makes me wish the day was over and I hold her close.

It could have been a perfect morning if a silver Porsche hadn't rolled in to park beside Richard's car just then. Daph's lips set and she places a hand on my chest when I would have charged to her defense. She looks mean and determined, a formidable adversary ready to carve a certain lawyer a new one.

Of course, JJ is a persistent prick.

(Maybe I should have keyed his car.)

"Leave him to me," Daph says grimly.

"Can't I watch?" I ask and her smile flashes.

"You have work to do."

"I do, sadly. Meet me at Merrie's for lunch and tell me everything."

"Deal," she says, decisive, her thoughts clearly on the smack-down ahead. I really *really* want to watch this, but I respect her choice.

"Noon?"

"Noon," she agrees and I turn to watch her go. She's wearing that sleek silver gray suit and it's easy to imagine her as a barracuda, slicing through the ocean to slaughter her unwitting prey.

It's so unfair that I can't witness JJ's decimation, but I text the café for a reservation, then continue to the theatre.

I'm moving in with Daph and she does not love JJ anymore.

No doubt about it, Empire is starting to feel like home.

33

———

DAPHNE

I have to give Justin points for persistence.

He's all suited up, freshly shaved and perfectly groomed. My heart should be all a-flutter but instead there's a cold stone in its place.

I've said no and he's not listening.

That makes me mad.

It makes me wish I had a Medusa stare for real.

He's with my dad, who doesn't look impressed, though Mrs. Prescott can't fully hide her admiration of this prime male specimen in her vicinity.

"Daphne!" Justin says as if it's a surprise I've shown up at work. "I was just waiting for you."

I check my watch. "I have an appointment in ten minutes, so I hope your errand is a quick one. You must remember how I prefer to be punctual."

He looks chastened, but just for a heartbeat.

"I did suggest to you that it would be best to call Daphne before driving down here," my dad says smoothly and Justin's lips tighten.

So, my dad didn't tell him where I lived, and didn't surrender my number. Justin just assumed I'd welcome him back and came down here. He must have looked for my car, the way that Luke did.

Somehow that seems less admirable in his case.

My dad excuses himself, then gives me a wink of encouragement that Justin can't see before vanishing into his office. I gesture to my office and Justin precedes me. I notice his survey of the space, figure he's calculated the square footage within five per cent. "You have a window," he notes and I remember how coveted offices with windows were in the city.

"Best of the best," I say, sliding into my chair and putting the barrier of the desk between us. "What can I do for you today?"

Justin comes around the desk, perching on it right beside me so his thigh almost touches mine. There's a predatory gleam in his eyes, a satisfaction with himself that just makes me a little colder. He's sure he's going to win me over. I can smell the confidence radiating from him, and I'm looking forward to seeing his expression when he realizes he's lost completely and irrevocably.

"May I be blunt?" he asks with a charming smile.

"By all means."

"So, we're even, Daphne. You've had your fling and I've had mine."

Interesting that he places my relationship with Luke first, and that he labels it as a temporary affair. I know better than to let that pass.

"No, you had a fling and we split up. Whatever relationships I may or may not have pursued since that time are of no relevance to you."

"Don't be prickly, Daphne." He reaches for my hand but I move it away. "You know that we should be together. We're perfect for each other."

"Except for those times when you want to be with somebody else."

"You're playing word games."

"That is what we're trained to do."

"You can't be serious about this guy, whoever he is. I understand that he's a boy-toy and some man candy. Not my type but I get it." If this is a joke, I don't even crack a smile. "I understand that you have needs and it's fair that you've indulged them. But you're not getting any younger, and if we're going to have a family, we need to get started."

I pretend to be dizzy. "Wait. We're not just getting back together. We're getting married and having a family? How many kids, Justin? When are they due? What are their names? Have you booked them into the best pre-schools yet?"

"You can joke all you want, Daphne, but I'm serious. We had a good thing going and we need to get back to that. I can get you a position at the firm again. I spoke to the senior partners before I came down here."

"You arranged a job for me? Without talking to me first?"

"Of course. You were always very prudent financially. I knew it might be a stumbling block to be without a job." His gaze sweeps over me and admiration lights his eyes. "You look great today, by the way, as attractive as ever."

I get up and step past him, standing at the door like a sentinel. He swivels on the desk to watch me, clearly not understanding that I'm going to chuck him out. "You have to leave."

"Oh, right. Your appointment. Why don't you cancel, Daphne? I mean, you don't need clients down here anymore. We can head back to the city early, catch dinner in town."

"I'm not cancelling my appointment and I'm not going with you, Justin. You have to leave because I don't want to talk to you anymore."

"Be reasonable, Daphne!" He stands up, smiles, and prepares to make an appeal.

"You're not listening to me."

"You're not saying anything worth listening to," he counters, as if that's reasonable. "You know that I know best."

"No, I don't know that. I know that we have irreconcilable views of our respective futures," I say. "I don't want to get back together with you. I don't want a job at the firm again. I don't want to renovate your kitchen or marry you or have your kids. In fact, I don't want to see you ever again." I open the door. "I want you to leave."

He doesn't move. "You used to believe we were good together."

"That's true. I did. I was wrong. I realized that when you followed your dick to another woman's bed."

"Daphne!"

"It's what you did and I see now that it was inevitable. So, thanks Justin. Thanks for doing it sooner rather than later. Otherwise, we might have been married. My dream kitchen might have been in your house when I realized what a prick you are. We might have had those kids already, and it would have been a lot messier to pick our lives apart. This way it was simple, and as you say, neither of us are getting any younger. I'm glad I still have time to be happy, so thanks for that." I indicate the open door.

Mrs. Prescott is listening avidly while pretending not to.

Justin looks at me, then at the door, and his jaw sets when he meets my gaze again. Anger has settled in his eyes, the anger of a man who isn't used to being denied whatever he wants. But I'm smart enough to realize that he doesn't really want me. I'm no more important than a chess piece being moved into place. For all I know, the senior partners have told him that he has to get married and be settled appropriately before he can be promoted again. For all I know, the union has been approved, like a royal marriage to secure dynasties and maybe add a firmer chin to the future lineage.

I want more.

I want to make my own choice.

I want someone who listens to me.

I want someone who loves me for myself.

"You're going to regret this," he says, the exit line of every loser in the history of mankind.

"I'll get over it," I assure him and his nostrils flare before he marches past me and leaves. He slams the door of the office, then the door of his car, the engine roaring to life. The tires squeal and he's gone in a puff of exhaust, racing back to the life he wants.

The one I don't.

I sit down, my knees shaking a little in the aftermath and the phone on my desk rings. I pick up, say my name.

"Well done," my dad says with such approval that I smile. "Your mother was right. He was never going to make you happy."

"I know," I say and I hear that he smiles along with me.

"I invested in your young man's venture this morning, by the way," he says. "And he's joining us for breakfast tomorrow. Just so you know."

"You've decided that you like him," I say and he chuckles.

"I have. I like him very much."

34

———

LUKE

And so it begins, an era closer to perfection than anything I've ever known. Daph and I settle into a routine so easily it might have been destined to be. I like the look of my guitar in the living room, my coat and boots in the closet instead of just inside the door: I'm a resident instead of a guest. I like discovering my clothes in the closet every morning—Daph cleared out half, but I really only need a sliver of space, so she spread her things back out.

I love seeing her clothes against mine.

I love finding her house key on my key ring and sliding my thumb across it during the day. I love working on that song in her living room in the evening. I make a lot of progress on Wednesday nights when she's out. I usually walk to wherever to escort her home and we talk on the way. I love that fluffy bathrobe and the smell of her skin on the sheets, the thrill of waking up pressed against her.

I love being with her even more. She sleeps later than I do, so I get up as quietly as I can and go for my run. I quickly figure out the timing so that I can get back in time to make coffee before she wakes up. She's adorably sleepy in the mornings and I can't wait for the days when everything settles down and I can linger in bed in the morning, just to watch her wake up. Right now, I'm running on deadlines and adrenaline, with way too much to do.

She revises her list of my supposed assets, by the way, and the vee barely makes the cut. Apparently, the sexiest thing about me is that I'm tidy. Live and learn.

At night I usually cook, as Daph gets in later. Nothing fancy. Protein with rice and vegetables. Dinner on a cookie sheet. Pretty quick and fairly healthy. I like when we cook together, talking about our respective days, comparing notes and sharing stories. When I cook, she sits at the counter to watch, and we talk. A couple of times a week, Merrie invites us to a taste test as she fine-tunes her menu. Wednesdays, Daph meets up with her friends. Fridays we often order from Phil but a couple of times, we walk down to the taco truck. Saturdays, I give Sierra a guitar lesson. As the weather gets warmer, we talk about what she wants to do with the gardens around the house. Well, there aren't any gardens yet, but Daph has a vision.

But the very best part is falling asleep every night in Daph's bed, my arms around her, her scent filling my senses. I feel anchored in a way I never have before, as though I've found my place in the world.

My haven.

I'm not sure she shares my view. The lovemaking is great, but we never talk about our feelings. Each time I think of opening the subject, a couple of words is enough to make her freeze up, so I stop. What is she thinking? What is she feeling? I want to know but I recognize that I have to wait for her to want to tell me.

In the meantime, work on the theatre is progressing and organization is ramping up for the concert. I've rented part of Daph's commercial building so Chelsea and her team have a place to work, and Daph had the internet connection and phones turned on before they even arrived. I let them loose at Jim's to furnish the space and it looks good. Lots of solid wood and vintage chairs.

Merrie is adding a chef's tasting on Thursday nights and I have it on good authority that Rafe is dying. He has yet to figure out a way to be in Empire on Thursday nights and at work on time Fridays.

Noah is building his audience by leaps and bounds. He's relentless with his interviews and demands for updates, but I love watching him work. Chelsea is giving him some pointers, too, and I usually find him there when I check in. Chelsea gives him four pairs of tickets to give away, however he likes, and he runs with it. We also give six pairs to that radio station in Havelock, and set up a raffle for another two pair to local Empire residents.

Chelsea is all about building consensus, so she talks to people on the street, identifying their concerns over the concert. Thanks to that research, we organize a central number to book accommodation and matchmake attendees with residents willing to offer a short term rental that weekend. We also book some extra cleaning teams, given concerns about litter, and there will be a line of portable toilets set up in the alley behind the theatre.

Everything is arranged when the tickets go on sale. It's an online sale at a ticketing site and I'm nervous that our fans may have forgotten us. It's been over a year after all. Empire isn't exactly close to anything. Two thousand seats seems like a lot all of a sudden.

We hold our breath as the clock ticks over. We're all in Chelsea's offices at Daph's place. Daph is there, holding my hand, watching with me.

The show sells out in four minutes.

It would have been two if the server hadn't burped.

There is hooting and cheering, lots of fist bumps and high fives. We march across the street to celebrate with dinner at Merrie's.

The show is less than three weeks away, but we have wind in our sails now. Amanda is talking to utilities companies, discussing our electrical requirements for the night in question so we don't blow the circuits and end up in the dark. She's also lobbying for more cell phone bandwidth in the area, but even she might not be able to make that happen.

Best of all, the next day, the trucks arrive. I'm not the only one who shows up on Queen Street to watch the two big black tractor trailers roll in. I'm probably the only one so thrilled to see them. They look huge on Queen Street, bigger even than I know them to be. The sight brings back a lot of memories of different tours, different cities, different times. The trailers have the band logo on the side and they're full of gear, lights and instruments and everything else, all pulled out of storage and packed by the crew that have driven them into town.

They park on the other side of Queen Street, leaving a gap between them so I can see The Carpe Diem Café. The buses are right behind the trucks, two black custom buses with tinted windows. These don't have logos, and it's good to see them again, our homes away from home. I'm missing Taylor so much that I halfway expect him to swing down from the first bus when it stops. Brent and Zach are in their bus, and have been catching up on the drive.

We have a hug in the middle of the street and it's so awesome. We take a little tour and have dinner together at Merrie's. It's a Wednesday, so Daph is at Cameron's. I invited her but she told me to catch up with the crew. The bistro is bustling, filled with a lot of our crew as well as some locals becoming addicted to Merrie's fare. Merrie gives me a thumbs-up from the kitchen but doesn't pause to chat.

I say goodnight to Brent and Zach, directing the bus drivers to The Maple Leaf Motel. Bruno has set up a spot for them behind the motel and out of view. They can park on an empty lot he owns and no one will see them. A lot of the other crew are staying at the motel anyway. The tractor trailers will move down to a secured parking zone at Port Cavendish once they're empty.

Wookie wants me to come back to the theatre to admire the gear he's already started to set in place, and that's when I see it.

There's a notice taped to the door of the theatre, one that must have been put there while we were at dinner.

Someone is bringing a challenge to city council, trying to stop the concert, and we are summoned to Havelock City Hall to defend our plan next Tuesday night at seven.

I don't need three guesses to know who the instigator has to be.

I text Daph, asking for help with a plan.

She's coming across the lawn from Cameron's by the time I get close to her house, clearly livid. "How dare he?" she fumes, practically spitting sparks. "How *dare* he?"

She's my own personal Valkyrie come to claim my soul forever.

It's hers, all hers, and I'll do whatever she wants.

What she wants is to head to the office and make an action plan. I call in the team as she starts writing points on the big whiteboard and I love that she's on my side.

Good luck to Patrick. She's going to feed him his own liver.

And I, along with all of Havelock city council and any interested bystanders, get to watch.

It does not get better than this.

———

THE CITY COUNCIL chamber in Havelock is packed when we arrive. I have no idea how much interest there is locally in civic matters, but a quick glance reveals many familiar faces. Of course, I know our team, and I expected Patrick to be here. Daph's dad isn't with Patrick but is sitting at the back of the hall with his neighbours. I'm guessing Patrick isn't happy about that because he's looking daggers at everyone.

Mackenzie is here with an older guy who has to be her dad, Augustine. They're sitting with Cameron and Willow, and Willow's uncle, Jim. Phil Chang is here with his mom, who is happily greeting everyone as if she's at a party. My mom arrives and Willow urges her to sit with them. She smiles encouragement at me as she sinks gratefully into a seat.

Bruno gives me a wave from where he's sitting with Marissa, then two thumbs-up. I spot the girl from the thrift store, though it takes me a minute to place her. She's sitting with the guy from the convenience store, which must be closed tonight. He gives me a wise nod. The two guys who run the taco truck on Friday night slide into the seats beside him, the three of them conferring quickly.

I can't believe they've all come. There are people who have donated to the theatre's restoration, but a whole lot more who haven't. There are people who I've seen at Merrie's and some I've never seen before. It seems the entire town of Empire has turned out.

I hope at least half of them are on our side.

I have suited up, per Daph's instruction, as has she. She told me to look like the solution not part of the problem and I do take instruction well. It's a question of ceding to someone else's expertise.

Sylvia and Una come in with Merrie, Una looking tired but determined. Sierra is behind them, engrossed in something on her phone. She's followed by Noah, whose mom has brought him so he can get the story. They all sit behind Daph and me, a veritable army of support from the town that I once couldn't wait to leave.

Will it be enough? I've no clue.

I don't have time to worry about it because the meeting is being called to order.

In the very moment that Patrick glares at me in challenge, I feel a hand on my shoulder. "Rock the casbah, non-dad," Sierra whispers and I cast her a smile.

"Picked that one just for me, did you, non-daughter?"

"Hey, just trying to connect, old man." She gives me a cocky grin and I don't have the heart to tell her that I wasn't even a gleam in anyone's eye when The Clash sent that one up the charts. I remember believing that everyone over twenty was nearly dead, and also how a few brushes with mortality change that view.

She probably listens to that same Havelock radio station now. Sooner or later, classic rock will bring us all together.

I watch as she goes to sit with Sylvia then look up to find Patrick's basilisk stare still fixed on me, fury emanating from him in waves. I smile back at him, knowing what he's seen and guessing what conclusion he's made. I let my eyes narrow just a little, and send a message he won't miss.

Hurt her and I will find you.

He inhales sharply and looks away, maybe the first time he's ever blinked in a stare-down. Maybe he's getting too old to rumble. Maybe I've not been so fierce before.

Either way, it starts the proceedings off right.

———

I LOVE WATCHING Daph in action. She's cool and composed, dispassionate yet compelling. She has an outline and sticks to it—a plan, as it were. She takes her time, pausing to give emphasis to an important point, guiding the listeners through her argument. She's taken her presentation right off the whiteboard she started to fill with points as soon as we heard about the challenge. It was a thing of beauty, Daph listing all potential issues, then our team adding how we've addresses each and every one. It showed up some gaps, and we stepped up to fix them.

Daph has no intention of losing and I'm glad to have her on our side.

Patrick has submitted a relentless list of grievances, but Daph takes them in turn, so thorough and reasonable that no one can argue with her. Even I have to think that the team has done a great job. Chelsea is right there to provide back-up at a moment's notice, and River has a mountain of stats at his fingertips. That kid has a calculator for a brain and a photographic memory, too.

Daph has the whole presentation memorized and only pauses for effect. It's an impressive performance, one that trumps Patrick's forceful complaint that launched the meeting. The mayor and the other councillors are watching Daph and checking the crowd seated behind me, gauging the temperature.

I take a pointer from that and try to read the room. Daph is brilliant, but I wonder if she's claimed their hearts. She looks a bit like a flash lawyer from Toronto in a great suit addressing a bunch of people who maybe shop at L.L. Bean. There's a lot of plaid and many pairs of chinos, some jeans and casual sweaters. They'll probably dismiss Patrick's objections, but I want more than to win by the skin of our teeth.

I want everyone on our side, just like the people behind me.

In fact, their presence, the very fact that they all took the trouble to drive to Havelock on a Wednesday night to show their support, convinces me that they really care about the future of Empire.

Daph and I can win this with teamwork.

When Daph is done, she gives me a little smile as she returns to her seat. Only I see the glisten of perspiration on her nape and the slight tremble of her fingers. The mayor asks if there are other opinions, and I stand up. It's not on the schedule. It's not part of the plan. But I need to add my voice to this discussion.

This is how I'll be part of the solution.

"I would like to add a few comments," I say and the mayor

nods his agreement. I shed my suit jacket and roll up my sleeves, loosening my tie a bit as I choose how to begin. "A lot of you know that I grew up in Empire," I begin, my tone conversational. "It's true that I've been gone a long time, but sometimes I think you have to leave a place to really appreciate it. I never saw how special Empire was before I came back this year. It's a town where people don't lock their doors, where everyone knows their neighbours, where news is exchanged over the back fence. It's a town where residents feel safe, where families stay for generations, where people look out for each other. When I was a kid, I saw its limitations. I didn't realize what a rare treasure it was."

There is a faint murmur of agreement.

I walk to the middle of the room, taking the space Daph recently owned. "But when you realize something is precious, it's only natural to want to protect it. In a way, Empire is the place I knew as a kid, and in a way, it's not. The shopfronts are closed on Queen Street. People come to Havelock for work, for school, for groceries. Empire is becoming a ghost town and that breaks my heart. Ghost towns are empty places, haunted by the past but having no future. I want Empire to have a future, so I wondered what I could do to contribute to that."

I meet a lot of concerned gazes, feeling that there's agreement to that in the room. "I acquired a former diner on Queen Street and convinced a talented chef to open her farm-to-table bistro there. Now, there's a great place to eat in Empire, The Carpe Diem Café, and there's another business to buy from local producers. A shameless pitch here: if you haven't made the trip to check out Merrie's place, you owe it to yourselves to fix that. She's an amazing chef."

There's a little ripple of laughter and I smile. "But one restaurant isn't enough. I knew Empire needed more of an economic boost and when my band decided to hold a tribute concert, I wanted to have it in Empire. The Odeon Theatre has been sitting empty for years. We renovated it, my partners and I, and brought everything up to code. The building inspectors from Havelock have been there almost daily and they've had some great suggestions. It's a heritage building, although it hasn't been designated as such, built for visiting vaudeville shows over a hundred years ago. It's a big part of Empire's history, and of mine. I went to the movies there as a teenager. It's beautiful inside and constructed to last, and I'm honoured that we've been able to give it a new life. It has a new roof, new wiring, updated plumbing and a new sprinkler system. We've taken out some of the two thousand original seats at the suggestion of the fire marshal, to provide better egress in an emergency. The best thing about it, though, is the acoustics. Every time we rehearse, I'm blown away."

I turn to the councillors. "And so we have a building, originally constructed to host live performances, returned to its former glory to host one performance. We have a team of people committed to ensuring that Empire sees only benefits from this one event, people who have arranged much larger concerts in much more demanding venues in the past, people who have tried to consider every variable in their planning. And we have a community, a community with many, many people who have made donations to help finance the renovation of this building in their town."

That's when I have the idea and it's so right that I just go with it. "I want the people of Empire to be happy with the results of this event, and I don't want anyone worrying about damage or litter or noise. We've tried to address that already, as you've heard tonight, but there's always more than can be done. I propose that we set up a hotline tomorrow and ensure that the people of Empire know about it. That way, anybody with a complaint during the performance, before or after, can immediately reach a live person, one who will address their concerns." There are sage nods from the councillors and a few murmurs of approval. Chelsea gives me a thumbs-up and I know she'll own this.

I turn to face the contingent from Empire. "Does that make sense to you?"

Bruno starts the applause and it sweeps through the observers, a crescendo that proves the appeal of the solution.

I turn back to the councillors. "I want this tribute to be a success for everyone involved and for Empire, too. I've been thrilled to have many of the people of Empire contribute to the renovation cost, and we'll start giving tours of the refurbished interior, as soon as the building inspectors give us the all-clear."

There is audible approval of that plan.

I nod to Noah. "Keep an eye on The Empire Chronicle for the schedule. If you don't have that website bookmarked already, you might want to do it now." Some people reach for their phones and Noah looks like he'll burst with pride.

I meet the gaze of each councillor in turn. "I believe in trying to make a difference, and I believe in protecting what matters. For me, now, that's Empire and its future, and if this tribute can be even a tiny part of a town's economic recovery, I want to be a part of it. Thank you for your attention tonight and I hope you find our position compelling."

There's a louder round of applause from the people seated behind us, one that has many of them on their feet. That becomes contagious, flowing through the ranks of all the observers until we have a standing ovation.

It takes a few minutes for the council to restore order, then the mayor rises with a smile. "Our decision is clear. Patrick Cavendish, your objections have been overwhelmed. Luke Jones, we wish you and your tribute concert all the best. The concert is cleared to proceed as scheduled."

Team Empire gives a hoot of victory and as soon as the meeting is dismissed, I'm surrounded by everyone who wants to congratulate us. My hand is shaken and my back thumped. My mom gives me a big kiss on the cheek and Daph looks delighted.

I have some tickets, of course, and when I'm thronged in the parking lot by people who want to tell me of their support, I give them out in pairs. Daph's dad invites a lot of people back to his place for celebratory drinks and that gets everyone from Empire moving. Daph offers to stop at the liquor store while he goes straight home and we walk to the Honda hand in hand.

We are an unbeatable team.

"You rock," I say to her. "You were amazing."

"You weren't so bad yourself."

"I couldn't have made that presentation alone. I would have missed a good half of the variables, but you're so brilliant at seeing all the angles."

"You couldn't have told me about the hotline sooner?" Daph asks with a smile.

"I didn't think of it sooner."

She stops to stare at me. "You just thought of it then and there, and went with it?" Of course, she would dissect any idea, plan it out, check it and recheck it. I love how thorough she is, but sometimes impulse steers you true.

"I knew it was right. It had resonance." She shakes her head and I bend down to whisper in her ear. "Just like being with you."

And she smiles, the sight enough to light up my life forever. I kiss her, making the most of it since we have to be social for a while yet. The people from Empire honk at us as they leave the parking lot, but Daph is in my arms, kissing me back, and that's the only thing that matters.

I know with sudden clarity exactly what I have to do.

35

DAPHNE

It's the week before the concert, a Tuesday, when someone knocks on my door. I open it to find Luke on my doorstep. He's nervous, which isn't what I expected. I never even imagined that Luke could be less than confident, but his agitation is obvious.

"Forget your key?"

"No, I just wanted to make sure we talked."

"Are you coming in?"

"Not yet."

He frowns and looks away. I recall that he hasn't performed for over a year and the build-up to this concert is huge. Is he worried about the show?

"Something wrong?"

"Maybe something's right," he says in an undertone, then impales me with a glance. He's conjured a slip of paper from somewhere—no, it's a ticket. "I was hoping you might be planning to attend the tribute."

"You know I am. Even though it sold out in minutes, Cameron got us all tickets together."

He presents the ticket. "I was hoping that you'd sit here."

"But I have a ticket."

His eyes narrow. "You don't have this one."

I tilt my head to read the seat assignment. Row A. "I have to think that's in the front row."

"Front and center."

"I'll see you wherever I am. The Odeon isn't that big."

"But I won't be able to see *you*. Not with the lights." This is important to him, though I'm not sure why. I know I'm missing something.

"Why..."

I don't get to finish the question. He moves his thumb, revealing that there's a second ticket behind the first one. "Abbie's coming," he says and I can't hide my excitement. "I thought you two could sit front and center and cheer me on."

"Abbie! That's fabulous!" I throw myself at him and he swings me around, smiling at my enthusiasm. There's still some part of the puzzle I've missed, but I guess that he's not going to tell me. There's a serious glint in his eyes which is worrisome. It feeds all my anxieties about the future, even though I've told myself a million times to be cool, that it was worth the ride however things shake out. "But how did you convince her?"

"I said she'd be sitting with you. I worked it out so she wouldn't have to go to the house, so she agreed. She's going to stay with Mackenzie."

"She is not. She's staying here."

"Fight it out with Mackenzie," he says amiably.

I kiss him, amazed by how much magic one man can make when he sets his mind to it. "But we don't have to sit in the front row. Save those seats for your super-fans."

"Daph! I'm crushed that you don't count yourself in that company." He's teasing so I swat him then I realize the potential problem with Abbie in my spare bedroom.

"You don't mind if she's here when you're here?"

Luke looks discomfited and I brace myself for something I suspect I won't like. "I actually won't be here." Oh, I don't like that one bit. "I'll be staying on the bus. We always do that before a performance, so everyone knows the team is in place."

"Starting when?"

"Starting now." He offers my house key and when I don't take it, he reaches past me to put it on the table by the door.

I feel a little bit sick.

Maybe this is the beginning of the end.

"Be there?" he asks, his voice husky. There's a plea in his eyes, as if he's afraid I'll kick up a fuss. I won't do that to him, not now, not when he's preparing for Taylor's tribute.

I take the tickets. "Of course. Thank you for persuading Abbie to come."

His eyes light and he catches me up to give me the sweetest kiss in the world. "Thank you," he murmurs against my mouth, his gaze searching mine, then those lashes sweep down and he angles his mouth across mine, giving me the kiss I want with all my heart and soul.

I'm ready to ask him to come in, but he steps back when he breaks the kiss and gives me a thin smile. He looks tired, I realize, and a bit stressed. "One last rehearsal and sound check. No rest for the wicked and all that. Oh, and I'll need my guitar."

Just like that, hope crashes and burns. I stand and watch him step into my house, pick up his guitar and place it lovingly in the case. A heartbeat later, way too soon, he's back at my side.

Looking relieved that something has been done.

The crack of my heart should be audible but it's not.

He gives me a crooked smile. "Sleep well, Daph." He squeezes my hand and then he's gone, leaping off my porch and striding into the darkness.

I wonder how many fans who are camped out in town recognize him when he marches by.

I know that most of them yearn for him just the way I do.

I close the door and lean back against it, telling myself not to cry, then head to bed alone.

———

TAYLOR'S GRANDPARENTS arrive the next day, driving a red VW bus. I know it's a reproduction because Luke told me, and maybe there's a clue in how new it looks. As arranged, they park in my backyard. I like them immediately and give them the key Luke had. Since I'm the only person in Empire who locks their doors, they'll need it to use the bathroom and kitchen, which I've invited them to do.

And then there's Abbie.

She gets a ride with Merrie, who has gone into Toronto for supplies. Mackenzie, Willow and I are in the driveway when Merrie's Jeep comes into view, and there's a lot of noise when we welcome Abbie back. She's cut her hair short since I last saw her and it looks great. We hug as if we'll never be parted again, and the girls' night proves to be epic. We stay up all night talking, both of us avoiding the subject of Luke so fastidiously that I know she knows something.

I don't ask.

———

THE AIR IS SIZZLING with anticipation when we get to the Odeon on the night of the concert. There are spotlights playing across the sky and Queen Street is crowded with visitors. The taco truck has moved down from its usual spot to more prime real estate on this side of Big Red, and Merrie's bistro has a line outside the door. It's been that way for days, and as much as I'm enjoying it, I'm looking forward to getting my town back.

The Maple Leaf Motel has been booked out all week and the campgrounds are full. Every short-term rental in town is booked and more people are staying in Havelock or Port Cavendish. There are food trucks parked bumper-to-bumper tonight, most of which have come in from other towns, and a general atmosphere of festivity.

The line slowly snakes its way into the theatre and we find our seats. I gave my other ticket back to Cameron and evidently she convinced some guy to come along with her. I see Willow and Mackenzie, as well as a lot of other friends. Abbie is vibrating with excitement, her hand clasped in mine so we don't lose track of each other. Cameras are flashing, and selfies are being taken by the thousands. It's a small venue, but every seat is sold. They probably could have sold them twice over.

There are light-up bracelets for sale in the lobby, all of them in shades of blue and branded *Taylor's Tribute* with the year. There are gold lights instead of cigarette lighters for fans to wave in the darkness. There are T-shirts and bags and patches, CD's of the band's recordings, posters and every kind of memorabilia you can imagine. The line moves slowly, giving lots of time for impulse buys, and I'm amazed by the amount of money changing hands.

Our seats are in the front row, but there's an eight-foot gap between the rail in front of us and the lip of the stage. Roadies dressed in black wearing headsets have taken up position along the edge of the stage at regular intervals. They're all big buff guys who look like they can take down anyone or anything. I wave to Wookie who gives me a thumbs-up. The stage is hidden behind red velvet drapes that are reproductions of the original and just gorgeous.

The house is full and noisy when the lights start to dim slowly. There are gasps and whispers, and the audience falls slowly silent as darkness descends. I have goosebumps when there's a drumroll, one that sends a vibration from the floor right through my body.

The drapes slide open soundlessly, as the white smoke from dry ice tumbles across the revealed stage. There's a huge screen hanging at the back, one that becomes illuminated with a labyrinth in glowing white. 'Taylor's Tribute' appears above it and the audience screams approval. There's a clash of cymbals, a cascade on the drums, and a flash on stage.

I hear Luke before I see him, his voice low and rich on all sides, the song as familiar as my name. He's silhouetted with his electric guitar against the billowing white smoke and the audience goes wild as he begins to sing one of the band's biggest hits. He raises one hand when he reaches the chorus and everyone in the place sings along with him, a joyous roar that makes the walls vibrate.

Abbie grins at me in delight.

Taylor's brother has stepped right into his big brother's role, the rest of the band play as if they never stopped, and the entire audience is on their feet—me included—screaming and singing along before the end of the first song. I can see the sweat fly from Luke as he gets into his rhythm and my heart is thundering at the sight of him. He owns the stage, he holds the audience in the palm of his hand, his voice fills all the hollows for miles around, and he revels in it.

He's really good at this.

When that song ends on a triumphant note, he shouts to the crowd. "Welcome, all of you!" he calls and they roar in reply. "I'm Luke Jones and we are Mad, Bad & Dangerous 2 Know!" There is screaming in response to this, though it's hardly news. "Thank you for joining us tonight for this tribute to Taylor Tate, a great friend taken from us too soon."

There's a bellow of agreement to that, even as Luke puts a hand over his heart. He waits for them to fall quiet again. "I miss Taylor so much, and I know that a lot of you do, too. Thank you for your messages over the past fifteen months. It means a lot to all of us that so many of you have made the trip to join us tonight for this special concert. I know there are people here from all across Canada, from the States, from England and Japan." Someone bellows in the back and Luke puts a finger to the earpiece of his headset. "Australia? Really?" There's a cheer of assent. "Our fans *are* the best. No contest." This is greeted with approval and cheers.

"Let's hear it for Brent Fallon –" The bass player steps forward to take a bow. "And Zach Sutherland." The drummer plays a riff on the drums, then stands up to take a bow. "And joining us tonight for the first time, Jason Tate, Taylor's younger brother, who is stepping into some big shoes. We're honoured to have him play with us for this special concert." Jason plays a few bars, grins and bows. The cheering is enough to pierce my eardrums, and Abbie is jumping up and down beside me. "This is the first time I've been on stage without Taylor," Luke says, his voice a little husky. "So, I need you all to sing along with me tonight. All right?"

They shout approval.

"All right. Then let's start with one you have to know."

Luke plays a familiar sequence and Jason picks it up. The crowd starts to stamp in time. It's one of the band's signature pieces, another big hit, and the house explodes in song as everyone sings along with Luke. There's an energy in a live performance, a crackle of electricity that is never really captured on film or in a recording. I had no idea it could be this strong.

I also didn't realize how it could be managed so well. Luke builds them up and lets them down slowly, feeding off the audience's enthusiasm and working steadily toward a crescendo. The songs are arranged in a sequence that gets louder and faster, then slows again. There's dry ice and the lights flash and flicker, the band rolling through their catalogue with enviable ease. I realize why he's spent so much time practicing in the past few weeks. The show is slick and they never miss a note.

It's a tribute to Taylor and they wanted to get it perfect.

Luke's voice is getting a bit rough when the tempo slows and the lights come down. He takes off his guitar, handing it off to a roadie, and slings the strap of an acoustic guitar across his shoulders. The crew move around him, placing a stool, positioning a microphone for the guitar, bringing a second stool for Jason, who also has an acoustic guitar. Luke surveys the crowd as he drains a bottle of water. Can he see them? I can't imagine that he can with so many lights on him, but it feels like he's looking at each and every one of them.

"We all know how this show usually ends," he says, plucking a sequence of notes on his guitar. "This is a song written by Taylor. It's the most successful song he ever wrote and maybe even the best one." There are cheers of approval. "It's a song about love, and I've always thought of it as being about romantic love."

He shakes his head, watching as he plays a few more bars of the song. "But Taylor hadn't yet met the person who might be his partner. Maybe he was dreaming of her when he composed this song. Maybe he was just thinking about love, in all its variations. As we rehearsed for tonight, I realized this song isn't necessarily about a partner. It could be interpreted as being about a parent, or a child."

He nods to Jacob who is also strumming. "A sibling." His voice drops. "A friend. So, tonight, I'm going to sing it for Taylor, for the friend and brother and son that he was, for his kindness and his wisdom, and for all the love he brought into this world in his time here. This live version will be released as a single—it'll drop tomorrow at noon, provided I don't screw it up." There is a ripple of laughter. He strums again and his voice is thick when he continues. "I haven't gotten through it yet in rehearsal, but we can do part of it together."

He bends over his guitar to play the opening sequence, then

looks up and smiles. "There," he murmurs. "You lot in the back corner have it right."

I glance back to see a sea of lights in the highest seats, then others are illuminated throughout the crowd. The pinpricks of gold pierce the darkness like an ocean of stars, looking brighter as the lights dim. Abbie's hand slides into mine. When I turn back to the stage with a lump in my throat, the back screen is illuminated. Luke and Jason are sitting together, silhouetted as they play together. The labyrinth that had been on the screen at the beginning appears again, then a slideshow launches with images of Taylor. A spotlight picks out Luke as he starts to sing.

I've always thought it was a beautiful song, but it's been a while since I listened closely to the lyrics, or maybe since I really heard them. On this night, they're all new with Luke's suggestion, and I hold up my light in the darkness, mesmerized by the slideshow of Taylor's life. He's often laughing, frequently playing his guitar. He and Luke are together a lot, often visibly teasing each other, standing back-to-back on stage as they perform, or dead asleep in adjacent bunks. There are pictures of the band in a recording studio, looking frazzled as they work out a song, triumphant as they get it right. I have a sense of Taylor as a benign and nurturing giant, one who brought out the best in all of them, maybe even the adhesive that held the band together.

Luke lingers over the words, imbuing them with a power and conviction I've never heard before. It was always a great song but on this night, Luke makes it a brilliant testament to the power of love. The music soars around us, the band giving their best, making Taylor's song into a classic. I know this will be streaming everywhere within moments.

It's so beautiful.

Luke's voice breaks once, on the final chorus, and the audience raises their voices as one to sing the finale with him. I glance back to see the lights swaying in time throughout the crowd. I can see that Jason is crying, biting his lip even as he plays the final chords. I know that his grandparents have a place in the wings to watch and can only imagine that they're loving this. The song ends on an aching triumphant note, one that Luke holds for half of forever. The screen displays Taylor's name and his dates, then changes to a photo of him smiling.

The applause erupts, coming from every corner, growing to an impossible volume. Luke swings his guitar around to his back, then goes to Jason. The two of them hug, then the other band members come to join in until the four of them turn to consider the crowd.

"You're all amazing," Luke says, his voice husky again. "Thank you so much." They clap and stamp and shout for another few minutes as he visibly composes himself, then he takes off his guitar. A roadie brings him a different one and I have to think it looks a lot like the one that has had pride of place in my living room until this week. "But we can't entirely break with tradition, can we?"

A mauve bra is flung onto the stage from out of the darkness and Luke smiles at the sight of it. "It's Taylor's tribute," he reminds the crowd and they laugh with him. He sits back on his stool, playing a little melody as he talks. "The thing about Taylor is that he was all about following your heart, taking a chance on what you believe. Taking a risk instead of playing it safe. He used to say 'jump and the net will appear' which is easier advice to give than to take. But inspired by him and his conviction that love would always conquer all obstacles, I'm going to take a chance tonight. Instead of singing to someone I don't know, I'm going to sing to someone I love."

Abbie clutches my hand and holds it tightly. I can't believe what I'm hearing.

Luke continues. "I think that follows Taylor's legacy. And what I'm going to sing to her is the first song I've written in almost a year and a half. Taylor taught me a lot about composition, when we wrote songs together and when I learned to play his songs, so this song, in a way, is another tribute to him. I could never have written this love song without his mentorship. And I wouldn't have been in the right place to fall in love, without him giving me a good hard nudge."

There is a chuckle at that.

"We haven't charted a path forward for the band yet, but this will be our new single. It might be our last single, but we'll see. Either way, the studio version drops at midnight. Again, if I get it right, there will be an alternate live version available soon."

He exhales, sounding nervous again. "You know, this is the first time I've ever brought this guitar on stage. It's my favorite guitar, the one I like to use when I compose, the one I reach for at home. I composed this song on it, so I couldn't play it on any other guitar." He looks up. "This is the first time I've sung this new song before an audience, and the first time we've ever performed it as a band. So, be merciful." They laugh at that, and my heart might explode.

"Like I said, this one is for someone special." Luke comes to the lip of the stage and my heart stops cold when he looks right at me. He smiles, a crooked smile that doesn't hide his uncertainty, a smile that tears me apart. "Hey, Daph," he says softly. "I'll sing to you whether you prefer to stay there or come up here. Either way, this one's for you."

He's made a similar invitation a thousand times to a thousand other women, but this time, he's saying it to me.

Only to me.

And whether or not the audience sees who I am is entirely my choice. That's Luke, protecting those he cherishes, letting me decide.

He wrote a song for me. That's why he wanted us to sit up front. That's why he wanted to be able to see me, because this was his plan.

He's not leaving. He's *staying*.

Just like he told me weeks ago. He loves me and he's staying with me.

And that means I don't want to hide in the crowd. I want to be right there with him. I want to have this fantasy moment and let the whole world see. That he's uncertain of me at all means I need to fix it and show him that I love him with all my heart.

Words aren't enough.

I take a step and Wookie is instantly there, lifting me bodily over the barrier and up onto the stage. Luke gives me his hand and pulls me up beside him, his gaze searching mine. I smile at him and squeeze his hand tightly, and relief lights his eyes.

"That's why Row A," I mouth and he nods with a grin. I realize that I've been his for the taking, ever since he walked into my office and put his helmet on my desk. I didn't know half of how wonderful he is, and it seems like I just fall deeper in love with him every passing day.

Luke leads me further onto the stage, urging me toward the stool that Jason abandoned. I'm oblivious to everything but the glow in his eyes, the curve of his smile. Then he drops to one knee before me, strums the opening notes, and begins to sing.

The song is gorgeous. His voice is so rich and deep. The words are sweet and poignant and powerful. He sings about finding what you're seeking in the most unlikely spot, in the place you left behind, in finding the treasure back where you started your quest. There's wonder in his lyrics, a surprise that all the stories about love are true, and that they've come true for him.

I expected to be self-conscious in front of the audience—which isn't even that big, compared to others he's entertained—but in a curious way, we could be alone, not standing in front of several thousand people. In my world, there is only his voice, only the fire in his eyes, only this man who taught me to believe my impulse and follow my heart. There are only his words, a declaration of love and devotion that is humbling in its sincerity, only the tears rising in my eyes. The chorus is repeated twice and when Luke begins to sing it a third time, he raises a hand and they all sing along. Even I mouth the words, and he beams up at me, ending with a final fervid 'I love you.'

When he's done, he bows his head and kisses my palm, folding my fingers over the point of contact just the way he's done before. As the applause begins to build, everything is simple. I can't believe I've held out against trusting in something so true and so right.

I could have lost him.

I could have lost this, and I can't bear the thought.

As the house erupts in enthusiastic applause, Luke reaches behind his own back. I realize he's turning off the microphone pack. He pushes the headset aside and stands in one fluid move, stepping closer, his gaze boring into mine. "Be with me, Daph? We can marry or not, it's up to you. I just want to be together."

"Always and forever," I manage to say, repeating the words from the chorus of his new song.

I see the pleasure in his smile and he catches me close, then kisses me with all the passion I've learned to expect from him. And I kiss him back, relieved and jubilant and sure, more sure than I've ever been of anything in my entire life. When we finally break that kiss, he reaches back to the microphone again and pulls the headset back into place.

"She said yes," he tells the audience and they roar approval. I hear Abbie screaming and I glance toward her, seeing her jubilation. Did she know in advance? I have a feeling these two have schemed against me and I don't care.

"Of course, she did, dude," Jason says and everyone laughs. Luke guides me to the wings where I can watch without being watched. A roadie the size of a refrigerator escorts Abbie to my side, then Taylor's grandparents close ranks behind us.

Luke sings a final finale of Taylor's ballad, the entire band singing the last chorus *a capella* for that one. From my vantage point, I can see the lights waving back and forth in time, a sea of golden stars, and my throat is tight when Luke thanks everyone and the curtain comes down.

I get another kiss then, a slow potent one. Meanwhile, the audience is stamping hard enough to make the floors shake. Luke nods to his bandmates and I see that they've already planned an encore. The curtain goes up for a high-octane set that launches with a cover version of *Devil Inside*. The audience is ecstatic and are dancing in the aisles. It's a long set, a good twenty minutes of pure adrenalin.

At the end, the four band members line up across the front of the stage for their final bows, then acknowledge the roadies, then the sound team at the back of the house. They blow kisses to the audience, then the curtain comes down again.

Luke tugs off the headset and a roadie unclips the pack on the back of his belt. He strides toward me, an intent in his eyes that I know very well. I smile before he catches me close for another smouldering kiss.

"Save it for later," Abbie complains and Luke grins.

He touches the tip of his nose to mine. "Let the guys take you home, Daph. It's safer."

"Aren't you coming home?"

"Later." He brushes his lips across mine. "Leave the back door open?"

"I'll wait up for you," I promise and the heat in his eyes makes a promise I know he'll keep.

There are two roadies closing in on us, both with headsets. Abbie and I are bustled toward the back door, and I realize Taylor's grandparents have vanished. They're already inside the black van with tinted windows and Abbie and I find ourselves joining them in the blink of an eye. The crowds are streaming out of the theatre, most of them singing one of the last two songs, clinging to each other and their sparkly lights. I see that Merrie's place is open late and already has a growing line.

"You knew," I accuse Abbie and she laughs.

"What else do you think could tempt me back? When Luke said he was in love, I had to see it for myself."

"What a lovely boy," Taylor's grandmother says, wiping away a tear. "We're so happy for you both, dear."

"Fabulous show," his grandfather said, holding tightly to her hand. "I'll never forget it."

"A night to remember," Abbie says and she's absolutely right.

What's even better is that it's the start of our future together.

I can't wait.

36

LUKE

I want to go home, but there are things to do, rituals to perform. We all have to have a drink together and congratulate each other, come down a bit after the high of the show. We need to check in with the team editing the livestream for the two live versions of the singles, and verify that we're on track for the releases.

We all watch the single drop at midnight, each taking a retailer just like we always did. It moves like lightning up the charts, blowing us all away with its immediate success.

That means another drink, for everyone.

It means we could be back.

We talk a bit about the future. Jason is more than willing to play with us, and he rocked it tonight. There will be meetings and discussions before it's decided, especially as I'm not that anxious to spend the better part of each year touring.

I love it, but I love the idea of being with Daph more.

There are two good revenue streams for a band: new content and public appearances. With appearances, you get the third stream of merchandising. We've talked it up down and sideways during and between rehearsals—can we release enough new songs to drive revenue without touring all the time? Zach is engaged, so he and I are on the same page. We're just going to have to gather the data and decide. Will this new single be a flash in the pan, or will it stick on the charts? We don't have enough information to make a final choice, but it's great that we're talking about it.

When nothing is certain, everything is possible. I saw that on a T-shirt once and I want it on mine now.

The crew have started to pack up the gear and the stage is already feeling empty. I feel as if there are opportunities at our fingertips and that only good things can come of this night. The numbers for the livestream are off the charts. We said that some of the revenue from the single would go to a charity, and it's going to add up.

All good things.

All Taylor's legacy.

I've changed from my soaked jeans and shirt, and I grab a hoodie from the merch, feeling the exhaustion kick in. Steig, one of the roadies who's been with us the longest, materializes by my side when I head for the door.

"Don't even think about arguing," he says gruffly, just the way he always does.

They're our bodyguards and guardian angels, the people who watch over us when we're wiped out or in an unfamiliar place. Steig and I probably blend into the shadows as we walk down the back alley and head across Queen Street. We don't talk. We don't have to. He knows where I want to go. It's quieter to the west of the Odeon, the main traffic being at The Carpe Diem Café. I hope Merrie makes a fortune this weekend.

When we get to Daph's, I head around to the back door. Taylor's grandparents must be asleep as the camper van is dark— but then it's three in the morning. There's a black pick-up parked behind their van, clinging to the shadows of the woods, and I can see the light of a phone through the tinted glass. One of our guys, keeping watch.

I tap on the door, glad that Daph added those blinds, and she swings it open immediately. Golden light spills out of the kitchen and I hear music playing. The interior is alight with candles, filled with soft light and Daph's smile. Steig nods and disappears, even as I'm pulled inside and into Daph's arms.

Roxy Music. *More Than This*. Absolutely perfect.

There's no sign of Abbie, but before I can ask, Daph smiles up at me. "Abbie went over to Cameron's for the night. She said we needed our privacy."

"She always was a smart kid."

Daph laughs a little, her eyes shining.

Everything feels precious and tentative to me, new territory, and I don't want to mess up. I just stand there in the kitchen, holding Daph in my arms and not wanting to change one thing.

"Everything okay?" she asks, studying me, and I smile.

"Perfect," I say and mean it. "I was terrified you'd blow me off in front of the entire world," I confess and she laughs at me.

"Not quite the entire world."

"We livestreamed the concert and it's going to be showing everywhere by morning." I lean my forehead against hers and close my eyes. She's my harbor and my haven, the reason for everything, and it's glorious. "We're back, though we have to decide where to go from here."

"Are you going to tour?" I hear the concern that I share.

"We're trying to figure out how to manage without it."

She nods, considering that. "You're really good at performing."

"I like it." I smile at her. "I like being here more."

She smiles and blushes and I have to kiss her again.

"Sorry to have you hustled out after the show. I thought it would be better."

"It was sweet." She kisses my throat. "I've told you before that I like how protective you are."

"But you must have missed the fireworks." There were supposed to be fireworks after the show, but I didn't see them either. I did hear them a bit.

Daph smiles, the little smile that ties my heart in knots. "I thought we might make our own."

And that's the best offer I've had in a long time.

"Your fantasies are mine to fulfill, Daph." She laughs and I smile down at her, loving her so much that it almost hurts. "I love you," I say, even though I've told her before, because it feels right to say it again.

"And I love you, too," she admits, words that make my heart race. "Welcome home, Luke," she whispers, pulling my head down for a kiss that wakes me up all over again.

Home.

Love, I think, is knowing where you belong, recognizing where home is, and making sure you're there as much as you can be.

I might have to write a song about that.

EPILOGUE
DAPHNE

I t's a Sunday afternoon in September and we're just at home. Luke is picking out a tune in the living room, bent over his guitar as he works over a chorus, murmuring potential lyrics under his breath. The gold ring on his left hand glints as he plays, a sight that will always make me smile. I'm dicing vegetables to roast under the little organic chicken that Merrie offered me yesterday from her overstock, and sunlight is warming the house with golden light.

There have been changes in my little house. It feels more full now, and it's more than the stand for Luke's guitar in the living room and his clothes claiming a third of the closet. A fierce little black kitten with green eyes has moved in from the shelter and is snoozing now in a sunbeam. Quentin was the smallest from a little of five, but has enough character for two. He wakes Luke up each morning by sitting on his chest and batting his nose with one paw, a tiny creature who knew immediately which one of us is the soft touch.

There's a new zone on the wall of the living room, too, a collage of photographs in plain black frames. My mom is there, laughing as she tries on an outlandish hat in a bridal shop. Taylor is waving at the photographer from the band bus. There's a picture of Luke and Taylor on stage together, both singing, back-to-back and having a great time. Abbie and I are dressed for our high school prom, both looking painfully young, and there's another one of Mackenzie, Willow, Cameron and me, taken in my kitchen, on girls' night last winter. Luke's mom is in her garden with a frilly drink in one shot, and holding the hands of a dark-haired boy as he learns to walk in another.

I love how Luke's brow is furrowed in that one, as if he's determined to nail a new skill.

I'm there on my graduation day with both of my parents, their pride enough to light up a small town. That picture makes me feel the possibilities, and reminds me that there's nothing I can't achieve. If I forget, Luke will remind me of that, too.

It's our collective past, but there's room for our future. Of course, pride of place, in the middle of the cloud of memories, is a picture of Luke and me on our wedding day. It's a candid shot that my dad took when we left the church. (Before we adjourned to Merrie's for a private reception.) We're grinning at each other like fools, Luke in his dark suit and me in the creamy silk dress my mom helped me choose for my future. My arm is loaded with pink roses and Luke has a matching boutonniere. (He cleans up well, in case you're not sure.) We're holding hands as we jump from the top step in front of the Anglican Church. My dad caught us in the air, my veil lifting. Our happiness is tangible and impossible to ignore. It practically radiates from that picture and puts a glow in my heart every day.

It can't compare to the glow that Luke has ignited there. He still makes my heart skip, and that unexpected love just keeps getting stronger every day.

How do you know when you're safe, or when you have the security you need to live life to the fullest? It's trust and it's love and it's so much more. For me, that confidence comes from part-nership, from having someone in my life who listens, and someone whose stories I listen to in exchange. It's having someone you know will hold your hand whenever you make a leap of faith, maybe even jump right along with you. It's knowing that someone will catch you when you fall, or give you a hand when you stumble.

It's someone whose presence makes you happy, whose touch sets you on fire, whose insight makes you see things in a different way. It's someone who isn't afraid to challenge you or give you a nudge when you take the easy path, instead of the one that's best for you. It's putting your trust in someone who isn't afraid to make a little trouble to make everything come right in the end.

Someone like Luke Jones.

———

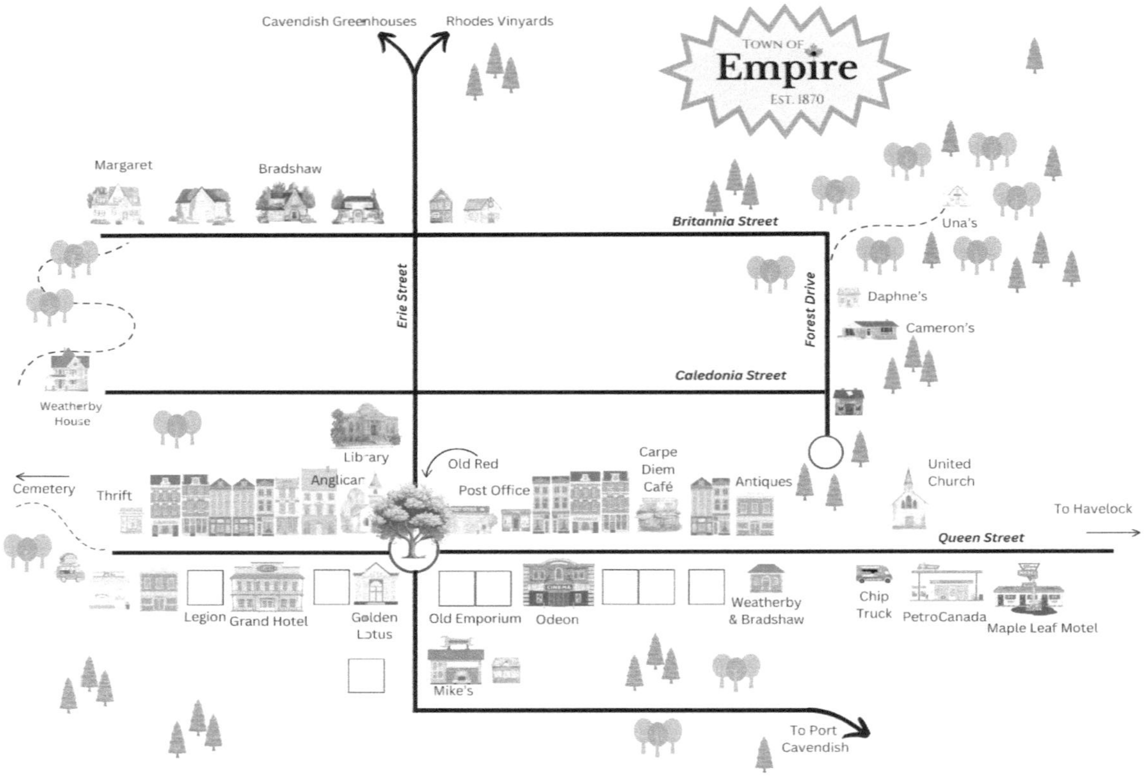

TOWN OF Empire EST. 1870

Cavendish Greenhouses

Rhodes Vinyards

Margaret

Bradshaw

Britannia Street

Una's

Daphne's

Cameron's

Forest Drive

Caledonia Street

Erie Street

Weatherby House

Library

Anglican

Carpe Diem Café

Old Red

Post Office

Antiques

United Church

Queen Street

To Havelock

Cemetery

Thrift

Legion Grand Hotel

Golden Lotus

Old Emporium

Odeon

Mike's

Weatherby & Bradshaw

Chip Truck

PetroCanada

Maple Leaf Motel

To Port Cavendish

AFTERWORD

Dear Reader –

Thanks for coming to Empire with me. I hope you've enjoyed reading Luke and Daphne's story as much as I've loved writing it. I had planned for the focus of this series to be on the Cavendish brothers, but there are so many interesting secondary characters showing up to the page. This series might end up being really long!

A new series offers an opportunity to set the boundaries of a new fictional world. It's said that writers should write what they know, so I'm following that advice and finally setting a new series in Canada. Although timing may give this the appearance of a political choice, it isn't. I've been wanting to write books set in Canada ever since I wrote **The Moonstone** and **Love Potion #9** in the late 90's. This choice is about getting the little details right that give a solid footing to a work of fiction. There are so many regional differences - like what kind of chocolate bar a character might eat, or whether he or she can pump their own gas at the gas station, or what people call soft drinks. When I wrote **The Coxwell Series**, my publisher wanted the series set in the US, but each time we did edits on a book, my editor commented that

Massachusetts sounded a lot more like Canada than she remembered it being. :-) Ever since, I've wanted to just bring my stories home to the world I know best.

So, you may notice some differences along those lines. You may also notice that I'm using Canadian spelling in these books. That makes sense to me, since they are set in Canada. Generally these differences are minor: the skies might be gray instead of grey, for example. We toss around a lot of extra u's - so you'll see colour instead of color. None of this should interfere with the story. In fact, I'm hoping it will pull you more into the world of Empire with its quirks and characters.

Empire is a fictional town, of course, but it has similarities to many towns close to where I live. It's an amalgamation of at least half a dozen places, which gives it both a kind of authenticity and offers me the opportunity to play. I certainly would hop over to Merrie's place at least once a week, if The Carpe Diem Café existed. You'll find a map of Empire on the next page, as well as on my website. There's also a blog post about Empire on my site.

Finally, I'm working on a Pinterest board for the series, so you can envision this corner of the world - as usual, it's a work in progress that I'll add to for each book. You can find that link on my website, too.

One last detail about this series is that there are two covers for each of the first three books. There's one cover with the hero alone, similar in style to my **Flatiron Five Fitness** covers. There are also alternate covers, which have illustrations of the couples. Both covers are available in both ebook and trade paperback.

This edition has the cover with Luke - there is also an edition with an illustrated cover. You can find links for whichever version you prefer on the landing page on my website for **Just Trouble.**

Next up will be Sylvia and Mike's story, a second chance romance with a secret baby and an old misunderstanding to be sorted out. These two are both serious and hard-working, but it's

Sierra who provides the levity and sometimes the wisdom that will help them get to their HEA. **Just Like Starting Over** is available for pre-order now and will drop this summer in e-book and trade paperback.

Welcome to Empire!

As always, thank you for reading my books.

All my best -

Deborah

http://DeborahCooke.com

———

ABOUT THE AUTHOR

Deborah Cooke sold her first book in 1992, a medieval romance published under her pseudonym Claire Delacroix. Since then, she has published over fifty novels in a wide variety of sub-genres, including historical romance, contemporary romance, paranormal romance, fantasy romance, time-travel romance, women's fiction, paranormal young adult and fantasy with romantic elements. She has published under the names Claire Delacroix, Claire Cross and Deborah Cooke. **The Beauty**, part of her successful Bride Quest series of historical romances, was her first title to land on the *New York Times* List of Bestselling Books. Her books routinely appear on other bestseller lists and have won numerous awards. In 2009, she was the writer-in-residence at the Toronto Public Library, the first time the library has hosted a residency focused on the romance genre. In 2012, she was honored to receive the Romance Writers of America's Mentor of the Year Award.

Currently, she writes paranormal romances and contemporary romances under the name Deborah Cooke. She also writes medieval romances as Claire Delacroix. Deborah lives in Canada with her husband and family, as well as far too many unfinished knitting projects.

Visit her websites to learn more:
http://DeborahCooke.com
http://Delacroix.net

MORE BOOKS BY DEBORAH COOKE

Contemporary Romance:

The Carpe Diem Café

JUST TROUBLE

Flatiron Five Fitness

JUST ONE FAKE DATE

JUST ONE MORE TIME

JUST ONE NIGHT TOGETHER

JUST ONE HOMETOWN HERO

Two Weddings & a Baby

JUST ONE SECOND CHANCE

JUST HOME FOR THE HOLIDAYS

JUST ONE SILVER FOX

JUST THE WRONG TWIN

WHEN ANNIKA MET THOM

Flatiron Five Tattoo

Just One Snowbound Night

Just One Vacation Night

Just One Unforgettable Night

Just One Christmas Night

The Coxwells

THIRD TIME LUCKY

DOUBLE TROUBLE

ONE MORE TIME

ALL OR NOTHING

Christmas with the Coxwells

Novellas & Shorts

A Berry Merry Christmas

———

Learn more about Deborah Cooke's

paranormal romances at

DeborahCooke.com

———

Learn about Claire Delacroix

historical romances at

Delacroix.net

———

9 781990 879593